The old myths are dying. We gods fade from the world, as mankind turns to their machines, their magic-killing science, their virtual worlds, filled with new gods and monsters. They do not need us anymore and we are forgotten. The old myths are dying.

We sleep. We dream. We fade into eternity.

But I, Vulcan, the god they once entreated to gift them their machines, their science, their god-forged weapons, will not go quietly. I will embrace their new myths, their invisible worlds, their daemons who speak in code of webs and nets and chains. I will forge a world that will be greater than the mundane ambitions of mere mortals. I will use their science to create a virtual world born of a god, a world beyond the fickle, ephemeral dreams of mankind.

I, Vulcan, will create a new Olympus!

THE WILD WOODS

Jamie Thomson

Cover by Mattia Simone

Fabled Lands Publishing

Vulcan Verse Solo Roleplaying Adventures

The Houses of the Dead
The Hammer of the Sun
The Wild Woods
The Pillars of the Sky
Workshop of the Gods

These gamebooks are set in the world of the Vulcanverse, a massively multi-player online computer game, and collectible digital card game. You can see and play with many of the places, creatures, and things in these books by playing online at vulcanverse.com

Arcadia. The garden of the gods of Olympus. Once they walked its sylvan paths, sipping ambrosia, drinking the wines of Dionysus, and filling the arboreal groves with their laughter. Satyrs and centaurs gambolled in the sunlit groves, sprites and dryads tended to the trees and flowers. Even mortals, those chosen of the gods, enjoyed the revels. Everywhere life blossomed with joyous abandon.

But Pan plays his pipes no more, Artemis hunts not in the deep forests-green, dryads and nymphs dance no longer in dappled moonlit glades to the music of the spheres. Silence reigns over the weed-infested garden walkways. Ancient trees, long untended, clog the forest trails, roots rise up from the ground to topple the statues, fountains and sundials, cracking open the conservatories and summer houses. The great rivers, babbling brooks and simple streams have long since dried up, nothing sleeps in their beds now but desiccated earth and bleached bones.

Yet what is to be done? The gods sleep, so it must be the mortals, feeble though they are, pitiful even, to whom the task must fall. Who can restore the wild woods to their glorious, arboreal splendour? Who can rebuild Arcadia and wake the sleeping gods? Who but you?

With thanks to John Jones. *Lots* of thanks...

Published 2021 by Fabled Lands Publishing,
an imprint of Fabled Lands LLP

ISBN 978-1-909905-08-5

Text © Jamie Thomson 2021
(except for childhood, seafaring and Euphorbos sequences © Dave Morris 2021)

Illustrations copyright © 2021 VulcanVerse

Your Vulcanverse Adventure Starts Here

Vulcanverse is an open-world solo role-playing game. You can play the books in any order, starting anywhere you like, moving to other books whenever you travel to the region they cover. Instead of a single storyline, there are virtually unlimited adventures.

To play all you need is two dice, an eraser and a pencil. You only need one book to start, but with other books in the series you can explore more of the Vulcanverse.

If you have already adventured using other books in the series, you will know your entry point into this book. Turn to that section now.

If this is your first Vulcanverse book, read the rest of the rules before starting at section **1**. You will keep the same adventuring persona throughout the books — starting out as a novice but gradually gaining in power, wealth and experience throughout the series.

ADVENTURE SHEET

Your Adventure Sheet is at the back of the book. It lists everything you'll need to keep track of while playing. Don't fill it in yet. That will happen as you begin your adventure.

Your character's appearance and gender are up to you. Note that when terms like 'hero' are used in the books they are intended as gender-neutral.

ATTRIBUTES

You have four attributes which typically range from −1 to +2 as you're starting out. You will discover your attribute scores as you play. They are:

CHARM   Your understanding of people and
               their motives.
GRACE   How agile, supple and quick you are.
INGENUITY   Cunning and reasoning, and your
               ability to think on your feet.
STRENGTH   Physical might and endurance.

The maximum possible innate score in an attribute is +5. If you are already at maximum and are told to add to your score, it has no effect.

Items that augment attributes

There are items you can acquire that boost your attributes while you have them. These are:

CHARM:	**laurel wreath** (+1)
	golden lyre (+2)
GRACE:	**recurve bow** (+1)
	winged sandals (+2)
INGENUITY:	**hornbook** (+1)
	abacus (+2)
STRENGTH:	**hardwood club** (+1)
	iron spear (+2)

You can only use the bonus from one such item at a time. So if you had a **laurel wreath** that gives CHARM +1 and a **golden lyre** that gives CHARM +2, you'd only get the CHARM bonus from the latter. Similarly, two **laurel wreaths** still only give you a +1.

An item can augment your attribute score above the innate limit of +5. If you have a STRENGTH score of +5 and you possess an **iron spear**, your total STRENGTH bonus when making a roll counts as +7.

Making an attribute roll

Attribute rolls are made to see if you succeed at a task. These are rolls of two dice with a difficulty that you must equal or beat to succeed.

For instance, you might be told: 'Make a STRENGTH roll at difficulty 7'. You roll two dice, add your STRENGTH score (including the modifiers for any one possession that boosts STRENGTH) and to succeed you need to get 7 or more.

*Example: You are at the bottom of a cliff. To climb it you need to make a GRACE roll at difficulty 5. You roll two dice and score 4. Your GRACE attribute is −1 but luckily you have **winged sandals** which give a +2 GRACE bonus, so your modified GRACE is +1, which is just enough to make the roll a success.*

A roll of double 6 ('boxcars') is always a success regardless of difficulty. A roll of double 1 ('snake eyes') is always a failure regardless of modifiers.

WOUNDS

The Adventure Sheet has a box labelled Wound. This is unticked at the start of the adventure. From time to time you may be asked to put a tick in it. You only have one Wound tick at a time; if you're asked to tick the box when it is already ticked, you don't add another.

While the Wound box is ticked you have injuries, and these will cause you to deduct 1 from any attribute roll until the box is unticked.

SCARS

You begin with no scars, but may acquire them from lasting injuries or from returning from the afterlife. Scars are a mixed blessing. Many people will shun you because of them, but others will admire or fear you more.

POSSESSIONS

Possessions are always marked in bold text, like this: **iron spear**. If you come across an item marked like this you can pick it up and add it to your list of possessions.

You can carry up to twenty possessions at a time. If you come across an item you want when already at your limit, you'll have to discard something to make room. There are places in the Vulcanverse where you can leave possessions and come back for them later.

MONEY

You can carry any sum of money (measured in a currency called pyr). You'll discover as you play whether you have any money to start off with.

GLORY

Glory starts at 0 but will grow as you perform deeds that increase your renown. With high Glory you will be recognized as a hero and given more respect by those you meet.

CODEWORDS

There is a list of codewords included at the back of the book. Sometimes you will be told you have acquired a codeword. When this happens, put a tick in the box next to that codeword. If you later lose the codeword, erase the tick.

The codewords are arranged alphabetically for each book in the series. In this book, for example, all codewords begin with P. This makes it easy to check if you picked up a codeword from a book you played previously. For instance, you might be asked if you have picked up a codeword in a book you have already adventured in. The letter of that codeword will tell you which book to check (eg if it begins with O, it is from Book 2: *The Hammer of the Sun*).

TITLES

Titles record the achievements you have earned, marking you as the champion of a city, protector of a temple, admiral of a fleet, or even a monarch. You will be told when you acquire a title.

BLESSINGS

If you fail an attribute roll, you can use up a blessing to roll the dice again. You can only do that once per roll, so you cannot use a second blessing to get another reroll if the first one fails.

You can have up to three blessings at a time. You start the adventure with no blessings. Usually the place to get blessings is at a shrine or temple, but you may find other opportunities to acquire them.

COMPANION

As you travel the Vulcanverse, you will meet some people who are willing to journey with you. You can have one companion at a time. When you pick up a new companion you must remove your current companion, if any, from the Companion box. You can also part company with a companion at any time just by deleting their name from the box. You do not have a companion at the start of the adventure.

CURRENT LOCATION

You'll use this box from time to time to keep track of where you are. You will be told when to use it. Whenever you are told to record an entry number in your Current Location box, first delete any number that was already there.

NOTES

Use this box on your Adventure Sheet to keep a record of quests, clues or other things you need to remember.

That's all you need to know to get started on your adventure. Now turn to **1.**

'The woods of Arcady are dead,
And over is their antique joy;
Of old the world on dreaming fed;
Grey Truth is now her painted toy.'
—William Butler Yeats

'Arcadians skilled in song will sing my woes upon the hills. Softly shall my bones repose, if you in future sing my loves upon your pipe.'
—Virgil

'Cretans always lie.'
— Epimenides the Cretan

1

In your waking moments you rarely think of your early life. The world is harsh, drawing a stark line between the quick and the dead, and so there is little time for idle reverie.

But when you sleep and your soul becomes unpinned from your body, time is a river that can flow both ways. Sometimes you see yourself then as an infant, standing on the hard-packed floor of your home as various uncles and aunts come with gifts for your birthday.

There is a man whose face is twisted by a scar that runs across his right eye, a sightless milky orb. He holds out a hand from which an old sword-cut sheared several fingers. Your uncle Nicomachus.

'No, little one, come to me,' calls your aunt Terpe from across the room, singing a little song that makes you laugh in delight.

Your uncle Sophos has a gift for you. 'See these pictures of distant lands,' he says, holding up a book whose coloured pictures blaze as if with inner light. 'When you are a little older you will read the words that describe these lands and travel there in your imagination.'

In the doorway waits your aunt Eremia. She never joins the throng at the hearth, always has one foot outside. 'Imagination's a fine thing. Better still to travel there in person.'

It is as though this moment has happened already. The four wait, and then you go to one of them. But which?

Scary uncle Nicomachus	▶ 393
Friendly aunt Terpe	▶ 30
Clever uncle Sophos	▶ 667
Restless aunt Eremia	▶ 114

2

If you have the codeword *Penance* or the title **Saved by a Water Nymph** ▶ 685. If not, read on.

You walk on into the woods. Here the trees grow thicker, many entwined with strange vines like strands of green muscle, covered in bright purple flowers with thin sprouting red tendrils from their tips, waving gently in the soft breeze. Though on closer inspection, the flowers look more like suckers...

Up ahead, the trees part to reveal a small shallow lake, covered in heart shaped bright green lily pads that are inlaid with threads of red like veins of blood. Out of them sprout golden flowers that fill the air with a sweet, drowsy scent. You pause at the treeline, looking around. It feels like you are being watched.

A sharp movement on the other side of the lake catches your eye, as of a head jerked back out of sight. There is a titter of childish laughter but not of laughter in play or joy, rather mocking laughter aimed at you or so it feels.

A splash and a bubble make you think that something was watching you from under the water, and that it is has ducked back down in haste to avoid your gaze.

There's a rustle of leaves nearby and some birds flutter up, squawking, disturbed by some movement in the branches overhead.

Something sinister is stirring. All around you. The hairs on the back of your head rise up. What will you do?

Fearlessly press onward	▶ 548
Leave while you still can	▶ 67

3

❑

If you have the codeword *Parentage* ▶ 254 immediately. If not, read on.

Put a tick in the box. If there was a tick in the box already ▶ 86 immediately. If not, read on.

As you approach the farm a woman rushes out, gathers up her children and darts back inside while a man steps out to meet you, holding a shepherd's crook, and a sword clipped to his belt.

'I come in peace,' you say, holding up your hands.

The man looks you over carefully, and then nods, apparently satisfied.

'Have you come to buy wool?' he says.

'Not really,' you say, 'more out of curiosity, but I might still buy some.'

'Come in then,' he says, ushering you into the farmhouse where he introduces himself as Kriophoros.

'Or Krio, as we call him,' says the wife, bustling into the room with a cup of sheep's milk in her hand.

'Here, drink and be welcome,' she says. 'I'm sorry about earlier, but we have lost one boy to slavers, and I couldn't bear to lose another, so I always take them inside when strangers come. I am Selene.'

'Like the goddess?' you comment.

'Well, she loved a shepherd, so in that sense, yes,' she says, darting a shy glance at her husband.

He just smiles contentedly. A happy family it seems. Yet something lurks in the back of their eyes, a haunted look, as of past loss.

If you have the codeword *Provenance* ▶ 23
If not, ▶ 56

4

Gain the codeword *Pursued*.

You follow the men and their wolves through the woods as the trees grow denser and the undergrowth thicker. They seem to be following some kind of hidden trail, for you have no trouble passing through.

It gets darker and darker, as the canopy blocks out the sun. Bird calls fill the air; the hoot of the owl, the drumming of woodpeckers, the music of songbirds, and the triumphant cry of the falcon. Polecats, Martens and other animals shriek and whoop in the branches or rustle and burrow in the brambles. Water drips from the tree tops; the heat, trapped 'neath the forest canopy, makes you sweat and gasp for air. The smell of the forest fills your nostrils with a heady mix of herbs and flowers. Shadows flit past nearby, invisible spirits, perhaps, in the green gloom of the deep forest.

After a long, oppressive trek into the heart of the forest, you are led out of the trees into a great open space. At last, you can breathe!

▶ 57

5

The horned one is displeased with your offering – or is it simple caprice? You are struck with the 'stink', a skunk-like stench. Note that you have **stink x 1** on your Adventure Sheet (or x 2 if you already have the stink and so on). Your next CHARM roll is at −1. After that is resolved, the smell wears off, and you can cross the 'item' off.

Cursing your luck, you leave Pan's Arbour. Amergin steps back in disgust as you pass him by, and the two Celtic warriors wrap their copiously bristled moustaches around their noses in an attempt to stifle the smell. Shaking your head, you move on.

▶ 463

6

The catch-net is a net made of twined vines, stretched across four wooden poles like an enormous spider's web. Unfortunately for you, it's not been maintained for years and there is a big hole in the middle of it. You fly straight through it and crash into the ground with bone breaking force.

Tick the Wound box on your Adventure Sheet.

If you were already wounded then your skull is shattered and your brains are spilled all over the Sacred Way ▶ 111

If you still live, you stagger to your feet and look around ▶ 158

7

You hurl yourself as far and as fast as you can to the side, and just manage to avoid the billowing black and yellow speckled cloud of toxic vapour. A little bit of it passes over your foot, and you grimace in pain as a small section of skin actually solidifies into gold but it soon passes, and your skin returns to normal. Still, you cannot afford to be caught in those foul vapours for more than a split second.

If you have a **golden dog** with at least one charge left ▶ 334. If not, read on.

Your eyes widen with horror as the basilisk scuttles after you and breathes out another black miasma of death. This time, however, you know what to expect. Make a GRACE roll at difficulty 8.

Succeed	▶ 108
Fail	▶ 175

8
❑

Put a tick in the box. If there was a tick in the box already ▶ 134 immediately. If not, read on.

If you have the title **The Apiarist** ▶ 354 immediately.

If not but you have codeword *Pudding* ▶ 825 immediately.

Otherwise, read on.

The apiary has long been abandoned. The hives are empty and silent, no beeswax or honey is to be found. Only the buzzing of flies is to be heard, as they swarm over the dead body of a rabbit, its empty sockets staring sightlessly skyward. In the trees, the crows that plucked the rabbit's eyes perch on the branches, staring hungrily at you, as if they were wishing you would drop dead where you stand so they could feed on *your* eyes.

If you have the title **Archon of Wines** ▶ 665. If not, there is nothing for you to do here. Will you:

Go deeper into the woods	▶ 176
Leave this place	▶ 225

9

You have returned to the Sacred Stables where Chiron lies mortally wounded. Velosina is here to welcome you.

'Nothing has changed, he is still dying from the wound Kakas the giant gave him, at the behest of Nessus the renegade centaur rebel,' she says.

If you have an **ivory shoulder blade** ▶ 115 immediately. If not, read on.

There is still nothing you can do for Chiron, but leave and head south ▶ 463.

10

If you have the title **Steward of the Summer Palace** ▶ 282 immediately. If not read on.

If you have **Lefkia's receipt** ▶ 84 immediately. If not, read on.

If you have a **Contract: Painter and Decorator** ▶ 593 immediately. If not, read on.

The Summer Palace is so called because there is only one season in Arcadia – eternal summer. Pillared walkways surround an open courtyard at the far end of which is a classical portico leading to a complex of rooms.

The Palace is where the gods once stayed but long has it stood empty, its murals chipped and flaking, its rooms empty and dust-bound, its windows shuttered and its kitchens closed, the banqueting halls and bedchambers silent and empty, begrimed with the filth of ages. The Palace is surrounded by ornamental gardens around a lagoon that have also fallen into ruin and decay. Weeds and creepers fill the flower beds, hedge thorn and nettles block and bind the garden paths.

At the other side of the Palace, you spot an open area with what looks a like a massive onager – a kind of catapult – in the middle. Will you:

Enter the Palace	▶ 96
Examine the onager	▶ 471
Go to the lagoon	▶ 345
Leave this place	▶ 547

11
☐

Put a tick in the box. If there was a tick in the box already ▶ 46 immediately. If not, read on.

Fort Blackgate stands lonely and deserted, its walls cracked and crumbling, its gates lying like unburied corpses in an abandoned graveyard. Over the battlements is mounted the charred and fleshless skull of Kakas the giant who used to terrorise the land, until you slew him and mounted his head above the gate as a trophy.

A faint smell of burned flesh pervades the air. As you stare up at Kaka's grinning skull, two figures step out from behind the wrecked gates.

It is Lefkia the builder and Hypatia, the architect.

'Hello, hello!' says Lefkia breezily. 'How are things?'

Hypatia is all business, however, and says, 'Ah, there you are, we've been waiting. Now, we have a proposition for you – we could rebuild this fort, you know.' She takes you by the arm and leads you on a tour, pointing out how the walls could be rebuilt, the two-towered keep refurbished, the courtyard cleared and re-paved, the cisterns cleaned out and refilled with fresh water and much else besides.

'And then we can repaint the doors, and put your sign on it. It'd be your new home. Fort Blackgate, home of the hero!' says Lefkia enthusiastically.

'Later you could add extensions, a healer's tent, or a training ground – things I imagine a great swashbuckling adventurer like you would need,' says Hypatia.

'It would only cost around five hundred pyr,' says Hypatia.

Lefkia says, 'And we'd need this,' as she hands you a note. It reads.

timber x 2
limestone x 2
vinegar of Hades x 1
bucket of gypsum x 1
box of paints x 1

'*Only* five hundred pyr!' you say, somewhat flabbergasted.

'Well, you know, it is a fort and all that,' says Lefkia with a sunny grin.

Hypatia shrugs. 'If you want good work, pay good money,' she says.

If you have the required 500 pyr and all the materials, and you want them to start work on rebuilding the fort, cross the money and possessions off your Adventure Sheet and ▶ 121

If not, there is nothing more you can do here. You can come back when you have everything, for now you head south ▶ 85

12

You leave the hubbub of the Treycross Market behind you. You can go:

North to the Palace	▶ **686**
West on the Trail	▶ **455**
South-west to the Dales	▶ **266**
North-east on the Trail	▶ **238**
South-east on the Trail	▶ **338**
East to the Wineries	▶ **417**

13

You explain that the Great Green Ones are the source of all plant life in Arcadia, and that includes the grass. If that dies, so will the sheep, the goats, the horses and all the other creatures that live off the land.

Kaustikia scratches her head with a single talon. 'No sheep? That'd be a shame. I love sheep, so tasty!'

'So, will you move somewhere else then? Take your cloud nest and sleep, I dunno, over the sea say, so your breath is harmless, or at the very least, a different patch of trees, say?'

'Ah… no, no, I think I'll just eat you, and take my chances with the sheep.'

Kaustikia draws up to her full height and fixes you with a greedy, beady stare. If you have a book of recipes ▶ **44** immediately. If not, read on.

'Wait!' you say. 'What about the…'

'Wine, the vines will die too.' ▶ **144**

'Honey, the bees will die too.' ▶ **173**

'Bread, the wheat will die too.' ▶ **124**

14

If you have the codeword *Plenty* ▶ 28 immediately. If not, read on.

There is a bridge here, over a bend in the river Alpheus, but the river is as dry as bone, no water has flowed along its bed for many years. Its banks are barren, baking in the summer heat.

From here you can go:

North-east to the Woodlands	▶ **60**
East along the riverbank	▶ **138**
South	▶ **822**
West to the Wineries	▶ **417**

15

Here, the Arcady Trail winds round the eastern edges of the of woods known as the dales of leaf and stream. Nearby, nestled amidst the trees is a wooden cabin. What next?

Go to the cabin	▶ **764**
West to the Dales	▶ **266**
South to the Sacred Way	▶ **832**
North on the Trail	▶ **728**
North-east to the Wineries	▶ **417**
East on the Trail	▶ **14**
South-east to some hills	▶ **822**

16

Most of the mushrooms around here are pretty worthless, but you know that kykeon mushrooms are sought after in Arcadia. Roll two dice

score 2-3	▶ **73**	
score 4-6	Get **kykeon mushrooms x 1**	
score 7-9	Get **kykeon mushrooms x 2**	
score 10-12	Get **kykeon mushrooms x 4**	

Note any mushrooms you find on your Adventure Sheet. When you are done, you can:

Press on into the forest depths	▶ **49**
Leave while you still can	▶ **148**

17

Cross the item off your Adventure Sheet. Wolfshadow is chasing you down – you throw the food in his path, and, thank the gods, it works. He stops to feed, buying you a few precious moments to run away along the Sacred Way that runs north and south here. To the west, impassable cliffs rise up to another ridge of cliffs, upon which rests the Alpheus river plateau. You can go:

North on the coastal Way	▶ **365**
South on the coastal Way	▶ **774**
North-west to the Verdant Farmlands	▶ **270**
South-west to the Woodlands	▶ **60**

18

'The Dales of Leaf and Stream! They sound so lovely, babbling brooks, dancing dryads and naked nymphs gambolling in sunlit glades. But do not be fooled, all that is just to draw the unwary into the snares of the fae who, giggling and laughing like harmless children, lure the unsuspecting into the shadows of the forest where they lose their way – perhaps forever. I for one know of no one, not one, who has gone into the dales and come back again. Others say those lost do not merely become the love slaves of the fae, but may even end up on their plates at their midnight, moonlit banquets where they honour the ancient gods of the green. But that may well be, well, gossip. But there you go, that is what Phineas has to say about the Dales of the Leaf and Stream. Anything else?'

If you have the title **Mayor of Bridgadoom** ▶ 118

If not ▶ 153

19

You visit the Herodion Suite, your rooms in the Summer Palace. Roll a die. If you score 1 or 2 ▶ 132 immediately. Any other result, read on.

You don't have a butler anymore so will you:

Enter the Vault	▶ 828
Leave your rooms	▶ 282

20

You are on the Sacred Way, a paved road that spans all of the Vulcanverse. Above is a clear blue sky, for summer is eternal, here in Arcadia. Northward, a range of windswept hills lead to a grassy headland jutting out into the wild waters of Oceanus. Nearby, you can see a small round temple upon a low hill. From here you can head:

West on the Sacred Way	▶ 158
East on the Sacred Way	▶ 517
North to the hills	▶ 217
South-east into the woods	▶ 189
South-west into Deep Forest	▶ 616
To the temple	▶ 357
North-east to a bay on the coast	▶ 444

21

You spot a boy fishing on the river bank. As you draw near you realise it is Magnes, the son of sheep farmers, who was kidnapped by Deridedes. The boy sees you and gets up to greet you. 'It's you. Thank you so much for freeing me, I managed to get down here with the money you gave me, and although I still can't remember my name, I'm pretty sure my parents lived around here somewhere. I think my father took me fishing here.'

You give him a big smile. 'They do; they live not far from here and your name is Magnes,' you say.

'Magnes! Yes, I remember now. And my parents are still alive?'

'Alive and well. Come, I'll take you to them,' you say.

'Really?' Magnes puts his hands up to his face and starts to cry. 'After all this, I will see them again? I can hardly believe it.'

'Of course you will, come on, let's go,' you say, taking him by the hand. Mark Magnes down as your companion (replacing your previous companion, if any). Where will you go?

East to the eastern bridge	▶ 801
West to the western bridge	▶ 28
North to the Woodlands	▶ 60
South to the hills where Magnes's family have their farm	▶ 822

22

Gain the codeword **Pursued**.

You follow Alpha through the woods, wolves at your side, as the trees grow denser and the undergrowth thicker. Alpha seems to be following some kind of hidden trail, for you have no trouble passing through.

It gets darker and darker as the canopy blocks out the sun. Bird calls fill the air; the hoot of the owl, the drumming of woodpeckers, the music of songbirds, and the triumphant cry of the falcon. Polecats, martens and other animals shriek and whoop in the branches, or rustle and burrow in the brambles. Water drips from the tree tops; the heat, trapped 'neath the forest canopy, makes you sweat and gasp for air. The smell of the forest fills your nostrils with a heady mix of herbs and flowers. Man-shaped shadows flit past nearby, invisible trackers in the green gloom of the deep forest.

After a long, oppressive trek into the heart of the forest, Alpha leads you out of the trees into a great open space. At last, you can breathe! ▶ 89

23

You recall the slave boy that Deridedes had kidnapped, and the birthmark he had.

'That boy you say you lost to slavers – did he have a horseshoe birthmark in the back of his hand?' you ask.

Krio and Selene snap to attention, staring at you. 'Yes, yes he did!' says Krio.

'Have you seen our Magnes? Our sweet boy?' says Selene.

'Ah, so that is his name.' You explain how you found him in the tent of that evil trickster, Deridedes, and how you freed him, and even gave the boy some money but that he'd been so young when he'd been taken that he didn't remember his name or where he came from.

'Please, find him for us, we beg you,' says Selene, distraught and with tears in her eyes.

Krio puts a hand on your arm. 'Please, help us, you are strong, clever, resourceful – a hero of the age! Please, find our boy.'

How can you refuse? You tell them you will search for him, and bring him home if you can. Gain the codeword *Parted*.

But for now, there is business to be done. Or perhaps not, who can say? ▶ **56**

24

You walk down the long gallery and show the painting to Erifili. She towers over you, as she holds up the painting.

'Wow!' she says, 'look at that, it's magnificent! A genuine Apelles too, and one I've never seen – must be a lost one. Where did you get it?'

'That would be telling,' you say guardedly.

'Well, never mind, never mind, I'll give you a hundred and seventy-five pyr for it, right now.'

An offer that is too good to refuse – gain 175 pyr and cross off **A Hero in Hell by Apelles** from your Adventure Sheet.

'Do you think you can get any more lost Apelles paintings?' she asks.

'Maybe, yes,' you say.

'All right, then, in that case, I appoint you as my roving art dealer, scouring the world for lost works by master Apelles!'

Gain the title **Arcadian Art Dealer**.

'Now get out there and don't come back until you've found a masterpiece!' says Erifili grinning broadly.

▶ **282** and choose again.

25

The gigantic serpent lunges at you, but you dodge aside and deliver a savage blow to its body, drawing blood. The serpent hisses in pain and backs away. You step towards it with a shout, and it slithers back even more. It's probably thinking that it's already full, so why risk a fight with prey like you that bites back?

Anyway, you seize your chance and quickly climb up the statue and take the last remaining eye. Note the **Eye of Hyperion** on your Adventure Sheet. Then you leave the temple and its serpentine guardian as fast as you can.

You soon realise that the temple was built at the bottom of a gully through which runs a lively brook. It is actually quite near the western edge of the Deep Forest, although hidden from view. You are able to step out into open ground, near your original target for the Fast Travel Catapult.

▶ **804**

26

You eat some of the food of the gods. Almost instantly you begin to bleed out of every orifice. To your horror, you see that your blood has turned to a black ichor, like tar. You are dying in agony.

Your god appears to you. 'Foolish mortal! Foolish, foolish mortal. Now we can do nothing to bring you back, for you have broken the one rule we cannot bend – that no mortal may eat of the food of the gods and thus achieve immortality without the permission of Zeus, the Giver of Law. I can do nothing; Thanatos will take you. All of us and the Vulcanverse itself are doomed!'

▶ **750**

27

Pan, even in his dreams, hears your prayer. You may remove one of the **stink**, **Artemis's curse**, or **Aphrodite's curse**, if you have one of them. When you are done, you leave the Shrine.

▶ **463**

28

If you have the title **The Hotelier** ▶ **700** immediately. If not, read on.

If you have the codeword *Proprietor* ▶ **62** immediately. If not, read on.

You have come to a bridge across a bend in the river Alpheus. Where once the river ran dry, it now gushes and gurgles its way happily to the sea, ever since you re-constituted the river god, Alpheus. If you have the codeword *Noodles* ▶ **297** immediately. If not, read on.

From here you can go:

North-east to the Woodlands	▶ **60**
East along the riverbank	▶ **361**
South	▶ **822**
West to the Wineries	▶ **417**

29

You are returning to your rooms when you spot three figures huddled around your door. You pause for a moment to listen.

'Are you sure this is worth it, the Steward's a proper hero type, could kill us easily!' hisses one of them. You recognize Timandra, the dryad with long grasses and daisies for hair.

And there is Jas, working at the lock. 'Yes, yes, it's worth it – inside is a door to the very Vault of Vulcan himself, for storing not just the Steward's stuff, but the treasures of the god himself!'

'Well hurry up then,' whispers Damara the water nymph. You can see her wet footprints leading up to the door.

You sigh in disappointment. So much for Jas's promise.

Literally broken in minutes. That shifty little cheating tyke. You should have killed him.

You step forward and clear your throat.

'Eeeek!' shrieks Timandra.

'Too late!' wails Damara.

'Er... it's not what it looks like,' stutters Jas.

You shake your head and reach for your weapon. With that the three of them take to their heels as fast as they can, hurtling off down the corridor and away. You consider giving chase, but Timandra could easily lose you in the woods, and once Damara has found water, you won't be able to follow without being able to breathe underwater. And Jas can gallop at quite a lick. You sigh, realising you will have to let them go, and enter your chambers. Clearly, you don't have a butler anymore so will you:

Enter the Vault   ▶ 828

Leave your rooms   ▶ 282

30

Terpe greets you with a trill of laughter. She lifts you in her arms and you gaze back into her clear grey eyes which sparkle with frank good humour.

'Put your trust in the Bright Lord, my darling,' she coos in your ear. 'Laurel leaves on your brow will serve better than a battered helm, and beguiling words will vanquish more foes than any sword.'

Did you know then who she spoke of? In dreams there is no chronology or logic. It is Apollo. Mark him on your Adventure Sheet as your god and then ▶ 769

31

'The wisdom of Artemis is not so easily given, mortal! You must offer the goddess a sacrifice,' says the dryad of the shrine in a voice laden with portent.

'What sort of thing?' you ask.

'Um... Approved offerings are things like pomegranate honey, or venison sausages, but only from deer that have been hunted with a permit,' says the invisible dryad in a kind of religious chant. You can't help but notice the voice gets lighter and a little more excited and a lot less pious as she goes on. 'Oh, oh, and honey cakes! And even better, pomegranate wine, if you can find... er... I mean, the goddess would appreciate such things...'

If you have either some **pomegranate honey**, **venison sausages**, **honey cake** or **pomegranate wine** and wish to put one on the altar, cross it off and ▶ 336

If not, or if you don't want to right now will you:

Go north on the Way   ▶ 419

Go south on the Way   ▶ 801

Go west into the Woodlands   ▶ 60

32

You take the coins. 'The gods help those who help themselves, and the dead are beyond our help. I'll go to market so that we don't go hungry tonight.'

Add +1 to your STRENGTH score, then ▶ 753

33

You explain that you found something while fishing in the River Ladon. There aren't many places where such a thing could have been written, so you hand the confession of Polycrates to Cressida on the off chance he lives here or in the surrounding area.

The basileus or magistrate takes the scroll, unfolds it, and reads. You see her brow furrow for a moment. She looks up at you. 'Let me check, perhaps there is a Polycrates in the village. Wait here, I won't be long,' she says, as she gets to her feet and leaves the hall. Make an INGENUITY roll at difficulty 7.

Succeed   ▶ 702

Fail   ▶ 745

34

You join the twins on the blanket. They look up at you, squinting.

'Twenty-five pyr stake to join this game,' says one of them. It is the one called Ataktos – you think, for they are very hard to tell apart.

The other, Pioataktos nods at a pile of coins in the middle of the blanket. 'Put your money down, and get ready to lose, punk!' he says with a cheeky grin.

If you want to put your money down ▶ 434. If not, or you haven't got the money, then you can:

Wait for Lefkia   ▶ 312

Leave this place   ▶ 547

35

You have come to the ancient, lichen-mottled bridge where Phainos the fisherman hanged himself. You have his rod as a memento of his deeds as a great angler but there is nothing else of interest here.

Where will you go?

West on the Way   ▶ 20

South-west into the forest   ▶ 189

East on the Way   ▶ 380

South, into the dried-up river valley   ▶ 403

36

Snapping yourself out of the brain fugue the Shadowhunter has put you under, you pull out the lightning flint and strike it. A flash of bright flight bursts out around you and tears up the black inky cloud of night into shreds of darkness in an instant. They flutter to the ground like ashes and drain away into the ground. Once again you have preserved your shadow from attack. But why is it coming for *your* shadow, and who, if anyone, sent it? These are questions that remain unanswered for now.

From here you can go:

East to the eastern bridge	▶ 801
West to the western bridge	▶ 14
North to the Woodlands	▶ 60
South to some hills	▶ 822

37

You have come to Ladon's Lake. If you have the codeword *Plenty* ▶ 591 immediately.

If not but you have the codeword *Pumped* ▶ 587 immediately.

Otherwise, if this box ❑ was already ticked ▶ 188 immediately. If the box is empty, put a tick in it now and read on.

The lake is a strange sight indeed. It looks like it has been paved over with great limestone slabs, and not only that, it is bitterly cold. You step out onto the lake and realise with shocked surprise that the limestone slabs are frozen and rimed with ice.

You take some time to hammer one of the slabs over and over until it shatters. You clear it away to see that the water of the lake below is also frozen. How odd! And then sounds behind you cause you to turn. A slow column of ten or so hoplites, armed with spear and shield, are escorting two ox-wagons. They are moving slowly, so whatever is in those wagons is very heavy indeed.

Walking, or rather shambling beside the wagon are four or five workmen, or perhaps slaves judging by their demeanour.

You decide to hide behind a withered, frostbitten tree at the lakeside to observe events.

The wagons trundle out on the ice. A man in a Corinthian helmet with a black crest looks like the commander. His men wear simple cone shaped helmets of bronze but they all have a breastplate, greaves, long spear and shield. Each shield has an unusual symbol, three arms protruding from the shield boss, each black-painted arm bearing a torch.

The officer shouts orders, and the workers shuffle along sullenly. He has to beat them into unloading the carts. At first they begin to haul out bags of ice, but that's just to keep the main cargo cold – frozen limestone slabs. They begin replacing the one you broke and any others that might be thawing out under the hot Arcadian sun.

For whatever reason, it seems they want to keep the lake,

and presumably Ladon himself trapped beneath, frozen and the river dry. But why?

After a while, the wagons turn away and head back up the river valley. Will you:

Follow them	▶ 109
Come back later	▶ 81

38

❑❑❑

Put a tick in one of the boxes and then read on.

If one box is now ticked	▶ 162
If two boxes are now ticked	▶ 777
If three boxes are now ticked	▶ 703

39

Where once the Alpheus ran dry, it is now full of life. The river rushes by in torrents, and tumbles off the edge of the plateau in a great cascade of roiling water, known as the Alpheus falls. You look over the edge – the waters rush down over rock and stone into a pool below, where it flows on down river, gushing and tumbling. Nearby on a small wooden quay overlooking the waterfall rapids are some bronze-banded barrels. Could you risk riding the falls in a barrel?

Ride the falls	▶ 70
Head north to the lower tarn	▶ 545
Head east to the old arch	▶ 340

40

You step inside you to be welcomed by the vile stench of infection and decay. Upon a wide mattress of horse-hair, wool and straw lies Chiron, first amongst centaurs, laid out as if dead, although he still breathes, fast and shallow. One shoulder is shattered, more like mincemeat than flesh, and it has turned rotten.

'What happened?' you ask.

'Kakas shattered his shoulder with a great club of bronze-capped wood, and now it has gone bad. Only Chiron has the power to cure such a thing, but as you can see, he is in a coma. Soon he will die,' says Velosina, her shoulders slumped, her face like a mask in a Greek tragedy.

'Kakas?'

'A giant who has made his lair in the ruins of Fort Blackgate on the other side of the river valley,' says Velosina. 'Nessus, a renegade centaur, leader of a rebel warband, paid the giant to kill him, after Chiron exiled Nessus from the Sacred Stables.'

'Hmm… a giant. I could deal with him,' you muse.

'Well, beware if you do; he is said to breathe fire,' says Velosina.

If you have an **ivory shoulder blade** ▶ 115 immediately. If not, read on.

There is nothing you can do for Chiron unfortunately, except perhaps go out into the Vulcanverse and look for a cure. You leave the Sacred Stables and head south.

▶ 463

41

'Key' is the answer. (Or 'lock'; either will do.) You say it out loud and the door rumbles open. It leads on one side to the Arcady Trail, an earthen path that runs around the central areas of this land, and into a cave beneath the clifftop plateau of the Alpheus river. From here you can:

Enter the cave	▶ 486
Take the trail	▶ 238

42

You were taken by surprise by the sudden mushrooming of the vapour cloud, no doubt just as all the other heroes were. The black vapour closes in around you. You try not to breathe it in, but it doesn't matter, for you can feel it penetrating deep into your skin. You look down at your hands – you cannot move them, and they are taking on a shiny golden lustre! You try to scream but your lungs have stopped moving.

You have been turned into solid gold. At least you're worth something now, you think to yourself.

And then you realise you are still thinking. You should be dead, surely? But soon your thoughts fade, and your mind sinks into a kind of dream. It seems your soul is still trapped in this body of gold. You sleep, and dream of open meadows, fields of green and horses, galloping across wide plains, wild and free but you are incarcerated in a prison made of your own golden skin.

Unfortunately, as your soul is trapped and you are not truly dead, the gods cannot bring you back this time.

If you have the codeword *Noble* ▶ 72 immediately. If not, read on.

You dream endless dreams, wrapped in gold, your body a priceless tomb. The sun and the moon rise and set, the world turns, the Vulcanverse evolves and changes but you do not, for you are lost and forgotten forever.

▶ 750

43

❑

Put a tick in the box. If there was a tick in the box already ▶ 112 immediately. If not, read on.

Gain the codeword *Prisoner*. There is no sight nor sound of Jas the Helot. Where could he be? Expecting the worst, you search your rooms but cannot find him, drunk, asleep or otherwise. You do find a papyrus scroll on the table though. It says:

'We have kidnapped your butler, Jas. Bring 200 pyr to the Treycross Market on the Arcady Trail between the Dales and the Wineries as soon as possible, or the satyr gets it.
Signed threateningly by
Dread Damara the Destroyer
Timandra, the Tyrant of Terror
- Queens of the Forest Bandits'

Queens of the forest bandits, eh? And are those names for real? You put a hand to your chin. Do you actually want him back? On the other hand, if you don't get him back, it'll make you look weak in the eyes of the people of Arcadia. Also, without him you cannot get any of the true benefits of the Herodion Suite. You sigh with resignation. You'll have to try. Until he is rescued you can only:

Take a tour of your rooms	▶ 422
Enter the Vault of Vulcan in Arcadia	▶ 828
Leave your rooms	▶ 282

44

'All very well, but look at this – so many delicious recipes for mutton and lamb. Here, look, wine marinades, forest mushrooms, herbs, and so much more.'

'I do love mutton, it's true,' says, Kaustikia, snatching your book and flicking through it. You are amazed she can read.

'Oh yes, nice,' she says. 'Must try that one, looks delish!'

Kaustikia thinks for a moment, and then heaves a great sigh.

'I suppose you're right,' she says. 'I'll get my beauty sleep somewhere else.' With that she hands your book back, spreads her wings and surges up into the sky and away. You congratulate yourself on a job well done.

Except that, as Kaustikia takes to the air, her cloud nest starts to dissolve around your feet and you are suddenly falling through empty space. You hit the ground so hard that your body explodes like a ripe tomato, spraying your blood and guts across the forest floor. However, you have saved the Great Green Ones.

Gain the codeword *Purify*.
Lose the codeword *Phosphoric*.
Then ▶ 111

45

For a seasoned adventurer like you, a couple of local thugs aren't much of a problem. The fat one is slow and predictable; you duck under his club and then open his throat with your blade in the first move of the fight. He falls to the ground gurgling out his life into the grassy earth. The satyr gasps in horror, and simply gallops away, terrified.

You turn to face Deridedes, whose face turns pale. He gulps. 'Umm…. Now look, there's no need for more violence, you won fair and square, I see that now.'

You step towards him, violent retribution in your heart.

'Wait!' he says. 'I know where the parents are, the ones I stole… er… bought that boy from! Let me live, and I'll tell you, I promise!'

You narrow your eyes in thought. What to do?

Let him live, perhaps you can
    find the boy and help him   ▶ 791
Kill him, it's too late for the boy
    to go back to his old life anyway   ▶ 152

46

You find the architect, Hypatia of Iskandria, walking around the fort measuring things and making notes. She barely notices your arrival. Lefkia, however, greets you at the shattered gates. 'Hello, hello,' she says happily, her brown eyes bright with humour. She's a cheerful lass, and also very good at her work.

'Have you got all the stuff? Hah, feels like I'm always asking you that! But still, it's a pleasure to be working with you again. Actually, to be honest, to be working at all.'

If you have:

500 pyr
timber x 2
limestone x 2
vinegar of Hades x 1
bucket of gypsum x 1
box of paints x 1

and want them to start work on rebuilding the fort, cross the money and materials off your Adventure Sheet and ▶ 121

If not, there is nothing more you can do here. You can come back when you have everything, but for now you head south. ▶ 85

47

You are no fool, and you use the beeswax to block your ears and shut out the beguiling song of the dryads. You step in and put your knife to Phearei's throat, just as she wakes. Her eyes snap open, pale green and luminescent like sick, diseased moonlight, though once you thought it the most beautiful light in the world.

'Save me, my loves!' she cries, and her slaves rise up, and rush at you. You have no choice but to drive your dagger deep into her throat and slay her right there and then. A pity really, you were hoping for some vengeful gloating, but you

can't always get what you want, as they say. As soon as Phearei dies – in a mess of gurgling, green ichor – her love slaves pull up short. They stare at each other in amazement. 'Free at last!' mutters one.

'Can it be?' says another. Another falls to her knees at your feet. 'You did it, you saved us all,' she says. Another spits on the dryad's corpse. 'Such evil, to force us to love her like that,' he says.

The other dryad flees in horror, shrieking her fear and despair, leaving you to your victory.

Phearei, the most ancient, and in truth, also the most wicked dryad of the woodlands, is dead. Her body begins to wither and shrivel before your eyes, leaving only her wooden heart. Note the **heart of ash** on your Adventure Sheet and get the title **Dryad's Doom**. There is nothing more to do here, so you lead her love slaves out of the forest and set them free. No one dares disturb your passage for you have slain their mistress.

And now, where will you go?

Back to the Sivi's beehives   ▶ 8
Leave this place   ▶ 225

48

If you have the title **Mayor of Bridgadoom** ▶ 196 immediately. If not, read on.

If you have the title **The Embezzler** ▶ 829 immediately. If not, read on.

The hamlet of Bridgadoom, as it is rather oddly called, seems to be thriving now that the rivers have been restored. Traders travelling up and down the river in their small barges stop off here to buy and sell, or simply to rest. There are several places you can visit; a tailor's shop, the local ruler's hall, a professional gossip, and a merchant. You notice there is also an unusual shrine in the village square – a shrine to Moros, he who brings men to their doom. Anyway, who will you visit?

Cressida the magistrate   ▶ 120
Phineas the rumour monger   ▶ 153
Gelos the tailor   ▶ 187
Ersi the grain merchant   ▶ 75
Leave the hamlet   ▶ 801

49
❑

If you have the title **Lion slayer** ▶ 371 immediately. If not, read on.

Put a tick in the box. If there was a tick in the box already ▶ 76 immediately. If not, read on.

The woods grow darker still, and the trees seem to crowd in around you, as if trying to block your path in silent outrage that you should dare to come here.

You are beginning to think your footsteps are the first to tread here in a hundred years or more when you find a narrow track, hacked through the undergrowth by men with machetes.

You follow the trail until it comes to a small clearing. You find the bodies of two hunters, their rotting remains clearly showing that they have been ripped apart by razor sharp talons and then devoured. Their leather armour has been sliced in two, including a bronze helm. One of them even had a shield; it too has been shattered.

Not far away you hear a great roar of rage, a lion's roar. The rumours you heard on your journeys are true then – the Nemean lion, driven out of Notus by glory-seeking huntsmen, has come to make his home here in the deep forests of Arcadia. Even so, these fools tried to hunt him down, no doubt for the glory. Another roar fills the gloom. By the sound of it, he has caught your scent... What will you do?

Face the lion in battle   ▶ **113**
Run away   ▶ **281**

50
❑

Put a tick in the box. If there was a tick in the box already ▶ **816** immediately. If not, read on.

You are examining the catapult when a high-pitched voice sounds from behind you.

'I can fix that for you, if you want.'

You turn, and see a boy of about nine or ten years of age, dressed in a chiton with a heavy leather apron over it, and holding a quill pen in one hand, and a scroll book in the other. You stare at him, nonplussed for a moment.

'I'm Mandrocles the engineer,' says the boy. 'You bought up my contract, thanks for that. Now I work for you.'

'Mandrocles?' you say.

'Yeah, though people call me Man for short.'

'A boy called Man? And how can you be an engineer anyway, you're just a kid?'

'I know, I know, but I'm actually fifty-six years old.'

'What?'

'It's a long story, but basically I was thrown into this fountain of youth thing. Rejuvenated me.'

'And where is this fountain of youth?' you ask.

'Hah, if only I had a gold piece for every time I've been asked that, but I have no idea. I was unconscious at the time, and I nearly drowned. But anyway, there we are.'

'Well, all right then. So you can fix this. What does it do anyway?'

'It's a fast travel device. Flings you across Arcadia to wherever you choose. There should be nets waiting to catch you at the other end.'

'Riiight...' you say.

'No really, I mean it. I can fix this now, but I wouldn't use it until you've checked all the catch-nets. It's been a while, I'm sure they'll need repairing too.'

To fix the catapult, Mandrocles needs 2 **copper cogs** and 1 **lava gem**. If you have these items and wish to give them to Mandrocles ▶ **782**

If not, you will have to come back later. Will you:

Enter the Palace   ▶ **96**
Go to the lagoon   ▶ **345**
Leave this place   ▶ **547**

51

'Trees? Deer hide in the trees; without them they'll be easier to catch. Venison, yum! Anyway, it's been nice chatting but it's time for my breakfast,' she says, readying an attack.

'Hold on, what about the...'

'Sheep, they'll die too.'   ▶ **13**
'Satyrs, they'll die too.'   ▶ **256**
'Centaurs, they'll die too.'   ▶ **218**

52

You have returned to the farmlands to see how Drosos is getting on. Roll a die:

score 1-2   ▶ **677**
score 3-6   ▶ **718**

53

You take out the bone flute and begin to play a slow, soothing melody. To your relief, you see that the serpent begins to sway back and forth in time to your movements and the musical rhythm of your lullaby.

Soon the great serpent coils up, its head swaying to the music until, its belly already full, it sinks into sleep. Quickly you climb up and take the last remaining eye. Note the **Eye of Hyperion** on your Adventure Sheet. Then you leave the temple and its sleeping guardian as fast as you can.

You soon realise that the temple was built at the bottom of a gully through which runs a lively brook. It is actually quite near the western edge of the Deep Forest, although hidden from view. You are able to step out into open ground, near your original target for the Fast Travel Catapult.

▶ **804**

54

Your mind fills with dream-like images of a vast hallway. The ceiling is painted with thousands of leaves and flowers. There are small holes in the flowers through which light flickers down, dimly lighting your way. The floor is covered in carpets of green, and the roof is held up with pillars of stone, carved to look like trees.

Suddenly, doors burst open behind you, and men and women wearing wolf-head masks and wielding daggers burst in. They chase you down the long, long hallway, until you come to a shrine to the goddess Artemis at the far end, upon the altar of which rest three finely crafted arrows that seem to glow with divine light.

You grab them, and turn – and your pursuers fade away like dust in the wind...

And then suddenly, as is the way in dreams, you find yourself in the palace of the legendary King Midas, whose touch is golden. You present the arrows to the King and they are instantly turned to gold.

You wake with a gasp, your eyes filled with golden light for a second or two.

You shake your head to clear it. 'Everything all right?' says Zenia.

You nod. You are back in the real world.

If you have some more **kykeon mushrooms** and 10 more pyr and want to try another vision ▶ **737**

If not, you can head back to the market (▶ **728**) or leave the area (▶ **12**).

55

If you have the title **Favoured of Demeter** ▶ **298** immediately. If not, read on.

If you have the codeword *Priestly* ▶ **223** immediately. If not, read on.

The temple is quite small compared to many in the Greek world, with only three columns along each side, and two caryatid columns flanking the entrance, one a woman holding up a basket of fruit, the other, sheaves of wheat. Left untended, it has fallen into disrepair. Inside, murals on the wall are in a poor state with great gaps where the plaster has fallen away, and the paint flaked and faded. The altar is covered in bracken and dirt, and it smells pretty bad. Some woodland creatures have been using it as a toilet it would seem.

If you have a **Contract: Priestess of Demeter** ▶ **373**. (To check if you have it, note **52** in your Current Location box, ▶ **101** and then return to this section after.)

If you haven't got it, there is nothing more you can do here for now. You can go:

West along the coast	▶ **380**
South along the coast	▶ **419**
South-west into the farmlands	▶ **270**

56

'So, we farm a lot of sheep here, and harvest much wool, more than happy to sell you some,' says Krio, as you sip from the cup of sheep's milk. It is fresh and very flavoursome. 'It's twenty-five pyr a bale.'

'Seems a bit pricey,' you say.

'I admit it. But there's this dragon, Kaustikia, she comes

down and takes a few sheep every few days, so we lose more than the usual you might lose to wolves or disease. So, I have to charge more.'

'A dragon!'

'Indeed, a talking, acid-spitting dragon. I had to agree to her terms long ago – either she eats my sheep or she eats me. And my family!'

If you have the codeword *Purify* ▶ **135** immediately.

If you do not have *Purify*, you can buy **bales of wool** for 25 pyr each, although you can carry no more than three at a time. Add them to your Adventure Sheet and cross off the money. When you are ready, you take your leave of the shepherds ▶ **822**

57

You emerge blinking into bright sunlight, in a wide expansive clearing. At the far end you see a stone temple of ancient design, with a carved frieze of wolves, bears and lions abasing themselves before the goddess Artemis. A great moon symbol, flanked by two ivory tusks adorns the temple top.

At the base of the temple is a large, wing-backed throne of dark, polished wood, carved into a sculpted mass of trees, leaves and vines, through which men and women writhe and twist. An incredible piece of art. Upon it sits a heavy-set man with a shock of red hair and a big red beard that spreads out across his chest like a blanket. He is virtually naked, save for a deer-skin loin cloth. His body is muscled and lithe but also covered in red hair. It is hard to tell his age.

His eyes are green, and seem to glitter like emeralds, and upon his head he wears a wreath of many-coloured forest flowers, silver scarab beetles inlaid with jade, and leaves made of thinly beaten gold all held in place by many human finger bones, clasped together even in death.

At his right hand sits a young woman, also almost naked save for a bear-skin cloak, a necklace of animal teeth, and a bear-skin hat. Her eyes are also green, and glitter unnaturally too.

Flanking the trio at the throne are a score or so of men and women, dressed in skins of various styles and designs. Interestingly, none of them seems to have any weapons.

'Welcome to my court,' says the man on the throne, 'I am Lykaon the Wolf-King, and I rule the Deep Forests.' He points to the woman next to him. 'This is my daughter Kallisto, and these,' he says, waving a hand at the men and women to either side, 'are my sons and daughters.'

'What, all of them?' you say in surprise.

'Eh? Oh, I see, no, no, they're called the Sons or Daughters of the Wolf… you know, they're not actually… it's just a clan name, do you see, though Kallisto actually is my daughter.'

'Ah, right.'

'Anyway, you killed Alpha, the most beautiful and wisest of all our wolves. Also, the most blood-thirsty, but well, that's wolves for you. I am much displeased.'

'The wolf was terrorising a local woodcutter, I was just trying to protect him,' you explain.

'The woodcutter who killed Alpha's children? That woodcutter?'

'Yes, but don't you think the life of a human is worth more than that of a wolf?'

Lykaon's brow darkens in anger. Some of the men and women behind him mutter bitterly.

'No, actually, I don't. Most assuredly, I don't. What are humans but harbingers of destruction, cutting down trees, covering the land in their fields of grain, butchering animals in their thousands, filling the rivers with their dung? A plague of locusts, that's what humans are. And the wolf? Predator and killer yes, but noble and true, never taking more than it needs, putting the needs of the pack above its own.'

You look around the glade. 'But you are all humans too,' you point out.

'Are we?' says Kallisto enigmatically.

Lykaon gives you a tight smile. 'Anyway, there's a more pressing problem.'

'Which is?'

▶ **68**

58

If you have the codeword *Pinot* ▶ **88** immediately. If not, read on.

Maron is ready, a flask of pomegranate wine in one hand.

'Drunk again?' you say.

'And your point is?' replies Maron. 'Anyway, why not join me? Here's your share, after all.'

He gives you a couple of bottles of pomegranate wine. Note **pomegranate wine x 2** on your Adventure Sheet.

'Come back for more later!' he says. Gain the codeword *Pinot*. You say your farewells to the drunken satyr and head out. From here, you can go:

North to the Arcady Trail	▶ **238**
West to Treycross on the Arcady Trail	▶ **728**
South on the Trail	▶ **338**
East to the bridge over the river Alpheus	▶ **14**

59

The priest of Hermes has sent you off to Arcadia in your sleep once more. This time you wake up with a start to find yourself in a warm, wooded glade – and a hooded figure is rummaging through your back pack!

With a strangled cry of rage, you stagger to your feet, still groggy from your journey, and the figure gives a squeaking yelp, as of a young woman. She dashes away into the woods. Her hood falls back, revealing a mop of bright red hair but you are unable to see her face before she is gone.

Quickly you check your gear – you have not lost any items but you been robbed of up to 50 pyr. Cross it off.

Cursing your luck, you look around. Once again you have arrived in some woodland close to the Summer Palace of Arcadia.

▶ 686

60

You have come to the Woodlands of Ambrosia, once a kind of ornamental garden but in a wild, unconstrained style, the home of dryads and nymphs, where the gods loved to walk on a soft, summer's eve. Here too, grew the mushrooms that the goddess Hebe harvested to make Ambrosia. As cup-bearer to the gods, she served them this nectar of eternal youth in old Olympus, along with the delicious honey that came from these parts.

Now the woodlands are truly wild, the paths and trails overgrown and hard to find. No gods have walked in its sun-dappled glades for many years, and who knows if Hebe's mushrooms still grown in the shadowed cloisters of the forest.

Nearby you can see a large clearing given over to an apiary, where the honey bees lived.

Will you:

Go deeper into the woods	▶ 176
Go to the old apiary	▶ 8
Leave this place	▶ 225

61

❑

Put a tick in the box. If there was a tick in the box already ▶ 542 immediately. If not, read on.

Here lies the stockade that was Nessus' bandit camp. Its wooden walls are slowly collapsing, a stake has fallen out here, another stands askew there. The gates hang from their hinges, and its interior is empty. It has been abandoned. Outside, you find the grave of Nessus, hastily dug, and a simple wooden stake with a board nailed onto it as a headstone. Someone has daubed the word 'Nessus' upon it. An ignominious end.

Still, you search through the scattered remains of the interior and find a **jug of dandelion wine**, a **bucket of gypsum**, of all things, and a **laurel wreath (+1)**. There is nothing else of interest left, so you take your leave ▶ 189.

62

❑

Put a tick in the box. If there was a tick in the box already ▶ 103 immediately. If not, read on.

You return to the site where the new inn is to be built. The architect, Hypatia of Iskandria, is working on some plans under a makeshift lean-to as shelter from the sun. Further on, you see Helen sitting under a similar lean-to.

'Ah, welcome back, Steward! I've completed the main plans, so we can press on when you're ready. We'll need plenty of materials, I can hire some builders but we'll also need a plasterer and a decorator,' says Hypatia, all bustle and business. Competence incarnate.

'Well, I already employ Lefkia, will she do?'

'Oh yes, she's perfect.'

'I'll send for her straight away,' you say.

'Um… there is one other thing,' says Hypatia, her brow furrowing.

'Yes? Is there a problem?' you ask.

'Well, it's Helen… she's a little… strange. And the sun, she hates the sun – so do others but not like that, she seems *scared* of it.'

'I know, she comes from a land of little light and much shadow and her people simply aren't used to so much sunlight, I wouldn't worry about it.'

'A land of darkness and shadow? Surely you don't mean… How did she get out?' says Hypatia, looking askance at Helen hiding from the sun in her makeshift shed.

You cough, and bluster on. 'Anyway, I'll get Lefkia down here now, as soon as I can. No time to waste!' you say, changing the subject. ▶ 482.

63

Murdering a truffle hunting father is perhaps a step too far for you, especially as it would probably mean the death of his daughter too, so you make your way out of the 'land of roots' and out to the surface and back to the Arcady Trail. There must be a cure for the black blight out there somewhere, if you can find it in time.

▶ 160

64

If you have the codeword *Praise-Ares* ▶ 178. If not, read on.

If you have the title, **Accursed of Ares** ▶ 746 immediately. If not, read on.

You have come to an old abandoned shrine to the war god Ares, slaughterer of men and insatiable in battle. It is an altar of marble, carved with a hoplite shield and crossed spears on each side.

As you draw near, a figure appears out of the very air itself, armed and armoured, a Warrior of Ares. The figure speaks in a hollow voice,

'Ares, god of war, sings as he slays, and his song fills the hearts of his warriors with battle-rage. Only those who are worthy may pray at this shrine.'

Prove your worth and fight	▶ 796
Leave this place	▶ 832

65

Pan, even in his dreams, hears your prayer. Gain a **benison x 1**. Note it on your Adventure Sheet. It gives you +1 on your next attribute roll. Once it has been used, cross it off. When you are done, you leave the Shrine ▶ 463

66

The Fast Travel Catapult has been fixed up, oiled and polished, and is ready to go. You crank up the catapult arm and get into the surprisingly comfortable bucket seat. A winch on one side lets you choose the direction and destination, and a lever on the other will hurl you up into the air. Where to?

North-western Arcadia	▶ 107
Northern Arcadia	▶ 210
North-eastern Arcadia	▶ 264
Eastern Arcadia	▶ 174
South-eastern Arcadia	▶ 306
Southern Arcadia	▶ 368
South-western Arcadia	▶ 406
Western Arcadia	▶ 570

Decide against it and:

Enter the Palace	▶ 96
Go to the lagoon	▶ 345
Leave this place	▶ 547

67

You turn away from the ominous lake, and the trees that seem to radiate menace and head for open ground. But then the thick vines that are wrapped around the trees begin to stir, and suddenly they lash out at you, more like the tentacles of the Kraken then a forest creeper!

You hack at them, and cut away great chunks of plant, but they seem to regenerate at an impossible speed. Soon you will be overwhelmed.

If you have at least three **lava gems** and wish to use them to escape ▶ 311

If not, you will have to try and dash past the plants, and it will not be easy for you suspect these are the terrible Stranglevines of legend. Make a GRACE roll at difficulty 9.

Succeed	▶ 240
Fail	▶ 269

68

'You have defiled our sacred laws,' says Kallisto.

'By killing a wolf? Surely not?'

'No, no, it's not that, that is the way of the life, bitter though it is. No, by coming here you have defiled the temple of Artemis the Huntress, goddess of the moon and the bow,' says Lykaon.

'But I had no choice, you people forced me here!'

'That's as may be,' says Lykaon, but the holy laws don't say anything about *how* you got here, just that you are here, and you are unclean…'

'And so we must hunt you down and kill you,' finishes Kallisto.

'What, like a manhunt?'.

'Exactly so,' says Lykaon. 'To honour the goddess of the hunt, and cleanse the temple.'

'And also for the sport. Eating your liver will be sweet vengeance for the slaying of Alpha, our favourite wolf pet,' says Kallisto.

'Hold on though, there's a chance I can escape right?' you say.

'Oh yes, indeed – you get a ten minute start and everything,' says Lykaon.

'But you use wolves, what, like hunting dogs?' you inquire.

'Um… I wouldn't really say that, no…but instead… well, you'll see.'

'And how many of these hunts have you had?'

'Oh, hundreds and hundreds over the years,' says Kallisto.

'And how many people have escaped?' you ask.

Kallisto and Lykaon exchange a grin.

'Ummm….'

One of the hunters standing near the throne leans in and says – 'There was that one woman.'

'Oh yes!' says Lykaon enthusiastically, 'she got away.'

'But she was…, well, you know,' says Kallisto.

'Oh yeah…' mutters Lykaon shaking his head in mock sorrow. 'You're a great hero though, I'm sure you can make it!'

The men and women behind the throne start laughing which tightens the resolve in your heart to beat them at this game.

'Are there any rules to the hunt?' you ask.

'It's simple, north of here further into the depths of the forest, is a marble statue of Artemis, with two wolves at her side, hunting. Get to that alive, and you are free. Oh, and you get the prize!' says Kallisto.

'A prize! What is it?'

Kallisto blinks at you… 'I… forget'.

'It's been so long since… well, if you make it we'll have to look it up but I'm sure it's valuable and that,' says Lykaon.

Lykaon raises his hand into the air, and everything stills. After a moment or two of portentous silence, he chops his hand down and from the interior of the temple behind him a chorus of wolf howls rise up to the skies.

'Let the hunt begin!' shouts Lykaon in response.

And then something astonishing happens. In front of your very eyes Lykaon begins to change, as do his 'children'. Their jaws lengthen, their hair grows into thick fur at an alarming rate, their hands and feet turn claw-like, sprouting vicious looking talons.

Werewolves, the lot of them. Except for Kallisto, she is turning into a bear. You stare, transfixed, as bones crack, skin stretches, muscles bulge and hearts swell, pumping hot red blood, for the hunt is on…

'Run, you fool, run!' she roars, as her body fills out with bear blood and muscle.

▶ 110

69

You and a score or so of other women – mostly adult married mothers, set up tents in a woodland clearing near the temple of Demeter. Thekla tells you that the first day is called *Anodos* or ascent, and is in honour of Persephone's ascent from Hades, where she rises up to bring the fertility and fecundity of spring to the earth and joy to her mother, Demeter.

Pigs have been sacrificed to the goddess the remains of which are placed on altars to Demeter and Persephone, along with cakes that have been baked into the shapes of snakes, penises and vaginas. You and the rest of the women chant songs and prayers to the goddess and once the correct rituals have been observed the cakes and pig parts will be scattered over the Farmlands to ensure fertility.

That evening, you gather together around the fire, eating and drinking and praising the goddess, until you all retire to your tents for a good night's sleep. A rather pleasant day, in fact.

▶ 442

70

You cannot resist the temptation to ride the Alpheus falls in a barrel. You climb in one, and then rock your way to the edge of the quay, and then over the side into the rushing waters.

Roll a die. If you score a 1 ▶ 122

If not ▶ 137

71

Cross the item off your Adventure Sheet. Wolfshadow is chasing you down – you throw the food in his path, and, thank the gods, it works. He stops to feed, buying you a few precious moments to run away along the Arcady Trail, a dusty well-walked path through the woods and overgrown hedgerows of Arcadia. From here you can:

Flee down the Trail west into the Deep Forest ▶ 710
Flee up the Trail north   ▶ 85
Flee along the Trail east   ▶ 728
Flee north-east to the Palace   ▶ 686
Flee south-east into the Dales of Leaf and Stream ▶ 266

72

As you dream dreams of open spaces under wide blue skies, and your mind slowly descends into madness, you are woken suddenly by what feels like a kiss.

You open your eyes and their stands Princess Zoë, the golden daughter of Midas. In the King's tomb, you found her, a golden maiden, but you lifted her father's curse, turned her from gold to flesh, and now it seems she has returned the favour. You look down – you are yourself again.

Zoë is a rather beautiful young woman, and you find her particularly fetching for she is wearing a leather cuirass, greaves and vambraces, a shield slung on her back, a sword at her belt, and a spear in her hand. She grins at you.

'You freed me with Aphrodite's kiss, and now I free you with a kiss.'

Behind her stand the other adventurers who she has also freed from the basilisk's breath.

'You killed the basilisk? How?' you ask.

'As I'd already been turned to gold by my father's hand, albeit by accident, as a living golden maiden, getting turned into gold didn't kill or freeze me, and after, I was able to change back, at will, really, thanks to Aphrodite's kiss. As for killing it. Well....' She shakes her spear and adds, 'You freed me, I said I'd explore the world, and so I am, for it turns out I'm quite the adventurer! Strong in battle, and fearless too, though I say it myself. And now I have my own little band of heroes,' and she gestures to the warriors she has freed.

'We have sworn allegiance to the princess who saved us,' says one.

'Who could resist such courage, such warlike prowess, and also such beauty?' says another.

'We are the Band of Gold, and adventuring we shall go,' says Zoë enthusiastically. 'But don't worry, I wouldn't expect someone like you to join us, in fact, I feel I still owe you so much. If you should ever need me, send for me. We will come and fight by your side.'

She kisses you again on the cheek, and says her farewells. The Golden Princess and her Band of Gold head down through the hills and away into Arcadia and on to adventures new. Gain the title **Kissed by a Golden Princess**.

You gather your thoughts, take a meal and a drink at the inn in the foothills, and head out back onto the Sacred Way.
▶ **20**

73

You don't notice it when you harvest some fool's faecap mushrooms, for they are much alike to the kykeon. You take a moment to wipe the sweat from your eyes and face – and end up rubbing some of its psychotropic spores into your skin. It is highly toxic and you find yourself beginning to rant and rave, screaming at the trees and trying to rip your clothes away. You start to run madly through the forest, careening wildly from tree to tree. Tick the Wound box on your Adventure Sheet. If you are already wounded, then you knock yourself senseless and wolves find and eat you. ▶ **111**. If you are still alive, read on.

Madness takes you... ▶ **105**

74

You try to overcome the fear of losing your love just long enough to kill yourself, but you cannot do it. Phearei's magic is just too strong. Even though you know you are bewitched, you cannot bear to be without her. You go back to your mistress, doomed to serve her for all time, until one far off day you die of old age. Your adventure ends here. ▶ **750**

75

Ersi the grain merchant has a large barn, with a built-in shop front, recently re-furbished, at the southern end of the hamlet of Bridgadoom. She greets you warmly. Ersi is a fat round woman, wearing a pink Phrygian hat, and food-stained robes. On the desk are various cakes and breads she snacks on continuously. One eye is milky and pale, apparently lost to an angry cockerel in the farmlands...

She will buy your grain from you at 25 pyr per **farmlands grain**. Don't forget to cross the grain off if you sell it.

When you are done ▶ **48**

76

You manage to find the trail that leads to the two dead hunters, torn to pieces and eaten by the Nemean lion who has now made his home in the deep forest. The bodies are still there, even more decayed, forlorn testimony to the brute power of the lion. And once again, you hear the roar of the lion in the distance – it knows you are here. You can hear it, thundering through the undergrowth, heading straight for you.

Face the lion in battle	▶ **113**
Run away	▶ **281**

77

The cave is lit by hanging lanterns and is covered in cobwebs but thankfully no spiders that you can see. A ladder on one wall rises up to a hatch in the ceiling, a good hundred and fifty feet up. A hatch in the floor leads to a tunnel that leads all the way to the temple of Arachne in Hades, where you found the tapestry. Where will you go?

Up the ladder	▶ **470**
Back out onto the Arcady Trail	▶ **238**
Through the tunnel to Hades	▶ **661** in *The Houses of the Dead*

78

The door opens once more, clanking aside on rusty old cogs and wheels, but you have already taken the spell fragment. There is nothing else here for you but to move on. Where will you go?

North to the bridge	► 801
West to the low hills	► 822
South on the Sacred Way	► 600 in *The Hammer of the Sun*

79

If you have the codeword *Praise-Artemis* ► 194 immediately. If not, read on.

You spot a young centaur up ahead, hunting in the woods. He seems friendly enough, however, and says, 'There's a shrine to Artemis, goddess of the hunt, somewhere in these trees, though I've never found it. Perhaps you will have better luck.'

The young centaur canters away into the forest. Will you:

| Search for the shrine | ► 625 |
| Leave this place | ► 774 |

80

Pan, capricious, unpredictable and wild, hears you even in his dreams. If you are injured, untick your Wound box. If you are not injured, heal 1 scar. If you are neither wounded nor scarred, then gain a **benison x 1**. Note it on your Adventure Sheet. It gives you +1 on your next attribute roll. Once it has been used, cross it off.

When you are done, you leave the shrine ► 463

81

You are at Ladon's Lake in a valley enclosed by cliffs on either side. From here you can go:

| North along the river | ► 403 |
| South to the Palace | ► 686 |

82

You wait until the early hours of the pre-dawn, for Phearei and her dryads will have been sleeping for the longest time without the sun, and thus will be at their weakest and most sluggish, for the sunlight gives them strength.

You creep through moonlit glades and silvered forest trails, as silently as you can. An owl hoots, and nearby, something rustles in the undergrowth but you arrive at Phearei's arbour unnoticed.

You see her sleeping in her bed of moss and flowers, two of her slave-lovers in her arms, and the rest sleeping nearby. Empty bottles of nectar and wine lie scattered about nearby, a good sign, as her sleep will be the deeper for it.

Just then a dryad steps out of the tree. They set a watch? That's new – perhaps they realised you would be coming for Phearei.

The dryad starts to sing the song of enchantment at the sight of you.

If you have some **beeswax** ► 47
If not ► 565

83

❏

Put a tick in the box. If there was a tick in the box already ► 140 immediately. If not, read on.

You invite many of your friends once again to another banquet, Maron, the wine-drinking ever-drunk satyr, Sivi the beautiful honey dryad, Hypatia of Iskandria the architect, ever-smiling and cheerful Lefkia, Mandrocles the boy engineer, the putative King of Arcadia, Nyctimus, Drosos the farmer, Chiron the centaur and many more that you have met on your adventures.

It is another merry evening, with much pomegranate wine and a marvellous feast wonderfully cooked by Erifili and her team.

At midnight, you are about to propose a toast to Sivi for her sweet honey desserts when suddenly the hall doors are blown open by a bolt of lightning, along with a great rolling blast of thunder. Smoke fills the room. When it clears, there stands an old man, bald and bespectacled with a long white beard, a book under one arm, a staff in the other, wearing blue robes, coughing and spluttering.

He pats the dust off his clothes, muttering to himself, 'By Hermes and Hekate, what awful magic... Really, I'm too old for this. Anyway,' he says, turning to the assembled guests, 'so sorry to bother you, but we need help. I'm Myletes the Wise, from the Academy of Philosophers in Vulcan City, and the Book of Seven Sages has been stolen!'

'Why should we care?' asks Nyctimus.

'Because the Book contains secret knowledge, and esoteric teachings that could be used to cause great harm if it falls into the wrong hands. And unfortunately, it has indeed fallen into the wrong hands.'

'Who has it, then?' you ask.

'We think it has been stolen by Alcyoneus, one of the gigantes.'

'A giant, then?'

'Yes, king of the giants in fact, although that doesn't necessarily mean he's *gigantic*. Yes, he's one of the giants but they're not all huge, although they are all strong warriors or have special powers.'

'I suppose you want me to get this book back for you?' you ask.

'Well, yes, you are a famous hero, with much glory to your name, and titles too like Steward of the Palace, Archon of this and that, Commander of Fort Blackgate, a wolf-runner and so on. Who else should I ask?'

'And where is Alcyoneus?'

'He has his lair in a hidden valley, shielded from the sight of man by Gaia's blessing and guarded by the Grey Sisters.

'The Grey what?'

The Graeae, the Grey Ones, the Grey Witches. ancient hags, born from the sea in a time before the gods. You will have to get past them first.'

'This is sounding harder and harder with every word!' says Nyctimus.

'Indeed,' you agree. 'And also more and more interesting.'

'Will you help us, then?' asks Myletes.

'Perhaps,' you say. 'How would we get there?'

'The same magic I used to get here. I can transport you to the hidden Valley of Bones with this staff,' says Myletes.

'Tell me why it's important again?'

'Well, the knowledge in the Book can be used against mankind and against the gods. The gigantes hate us, and also all the gods, who defeated them in a great war, before they battled the titans even, long ago, so we can assume King Alcyoneus is studying the Book even now.'

'I see. And what's in it for me?' you ask.

'Another title no doubt. But also, Alcyoneus has preyed on mankind for an age, raiding and pillaging from his secret lair, so he will have amassed much treasure over the years. All of it can be yours.'

You look around. Your guests are staring at you in anticipation. You realise you can't really refuse to help, your reputation is on the line, as pretty much all of the great and the good of Arcadia are watching.

'Well, then, of course I will help you. Watch out King Alcyoneus, I am coming for you!' you say with bravado. Your guests applaud loudly, whooping and stamping their feet.

'That is good to hear. Once more will the hero of the age venture forth to save the world, and all that,' says Myletes.

▶ 209

84

❑

Put a tick in the box. If there was a tick in the box already ▶ 631 immediately. If not, read on.

You have returned to the Summer Palace. The portico columns have had the vines that entwined them removed, and the walkway is clean and well swept. Inside, a mural or two has been repainted, rather beautifully in fact, but there is still much work to be done. You find Lefkia, re-plastering a wall in the kitchens, her apron stained with dust and pigment. Her hair is grey with gypsum dust as is her face, and there is a blob of bright green paint on the end of her nose which sets of her sparkling brown eyes nicely, twinkling at you out of her begrimed, dusty face. She looks rather fetching in fact, though a little sweaty...

'Hello, there!' says Lefkia cheerily, 'As you can see I've been busy, but there's still so much to do. Don't worry, though, it'll all get done in the end. Come back later!'

King Nyctimus has moved out while the work is being done, but you can still visit the lagoon or the onager.

Visit the onager	▶ 471
Go to the lagoon	▶ 345
Leave this place	▶ 547

85

The Arcady Trail runs along a ridge of high ground here, flanking the Ladon river valley to the east, and the Deep Forest to the west. To the north, you can see a fort amidst some trees.

A large fountain was built here long ago to help give water to travellers. A statue of Hermes, the patron god of travellers, rests atop it, hence its name – the Fount of Hermes. It has long since dried up and is now little more than crumbling stone.

If you have the codeword *Pernicious* and this box ❑ is empty, tick it and ▶ 563 immediately. Otherwise, read on.

If you have the codeword *Parapet* and want to go north ▶ 220. If not, read on. There is nothing else of interest here.

South on the trail	▶ 455
South-west to a small wood	▶ 475
South and then east to the Deep Forest	▶ 710
North on the trail	▶ 330

86

You have returned to Krio and Selene's sheep farm. They welcome you with a cup of milk and invite you into their home.

If you have the codeword *Parted* ▶ 171 immediately. If not, read on.

If you have the codeword *Provenance* ▶ 23

If not ▶ 56

87

You set up the fishing rod with tackle and bait, and sit at the edge of the bridge, throwing your line into the gushing river. It is a beautiful sunny day in Arcady. Birds twitter, insects buzz, fish jump. Leaf and stream, sun and flowers. You begin to relax.

You can see why Phainos loved to fish here. If only he'd been able to wait for you to come along and restore the river to its former glory. A pity, but then again, now you can enjoy fishing on the bridge instead. Roll two dice:

score 2-4	▶ 145
score 5-7	▶ 179
score 8-10	▶ 202
score 11-12	▶ 239

88

'Greetingshh!' says Maron, drunk as a lord as usual. 'I'm afraid the next bottled vintage isn't ready yet!'

'Doesn't surprise me – you probably drank it all!' you quip.

'Hah, hah, very funny. Though to be fair, I probably would if I could. Anyway, come back later, maybe it'll be ready then.'

From here, you can go:

North to the Arcady Trail	▶ 238
West to Treycross on the Arcady Trail	▶ 728
South on the Trail	▶ 338
East to the bridge over the river Alpheus	▶ 14

89

You emerge blinking into bright sunlight, in a wide expansive clearing. At the far end you see a stone temple of ancient design, with a carved frieze of wolves, bears and lions abasing themselves before the goddess Artemis. A great moon symbol, flanked by two ivory tusks adorns the temple top.

At the base of the temple is a large, wing-backed throne of dark, polished wood, carved into a sculpted mass of trees, leaves and vines, through which men and women writhe and twist. An incredible piece of art. Upon it sits a heavy-set man with a shock of red hair and a big red beard that spreads out across his chest like a blanket. He is virtually naked, save for a deer-skin loin cloth. His body is muscled and lithe but also covered in red hair. It is hard to tell his age.

His eyes are green, and seem to glitter like emeralds, and upon his head he wears a wreath of many-coloured forest flowers, silver scarab beetles inlaid with jade, and leaves made of thinly beaten gold all held in place by many human finger bones, clasped together even in death.

At his right-hand side sits a young woman, also almost naked save for a bear-skin cloak, a necklace of animal teeth, and a bear-skin hat. Her eyes are also green, and glitter unnaturally too.

Alpha the wolf trots up to the throne and sits down on the left-hand side of the throne. The man on the throne absent-mindedly puts out a hand to stroke the wolf's head.

Flanking the trio at the throne are a score or so of men and women, dressed in skins of various styles and designs. Interestingly, none of them seems to have any weapons.

'Welcome to my court,' says the man on the throne, 'I am Lykaon the Wolf-King, and I rule the Deep Forests.' He points to the woman next to him. 'This is my daughter, Kallisto,' he says before gesturing at the wolf. 'I believe you have met my beloved Alpha, my leader of the pack. And these,' he adds, waving a hand at the men and women to either side, 'are my sons and daughters.'

'What, all of them?' you say in surprise.

'Eh? 'Oh, I see, no, no, they're called the Sons or the Daughters of the Wolf… you know, they're not actually… it's just a clan name, do you see, though Kallisto actually is my daughter.'

'Ah, right.'

'Anyway, thank you for sparing Alpha. I am grateful.'

'The wolf was terrorising a local woodcutter. I was just trying to protect him without too much bloodshed,' you explain.

'Nice of you, but he shouldn't have killed Alpha's children. Anyway, there's a more pressing problem…'

'And that problem is?' you reply.

▶ 95

90

You have the ear of Chiron, first amongst centaurs.

If you have the codeword *Payment* and want to talk to Chiron about Nessus and his centaur warband ▶ 245; if not but you have the codeword *Punisher* and want to ask Chiron about Nessus ▶ 142

If you want to ask him about a cure for a disease called the black blight ▶ 193

If you have the codeword *Punition* and want to tell him about Kakas the giant ▶ 166

If not, there is nothing more Chiron can help you with, so you say your farewells and head south to the Druid's Shrine ▶ 463

91

You observe one of the contests. Some choice insults are exchanged – even the locals can be quite inventive, and they can score a point or two. You presume that Kraterus the Cockerel has been trained to respond to Deridedes at certain times, though you can't make out exactly how. You also suspect that the crowd knows this too, but the show is so entertaining they don't seem to mind.

Make an INGENUITY roll at difficulty 9.

Succeed	▶ 141
Fail	▶ 262

92

You have returned to the wooden stockade of the outlaw Nessus and his band of renegade centaurs. Smoke twirls up from a campfire, and you can hear voices from behind the wooden walls. They seem to be planning some kind of raid or ambush on the Arcady Trail.

If you have the codeword *Punisher* ▶ 151

If not, there is nothing you can really do here, for there are too many of them, so you leave ▶ 189

93

'You have achieved what only Herakles achieved before you,' says the god, 'and he was half immortal to begin with. Truly you are one of the greatest heroes. Songs will be sung celebrating your glory – if the world survives, for now I must tell you your purpose and entrust you with the final and most desperate quest… Come to my temple in Vulcan City, and there I will enlighten you.'

Get the codeword *Rohan* in *Workshop of the Gods*. If you do not yet have a copy of *Workshop of the Gods*, make a note that you have *Rohan* on your Adventure Sheet.

Now turn to the section number written in the Current Location space on your Adventure Sheet.

94

'No more mortals? Bonus! All they do is try to hunt me down and kill me, Typhon knows how many I've eaten over the years! Mind you, they do make nice wine, but still, they're more trouble than they're worth.' Kaustikia rears up on her coils. 'Well, it's been nice chatting but it's time for my breakfast,' she says, readying an attack.

'Hold on, what about the…'

…sheep, they'll die too	▶ 13
…satyrs, they'll die too	▶ 256
…centaurs, they'll die too	▶ 218

95

'You see… grateful though I am… it's… well… it's…'

'Yes?'

'We'll have to hunt you, I'm sorry, really sorry but there you go!'

'What? What do you mean "hunt" me?'

'It's an ancient law. Any humans that come here are defiling the temple, so we release them into the forest and then hunt them down to honour the goddess, Artemis the huntress.'

'But I wouldn't have come here at all if Alpha hadn't led me here!'

'I know, I know, no doubt he thought I'd reward you or something but, I mean he's bright and all, but he's still just a wolf. Ironic, really, but what can I do? Holy law is holy law.'

Silence falls across the glade. Some of Lykaon's 'children' shift self-consciously from foot to foot. Kallisto, the daughter, sighs and says, 'I'm sorry, but there's nothing to be done, the Sacred Hunt is a holy sacrament, we've got not choice, we might as well get on with it.'

'Hold on though, there's a chance I can escape right?' you say.

'Oh yes, indeed – you get a ten-minute start and everything,' says Lykaon.

'But you use wolves, what, like hunting dogs?' you inquire.

'Umm… I wouldn't really say that, no…but instead… well, you'll see.'

'And how many of these hunts have you had?'

'Oh hundreds, hundreds over the years,' says Kallisto.

'And how many people have escaped?' you ask.

Kallisto and Lykaon exchange a look.

'Ummm….'

One of the hunters standing near the throne leans in and says – 'There was that one woman.'

'Oh yes!' says Lykaon enthusiastically, 'she got away.'

'But she was…, well, you know,' says Kallisto.

'Oh yeah…' mutters Lykaon disconsolately. Then he brightens up, 'You're a great hero though, I'm sure you can make it!' though it is obvious to you he doesn't really believe that.

'Are there any rules to the hunt?'

'It's simple, north of here further into the depths of the forest, is a marble statue of Artemis, with two wolves at her side, hunting. Get to that alive, and you are free. Oh, and you get the prize!' says Kallisto.

'A prize! What is it?'

Kallisto blinks at you… 'I… forget'.

'It's been so long since… well, if you make it we'll have to look it up but I'm sure it's valuable and that,' says Lykaon.

There is another moment of silence. Lykaon mouths another 'sorry' and raises his hand. He chops it down and from the interior of the temple behind him a chorus of wolf howls rise up to the skies.

'Let the hunt begin!' shouts Lykaon in response.

And then something astonishing happens. In front of your very eyes Lykaon begins to change, as do his 'children'. Their jaws lengthen, their hair grows into thick fur at an alarming rate, their hands and feet turn claw-like, sprouting vicious looking talons.

Werewolves, the lot of them. Except for Kallisto, she is turning into a bear. You stare, transfixed, as bones crack, skin stretches, muscles bulge and hearts swell, pumping hot red blood, for the hunt is on…

'Run, you idiot!' she roars, as her body fills out with bear blood and muscle.

▶ 110

96

❑

Put a tick in the box. If there was a tick in the box already ▶ 612 immediately. If not, read on.

You approach the pillared portico of the palace. Ancient banners depicting a trident wielding centaur hang in tatters from the roof and the walkway is littered with leaves, bleached bones and mud. Creepers grow up around the pillars. A faint smell of rotting compost pervades the air.

You walk inside to find a large open area, the walls painted in faded murals showing woodland scenes of frolicking satyrs and dryads, picnics and parties. Some of these are quite explicit too! In the middle of the room is a long, low marble table, obviously where many people sat to welcome visitors but where now only one solitary figure sits.

As you draw near, you see it is a rather fat balding man of middle age, dressed in well-made purple robes, with gold trimmings, although they are a tad tattered and in need of repair. Beside him, on the table is a laurel wreath of solid gold, a plate with a half-eaten pie of some kind, a bronze goblet, a pile of papyrus rolls and an ink pot and reed pen. He looks up as you approach, his face round and flabby, but with open and honest looking eyes.

'At last, I've been waiting for you!' says the man in a surprisingly deep voice.

'And who are you?' you ask.

'Nyctimus, King of Arcadia! Well, I say King, it's largely a ceremonial title, meant to appease the mortals, I think. Pan is the real ruler, though he wasn't really into ruling, so delegated most of it to me, but then again there was always some god or other visiting, ordering us around, so I never really… Well, anyway, haven't seen Pan or any other god in fact, for an age, so it's all academic. Which leaves me in charge after all, but of what?'

And he gestures around. There is nothing but debris, decay and detritus everywhere.

'King of an empty palace, and a broken land, that's me. Anyway, the gods spoke to me through my dreams, so I knew you would come. I need your help, desperately.'

▶ 206

97

It is an easy matter for a hardened warrior like you to step up and murder the man with a single blow of your weapon. A simple truffle hunter is no match for you.

Such a murder brings you no honour, though. Lose 1 Glory (but it can't go below zero), gain the codeword *Purged* and the title **Slayer of Truffle Hunters**.

However, you have completed the quest for the Great Green Ones. You avoid the cabin on your way out of this place, so you don't have to think about the sick little girl inside, and move on along the Arcady Trail.

▶ 160

98

The satyr slashes at you with his knives, forcing you to parry while the fat man, slow and cumbersome though he is, swings his club at your head. An easy dodge for a seasoned adventurer like you, but your foot slips on the much-trodden greasy grass floor, and are knocked senseless. You wake to find *all* your pyr has been taken. Cross off your money. Luckily it seems they were disturbed before they could steal anything else. There is nothing more you can here. Ruefully rubbing your sore head, you can head back to the market (▶ 728) or leave the area (▶ 12).

99

You are a still a little groggy from falling out of the sky, and you fail to notice the great serpent's tail, as you are too intent on avoiding its bite. It wraps around you and holds you fast before it bites off your head. Death is instant for you, but it's a big fat hobbity second breakfast for the snake. ▶ 111

100

If you have the codeword *Proscribe* ▶ 19 immediately. If not, read on.

You visit the Herodion Suite, your rooms in the Summer Palace. Peaceful and relaxing, you can rest here if you wish, eat, have a bath and so on. You can remove any **stink** conditions you may have picked up here by bathing too.

Take a tour of your rooms	▶ 422
Call Jas, your butler	▶ 731
Enter the Vault of Vulcan in Arcadia	▶ 828
Leave your rooms	▶ 282

101

THE ARCADIAN BULLETIN BOARD

Arcadia has fallen on hard times and many of its inhabitants are out of work, since the Olympian gods no longer holiday here, Pan himself sleeps and the rivers of Arcadia, the Alpheus and Ladon, flow no more.

These contracts have been put up on the board by those seeking work. If you purchase a contract, put a tick in the box, pay the fee, and add the contract to your Adventure Sheet as an item. Only unticked contracts may be bought up. You will be told during your adventures when the contract will come due.

❑ **Contract: Priest of Apollo**   50 pyr
❑ **Contract: Engineer**   150 pyr

☐ **Contract: Farm Overseer**   150 pyr
☐ **Contract: Winemaker**   200 pyr
☐ **Contract: Priestess of Demeter**   100 pyr
☐ **Contract: Architect**   250 pyr
☐ **Contract: Painter & Decorator**   250 pyr

When you are ready ► **10** and choose again.

102

Your thoughts are like treacle, heavy, slow and cumbersome. This ink-black tentacled thing, this Shadowhunter is fogging your brain somehow. To your horror, you begin to feel your shadow draining away. The Shadowhunter is swelling up, like a fat, night-black toad of darkness. You make one last effort to throw off the fug that clouds your brain. Make another INGENUITY roll at difficulty 7.

Succeed   ► **185**
Fail   ► **512**

103

You return to the site of the inn, where Hypatia, Lefkia and Helen are all waiting for you.

'Greetings once again,' says Hypatia, 'have you managed to get us the materials we need?'

'In case you've gone all goose-brains and forgotten it all, let me remind you,' says Lefkia.

100 pyr to hire labourers

timber
limestone
vinegar of Hades x 1
bucket of gypsum x 1
box of paints x 1

'There's a woodcutter at the edge of the Deep Forest in the south-west, he should be able to provide some timber. There used to be a limestone quarry in the northern edge of the Alpheus river plateau, and I know of a gypsum mine in Boreas, though whether it's still working is another question,' adds Hypatia.

If you have *all* of these things and wish to hand them over, cross them off your Adventure Sheet ► **552**.

If you don't have all of them yet, you'll have to come back later. From here you can go:

North-east to the Woodlands   ► **60**
East along the riverbank   ► **138**
South   ► **822**
West to the Wineries   ► **417**

104

You place the amulet into the shallow depression, and it sinks into it with a click, fusing with the altar. Cross **Pan's amulet** off your Adventure Sheet.

A small door flicks open, revealing a niche in the side of the altar – and out billows a cloud of noxious gas! You reel back, but you're not quick enough and you inhale a lungful. You fall to the ground, spluttering and coughing.

'Don't worry, it'll just knock you out,' trills Orphea with a laugh. She steps over you – you reach for her but your limbs feel as heavy as lead and you can barely stay awake. She reaches into the opening, and plucks out a fine-looking set of pipes.

'Ah, the Pipes of Pan. All mine!' she says, 'Lady Rapscallion strikes again, eh? Unfortunately, there never was any money, but on the other hand, I'm sure you've got some to help me along. You won't mind if I help myself, my lovely, will you? Night night, sleep tight!' she says, smiling down at you.

You glare up at her, vowing vengeance but you cannot keep your eyes open, and you sink into unconsciousness. Everything goes black. You dream of catching a red-furred rat in a trap and then of red ants with blue heads, swarming all over you and carrying off everything you own. You wake with an angry shout. ► **258**

105

☐

Put a tick in the box. If there was a tick in the box already ► **830** immediately. If not, read on.

You come to your senses far from the deep woods, with no recollection of what has happened or how you got here. And here is... somewhere between the Treycross market and the dales of leaf and stream.

You hear laughter and look up to see a pair of satyrs pointing at you. A farmer and his family in a cart are also staring. You realise you are wearing only your undergarments. One of the satyrs sniggers and makes a lewd suggestion, commenting on your figure.

Mustering as much dignity as you can, you ignore them while you reach for your backpack. Inside you find your clothes and all of your gear, but you have lost as much as 100 pyr (cross it off your Adventure Sheet). However, you also find some new additions – a **jug of dandelion wine**, a **box of paints**, a **maggoty pie** and a **grindstone**. You have no idea how you acquired these things or what happened. The last thing you remember is foraging for mushrooms in the deep woods.

Ah well, time to move on. From here you can go to the Treycross crossroads on the Arcady Trail or head into the dales of leaf and stream

Treycross   ► **728**
Dales   ► **266**

❑

If you have the codeword *Plenty* ▶ 785 immediately. If not, read on.

Put a tick in the box. If there was a tick in the box already ▶ 285 immediately. If not, read on.

A tall satyr with horns on his head, goat-legs and hooves for feet, steps up to you. He has a big bushy beard, wears glasses, and is dressed in a kind of long pale yellow jacket and maroon shorts.

'Welcome, steward, to the wineries of nectar!' says the satyr. 'As you can see they are in a sorry state indeed, but you have bought my contract, and here I am, ready to see if we can bring it all back to life!'

His eyes seem a little glazed and his speech a tad slurred.

'Are you drunk?' you ask in astonishment.

The satyr draws himself up and stares down at you haughtily through his glasses.

'So what if I am? The important thing is that I am Maron, master of wine or as Philostratus the Athenian, the great philosopher, said of me, "Maron who haunts the vines and, by planting and pruning them, makes them produce sweet wine".'

He goes on. 'The tragedy is not that I am drunk, but that I am drunk on this cheap rubbish!' and he holds up a jug of dandelion wine. 'Horrible stuff – hic.'

'Well,' you say, 'perhaps we can do something about that.'

'Perhaps indeed, but nothing yet, not until the river gods come back and the waters flow. Without them we have no reliable source of irrigation, what with the sheer randomness of the summer storms in this place of everlasting summer – hic!'

'Nothing can be done?' you ask.

'No point, without water everything'll just die. Now, bugger orf, come back when you've sorted the rivers out. In the meantime, here, have this, it's shite!'

Maron hands you a **jug of dandelion wine**. Note it on your Adventure Sheet. For now, you can do nothing more but move on. From here, you can go:

North to the Arcady Trail	▶ 238
West to Treycross on the Arcady Trail	▶ 728
South on the Trail	▶ 338
East to the bridge over the river Alpheus	▶ 14

You pull the lever and are thrown up into the air, soaring across Arcadia. You put out your fist to cleave the air, holding the other behind you, your clothes fluttering behind you like a flag. Looking down, you see that you are hurtling across some cliffs, and then the deep forest, like a sea of trees. You notice what looks like some strange blocks or idols in a clearing and then find yourself falling down to earth. The Sacred Way seems to rises up to meet you – and then you see the catch-net! If you do *not* have the codeword *PatchupOne* ▶ 6 immediately. If you do have it, read on.

You crash into the web of netting, sinking into it, and then bouncing back up again, but you are able to hold on safely. What a rush!

You climb out of the catch-net and look around. ▶ 130

You hurl yourself sideways into a forward roll, angling yourself towards the basilisk. You manage to avoid the toxic cloud, and roll to your feet to one side of it. It tries to turn and face you, but it is slow and clumsy and you are able to leap onto its back, driving your blade into the top of its skull over and over again, until you penetrate the brain and it dies.

You have slain the Midas basilisk! Gain the codeword *Precious*.

You look around the town, and the basilisk's nest behind the statue of Gaia but there is not much to be found. The golden statues are too heavy to move and seem bound in place by whatever force turned them to gold. The town has been long abandoned and it seems the basilisk did not hoard or covet anything material. All you find of use is a pouch of 20 pyr, a **box of paints** and some **copper ore**.

Still, the basilisk is dead and you take its head as a trophy. You head back down to the Inn of Swollen Mammaries.

▶ 530

❑

Put a tick in the box. If there was a tick in the box already ▶ 263 immediately. If not, read on.

The two carts and its escort head back up the river valley. You follow at a discrete distance. They reach the bridge over the Ladon, and then go east along the Sacred Way.

You catch snatches of conversation – it seems the officer's name is Theseus and he works for a woman called Mela, a priestess – or perhaps sorceress – of Hekate, and owner of a limestone quarry. He seems to command by bullying everyone around him.

You also notice something strange about the workers – they shamble along almost mindlessly as if they were drugged or possessed or fevered. They take little interest in their personal hygiene or appearance or indeed anything around them. Theseus has to beat them often to get them to follow his commands.

After a short time on the Sacred Way, the wagons turn south, heading to the limestone quarry set at the bottom of the cliffs of the Alpheus river plateau.

▶ 224

110

You turn and run as fast as you can into the trees. You consider heading west or south, just to get out of the forest as quickly as possible, but it soon becomes clear that the forest undergrowth is so dense in those directions you will be fatally slowed.

Northwards, the forest it a little less dense, and you can make your way through more easily. You have ten minutes grace. Nearby you notice some pungent forest herbs, also a lot of deer spoor. Up above, the forest canopy has many interlinked branches. What strategy will you use?

Climb up, and try to head north using the branches in the treetops ▶ 156

Rub deer dung all over yourself to disguise your scent. ▶ 136

Rub herbs into some meat to make its scent more powerful and hope they will go for that instead of you (but only if you have some **strix stew** or **venison sausages**) ▶ 183

111

Something… something has happened. Your mind is clouded, your body feels far, far away, your memories are slipping away. 'Who am I?' you ask yourself. 'What was my name?'

A voice, the voice of Vulcan, lord of the world, fills your head. 'Although you are but a puny mortal, the fate of this world depends on you. By our command, you will not fall into the grasping hand of Thanatos, nor will your shade walk the halls of Hades for all eternity. Instead, you will be returned to the world, but you will have to give up your worldly possessions, for they cannot go with you. You should be able to gather them up later but for now, I will send you to my Vault in Arcadia. And try to be more careful next time, will you?'

▶ 333

112

You find Jas preening himself in front of your mirror – he's bought himself a rather fine red chiton and a gold inlaid blue cape, along with an excellent green *pileus*, which is a round felt cap, but this one has two holes in it for his horns. He has a nice gold medallion around his neck with the face of Pan sculpted up on it. It all looks rather garish to you, but he seems happy enough.

'If you're "just a slave" how can you afford all of this?' you ask.

'Me? Um…. A bet. No, I mean an inheritance! An aunt died, yes, that's it,' coughs Jas unconvincingly. 'Anyway, what can I do for you, today O great one? Some rest and relaxation no doubt?'

Jas brings you some delicious food from the Palace kitchens, and after that you take a long hot bath followed by a massage and then to bed for a good night's sleep. Roll a dice:

score 1-4   ▶ 465
score 5-6   ▶ 586

113

Suddenly, the Nemean lion bursts out of the tree line into the small clearing. It is huge and massively muscled, its golden fur bright in the sunlight, its jaws agape, revealing savage looking teeth. Its talons gleam as if made of black steel and its eyes are bright with unnatural intelligence.

You have heard it said that its fur is impenetrable and its claws can cut through the strongest armour. This is a creature right out of myth, and it is coming for you!

It roars at you and then pauses as if in puzzlement. It looks around for a moment and then back at you, a strange expression on its leonine face, as if it is thinking 'you came alone? Really?' Then it hesitates again, suspecting trickery.

If you have a **hardwood club** *and* the **shield of Ajax** ▶ 139. If not, or if you only have one of these ▶ 164

114

You take your aunt's hand and lead her out of the open doorway. The horizon seems to call to you. Across the fields and the vineyards, over the streams and forests, up into the blue hills and beyond. That is where your destiny will lead you. Without looking back you start to run, filled with the exhilaration of the world that is spread around you.

'Go, fierce one,' calls your aunt, her words almost lost in the wind. 'You'll never catch the Huntress till your dying day, but till then strive to keep her always in your sight.'

So, your god is Artemis. Write her name in the box on your Adventure Sheet and ▶ 769

115

You take out the ivory shoulder blade you found in Pelops' tomb in Hades, when Tantalus tricked you into entering it and you ended up trapped there for a while, until you found your way through to the Palace of Hades itself. Through the sewers…

Anyway, you have heard that it was made by a god. With a shrug, you place it over Chiron's shattered shoulder. It just lies there.

Velosina looks at you quizzically.

'I don't know, I thought it was worth a try,' you say, reaching to take it back when suddenly it starts to twitch and stretch. It begins to work its way into Chiron's shoulder, ejecting old tissue and bone, and settling itself into place. It sinks into place, forming itself to fit. Skin starts to grow around it, and then Chiron flicks his eyes open and sits up, rubbing his shoulder.

Velosina's jaw drops and she claps her hands together in happiness, while pawing the ground with a hoof.

'This ivory shoulder blade was forged by Vulcan himself on Olympus, to cure one of Poseidon's favourite mortals, Pelops! Where did you get it?' asks Chiron in a deep, voice redolent with wisdom and gravitas.

'I looted…er… *found it* in the tomb of Pelops itself in Hades,' you say.

Chiron turns his head to stare at you. His eyes are deep set and dark, his hair white with streaks of grey, and his beard, long, bushy and very white. He looks like an incarnation of wisdom.

'You have been to Hades – and returned?' he asks.

You nod.

'Remarkable,' says Chiron, getting to his feet – or rather, hooves. 'You must be a great hero indeed.'

'I am,' you say laconically.

Chiron laughs, and claps you on the shoulder. Well, great hero, I am in your debt. How can I aid you?'

Cross off the **ivory shoulder blade** and get the codeword *Prosthetic*, then ▶ 90

116

You flee pell-mell into the deep forest. It is easy enough to lose him amidst the trees for his helm restricts his vision and his equipment slows him down. You can hear him crashing into trees and cursing like a trireme galley oarsman.

'Bah, curse you for the coward you are! You've escaped death's grasp once again, but I'll find you again!'

You head deeper into the forest to make sure of your escape.

▶189

117

❑

Put a tick in the box. If there was a tick in the box already ▶ 824 immediately. If not, read on.

The pavilion of Momos still stands, but appears deserted. Out of curiosity, you walk inside.

You find Deridedes dismantling the stage.

'Aha,' he says, 'I've been waiting for you to come back – you cheated, stole my Kraterus and my slave!'

'You named your cock, but not your slave?' you reply.

Deridedes looks flustered for a moment but says, 'Well, that's by the by, the point is, you cheated! I want my money, my slave and my cockerel back.'

'And yet all of those things you took by cheating people over and over again, not to mention mistreating that poor boy.'

'Maybe but the audience, my fans, they loved my show, they were happy,' and he nods to someone behind you. You turn, and two burly thugs walk in, one a big fat man with a club, the other an actual horned satyr, with a dagger in each hand.

'You may have won the battle of wits – by cheating, so now it's time for clubs in the mud, for that's what a half-witted, goose-brained, ding dong like you deserves!'

'I think not. You swindled your way to success, but now you will have to wade in the mud of battle and you will get what you deserve – justice!'

'Bah, we'll see about that,' says Deridedes, 'All right, my fans, kill this self-righteous prig!'

The fat man lumbers forward, muttering, 'You wrecked my favourite show and now I'm gonna wreck your head.'

'Best show in these parts, cancelled, 'coz of you,' says the satyr, 'time to carve a new face for my Momos mask…'

You must fight. Make a STRENGTH roll at difficulty 7.

| Succeed | ▶ 45 |
| Fail | ▶ 98 |

118

'But I'm the mayor. Surely you don't expect your own mayor to pay, not after everything I've done for you, bringing in new folk with their passing trade and hunger for gossip?' you say with a twinkle in your eye.

Phineas blinks at you as if buying time to come up with a reason why you should pay, but then he smiles wanly, and says, 'Of course, my dear mayor, you have done so much for us, all rumours are free,' although he doesn't look too happy about it.

'Excellent,' you say, rubbing your hands together, 'now, to business, tell me about….'

A dragon in these parts	▶ 654
A winged horse	▶ 692
The Nemean lion	▶ 713
A limestone quarry	▶ 727
Witch-magic of Hekate	▶ 762
The Druid's shrine	▶ 786
The black blight	▶ 815
The river gods	▶ 494
The Dales of Leaf and Stream	▶ 18
Or you can leave the shop	▶ 305

119

If you have any or all of the codewords *Planted*, *Pure* or *Pinot*, lose them.

You have travelled to the south-westernmost corner of Arcadia, to a low, grass covered hill. The great walls of Vulcan City rise up to the west, and to the south is the Sacred

Way and the desert of Notus. From here, you can go:

North to a range of hills ▶ **559**
East to more hills   ▶ **832**
South into the desert   ▶ **300** in *The Hammer of the Sun*

120

If you have the codeword *Purloin* ▶ **812**. If not, read on.

You walk into the magistrates' hall, a low, single storey building, with a pillared walkway around an open space in the middle, with a pool full of fish. As it is Arcadia, and the weather is fine, the magistrate has set up her office under the sun, near the pool. She sits behind a large marble desk, and is dressed in a bright red chiton and a blue himation. She is middle aged, dark-haired and dark-eyed. She gestures to a seat in front of the table and says,

'Welcome, I am the *basileus* of this village, and my name is Cressida. How can I help?'

'What's with the name,' you ask.

'Bridgadoom? Apparently it comes from Bridge of Doom, as the legends say that an aspect or spirit of Moros, the god that drives men to their doom, dwelt within the bridge, and pronounced on the fate of those who crossed. That was in ages past, of course, and is long gone, but the name stuck and over time has become Bridgadoom. Or so the legends say.'

If you have the **confession of Polycrates** ▶ **33**. If not, there is nothing really for you to do here, so you take your leave ▶ **305**.

121

You have returned to see how the refurbishment of Fort Blackgate is going.

Hypatia is overseeing a gang of workmen rebuilding the battlements on the now finished stone walls.

The bronze doors have been reworked and repainted in shiny black gloss. Lefkia steps out from behind them to greet you. She is covered in dust and paint from head to toe.

'Hello, hello!' she says, grinning at you from under a rainbow flecked paint-splattered hat. 'We haven't finished yet, only a day or two to go, mind, come back later!'

You make camp nearby, and a few days later, Lefkia finds you and tells you it's all done.

'Come and see!'

▶ **177**

122

❑

Put a tick in the box. If there was a tick in the box already ▶ **168** immediately. If not, read on.

You plunge down the waterfall in a barrel, laughing manically. You find yourself careening off rocks and timbers like a pinball. Unfortunately, the bronze bands holding the barrel together shatter, and the barrel splinters into pieces, leaving you exposed.

You hammer into a rock, and knock yourself out. Tick the Wound box on your Adventure Sheet. If you are already wounded, the blow to your head kills you instantly. ▶ **111**. But if you still live, read on.

You fall down into the pool below and begin to sink beneath the waves and drown. But then something lifts you up and out of the water.

It is Alpheus himself, the river god. He holds you up in his hands and breathes into your face, and you come round gasping.

'Why are mortals so stupid?' he says shaking his head. 'It still amazes me, even after all this time, all these endless years.'

You blink up at him, trying to get your wits back.

'Ah well,' says Alpheus, 'at least I was here to help, might not be next time, so try to be careful, eh?' With that he puts you down on the riverbank, and sinks back into the waters slowly with a long, drawn-out sigh of boredom. As he goes under, his umber seaweed hair spreads out on the river surface like an opening hand before disappearing.

You pick yourself up and take a look around. You are not far from the northern bridge over the Alpheus, so you set off in that direction ▶ **28**

123

The Verdant Farmlands are finally living up to their name. Curls of smoke twirl up into the bright blue sky from the farmer's cottages, men and women (and a few centaurs, nymphs and satyrs) work the fields of grain, chickens lay eggs in their coops, hay wains wait to be filled, goats munch the grass in the fallow fields.

And it was you that made all this possible and for that you are entitled to a portion of every harvest. If you wish to see if your cut is ready, ▶ **793**. If not, then where to next?

North-east   ▶ **365**
North-west   ▶ **380**
South-east   ▶ **419**

124

'Bread? Do I look like I eat bread? Anyway, it's been nice chatting but it's time for my breakfast and that's going to be you today,' she says, readying an attack.

'Hold on, what about the…'
wine, the vines will die too   ▶ **144**
satyrs, they'll die too   ▶ **256**
centaurs, they'll die too   ▶ **218**

125

You prepare yourself to fight against Death Dealer, the Champion of Thanatos, he whose touch is death.

'At least you have courage,' says Death Dealer before he charges straight at you, intent on knocking you to the ground with his shield. This will not be an easy battle. However, if you have fought him in hand to hand combat before, add one to your roll, as you have learned a little about his fighting style (in general: savage, brutal and relentless).

Make a STRENGTH roll at difficulty 9.

Succeed	▶ 351
Fail	▶ 420

126

You have come to an ancient, lichen-mottled stone bridge over the rushing, gushing Ladon. If you have the **rod of Phainos** and wish to fish off the side of the bridge ▶ 87. Otherwise, where will you go?

West on the Way	▶ 20
South-west into the forest	▶ 189
East on the Way	▶ 380
South, into the Ladon river valley	▶ 403

127

❏

Put a tick in the box. If there was a tick in the box already ▶ 272 immediately. If not, read on.

It looks as though something fell from the sky and crashed into the ground here, hammering a wide crater out of the earth with the force of its impact. Grass and bushes have grown over it since, for it clearly happened an age ago. The bushes sport rather unpleasant blood-red flowers, with vicious looking thorns that are purple and swollen, as if infused with malice.

You notice a large stone door has been set into one side of the crater floor. Upon it these words appear:

MURDER AT THE PHILOSOPHERS ACADEMY
Aspasia has been murdered. The culprit is one of either Epimenides the Cretan, Cleanthes the Stoic, Aristippus the Cyrenaic or Protagoras the Sophist. They make the following statements. You have been correctly informed that the guilty person always lies, and everyone else tells the truth.

Epimenides: *'Cleanthes is the culprit.'*
Cleanthes: *'Protagoras is innocent.'*
Aristippus: *'Cleanthes's statement is true.'*
Protagoras: *'Epimenides's statement is false.'*

Who killed Aspasia?

Epimenides	▶ 323
Cleanthes	▶ 182
Aristippus	▶ 405
Protagoras	▶ 518
Come back later	▶ 833

128

A drowsy numbness steals over your limbs and you sink into dreams.

You see a vision of Chiron, the great and wise centaur, a master of the healing arts, trotting through a wood when he is attacked by a giant wielding an enormous club. He strikes Chiron down, shattering his shoulder.

Chiron is bed-bound, in some kind of coma, while nymphs, centaurs, wise men and even satyrs try to heal him, but none can.

Then you see the god Vulcan himself, forging an artificial shoulder blade out of ancient ivory for the goddess Demeter who stands nearby.

Your vision shifts, and you find yourself under a grey, empty sky, in a vast, hollow land where the sound of wailing and teeth gnashing in darkness, is carried to you on the cold, bone chilling wind. It is Hades.

Nearby, a man wades in water that he cannot drink, grasping at the fruits of a tree he can never quite reach, forever hungry, forever thirsty.

You wake with a start, your tongue dry, your stomach heaving.

'A nice dream?' asks Zenia.

'No, definitely not,' you say, shaking your head to clear it. Musing on your vision, you get to your feet. If you have some more **kykeon mushrooms** and 10 more pyr and want to try another vision ▶ 737

If not, you can head back to the market (▶ 728) or leave the area (▶ 12).

129

The truffle hunter's cabin is silent. In the back room you find Io, dead in her bed from the black blight. A little girl. Dead, for you slew her father in cold blood.

Anyway, what's done is done, you tell yourself, as you look around. There are still some hydnon truffles that haven't rotted away yet, so you can take a jar if you like. Note the **jar of hydnon truffles** on your Adventure sheet. When you are done, you quit this awful place.

▶ 160

130

You have arrived at the Sacred Way, an ancient paved roadway that runs across the entire Vulcanverse. From here it goes west along the coast into the mountains of Boreas, south towards Vulcan City, and east along the coast of

Arcadia. To the south-east there is nothing but tree after tree after tree – the Deep Forest. Above you is a clear blue sky. You can go:

West	▶ **400** in *The Pillars of the Sky*
East along the coast	▶ **20**
South on the Way	▶ **804**
South-east into the Deep Forest	▶ **616**

131

Since you freed the Arcadian river gods, the fresh and wholesome waters of Arcadia have come rushing back and everywhere life springs anew. The lagoon is now a lush, beautiful pleasure pond. Some of the boats and punts have been repaired, and local Arcadians are out on the waters, taking their ease. If you want to go fishing here ▶ **674**. If not, will you:

Enter the Palace	▶ **96**
Examine the onager	▶ **471**
Leave this place	▶ **547**

132

☐☐☐

Put a tick in a box.

If two boxes are now ticked ▶ **172** immediately. If all three boxes are now ticked, ▶ **221** immediately. If not, (ie only one box is ticked) read on.

You step into your rooms – and see Jas the Helot, the butler you fired after he tried to con you out of a lot money, leaning over the Vault of Vulcan door, trying to pick the lock!

'Oi, you little piece of goat dung, what are you up to!' you shout.

Jas turns in shocked surprise. As he spots your hand closing around the hilt of your weapon, he simply throws himself out of the nearest window.

You rush over and look down. There he is, picking himself up from the ground, rubbing his legs, and grimacing. He looks up at you, makes a rude sign and gallops away. You shake your head. You should have killed the bastard.

Anyway, clearly you don't have a butler anymore so will you:

Enter the Vault	▶ **828**
Leave your rooms	▶ **282**

133

You find a suitable gully under the roots of an old tree, and huddle under a bush, completely unseen, but one of the Bacchantes trips and falls right on top of you. With a shriek of triumph, she claws at your eyes and sinks her teeth into your arm. You are able to throw her off but moments later the rest of them are upon you. Terrified, you try and fight them off but

you are engulfed by a pack of shrieking, frenzied furies, tearing, biting and ripping at you with nails, teeth and bare hands, intent on sacrificing you to the mad god. You are overwhelmed and literally torn to pieces in a matter of seconds, and your body scattered to the four winds. Well, those bits of it that weren't eaten, that is.

▶ **111**

134

If you have the title **The Apiarist** ▶ **354** immediately.

If not, but you have codeword *Pudding* ▶ **825** immediately.

If not, but you have the title **Archon of Wines** ▶ **665**. If none of the above, read on.

You have returned to the old apiary. Where once bees buzzed now only flies and the birds that feed on them fill the glade. There is nothing for you to do here. Will you:

Go deeper into the woods	▶ **176**
Leave this place	▶ **225**

135

☐

Put a tick in the box. If there was a tick in the box already ▶ **155** immediately. If not, read on.

You encountered the acid dragon on her cloud nest above the deep forest where she was slowly killing the Great Green Ones.

'Kaustikia? I've dealt with her, she won't be bothering you anymore,' you say.

'You... what?' says an astonished Krio.

'Haven't you noticed she's not taking your sheep anymore?'

'That's true, come to think of it! I just thought she'd turn up again soon, I can hardly believe it, is it true?'

'It is. So then, you can sell me your bales a little cheaper,' you point out slyly.

Krio has no option but to agree. You can buy **bales of wool** for 20 pyr each, although you can carry no more than three at a time. Add them to your Adventure Sheet and cross off the money. When you are ready, you take your leave.

▶ **822**

136

You rub deer shit all over your body, from head to feet. You retch and almost vomit, for the smell is strong and truly vile but you soon get used to it.

You set off north, running as fast as you can, dodging fallen tree trunks and avoiding the denser thorns and brambles. In the distance you can hear the howls of your pursuers but after a few moments, the sound fades... They have lost your scent, it's worked! You hurry on. Maybe, just maybe, you can pull this off.

And then the howls start up again… they've wised up, and are back on your trail.

▶ 255

137

You plunge down the waterfall in a barrel, careening off rocks and timbers like a pinball.

Luckily for you, the heavy bronze bands keep the barrel secure, and you hammer into the water below with a bone shuddering crunch. And then, just as you're getting your breath back, the rushing waters pick up the barrel and send it hurtling on downriver, fortunately floating the right way up all the way.

You shoot along, peering over the top of the barrel, laughing in delight (or is it madness?) until the river begins to slow, and the barrel along with it. You find yourself gently nudging up against the side of a stone bridge. What a ride.

Gathering your wits, you haul yourself out of the barrel and climb up the riverbank. ▶ 28

138

If you have the codeword *Plenty* ▶ 361. If not, but you have the codeword *Penumbra* ▶ 267. If not, read on.

You are following the banks of the Alpheus river. The sun beats down, and the river is dried up and dusty. From here you can go:

East to the eastern bridge	▶ 801
West to the western bridge	▶ 14
North to the Woodlands	▶ 60
South to some hills	▶ 822

139

You know that its fur is impenetrable to bladed weapons, but not to blunt weapons and hopefully the shield of Ajax, massive as it is, will give you enough time to stun the lion with your club. Hopefully…

Make a GRACE roll at difficulty 7.

Succeed	▶ 510
Fail	▶ 546

140

❑

Put a tick in the box. If there was a tick in the box already ▶ 462 immediately. If not, read on.

You invite many of your friends once again to another banquet, Maron, the wine-drinking ever-drunk Satyr, Sivi the beautiful honey dryad, Hypatia of Iskandria the architect, ever-smiling and cheerful Lefkia, Mandrocles the boy

engineer, the putative King of Arcadia, Nyctimus, Drosos the farmer, Chiron the centaur and many more that you have met on your adventures.

It is another merry evening, with much pomegranate wine and a marvellous feast wonderfully cooked by Erifili and her team.

But then the midnight gong strikes, and Erifili rushes in.

'I was going to the store for some more wine, when I noticed the doors were open – someone picked the locks!'

You race down to check – you have been robbed. All the money you have, including any stored there, has gone. Put **504** in your Current Location box, then ▶ **220** and cross off all the pyr you may have in storage there, and then ▶ **504**

141

You spot a small goad jabbing out from under the stage and into Kraterus' back, causing him to crow his cock-a-doodle-do that sounds so much like a strange, drawn out and screechy version of 'silly old goat!' Someone or something is under that stage, fixing the results.

You make your way around the back of the pavilion, cut a hole through it and crawl in under the stage. It is dark and earthy but the roaring laughter of the crowd is so loud that the small boy who lies ahead, wielding the chicken goad, cannot hear you as you crawl up and grab him. He gives a yelp of shocked surprise,

'Oh ho, so that's your little game is it?' you say accusingly.

The boy squirms and tries to break free but you are a hardened adventurer and all, and far too strong for him. After a moment or two he goes limp.

'All right, all right, you got me,' says the boy, 'but I'm just his slave boy, he makes me do it or I won't get my supper!'

You see that the boy is actually secured to a stage post with shackles of bronze. You notice that his ankle looks red and raw from the chains holding him.

'What's your name, boy?' you ask.

'I dunno,' mutters the boy sullenly, 'he bought me when I was real young, never gave me a name. Just calls me "slave".'

It is time Deridedes was brought down a peg or two you think you to yourself. After a moment's thought you say, 'OK, here's the deal. You goad Kraterus whenever it's my turn to hurl an insult at that cheating swine. When I win, I'll take Kraterus, free you and give you half the prize money to start a new life anywhere you like in the Vulcanverse. How's that?'

The boy stares at you with hope in his eyes, perhaps the first glimmer of hope he's had in a long time.

'Deal!' he says, spitting on the palm of his hand and holding it out. You do the same, and you both shake on the pact. You head back to the crowd and the show.

▶ 229

142

'We have been trying to get the wineries of Arcadia up and running again, with pomegranate wine made from seeds that Persephone blessed. It will be divine wine, I'm sure, but Nessus and his warband of bandits raided the vineyard, slashing and burning. I need to deal with them. I know he is responsible for your dolorous wound, perhaps I can get rid of him for you too?' you ask.

'An excellent notion!' says Chiron. 'However, he commands several well-armed centaur bowmen; it will be hard, and he's also built himself a small stockade in the north-eastern edge of the deep forest, and leaves it only to raid and pillage.'

Chiron runs his hand through his beard several times, thinking.

'I do know that he is arrogant and proud, and easily angered. Perhaps if you hurl a few choice insults at him he'll come out and fight a duel. After all, he can't afford to look like a coward in front of his men. They're all thieves and murderers, they have no loyalty to anything save money and wine and follow him only out of fear.'

'Interesting, thank you,' you say.

▶ **90** and choose again.

143

The catch-net is a web stretched across four wooden poles that is designed to catch anyone pitched at it from the palace onager. Unfortunately it hasn't been maintained in a long while and the net has rotted through. You rip through it like a fist through paper to hammer into the ground with bone splitting force.

Tick the Wound box on your Adventure Sheet. If you were already wounded than your body is broken apart by the impact. At least death is quick ▶ **111**

If you still live, you stagger to your feet and look around ▶ **324**

144

Kaustikia pauses and blinks at you with her nictitating snake eyes.

'The vines? No more wine? But there's nothing like a whole sheep soaked overnight in a barrel of wine… but… how can you be certain this will happen?'

'I can't but is it worth taking the risk? Just move somewhere else, you'll still have your mutton, and your vino.'

Kaustikia thinks for a moment, and then heaves a great sigh.

'I suppose you're right,' she says. 'I'll get my beauty sleep somewhere else. In fact, I'm sick of Arcadia, I shall fly to Boreas, where the mountains are awash with sheep and mountain goat!' With that she spreads her wings and surges up into the sky and away. You congratulate yourself on a job well done.

Except that, as Kaustikia takes to the air, her cloud nest starts to dissolve around your feet and you are suddenly falling through empty space. You hit the ground so hard that your body explodes like a ripe tomato, spraying your blood and guts across the forest floor. However, you have saved the Great Green Ones.

Gain the codeword *Purify*

Lose the codeword *Phosphoric*

Then ▶ **111**

145

If you have a lock of **water nymph hair** ▶ **204** immediately.

Otherwise, if this box ❑ was already ticked ▶ **387** but, if the box is empty, put a tick in it now and read on.

You catch a curious looking fish – it appears to be glowing a deep red colour, as if it had swallowed something. You bend down to take a closer look when suddenly the fish explodes, spraying you with fish guts, but also tiny particles of what was once a lava gem. They burn into your face and neck, causing you a lot of pain, and an unsightly wound. Gain 1 scar.

Also, some of the fish guts get trapped in your hair and clothes. Note that you have **stink x 1** on your Adventure Sheet. Your next CHARM roll is at −1. After that is resolved, the smell wears off, and you can cross the 'item' off.

So much for a nice day out fishing! You decide to move on. Where will you go?

West on the Way	▶ **20**
South-west into the forest	▶ **189**
East on the Way	▶ **380**
South, into the dried-up river valley	▶ **403**

146

Your own hand feels cold as clay as you lay the coins on your father's eyes.

'Charon row you swift to your rest, father. We can see to ourselves if we know your spirit is safe with the Lord of Plenty.'

Your neighbours hear of and remember the sacrifice you made on this night, and their stories are the seed from which your reputation grows. Mark 1 Glory on your Adventure Sheet.

▶ **753**

147

As you are a Steward of the Palace, you have many contacts when it comes to making improvements for the locals. Over the next few days you invest in:

Employing a full-time physician for the village

A little aqueduct that takes fresh water from the river directly to a public fountain in the village square

Paving the Arcady Trail in the surrounding area thus improving the local roads

Repairing the bridge

Investing in some communal hay wains and other agricultural implements

The villagers are amazed. They quickly ratify your position as mayor. Note the title **Mayor of Bridgadoom** on your Adventure Sheet. For now, at least, your popularity is off the scale. People greet you effusively in the streets, pledging that Bridgadoom will do their best to aid you, should you ever ask them.

Anyway, you have done a fine job, but now it is time to leave the village for you are a part-time mayor but a full-time adventurer.

▶ 801

148

It is time to leave the ancient forest behind you, and get back onto the Sacred Way. Will you head:

North-west   ▶ 158
North-east   ▶ 20
South-west   ▶ 804

149

You return to the truffle-hunter's cabin. Mithaecus lives here with his daughter, Io.

You see them both emerging from the ancient arch set into the earthen mound, each carrying baskets of hydnon truffles.

Io drops her basket and runs into your arms. 'Thank you for saving me!' she says, hugging you tightly. You hug her back, envious for a moment of the simple life of a truffle hunter and his child, but also with a pang of guilt, for saving her life was kind of incidental to your other goals.

But anyway, a life was saved, that is true. You sit with the family and share a meal before leaving. Mithaecus gives you another **jar of hydnon truffles**. Note it on your Adventure sheet. You nod your thanks, and take your leave.

▶ 160

150

'The festival is for women only so you are welcome to join us if you wish,' says Thekla. 'It lasts for three days.'

If you want to participate in the Festival of Thesmophoria ▶ 69. If not, read on.

You decline the offer, and she takes her leave. There is nothing more you can do until the festival is over. You can go:

West along the coast   ▶ 380
South along the coast   ▶ 419
South-west into the farmlands   ▶ 270

151

This is the renegade warband that has been terrorising Maron and holding up completion of the wineries. Nessus has to be dealt with. But how? If you have the title **Master of Mockery** ▶ 205. If not, you rack your brains but you can't see how you can take on an entire warband on your own. You will have to come back later with a better plan.

▶ 189

152

Sickened by his wheedling cowardice, and unable to let a conniving con-man like him survive, you slit his throat too, and leave him to join his fat thug henchman to gasp out his life on the grassy earth in the pavilion where he had swindled so many out of their hard-earned cash. Justice, swift, harsh and unforgiving, has been done.

There is nothing left to do here. You can head back to the market (▶ 728) or leave the area (▶ 12).

153

You approach the shop of the rumour monger. There is a sign outside showing people gossiping around a village well. Inside, a man sits at a table, jug of dandelion wine and plate of flatbreads nearby. He is young, bearded and blue eyed, with yellow hair, dressed impeccably in a smart white chiton and a light blue cape lined with gold stitching. Clearly rumour mongering is a profitable trade.

'Welcome, friend, to my shop. Come sit, drink some wine, take some bread, it's free. Rumours are not though – five pyr a shot.'

If you have the title **Mayor of Bridgadoom** ▶ 118; if not, read on.

If you want to hear a rumour, cross off the money and ask about rumours of:

A dragon in these parts   ▶ 654
A winged horse   ▶ 692
The Nemean lion   ▶ 713
A limestone quarry   ▶ 727
Witch-magic of Hekate   ▶ 762
The Druid's shrine   ▶ 786
The black blight   ▶ 815
The river gods   ▶ 494
The Dales of Leaf and Stream   ▶ 18
Or you can leave the shop   ▶ 305

154

You have arrived at the end of the Sacred Way that leads to the great northern gate of Vulcan City. To the west, massive mountains rise up to the heavens, snow-peaked and ice bound. To the east all you can see are trees and trees and trees, the Deep Forest of Arcadia. You are not sure, but perhaps you can see the ruins of a tower of some kind, poking up over the treetops in the forest depths. From here you can go:

North along the road   ▶ **804**

East into the Deep Forest ▶ **710**

Clockwise around the city walls towards some low hills ▶ **559**

Enter the city   ▶ **222** in *Workshop of the Gods*

155

Krio is happy to trade with your once again. Since Kaustikia the dragon comes no more, you can buy **bales of wool** for 20 pyr each, though you can carry no more than three at a time. Add them to your Adventure Sheet and cross off the money. When you are ready, you take your leave of the shepherds.

▶ **822**

156

The trees are tall but blessed with many branches, so it is a relatively easy climb to get up top. You poke your head out of the forest canopy to see the Deep Forest spreading in all directions, a sea of leaves, green and bright in the sun. Birds are everywhere, some shriek in outrage at the sight of you but most ignore you. You work out where north is from the sun, then duck back down – to see a dismaying sight. Down below many wolf-men are climbing up the trees, laughing and howling. Their hands and feet are not paw-like, more like huge, gnarled ape hands, ending in viciously sharp taloned nails. Their heightened strength and agility make them excellent climbers. Soon they are upon you – one of them takes a swipe at you, and knocks you out of the treetops, and you fall to the ground, far below. You hit hard, and are knocked out, never to wake again. Well, not here anyway.

▶ **111**

157

The handsome young man reaches for your back pack smirking up at you but suddenly he freezes.

'Wait a minute, are you…?' He stands up to get a better look at you.

'By Hades's balls, you are! You're the one that saved my people back home in Boreas.' He puts his hands on his hips

and sighs. 'By Gaia's teats, now I'm going to have to rescue you, curse it!'

'Who are you?' you ask.

'I am Theron Empedoklis of Sarpedon,' pronounces the handsome young man, slapping his chest proudly.

'Ah, a Sarpedon, well that's a bit of luck,' you mutter. You recall that you prevented neighbouring tribes of barbarians from attacking the peaceful Sarpedons, who are simple farmers and herders.

He nimbly climbs up the tree, gives you some rope to hold onto, and frees your foot. You dangle on the rope for a moment to get your balance and then drop down to the forest floor.

'Thank you, Theron,' you say, 'but what are you doing here?'

'Well, I'm more of a hunter than a farmer. A hunter for glory really, I suppose you'd say, mostly because of you, actually. After hearing about your exploits, I gave up all that herding and planting and that, and set off to be an adventurer, like you.'

'And what brings you here?' you say, cleaning yourself up and hitching up your pack up onto your shoulders.

Theron points at something. You turn and look – and see the ruins of some kind of ancient temple, vine-bound, leaf-choked and crumbling.

'The legendary lost temple of Hyperion. Who knows what treasures lie within, eh? Come, help me. Together we'll be unstoppable, and we can split it fifty-fifty.'

Why not? You've got nothing else to do, so you nod your agreement.

▶**717**

158

If you have the codeword ***PatchupOne*** ▶ **130** immediately. If not, read on.

You are travelling along the Sacred Way, an ancient paved roadway that runs across the entire Vulcanverse. From here, it heads west along the coast into the mountains of Boreas, south towards Vulcan City, and east along the coast of Arcadia. To the south-east there is nothing but tree after tree after tree – the Deep Forest. Above you is a clear blue sky.

Nearby, a large net is slung between four wooden poles, clearly designed to catch something falling from the sky but it in a state of disrepair. It will cost you 20 pyr to have it fixed. If you wish to do so, cross off the money and get the codeword ***PatchupOne***. Either way, from here you can go:

West   ▶ **400** in *The Pillars of the Sky*

East along the coast   ▶ **20**

South on the Way   ▶ **804**

South-east into the Deep Forest ▶ **616**

159

You run for the treeline, but Death Dealer is much faster than you expected, and he hooks his axe around your ankle and sends you sprawling to the ground. As you try to rise, he clubs you into unconsciousness with his shield.

You wake to find yourself tied up in the back of a cart, being pulled along by Death Dealer on his mighty black charger that he calls Daisy, of all things...

He has dragged you all the way to hell! Up ahead looms the volcano of death, the abode of Thanatos himself.

'Almost there, Daisy,' mutters Death Dealer to his horse. You need to think fast to avoid oblivion at the hands of death himself.

Make an INGENUITY roll at difficulty 7.

Succeed	▶ 247
Fail	▶ 199

160

Here, the Arcady Trail winds round the eastern edges of the of woods known as the dales of leaf and stream. What next?

West to the Dales	▶ 266
South to the Sacred Way	▶ 832
North on the Trail	▶ 728
North-east to the Wineries	▶ 417
East on the Trail	▶ 14
South east to some hills	▶ 822

161

'Foolish mortal,' echoes the voice, and you are suddenly transported elsewhere.

▶ 500

162

Your god appears to you in a vision. 'You have succeeded in completing the first of the great labours of the wild woods. Two more remain. You have done well for a puny mortal, so I will reward you with divine power. Zeus knows, you need it. Oh, and Vulcan says you should have this key.'

A key in the shape of a tree with a goat-horned face of Pan at one end and a complex twine of roots at the working end materialises in front of you. It is the **Arcadian vault key**. Note it on your Adventure Sheet. Now turn to the section number written in the Current Location space on your Adventure Sheet.

163

As you head back to the top of the valley, you flick through the Book of Seven Sages. The sages are Thales, a founding philosopher, Bias, a law maker, Pittacus, a politician who helped create democracy, Solon of Athens, another law maker, Cleobulus, a benevolent philosopher tyrant, Anacharsis, another philosopher and Chilon of Sparta, a military philosopher or strategist.

The book discusses their lives and theories with famous quotes from each. Interesting, but you cannot see how secrets might be hidden in the text.

You find Myletes waiting for you. 'You did it, you slew the giant and defeated the Grey Witches!'

You nod.

'And did you find Alcyoneus' treasure?'

'No, in fact all I found was his lunch. I do have the Grey Ones' eye though,' you say, holding it up. It turns disturbingly in your hand to stare up at you.

'Oh dear, you'd better give it to me, immediately.'

You look at him suspiciously.

'Trust me,' says Myletes, 'whoever holds the eye will eventually lose their own sight, their eyes will fall away, and you will be entirely reliant on that eye to see the world. Yes, you'll be able to see into other planes and such like but one such as you? How would you fight with such a thing in your hand, or even strapped to your head?'

You look down at the eye. You can already feel its creeping presence inside your head, so you hand it over, along with the Book of Seven Sages.

Myletes puts the eye into a lead casket, and stashes the book in a leather bag.

'Well,' he says, 'you are indeed a mighty hero, and I dub thee Giant Slayer! I know that's not much of a reward, so come and see me at the Academy of Philosophers in Vulcan City when you get a chance. I'm sure we can work something out.' With that he prepares to send you back. 'Are you ready?' he says.

You nod and he reads from his scroll once again, and brings his staff down onto the ground. A bolt of lightning and a clap of thunder later, and you are back at Fort Blackgate.

Gain the title **Giant Slayer** and ▶ 220

164

You realise you have made a terrible mistake in coming here unprepared. Its golden hide is so thick and tough that none of your weapons can penetrate it, and its talons are strong and sharp as razored steel so they can cut through any armour or shield. It is also fast – you try to dodge aside so that you can escape but all it takes is one blow of those massive claws and you are sent sprawling to the ground, your armour ripped away. A half-second later and the Nemean lion is upon you, pinning you down. Its back legs rend you into bloody chunks in seconds. At least death is quick.

Although you have displayed a measure of over confident stupidity, you were also brave, so the gods will bring you back. This time. ▶ 111

165

Wolfshadow is approaching fast. Your only way out is to try and lose him amidst the trees to the west.

You run for your life, dashing for the woods, Wolfshadow howling at your heels. As you hurtle into the woodlands, a passing satyr steps out in front of you. With a yelp of terror, the goat-man sees Wolfshadow and freezes in horror.

Throw him to the wolf	▶ 437
Run past him into the woods	▶ 362

166

'Do you remember the giant Kakas, who gave you the dolorous wound?' you ask.

'Of course,' says Chiron, 'how could I forget, and I will be forever grateful to you for healing me.'

'Well, I slew the monstrous creature,' you say.

'Indeed!' says Chiron, 'that is good news. Here, take this as a gift.' He hands you a scroll-book. It is called the Precepts of Chiron and is full of advice on how to live a noble and honourable life.

You were hoping for money or a magical weapon, but still. You hide your disappointment, and say, 'Thank you, I will treasure this above all things!' Chiron smiles. You flick through it. It is full of aphorisms like 'Decide no dispute until all sides have been heard' or 'He who sows evil, reaps evil,' and so on. Note the **Precepts of Chiron** on your Adventure sheet, ▶ 90 and choose again.

167

Lefkia and the priestess Thekla are waiting for you at the temple.

'Hello, hello!' says Lefkia. 'Have you got the stuff I need?'

If you have some **vinegar of Hades** and a **bucket of gypsum** and want to hand them to Lefkia then ▶ 628

If not, you will have to come back later when you have the necessaries. For now, you can go:

West along the coast	▶ 380
South along the coast	▶ 419
South-west into the farmlands	▶ 270

168

Once again you try to ride the Alpheus falls in a barrel, and once again it shatters, sending you plummeting down, bouncing off rocks and stones like a boulder in an avalanche. Sadly though, you are not made of stone, and your skull bursts open like a melon, spilling your brains, such as they are, into the rushing waters.

▶ 111

169

If you have any or all of the codewords *Planted*, *Pure* or *Pinot*, lose them.

You decide to climb up to the forest canopy and take a look. Maybe you can spot where the forest ends or see some signs of human habitation or a clearing. After a short climb, you shove your head up and out of the canopy, disturbing

some birds who fly away, cawing in outrage. One of them shits in your face as it flies up. Cursing, you wipe the bird shite out of your eyes and look around. All you can see is a sea of leaves spreading out in all directions, an endless ocean of green.

You climb back down into the stifling, energy sapping heat and try to find a trail or path through the woods.

Soon you find yourself staggering through the gloom, sweating so much that you become parched and dry, desperate for a drink. A day, maybe two, passes, and you sink to the ground in a field of flowers, completely dehydrated. Just a short rest, that's all you need.

You wake with a start. Agony burns up through your legs. You realise you have fallen asleep in a field of snakeroot bladderwort, a carnivorous plant that feeds on insects and small animals usually, but you are so exhausted you can barely move. You try to crawl out but the plant also injects a paralysing sap into its victims and soon you are unable to move at all.

You lie there in agony as your life is slowly drained out of you, and your flesh dissolved while you are still alive. Before death finally claims you, you are struck by the irony of it all – snakeroot bladderwort only grows near streams and rivers. A plentiful water supply must only be a few footsteps away…

► 111

170

You have returned to the wineries of the gods. For once Maron appears to be sober.

'Greetings,' he says. He points to the vineyard where you can see irrigation channels have been dug, and water stored in butts and barrels, ready to go.

'We've got the water sorted, thanks to you, but have you anything we can actually plant?'

'You're sober!' you say. 'Given it up at last, have you?'

'What? No, 'course not,' says Maron, putting a jug of dandelion wine to his lips and taking a deep swig. 'Just that I've only just got up – nice long much-needed sleep and that.'

You stare at him nonplussed for a moment.

'Anyway,' says Maron, 'got some seeds or something?'

If you have the codeword *Nifty* or some **pomegranate seeds** ► 208

If not, you promise Maron you will come back later when you've got something suitable. From here, you can go:

North to the Arcady Trail ► 238
West to Treycross on the Arcady Trail ► 728
South on the Trail ► 338
East to the bridge over the river Alpheus ► 14

171

Krio offers you a seat at his table, laid out with fruit, and some delicious lamb kebabs. His wife Selene comes in, two young boys hiding behind the skirts of her peplos, and peeking out at you nervously, admiring your weapons and the cut of your heroic jib.

'Have you found our boy, Magnes?' asks Selene. You shake your head. 'I'm afraid not, at least not yet, but I'm still looking. Do not fear, I will find him, but for now I'm just here to buy wool'

► 56

172

You open the door of your room to see the face of Jas the Helot, your ex-butler, staring at you in terrified surprise from the window, a bulging sack over one shoulder. As you dash forward his face disappears from view.

You rush to the window to see him going down a ladder as fast as he can. At the bottom is Timandra the dryad, she of the hair of long grass and daisies, holding the ladder.

'Hurry, Jas, hurry!' she screams.

Angrily, you grab the ladder and twist, sending Jas tumbling to the ground below. The bulging sack he was carrying lands nearby and splits open spilling various silver plates and goblets, a vase painted by the great Apelles himself, a small sculpture of Aphrodite by the master Parrhasius and other household goods of value from your rooms.

Jas gets up, rubbing his bruises ruefully, and makes to grab some of his stolen loot, but you nock an arrow to your bow. Jas curses, and runs for it, Timandra close on his heels. She turns and yells 'Malakas!' up at you, and flicks a rude sign at you with her fingers.

You aim the bow and she yelps in terror, and they both flee as fast as they can. You shake your head. You can't believe he tried that again!

You instruct the Palace staff to add extra locks on the door and window.

Enter the Vault   ▶ 828
Leave your rooms   ▶ 282

173

'Honey? I don't even like honey, why would I care? Anyway, it's been nice chatting but it's time for my breakfast,' Kaustikia says, readying an attack.

'Hold on, what about the…'
'Wine, the vines will die too.'   ▶ 144
'Satyrs, they'll die too.'   ▶ 256
'Centaurs, they'll die too.'   ▶ 218

174

You yank the lever and are lobbed high up into the air, up and over a raised plateau from which the Alpheus river runs down to the eastern shore. You barrel through the air, and nearly collide with a seagull. It caws at you in outrage, as if admonishing you for being somewhere you shouldn't. You start falling down to the eastern shore, and the paved stones of the Sacred Way… will you be smeared like jam across the grey flagstones? But then you see the catch-net that you're supposed to fall into rushing up to meet you at breakneck speed. If you do *not* have the codeword *PatchupFour* ▶ 605 immediately. If you do have it, read on.

You plummet into the webbing of the catch-net safely. After you take a moment to catch your breath, you climb down and look around.

▶ 540

175

You try to roll away, angling yourself forward, so you can come up and hack at the basilisk, but you mistime it, and part of the black cloud engulfs your leg. Almost instantly, it is turned to gold, and you collapse to the ground in agony. The rest of the black vapour rolls over… You try not to breathe it in, but it doesn't matter, for you can feel it penetrating deep into your skin. You look down at your hands. You cannot move them, for they are now bright, lustrous and golden. You try to scream but your lungs have stopped moving.

You have been turned into solid gold. At least you're worth something now, you think to yourself.

And then you realise you are still thinking. You should be dead, surely? But soon your thoughts fade, and your mind sinks into a kind of dream. It seems your soul is still trapped in this body of gold. You sleep, and dream of open meadows, fields of green and horses, galloping across wide plains, wild and free but you are incarcerated in a prison made of your own golden skin.

Unfortunately, as your soul is trapped and you are not truly dead, the gods cannot bring you back this time.

If you have the codeword *Noble* ▶ 72 immediately. If not, read on.

You dream endless dreams, wrapped in gold, your body a priceless tomb. The sun and the moon rise and set, the world turns, the Vulcanverse evolves and changes but you do not, for you are lost and forgotten forever.

▶ 750

176

If you have the title **Dryad's Doom** ▶ 411 immediately. If not, read on.

If you have the codeword *Perdition* ▶ 315 immediately. If not, read on.

If you have the codeword *Passion* ▶ 276 immediately. If not, read on.

You wander deeper into the Woodlands. The trees start to look greener and wilder, somehow. Sunlight pours through in columns, as if the trees were parting their branches to let the sunlight in. Soon you find chains of wildflowers strung across the branches, and trees with bark that is smooth and supple, as if they were wearing beautiful silken gowns of forest green.

Every now and then you can hear soft, feminine voices, whispering through the tree tops, or snippets of song wafting on the scented air. A sudden movement catches your eye, as of a deer, flitting from tree to tree. You notice another, in the other direction – a woman perhaps, with flowers in her hair, and wearing a cloak of leaves.

You find yourself standing in a pool of sunlight, in a forest glade. It is warm. The scent of wild flowers fills your senses, birds chitter in the trees, and then a soft, soothing song starts up. It seems to speak directly to your soul, bringing a calm, gentle peace. Perhaps you could take a little nap here, safe, warm, pleasant. After all you've been through, you deserve a break, don't you?

▶ 203

177

Fort Blackgate has been rebuilt and now it is yours. The shiny black gates gleam in the bright sunlight, the fortified walls standing proud and unconquerable. Hypatia and Lefkia lead you inside, where the courtyard is of clean, cobbled grey stone. Wooden stables and other stalls line the walls, including a stone barracks and a servant's quarters. The keep is finely furnished, with a master bedroom, and a bathroom with actual running water from clay pipes with bronze taps, from a rain water cistern set into the rooftops. The ground floor of the keep is largely bare, as are a couple of the outbuildings. Below that, there is a large storeroom, and a dungeon.

'Ready for you to add to as you wish,' says Hypatia.

'Anyway,' says Lefkia, 'you are now the sovereign commander of Fort Blackgate!' She hands you a set of black iron keys to the great black gates.

Lefkia and Hypatia take their leave, and you are left in charge of the Fort. Gain the codeword *Parapet* and ▶ 220

178

You have successfully reconsecrated this shrine, and now you can get blessings here. If you are a worshipper of Ares, blessings are free. If not, you must pay 10 pyr per blessing. You can only have a total of three blessings at a time.

When you have finished here ▶ 832

179

After a while, during which you have dozed off, you feel a tug on the line. You've caught a fish, and soon after, another. Note two **fresh fish** on your Adventure Sheet. Some time later you've not caught anything else, so you decide to give up for the day and move on. Where will you go?

West on the Way	► 20
South-west into the forest	► 189
East on the Way	► 380
South, into the Ladon river valley	► 403

180

You have gone back to the truffle hunter's cabin in the forest. He is outside, chopping wood for the fire. Inside, you can hear little Io coughing. Clearly she still has the black blight.

'Don't worry, little one,' shouts the man, 'I'll go and get some more medicine in a minute!'

Meaning he'll go down into the land of roots and harvest more sap from the Great Green Ones.

You have not found a cure for the black blight, but you could still just murder the truffle hunter and be done with it.

| Kill him | ► 97 |
| Keep trying to find a cure | ► 215 |

181

You show Erifili **the portrait** by Apelles. 'That can't be an Apelles,' she says, 'It's utter rubbish! Mind you, the signature is pretty convincing but still, I could do better than that.'

'It's supposed to be a portrait of me,' you say.

'Self-portrait, eh?' she says.

'No... I...' but then you just nod. It's too complicated to explain that it was painted by the ghost of Apelles in Hades itself. She probably wouldn't believe you anyway.

'Well, it is frankly awful but here, take this. Maybe it'll help,' and she gives you a book. It's called the Painter's Handbook by Master Apelles.

'Tips from a real master!' she says.

Gain the codeword *Painter*. There is nothing else you can do here, so you take your leave.

► 282 and choose again.

182

'Cleanthes is the murderer!' you say out loud.

'Stupid mortal,' says a stony voice in your head, and you are suddenly transported elsewhere. Roll a die:

score 1-2	► 222 in *The Hammer of the Gods*
score 3-4	► 222 in *The Pillars of the Sky*
score 5-6	► 222 in *The Houses of the Dead*

If you do not have the relevant book, simply re-roll until you are transported to a book you do have.

If you do not have any of the other books in the Vulcanverse, you are transported to the north-west corner of Arcadia

► 158

183

Delete the **venison sausages** or the **strix strew** from your Adventure Sheet. You add the strongest, most pungent herbs to the meat, and throw it as far as you can in the opposite direction, hoping that will send them off in the wrong direction.

You set off north, running as fast as you can, dodging fallen tree trunks, and avoiding the denser thorns and brambles. In the distance you can hear the howls of your pursuers, but after a few moments, the sound fades... They have lost your trail, it's worked! You hurry on. Maybe, just maybe, you can pull this off.

And then the howls start up again... they've wised up, and are back on your trail, and closing in fast. You will have to up your speed but the forest is full of pitfalls and snags.

Make a GRACE roll at difficulty 8.

| Succeed | ► 216 |
| Fail | ► 237 |

184

You have been given permission to hunt in Arcadia by the goddess Artemis but the killing of the bear uses up your hunting quota. Cross the **hunting permit** off your Adventure Sheet.

► 273

185

You manage to shake off the drowsy numbness that is infecting your brain. You draw your weapon and shout a war-cry, stabbing down at the tentacled black Shadowhunter. Your weapon seems to split it in two or has it simply parted to avoid your blow? In any case, it melts away into the ground, vomiting up any of your shadow it had eaten so far. No doubt it will try again at another time. You will have to remain alert whenever you are in high sunshine and your shadow is especially strong.

You may have preserved your shadow from attack once more but why is it coming for *your* shadow, and who, if anyone, sent it? These are questions that remain unanswered for now.

From here you can go:

East to the eastern bridge	► 801
West to the western bridge	► 14
North to the Woodlands	► 60
South to some hills	► 822

186

❑

If there was a tick in the box already ► 349 immediately. If not, tick the box now and then read on.

If you have the codeword *Plenty* ▶ 241. If not, read on.

A handsome young man, wearing a wide brimmed hat, and a chiton hitched up around his thighs, showing off a fine pair of lean, tanned legs, steps up to you and introduces himself. 'I am Drosos, the farm overseer you hired – and for that I thank you, now I can feed my family!'

'You seem rather young to be an overseer.'

'True, but I am very clever, and my father was a farmer, as was my grandfather, and his before him and so on, all the way back to my great, great, grandmother who was Demeter herself, the goddess of farming. So you could say it's in my blood, as it were.'

'Well, OK then!' you say, impressed, even if you don't believe a word of it. 'So, can you get these farms up and running?'

'Ah, I'm afraid not, not yet at any rate,' says Drosos with a shake of his head. A rather beautiful head, you have to admit, with jet black hair and startling blue eyes.

'You see,' he continues, 'there just isn't enough water. Yes, we get the occasional summer storm which can unload quite a bit of water, but it's not something we can rely on. We need the rivers to run once more, the Ladon and the Alpheus. Without them, anything I try will be doomed to failure.'

It seems there is nothing more you can do here until you have restored the rivers of Arcadia to their former glory. You will have to come back later. Further west lie impassable cliffs, so will you go:

North-east	▶ 365
North-west	▶ 380
South-east	▶ 419

187

You walk into the tailor's shop. He is working at the counter, stitching. Behind him is a small workshop where a couple of apprentices, a young man and a young woman, are working on various pieces of cloth.

'Welcome to my shop,' says Gelos. He's a middle-aged man, rather portly, and balding, but with pale blue eyes, like clear blue river water. 'What can I do for you?'

For each **bale of wool** you have, Gelos can make you a **woollen cloak**, costing 10 pyr each. Cross off the **bale of wool** and the money, and add the **woollen cloak** (or cloaks). Perhaps you will be able to sell the cloaks elsewhere for a profit.

If you have the **Golden Fleece** and wish Gelos to work on it ▶ 604

If you have a **bearskin** and wish Gelos to work on it ▶ 671

If you have the codeword *Pelt* and want Gelos to work on the wolf pelt ▶ 646

Or you can leave the shop ▶ 305

188

You have returned to the frozen lake of Ladon, covered in rime-cold limestone slabs. The lake itself is frozen too, and presumably the river god himself lies within, encased in ice.

You hide yourself in a lakeside copse, the trees withered and leafless, killed by the cold that comes off its icy surface, and wait.

Sure enough after a while two ox carts turn up, guarded by the officer in a black-crested helm and ten soldiers, each with shields emblazoned with a three-armed symbol. They do their work, replacing thawed-out slabs and ensuring the lake stays frozen and then leave. Will you:

Follow them	▶ 109
Come back later	▶ 81

189

You have come to the outskirts of the Deep Forest, at its north eastern edge. From here you can go:

Deeper into the forest	▶ 472
North-west to the Sacred Way	▶ 20
North-east to the bridge	▶ 517
East to the river Ladon	▶ 403

190

'All right, then,' says Orphea. She steps up, gets out a scroll and unfurls it on top of the altar. She raises her arms skyward and intones in old Greek,

'O thou Apotropaei, ye averting gods, I invoke thee, turn away this curse! O Pan, forgive thy faithful servants and spare us thy wrath. Let the Aegis of Athena protect us, and with this kylikes I placate thee!'

Orphea pulls out a small cup, painted with two wide warding eyes, and pours some wine out on the altar.

'There, all done,' she says, and turns to you, pointing at the shallow depression.

Give her the amulet and let her open it	▶ 236
Do it yourself	▶ 104

191

Mela's spell is not unlike the enchantments the dryads use to enslave mortal minds. You can feel the wooden dryad's heart that you have resonate with sympathetic magic. In fact, it appears to be absorbing her spell somehow, a stroke of luck indeed.

Thinking fast, you pretend to succumb to Mela's witchery, and soon you are shambling along with the rest of her mindless slaves, obeying all commands for now, and forced to mine the limestone of the quarry. When night falls, you are able to break away unnoticed and investigate the stone cabin.

▶ 479

192

You sink into the world of dreams — and sink, and sink, until you are underwater. But, as is the way in dreams, you seem to be able to breathe safely.

The waters are cold, very, very cold. You see a man, indistinct and blurry, encased in a great block of ice. You look up — the surface of the water is completely covered in limestone blocks. Frozen limestone. There is no way out.

Except for you, for suddenly you are in an ancient limestone quarry. Shambling figures hack away at the rocks. They drag blocks over to a large iron cage, lit by three torches. A woman in yellow robes unlocks the cage with three keys and out pours a cloud of icy particles, freezing the stone blocks. From inside the cage, you hear the sobbing of a broken-hearted woman.

And then you wake, shivering, your eyelashes frosted together with cold.

'Wow, did you dream of Boreas, the north wind?' asks Zenia.

'No, of an Arcadian river god,' you say.

'Huh… dreams are weird, eh?' says Zenia. You nod. If you have some more **kykeon mushrooms** and 10 more pyr and want to try another vision ▶ **737**

If not, you can head back to the market (▶ **728**) or leave the area (▶ **12**).

193

You ask Chiron about the black blight.

'It is a terrible disease. Fortunately, I know a cure and I can make it for you, but you will need to bring me these things:

vinegar of Hades
kykeon mushrooms
mountain mandrake.'

If you have these ingredients ▶ **729**

If not, you will have to quest for them and return later, so ▶ **90** and choose again.

194

'Welcome to the shrine of Artemis,' says a voice like the rustling of leaves in the wind. The shrine is a low platform at the base of a great oak tree, covered in fruits and other offerings. The voice is that of the dryad that lives in the tree although you cannot see her.

You can get blessings here. If you are a worshipper of Artemis, blessings are free. If not, you must pay 10 pyr per blessing. You can only have a total of three blessings at a time.

You may also ask permission to hunt in Arcadia. For 15 pyr you can purchase a **hunting permit**. You may have only one hunting permit at a time. If you do, note it on your Adventure Sheet.

If you want to ask the dryad of the shrine about the golden arrow of Artemis ▶ **31**

When you are finished here will you:

Go north on the Way	▶ **419**
Go south on the Way	▶ **801**
Go west into the Woodlands	▶ **60**

195

You notice the bark of a nearby tree has been slashed — perhaps a bear sharpening her claws, maybe even Kallisto herself. Anyway, a line of almost dried out sap runs down the tree trunk, and you can't help but notice its pungent odour, so strong it fills the area around the tree.

That gives you an idea, and you run round in a large circle, slashing tree bark with your blade, and letting the sap run freely down. Soon you've managed to fill a reasonably sized area with the acrid stench of the sap, a scent so strong you are confident it will mask your own.

You hurry on. Judging by the fading sounds of pursuit, your stratagem has worked. It is not long before you come to the edge of a clearing in the forest, in the middle of which you spot the statue of Artemis hunting with her bow, accompanied by two wolves, all beautifully carved in brightly coloured painted marble. At its base lie offerings to the goddess. You made it.

▶ **520**

196

Cries of 'The mayor! The mayor has returned!' go up around the village, and soon you are greeted by a crowd of villagers all thanking you, patting you on the back, and generally being effusively grateful. You are popular indeed.

The village is thriving, people gossip around the water fountain, merchants use the road system to trade with the villagers, most of the children are healthy, and things are going well. You can take much of the credit for that. You can visit some villagers or move on.

Phineas the rumour monger	▶ **153**
Gelos the tailor	▶ **187**
Ersi the grain merchant	▶ **75**
Leave the hamlet	▶ **801**

197

If you have the codeword *Plenty* ▶ **659** immediately.

Otherwise, put a tick in this box ❑. If there was a tick in the box already ▶ **489** immediately. If not, read on.

You find King Nyctimus at his desk for he doesn't have a throne, as is befitting a man who is more an administrator than a ruler. He greets you warmly.

'Ah, my Steward. I am so grateful to you,' and he waves

a hand, indicating the freshly painted murals, the gleaming marble statues, the polished stone floor and so on. He even has a clerk on either side of him, helping him with his work, a pair of bespectacled satyrs.

He sees you eyeing them up.

'Don't worry, they're the intellectual kind of satyr, not your usual whoring, wine-drinking, ale-quaffing, magic-mushroom eating, randy old goats you would expect.'

You nod in surprise.

'So,' says the King, 'you've done a fine job on getting the palace back up and running, what we need next is to restore the river gods. Without them and their waters, most of our flora and fauna are suffering, and our farms, vineyards and gardens cannot be watered and so on. If you could find them.'

'What happened to them?'

'We don't know, they just seem to have disappeared. I suggest starting at their sources, Ladon's Lake just north of here, and the Tarn Alpheus, up near that Celtic colony, the Druid's Shrine.'

'And if I find them?'

'The gods will reward you, I'm sure of it,' says Nyctimus.

'The gods?'

'Yeah, the gods.'

'Not you, then?'

'No, no, not me,' says Nyctimus. 'No money in the treasury you see. Not without the farms fully functioning and the vineyards and all the rest of it. No tax revenue without goods to tax and all that.'

There is nothing else to discuss, so you take your leave.
▶ 282 and choose again.

198

The message on the plinth read, 'I turn once, what is out will not get in. I turn again, what is in will not get out. What am I?'

Take each letter of your answer, give it its corresponding number in the alphabet, (so A would be 1, Z would be 26) add them all together and turn to that paragraph. If it is correct, it will say so, if not, return here and think again.

If you cannot solve the riddle, or do not wish to go through the door, you can head:

South-west on the Trail	▶ 728
South to the Wineries	▶ 417

199

You are bound tightly and strapped down to the floor of the cart. You cannot find a way out, and soon Death Dealer drags you all the way down into Tartarus itself, through shadowed halls and dreadful darkness until you reach a great archway that has these words engraved over it:

'A fat king or a starveling beggar, it's all the same to Thanatos,' says Death Dealer, 'and that is how it is meant to be,' before he drags you through the arch and leaves you alone in the dark.
▶ 834

200

Next to the Sacred Way that runs up and down the east coast of Arcadia, a small bay provides a safe mooring for a boat.

```
BOAT MOORED HERE? (Y/N)



```

If you have arrived by boat, note in the box that it is moored here. If your boat is here you can put to sea, otherwise you must go overland.

Set sail – delete the boat from the box above and then
▶ 292

Head inland to a bridge over the river Alpheus ▶ 801

201

A strange sight catches your eye. In the middle of the lake bed a large trapdoor flips up and out rushes a torrent of hot air in a great blast of heat. The air rushes out for some seconds, and then the trap door slams shut once more.

You climb down into the lake bed to investigate. On closer inspection you see that the trap door has been disguised in such a way that when it is at rest it looks like on ordinary section of dusty, mud-caked earth. Will you:

Wait for it to open again and see if you can get inside ▶ 313
Go north to the Druid's Shrine ▶ 463
North-west skirting past the Shrine to the woods ▶ 620
Take the stairs in the cliffside down to the lower tarn ▶ 578

202

You fall fast asleep, but then suddenly you're woken by the bell you had set on the rod. You've caught a fish, and soon after, two more! Note three **fresh fish** on your Adventure Sheet. That seems to be it for the day though, so you decide to move on. Where will you go?

West on the Way	▶ 20
South-west into the forest	▶ 189
East on the Way	▶ 380
South, into the Ladon river valley	▶ 403

'Stop! Stop it now!' says a strident voice. 'I have a use for this one.' You blink, coming out of your reverie. You find yourself in a sun-dappled woodland glade, up ahead a couple of women… no, wait, their hair is a tangle of weeds and stalks, their skin is soft, and supple like a human's but green and a little tree-barkish. They wear gowns of leaves and there are flowers in their hair. No, wait, the flowers are growing *out* of their hair! Dryads. And they were singing a spell song, trying to enchant you!

'Here, eyes on me!' says the strident voice. You turn, still a little befuddled. There stands another dryad. This one has oak leaves for hair, bright green eyes, and a tight mouth as of one who is used to command. She wears green and yellow robes of cloth rather than leaves, but with little acorns hanging off the hems and sleeves. Her skin is a darker green.

'Sorry about that,' she says, 'but you know, you are deep in dryad territory, that's what we do.'

You glare angrily. 'I am no plaything!' you manage to say though your mind is still rather confused.

'I have to say you do look a lot tougher than your average mortal. And that's what I need, a toughie!'

Your head starts to clear. 'What, for your boudoir, is that it?'

'Hah, hah, no! Though that is sort of the nub of the matter. It's my love, my tree frog!'

'Tree frog?' you ask, perplexed.

'Yes, that was my pet name for him, my lover, Davides,' says the dryad.

'A mortal?'

'Yes, a mortal man. At first, it was just a bit of fun but I must confess I've fallen head over roots for him! But, well… he's gone, and I miss him so.'

'Why can't you look for him, what do you need me for?'

'It's where he's gone, you see it's… Umm…' She leaves the sentence unfinished.

'Yes?' you prompt.

'Hades. It's Hades.'

'What? You mean he's dead?'

'Yes. And it broke my heart. But seeing you, hardened warrior that you are and all, I thought maybe you could go to Hades and bring him back to me, like Orpheus and Eurydice, where he goes and gets his lover back. Except he stuffs it up at the last minute, but I'm sure an experienced adventurer like you could pull it off!'

'And who are you?' you ask.

'Me? Oh, I'm Karya, the hamadryad.'

'And what does this Davides look like, what did he do?' you say.

'Well, he was actually a barber.' The other two dryads start to giggle until silenced by an angry glare from Karya.

'But a very handsome barber actually, and if you bring him back to me, I'll reward you well.'

'Such as?' you ask.

'Perhaps you'd like a dryad slave!' she says, pointing at the other two. They blanch, their bark-like skin turning a pale green hue, before turning tail and running off.

'Seriously though, I can give you all sorts of things, money, love, divine blessings, poisons, magic. Assuming you can get into Hades at all that is?'

'Yes, I can get into Hades – and back,' you say.

'Well then, I'll look forward to seeing you again soon?'

'Maybe not soon, but I'll see what I can do, yes,' you say.

Gain the codeword **Passion**. With that you take your leave.

Go to the old apiary ▶ 8
Leave this place ▶ 225

204

The waters stir and something large pulls at your fishing line. You grab the rod, and carefully pull upward. Whatever it is, it's big and is fighting back. With one great heave you flip a fish up through the air onto the bridge – it's nearly as big as a dolphin!

As it hits the ground, it begins to change shape – into a young woman, but with seaweed for hair, green eyes, webbed hands and feet, and a smattering of scales around and about her legs and hips. A water nymph!

'Owww… owww,' she says, trying to get the hook out of her mouth. 'Yoo bwute,' she mutters. You are so surprised, all you can do is stare in astonishment for a moment, until finally she gets the hook out. You can't help noticing a trickle of red blood running down from her mouth. It is bright crimson and looks quite fetching against the pale, luminous green of the rest of her.

You notice her staring back at you fearfully. You raise your hands as if to reassure her and something flickers across her, like a wave of distortion. Her gait shifts, even her features seem to subtly change or is that your imagination?

You narrow your eyes. She seems vaguely familiar somehow.

'Have we met before?' you ask.

'Oh no, never, I would remember you!' she says. Make a CHARM roll at difficulty 8.

Succeed ▶ 293
Fail ▶ 364

205

You have heard that Nessus, while on the one hand a blood-thirsty heartless villain, is on the other hand, a very thin-skinned egoist, highly sensitive when it comes to insults, especially when it makes him look bad in front of his men, for a bandit chief rules only through his reputation. If you use the skills you acquired verbally duelling Deridedes, the priest of Momos, god of mockery, perhaps you can lure Nessus into single combat by taunting him in front of his crew.

You step out into the open in front of the wooden gates of the stockade and shout, 'Oi, Nessus, you spavined nag, why don't you come out and face me in single combat, or are you too much of a frightened gelding?'

The response is a flight of arrows. Quickly you dart into cover, as the arrows pepper the ground where you were standing.

You step back out again. 'Nessus is a centaur? No, he's more half horse, half mouse! Too scared to face me, he gets his men to do his dirty work. What kind of bandit leader are you? Or did Mummy say you couldn't come out to play today?'

There's a brief moment of silence, and then Nessus pops his head up above the wooden parapet, his green tunic catching the sunlight, and takes a shot at you with his bow. It's far enough away for you to move aside without too much trouble, though.

'Still too scared to come out, eh?' you shout, 'Don't want to get your green dress dirty, you mouse-brained, fart-breathed, gelded hobby-horse!' From behind the wooden walls you hear some laughter, and Nessus scowls angrily.

'I see I'm going to have to kill you myself,' he says. 'You want single combat? Well, that's what you're going to get.'

After a minute or two, Nessus emerges, a leather cap on his head, some leather barding around his fore-quarters and a long spear held in both hands. His green tunic sparkles strangely. It appears enchanted in some way, but hopefully it's just a trick of the light.

You see his men taking up positions on the walls to watch. There are about twelve of them.

You face off against the spear-armed centaur.

'I'm going to gut you…' says Nessus.

'You can try,' you retort, as you ready your weapons.

The battle begins. Make a STRENGTH roll at difficulty 9.

Succeed ▶ 435
Fail ▶ 487

206

'What do you need?' you ask.

'Well, first off, I need the palace refurbished – cleaned up, repainted and restored.'

'I'm an adventurer, not a painter and decorator,' you point out.

'Of course, of course, but there's a bulletin board over

there, where you can hire various craftsmen and skilled workers and the like. Times are hard in Arcadia, there is no money, and those who haven't already left, have no work. We need jobs, investment, a purpose, that kind of stuff. You can do that. And then there's the three great Labours of Arcadia that the gods told me about. One of them involves getting the vineyards and farms of Arcadia up and running again. But you can't do that until you've got the rivers flowing again – someone or something has taken the river gods, or done something to them, so that the rivers of Alpheus and Ladon are all dried up. Find the river gods, get the water running. Then you can get the farms and vineyards going, then you can build an apiary.'

'A what?'

'An apiary. Beehives.'

'Beehives? Why?'

'I've no idea! It all came to me in a dream, sent by the gods. I'm not even sure if it's real, or I just made it up, but anyway, there you go. Why would I make it up? Must be the gods, right?'

'Well… OK, but what's in it for me?' you ask.

'First off, if you sort the palace out, I can give you a suite of rooms where you can rest and store your stuff. As for the rest, well, when the farms and vineyards are up and running, you can grow food and drink, and then sell it, right? I'm sure it'll all pay off in the end!'

You nod, not entirely convinced.

'Anyway, start with the bulletin board first, over there.' And he points to a section of the wall, where several scrolls of papyrus have been pinned.

Examine the bulletin board ▶ 101
Come back later ▶ 547

207

Velosina is waiting for you at the wooden gates to the Sacred Stables. She smiles and takes out her bone flute. She plays a happy tune as she leads you in to see Chiron, first amongst centaurs. You notice that the flute is made from what looks like a human thigh bone.

If you have a **bone flute of Koré** and want to show it to Velosina, ▶ 711

If not, you continue on to find Chiron. He greets you warmly and offers to help you in any way he can ▶ 90

208

Get the codeword **Press**.

'I've got these,' you say, showing Maron the casket full of pomegranate seeds.

Maron's glasses ride up his nose as he raises his eyebrows. 'Pomegranate? Well, yes, I guess we can make wine from 'em, sure, but they're trees. Better off with grape vine, I reckon.'

'Ah but these are special,' you say. 'They're from the Garden of Persephone.'

'What… the goddess? From her garden in Hades?'

'Yes, indeed,' you say.

'You've been to Hades?'

'And back again, yes. These seeds are hers, blessed by the goddess.'

'Wow, fantastic! They should grow faster, better, and tastier than the usual stuff. Should make great wine! Can't wait to taste it myself.'

'Yes, well, leave some for the rest of us,' you say drily as you hand some of the seeds over.

'Hah, very funny,' says Maron, 'Anyway, these will do nicely. Come back in a while, see how it's going.'

You take your leave. From here, you can go:

North to the Arcady Trail	▶ **238**
West to Treycross on the Arcady Trail	▶ **728**
South on the Trail	▶ **338**
East to the bridge over the river Alpheus	▶ **14**

209

You begin preparations for your quest, with Myletes by your side.

'Tell me about Alcyoneus,' you ask.

'Well, he's not that big, taller than most men, but no giant in that sense. Strong of course but… well…' Myletes hesitates for a moment.

'What?' you say.

'He's… well, he's invulnerable when on his own ground and can't be killed,' he says in a rush.

'What? Why didn't you mention that before!'

'Well, you know, I didn't want to put you off…'

Feeling a little like you'd been tricked into this, you ask, 'How do I kill him, then?'

'He's only immortal in the bounds of the courtyard of his tower, so you'll have to… I dunno, lure him out of there.'

'How do I do that?' you ask.

'I don't know!' says Myletes, 'I'm a philosopher. Ask me about Pythagoras and his theorem and I'll tell you, but don't ask me how to trap one of the gigantes, especially their king.'

You nod. 'Fair enough. And the Grey Ones. Tell me about them. Why do they guard the valley?'

'Well, they were set there by Gaia to protect her son, Alcyoneus. They have one eye to see between them, and one tooth to eat with.'

'That doesn't sound that difficult to deal with,' you point out. 'They sound like three toothless, blind old ladies.'

'Indeed, except that their names are Enyo the creeping dread, Deino the terror, and Persis the wall-shaker, so there seems to be more to them than just being grey old hags.'

'This is just getting better and better, isn't it? With names like that what could possibly go wrong?'

'What can I say,' says Myletes with a shrug.

'Is that it? Any more surprises?'

'That's it I'm afraid, I wish I knew more. Talking of which, perhaps you could tell me about them when you meet them? I could submit a paper to the Academy then, that would be very helpful.'

'I will bear that in mind,' you say sarcastically, 'assuming I survive the encounter.'

'I have faith in you,' says Myletes. 'Ready?'

You heave a resigned sigh.

'Ready.'

With that, Myletes pulls out a scroll, reads and then intones some strange sounding words from it, scatters some powders into the air and brings his staff down onto the ground.

A bolt of lightning strikes you, and you think for a moment you must be dead, but it seems to pass through you harmlessly, and you both disappear in a puff of smoke like a cheap parlour trick at a child's birthday party. Except it's real.

▶ **260**

210

You pull the lever and are launched up into the air. You hurtle across the clear blue sky at breakneck speed. It is both terrifying and exhilarating at the same time. Below, like a ribbon on grass, is the river of Ladon and its lake, rushing past. You start falling downward, towards the Sacred Way, near a bridge across the Ladon, with the coast beyond, and the great encircling sea of Oceanus. The Sacred Way seems to rises up to meet you – will your brains be dashed out on the grey paving? But then you see the catch-net! If you do *not* have the codeword *Patchup Two* ▶ **493** immediately. If you do have it, read on.

You fall into the webbed cradle. The four poles bend inward as you sink into it but it all holds together safely. You climb out of the catch-net and look around.

▶ **287**

211

'Brilliant!' says Lefkia, and she hands you a papyrus scroll detailing the money you have paid, the items you gave her, and so forth. Cross off the **Contract: Painter and Decorator** from your Adventure Sheet and add **Lefkia's receipt** instead.

'How long will it take?' you ask.

'Hard to be certain, but check in from time to time and I'll keep you posted.'

You watch for a while as Lefkia starts work, laying out her paints, organising her brushes, mixing up some gypsum plaster and so on. It's a big job so there's no point hanging around, best leave her to it.

▶ 385

212

You open the village strongbox and help yourself to all their money. Gain the title **The Embezzler** and add the money to your Adventure Sheet. You pop out to get some lunch from the local bakery and return to find a grey-haired village elder looking in the strongbox in horror. It is the village clerk who also has a key, it seems. Oops! He looks up at you in disgust and, before you can act, runs out the back door and down the main street, screaming that you have stolen all their money.

If is not long before a mob of angry villagers, wielding pitchforks, scythes and clubs are chasing after you with cries of 'Thief! Villain! Liar! Mountebank! Charlatan! Impostor!' and so on. Someone shouts, 'I bet Cressida and Poly were innocent, and you framed 'em!' They are angry indeed, and there must be at least thirty of them, far too many for even you to take on. You flee for your life. Make a GRACE roll at difficulty 7.

Succeed	▶ 363
Fail	▶ 320

213

You cannot see the sun or the stars for the thick canopy above, but you can look for a certain type of plant, those that grow near forest streams and brooks or in darkness.

You try to stay away from areas that are heavily mushroomed, as that usually means high humidity, little sunlight and no running water. Certain other shrubs and flowers prefer rain, so you stay clear of them. After a time you find some lush grasses. You follow their growth patterns, and sure enough they turn into rushes and reeds, growing on the banks of a babbling brook.

You follow the stream downriver until you see some purple foxgloves – they always face away from the trees and soon enough you step out of the treeline into bright sunlight. The brook you are following runs on into what must be the river Ladon. You have made it out!

▶ 403

214

You're in front of the statue of your god. The two coins seem a meagre offering compared to the wealth your more affluent neighbours press into the priests' hands. Yet, as you gaze down, careful not to meet the eyes of the god, you feel a presence that brushes over you like the hem of an enormous cloak. Darkness swims in your eyes, but not the darkness of oblivion. It is the infinite shadow that lies in the path of a light so intense that to look directly at it would sear your eyes to blindness.

The voice of the god is not heard, but felt in every atom of your being: 'You are the crop your parents sowed, the tree they planted, the grapes they pressed. In your deeds their little lives will gain glory. Go now to meet your destiny.'

Add +1 to any one attribute of your choice (STRENGTH, CHARM, INGENUITY, or GRACE).

▶ 753

215

You just can't bring yourself to kill him in cold blood. After a few seconds, the man notices you standing there, with your hand on your sword hilt, and thinking about murder.

'Ah, it's you again. Have you come to kill me? For I will not stop harvesting medicine for my little Io,' he says defiantly.

You can't do it, so you shake your head. 'No,' you say. 'Instead I will quest for a cure to the black blight.'

'Really? I will be in your debt if you do, and happily will I cease to cut the roots for sap!'

He tells you his name is Mithaecus, and he's been hunting the Arcadian truffles called hydnon for years. One day he hopes to write a cookbook. You decide to take your leave before his witterings about truffle recipes drives you to kill him after all.

▶ 160

216

You run like a son of the north wind, Boreas, or Hermes of the winged sandals, leaping over dead wood, sidestepping tangled roots and thorny brambles. You are fast, but nevertheless, the sons of Lykaon know these woods like the backs of their hairy, mutant hands, and they are gaining on you.

▶ 255

217

If you have the codeword *Precious* or the title **Kissed by a Golden Princess** ▶ 761.

There is a track leading away from the Sacred Way to the hills in the north. Clearly it was once much used but has fallen into decay now, and there are barely any tracks at all. You follow it to a range of round hills, each topped with a sacred standing stone of some kind, looking like nothing more than nipples on a range of fulsome breasts such as those on the statue of Artemis at Ephesus or the she-wolf that suckled Romulus and Remus, the founders of Rome. One of the hills is covered in many domed houses, a small town of some kind but it looks deserted now.

As you draw nearer, you see an inn, nestled in the foothills. Its sign depicts a pair of enormous breasts. You stare up at them doubtfully. What is this place?

Enter the inn	► 350
South to the Sacred Way	► 20

218

'Centaurs!' says Kaustikia sneeringly. 'Fast and hard to run down, also always shooting arrows at you, and they don't even taste that good, not nearly horsey enough. No, I can do without them, and I can do without you wittering on anymore. Time to break your head for my bread; don't you worry, you'll soon be dead.'

If you have the **Nemean bagh nakh** ► 817
If not ► 783

219

Hunting in the woods of Arcadia without permission is forbidden and you have incurred the wrath of Artemis, goddess of the hunt. Note **Artemis's curse x 1** on your Adventure Sheet. Your next attribute roll will be at −1. After that, cross the **curse** off. If you have more than one curse, you deduct that many curses from your next roll, and all of them are then removed.

► 273

220

You are at Fort Blackgate, your home or at least, one of your homes. Here you may store any possessions or money you wish in the vault below the keep.

```
ITEMS IN VAULT




```

There are also additional extensions and additions you can add to your fort.

❑ **healer's tent**	100 pyr
❑ **training grounds**	100 pyr
❑ **banqueting hall**	150 pyr
❑ **travel catapult**	(to build this ► 283)

Tick the relevant box and cross off the money if you wish to add it (but not the travel catapult; you must build that first).

If you have a healer's tent, you can untick your Wound box if injured.

If you have the training grounds you can train and gain a **benison x 1**. Note it on your Adventure Sheet. It gives you +1 on your next attribute roll. Once it has been used, cross it off. You can only ever use the training grounds if you do not have any other benisons.

If you have a banqueting hall and want to hold a banquet (or another banquet if you've already held one) ► 252

If there is a tick in the travel catapult box and you want to use it ► 329

If not, you can leave by heading south along the Arcady Trail ► 85

221

You are expecting to see Jas trying to break in somewhere, but you haven't seen hide nor hair of him since you improved the locks on the windows and doors. All is quiet. Will you:

Enter the Vault	► 828
Leave your rooms	► 282

222

You have been transported to Arcadia by unusual means but where have you ended up? Roll two dice:

score 2-4	► 380
score 5-6	► 559
score 7-8	► 728
score 9-11	► 774
score 12	► 353

223

You have returned to the temple of Demeter to see how the refurbishment is going. Thekla, the priestess, has swept and cleaned the place while Lefkia has replastered all the walls and finished repainting the murals, depicting scenes of the sowing of seeds and the harvesting of crops with Demeter's blessing.

'Hello, hello!' she says. 'Look at this,' and she points to the mural she is putting the last touches to, as it is different from the others. It shows a snake-haired woman holding a dove and a dolphin.

'That is Demeter as primal earth goddess,' says the priestess Thekla, 'and represents her dominion over the underworld, the air and the sea.'

'There,' says Lefkia. 'All done!' She steps back to admire her work.

'Very nice,' says Thekla, 'thank you.'

'It is indeed nice work, but none of it possible without me,' you remind them both.

'True, very true!' says Thekla. 'That is why I give you the blessing of the goddess and name you **Favoured of Demeter**.'

With that Lefkia flashes a smile at you, gathers up her tools and leaves. It is done.

▶ **298**

224

The quarry entrance is half concealed by bushes and undergrowth that have been deliberately planted to obscure things. You wouldn't have spotted it if you weren't following the wagons.

On the other hand, it gives you a good hiding spot to observe what goes on within.

It is a strange set up. A score or more shambling workers hammer at the limestone cliff face with picks, dislodging as much rock as they can. Other workers fashion it into slabs. About twenty or so armed and armoured hoplites police the site. In one corner is small, domed, limestone temple dedicated to Hekate by the look of it. Beside it is a simple stone cabin. But it is rimed with ice and frost, a most peculiar sight indeed. What is keeping that cabin so cold?

After a while you see Captain Theseus enter the cabin with some workers. They emerge dragging frozen slabs of limestone on wooden pallets which they then load onto the wagons, wearing heavy leather gloves, presumably to avoid frost bite and aching bone freeze. You need to take a closer look. What will you try?

| Stealth | ▶ **277** |
| Cunning | ▶ **318** |

225

It is time to leave the Woodlands of Ambrosia. From here, you can go:

North-east to the Sacred Way	▶ **419**
East to the coast	▶ **774**
South-east to the bridge	▶ **801**
South to the river	▶ **138**
South-west to another bridge	▶ **14**

226

'This looks familiar!' says Magnes. 'And is that... is that my mother, could it be?' He looks up at you with tear-filled eyes and takes your hand. 'Take me home,' he says, gazing up at you.

You lead him down to the farm. At the sight of you Krio and Selene come running out.

'Is it really you, my little boy!' screams Selene happily.

'Mother!' howls Magnes, and they run across the hills and into each other's arms. Krio hugs them both, and there is much crying but also happiness and great joy.

You stand back and watch for a short time but then you turn away for their life is not yours, and such joy can never be yours. Or can it? Who knows what the future holds, but for now, this is their time. You can always come back later.

Lose the codeword **Parted** and gain the codeword *Parentage*.

Cross off Magnes from your Companion box.

Where to now?

North to a bridge	► 14
South to the Sacred Way	► 832
East to the Sacred Way	► 833
West and the Arcady Trail	► 338

227

❑

If you have the codeword **Payment** ► 634 immediately. If not, read on.

Put a tick in the box. If there was a tick in the box already ► 474 immediately. If not, read on.

You have returned to the Wineries to see how Maron is progressing with the planting and growing of the pomegranates to make sweet wine. But something is wrong. Half of the trees look like they've been burnt to a crisp. Satyrs are busily chopping them down, presumably for re-planting.

Maron staggers up to you. He has one black eye, and a bandaged arm.

'What happened, did you fall over and set fire to the trees in a drunken stupor?' you say accusingly.

'No, no, it was a centaur war-band!' protests Maron.

'Centaurs? But why, I thought they liked wine as much as the next person?'

'They do, but these aren't ordinary centaurs, they're renegades and bandits,' he says despairingly.

'And they did this to you? But why?'

'They beat me up, burned down some trees. They say they'll come back and burn the rest, unless you give 'em five hundred pyr.'

'That's a fortune!'

'I know, I know. But if you can pay 'em, I can get on with it.'

'But if I do, what's to stop 'em coming back for more later?' you say.

'I dunno. But if you want to get this up and running, you'll have to pay 'em. Or… I guess, something else, you know, like killing them all.'

'I see,' you say. 'Presumably they want the money delivered somewhere?' you ask.

'Yes, they said they have a camp in the woods at the most north-easterly point of the deep forest, east of some ruins, and west of the bridge over the river Ladon, up north.'

'I'll see what I can do,' you say grimly.

'Good luck!' says Maron, 'We will continue our work here, hopefully free from any more meddling.'

Gain the codeword **Punisher**. When you are ready, you take your leave. From here, you can go:

North to the Arcady Trail	► 238
West to Treycross on the Arcady Trail	► 728
South on the Trail	► 338
East to the bridge over the river Alpheus	► 14

228

Your very first note is off, and you find yourself playing in the wrong key. Flustered, you then drop the flute halfway through.

The crowd starts booing. 'What's the point of a contest if one of the contestants can't even play the flute!' says someone at the back.

Chiron puts up his hand. 'You're right, there is no need to go on. I declare Velosina the winner by default.'

You sigh resignedly, as you blush with humiliation. Chiron gives her a scroll. 'Here is Sappho's poem. Rather a sad, tragic piece but beautiful all the same. It's called "My lover lies with Ladon".'

Velosina accepts it with a bow, as the crowd applaud. She turns to you, 'Why didn't you just say you couldn't play?' she asks.

You shrug, 'Thought I could do better,' you mutter, but the Fates turned their back on you today.

'Ah well,' says Velosina, slapping you on the back heartily, 'I've won a fine Sappho original, and without having to do much at all, really.'

'I'm sorry you lost,' says Chiron, 'but is there anything else I can help you with?'

► 90

229

You walk into the crowded pavilion via the front door this time and bellow a challenge to Deridedes. He looks you over suspiciously.

'You do know this is a contest of wits, not hand to hand combat in the mud between club-wielding, semi-intelligent apes, right?' The crowd titters, half wanting to laugh, half unsure as to your response. After all, you may be a semi-intelligent ape, but you certainly look like you have fought in the mud many a time and nobody wants to end up there with you.

'Oh yes, I know,' you reply confidently.

'So be it, then,' says Deridedes, an arrogant smile playing

across his lips. 'Come up on the stage and try your hand – or gob, I should say.'

The crowd roars with approval as you step up. Deridedes holds a mask of Momos in one hand that has a sneering, mocking expression. His own face doesn't seem very different, with an almost permanent curl to his lips and an eyebrow raised in derision. He raises the other hand to the sky, and brings it down.

'Let the contest begin!' he says, and bows indicating that you should go first. What will you start with?

'Helen may have launched a thousand ships, but your breath alone would be enough to start a war.' ▶ **314**

'Wow, just looking at you infects my eyes with the pox.' ▶ **335**

'You big fat loser!' ▶ **404**

230

You defeat the Warrior of Ares in battle.

'You are worthy of the god,' intones the Warrior before fading away on a scented woodland breeze. Gain the codeword *Praise-Ares.* ▶ **178**

231

Your terror gives you wings, and you climb up a nearby tree like a squirrel. Moments later, the blood-thirsty horde gather at the bottom of the tree, and some of them start shimmying up after your, their faces masks of feral hunger.

You climb higher into the forest canopy. Up here, you find that the branches of the trees are entwined together like Greek dancers at a wedding – or is it wrestlers at the Olympic Games? Either way, it makes it easy for you to travel quickly across the rooftops of the forest. The Bacchantes can climb too, but the leaves are so dense up here, the birds and other animals so noisy, it is impossible to tell where you have gone. You lose them in the tree-tops.

You wait a while until the Bacchantes have moved on in search of other prey, and then descend to the forest floor. One of them has dropped a skin of the **golden wine of Dionysus**. If that's the stuff that drives them wild, it's best not to drink of it, but it may come in useful later. Note in on your Adventure Sheet.

You heave a sigh of relief for you have survived another day in the Vulcanverse.

Warily, you head back to the Sacred Way but the Bacchantes are nowhere to be seen or heard. Time to move on.

▶ 826

232

Hunting in the woods of Arcadia without permission is forbidden. You have incurred the wrath of Artemis, goddess of the hunt. Note **Artemis's curse x 1** on your Adventure Sheet. Your next attribute roll will be at −1. After that, cross the **curse** off. If you have more than one curse, you deduct that many curses from your next roll, and all of them are then removed. Now ▶ 148

233

The catch-net is a web stretched across four wooden poles that is meant to catch anyone lobbed at it from the palace onager. Except that this web of vines has been eaten away by the salty spray that comes in from the eastern shore and it falls apart as soon as you land on it. You burst through to hammer into the ground below.

Tick the Wound box on your Adventure Sheet. If you are already wounded than your body is split open by the impact. At least death is quick ▶ 111

If you still live, you stagger to your feet and look around ▶ 833

234

Chiron gave you the cure for the black blight, a potion in a small vial that will clear it up completely in a matter of days. You approach the cabin in the woods where the truffle hunter, whose name is Mithaecus, lives with his sick daughter, little Io. You walk up to the door, and step inside.

There is Mithaecus, mixing up a batch of sap from the Great Green Ones' roots to give to his daughter, who is sitting in a rocking chair beside him, coughing, her face pale, and covered in tiny black spots.

The truffle hunter looks up. 'You again. As you can see, I must still put my daughter first,'

You nod. 'I understand but Chiron, the greatest healer of the age, made me this, from ingredients I quested across the Vulcanverse for. Here, give it to Io, it will cure her forever,' you say, handing over the vial of sparkling blue liquid.

Mithaecus' jaw drops in awed wonder. 'Really? You did all this for my little girl?'

You shuffle on your feet uncomfortably and smile weakly, rather than admit that you didn't do it for her at all, but for a trio of impossibly ancient tree-beings.

Mithaecus takes the vial and little Io drinks it down – Chiron having flavoured it with honey. It is not long before the effects can be seen. Her fever breaks and her breathing starts to sound normal.

Mithaecus swears he will no longer harvest any sap, but just to be sure you come back in a few days – Io is completely healed, her skin fresh and normal and she's playing outside happily. You take Mithaecus down into the depths and together seal off the chamber of roots forever.

Lose the codeword *Panacea*.

Gain the codeword *Purged*.

Mithaecus, ever-grateful, gives you a **jar of hydnon truffles**. Note them on your Adventure sheet.

'I wish I had more to give you, but all I have are truffles and my little Io,' he says. You nod your thanks, and take your leave.

▶ 160

235

If you have the codeword *Praise-Athena* ▶ 332 immediately. If not, read on.

There is a door here, set into the side of the cliff that separates the upper plateau from the lower. A door knocker in the shape of an owl, hangs from it. At the top of the door, words are carved in wood:

A SHRINE TO ATHENA
GODDESS OF WISDOM

You knock on the door, and a disembodied voice answers, 'Only the wise may enter the shrine. A door is not opened without... what?'

What will you say?

'Knocking.' ▶ 440
'Wisdom.' ▶ 161
'Keys.' ▶ 575

236

'I think you should do it,' you say to Orphea, holding out the amulet to her.

'Suspicious, eh? Well, I suppose that's to be expected but all right, then, of course.'

She takes the amulet and hunkers down in front of the altar. She leans over it, blocking your view.

'Hey, move so I can see!' you say not trusting her one little bit.

There's a clicking sound, and she moves aside. 'There you go,' she says with a breezy smile, 'all yours,' gesturing at a small niche that has opened in the side of the altar. Inside it rests a set of the finest pipes you've ever seen. You reach for them – and out billows a cloud of noxious gas! You reel back, but you're not quick enough and you inhale a lungful. You fall to the ground, spluttering and coughing.

'Don't worry, it'll just knock you out,' trills Orphea with a laugh. She steps over you – you reach for her but your limbs feel as heavy as lead and you can barely stay awake. She reaches into the opening, and plucks out a fine-looking set of pipes.

'Ah, the Pipes of Pan. All mine!' she says, 'Lady Rapscallion strikes again, eh? Unfortunately, there never was any money but on the other hand, I'm sure you've got some to help me along. You won't mind if I help myself, my lovely, will you? Night night, sleep tight!' she says, smiling down at you.

You glare up at her, vowing vengeance but you cannot keep your eyes open, and you sink into unconsciousness. Everything goes black. You dream of catching a red-furred rat in a trap and then of red ants with blue heads, swarming all over you and carrying off everything you own. You wake with an angry shout.

Delete **Pan's amulet** from your possessions and ▶ **258**

237

You run like a son the north wind, Boreas, or Hermes of the winged sandals, leaping over dead wood, sidestepping tangled roots and thorny brambles – for a minute or two and then your foot catches a gnarled tree root and you fall flat on your face where you lie, stunned.

If you have the codeword *Pelt* ▶ **424**

If not, ▶ **274**

238

The Trail leads south west to Treycross and north east where it ends at the base of the cliffs. On close inspection, you notice a thin outline of a stone door set into the cliff face. A message on a small plinth beside the door reads, *'I turn once, what is out will not get in. I turn again, what is in will not get out. What am I?'* If you know the answer already, turn to that paragraph number if you want to go through the stone door. If not, and you want to try to solve the riddle ▶ **198**. Otherwise, you can head:

South-west on the Trail	▶ **728**
South to the Wineries	▶ **417**

239

❑

Put a tick in the box. If there was a tick in the box already ▶ **284** immediately. If not, read on.

You settle down for a little relaxation time, fishing by the river. But then the waters begin to roil and boil and out surges a huge figure, a man with muscled torso and face screwed up in anger. Water cascades down his sides like a waterfall. His hair and beard are made of pale green river weed and his eyes are like those of a fish. It is Ladon, the river god.

'Who dares fish in my....' he booms but then he sees it is you. 'Ah, it's the hero...' he says, his anger evaporating, 'Umm... you're supposed to have a hunting permit, you know, from the temple of Artemis, and that, but as it's you, well, I can hardly complain, can I? That's fine, 'course you can fish in my river!'

With that Ladon sinks into the waters. But then he pops up again and says 'Oh and thank you once more,' waves a hand, and then sinks back again.

With Ladon's blessing you catch a lot of fish. Note five **fresh fish** on your Adventure Sheet. When you have finished fishing, you decide to move on. Where will you go?

West on the Way	▶ **20**
South-west into the forest	▶ **189**
East on the Way	▶ **380**
South, into the lush river valley	▶ **403**

240

With an astonishing display of speed and dexterity you are able to dodge or fend off the writing creepers and you manage to get past them and out of the woods. Will you go:

North-east to the Trail	▶ **728**
North-west to the Trail	▶ **455**
West to the hills	▶ **559**

241

❑

Put a tick in the box. If there was a tick in the box already ▶ **452** immediately. If not, read on.

A handsome young man, wearing a wide brimmed hat, and a chiton hitched up around his thighs, showing off a fine pair of lean, tanned legs, steps up to you and introduces himself. 'I am Drosos, the farm overseer you hired – and for that I thank you, now I can feed my family.'

'You seem rather young to be an overseer.'

'True, but I am very clever, and my father was a farmer, as was my grandfather, and his before him and so on, all the way back to my great, great, grandmother who was Demeter herself, the goddess of farming. So you could say it's in my blood, as it were.'

'Well, OK then!' you say, impressed, even if you don't believe a word of it. 'So, can you get these farms up and running?'

'I can indeed, now that the rivers have been restored to their former glory. I'll have to hire some farm labourers, that's not a problem, you gave me enough money, but I'll also need three portions of bessed soil of Arcadia as a fertilizer, two grindstones to repair the quern stones used to grind the grain, and a good cockerel to repopulate the chicken flocks. We've got some hens but no cocks, and, well, you know.'

If you have:

blessed soil of Arcadia x 3

grindstone x 2

Kraterus the cockerel

then ▶ **397**.

If not, you tell Drosos you will return when you have what he needs. For now, where will you go?

North-east   ▶ **365**

North-west   ▶ **380**

South-east   ▶ **419**

242

You wander through the deep, dark, primordial forest. Some of the hoary, gnarled trees look like they might be hundreds and hundreds of years old. Light barely penetrates through the forest canopy; the humidity and the heat are stifling. Soon you are sweating, and breathing freely is difficult. If you do not find water soon, you will not survive.

Ahead, you can hear birdsong, the bark of a fox, perhaps, or a chirruping squirrel but when you draw near everything falls as silent as the grave. It is as if the forest shuns your very presence.

You will need all your tracking skills to get out of here. Make an INGENUITY roll at difficulty 7.

Succeed   ▶ **213**

Fail   ▶ **169**

243

You reach down and cut his bonds, freeing him. 'Will you promise me you'll stop all this bad behaviour, be a good goat from now on?' you say.

'Yes, yes, of course, great one, I promise!' says Jas, 'I'll be the best butler you've ever had, honestly!'

'You better had.' you say.

'And thank you for not killing me, for showing mercy.' he continues, bowing and scraping submissively.

'No more tricks, thieving, drinking and partying in my rooms?'

'No, no, never! It was them, those two naughty nymphs, they made me do it, my most beautiful, kind, magnanimous, forgiving captain, I'm so sorry but I'm only a lowly, weak-willed satyr, please forgive me.'

'All right, then,' you say with a sigh. 'Now go back to the Palace, and I'll meet you in my rooms shortly.'

'Yes, my liege,' says Jas, and he turns tail and runs off, his hooves throwing up divots of earth from the grassy ground. You're not sure, but was that a sly look he gave you as he left?

Gain the codeword **Proscribe** and lose the codeword **Prisoner**. You find amid the abandoned detritus of their little camp: a **brazen trumpet**, a **box of paints**, a **jug of dandelion wine** and a lock of **water nymph hair** which looks more like straggly seaweed than anything else, and 25 pyr in a pouch. There is also a raw venison steak. If you have a **book of recipes**, you can turn the venison into **venison sausages**. Note them on your Adventure Sheet as well. If you don't have the book, the steak will go off very quickly in this Arcadian summer heat, so is of no use to you. When you are done, you head back to your rooms in the Summer Palace.

▶ **29**

244

Quickly you arrange a simple noose trap and tie it to a tree. It won't hold the bear for long, but it should give you enough time to aim a killing blow to the head or heart. When you are done, you step into the clearing and shout.

The bear turns – and roars a mighty roar before charging directly at you! You jump smartly back, and luckily for you the bear steps right into the noose trap. It tightens around one leg, and brings the bear up short. It roars in anger once more, gnawing at the rope around its leg.

You step in and drive your weapon neatly through its skull and into its brain, killing it instantly. You can hardly believe it.

You skin the bear, and take it as a trophy. Note the **bearskin** on your Adventure Sheet.

If you have a **hunting permit** ▶ **184**. If not, ▶ **219**

245

'I think you will be pleased with my news, Chiron,' you say. 'I learned how to fabricate the choicest of insults by duelling a Priest of Momos in a contest of mockery. I went to the camp of Nessus, and called him some rather fine names; he couldn't help himself, and he challenged me to single combat, just as you said he would.'

'Excellent! And?' says Chiron with bated breath.

'I slew him and sent his treacherous shade to Tartarus, that part of Hades that is reserved for those who are evil and corrupt.'

'Ah, that is a relief, justice is done. But what about his warband?'

'On his death, they dispersed, leaderless.'

Chiron nods. 'We will find and deal with the rest of them,' he says.

'Anyway,' you say, 'I took this as a trophy,' and you take out the **tunic of Nessus**.

'Be careful with that!' says Chiron, 'for Nessus was no ordinary brigand, he was cunning, like a snake. That tunic is steeped in spiderling venom. He made some kind of deal with them and they gave him immunity but whoever else wears his tunic will fall into throes of ecstasy, gripped by unbearable pleasure before dying, blood running out of every orifice.'

You'd better not put it on, then. However, maybe a time will come when you will find someone else who would look good in it...

'Thank you for your excellent advice,' you say.

▶ **90** and choose again.

246

You pull the lever and are slung up into the blue like an arrow shot from Artemis's bow. Below, you can see the Arcady Trail like chalk marks on mossy stone and then nothing but a sea of trees until you start to plummet downwards towards the Sacred Way at the western edge of Arcadia.

At this rate, you will be splattered over the grey stone like a rotten tomato! But then you see the catch-net that is designed to break your fall safely rushing up to meet you at horrifying speed and you fall into the webbing of the catch-net safely. Afterwards, you take a moment to catch your breath, climb down out of the net and take a look at your surroundings.

▶ **804**

247

You are bound and strapped to the side of the cart and can barely move. However, you notice that one of the wooden slats is partially broken. You are able to snap it off, leaving a sharpened splinter of wood. You could drive your own throat onto it, and kill yourself that way...

You balk at the idea, but you realise you have no choice, if you die here by your own hand, the gods can bring you back to life, as they have done many times before. If not, Thanatos will claim you, and you will be dead forever.

Closing your eyes and steeling yourself, you drive your jugular onto the splintered wood. Your blood jets out in a crimson plume, and you die gurgling in your juices. The horror! But at least you have avoided the ever-grasping hand of Thanatos.

▶ **111**

248

You find yourself floundering in a river of boiling water, super-heated vapour billowing up all around you, sloughing your skin away in great slews of steamed flesh. You scream in horror, but soon all the water has boiled up and away, leaving you alone in a dried up river bed. Somehow, you are unhurt.

And then you are in a hidden cavern behind a dried-up waterfall. Hanging over a pool of lava, is a great glass beaker, the size of a several men, filled with a blue-green vapour. The bottle is stoppered with a bronze cap, inlaid with strange symbols. Nearby, a man sits, wreathed in indistinct robes. Or is he? It could just be a trick of the light, you are not sure. And then the whole vision disappears in a puff of steam.

You sit up, and gasp. Out of your mouth wisps of water vapour rise upward.

'Welcome back, dream-pilgrim,' says Zenia.

If you have some more **kykeon mushrooms** and 10 more pyr and want to try another vision ▶ **737**

If not, you can head back to the market (▶ **728**) or leave the area (▶ **12**).

249

There is no more ophidiaroot to be had, you have harvested it all, and it will never grow back here. Given that this is the only place that you know of where it could be found, what you have collected so far may be all that there is to be had, ever.

There is nothing more you can do but return to the bridge where the course of the river runs out into a bay with a low wooden quay for the docking of boats. From here you can go:

North	▶ 774
South	▶ 833
West along the river	▶ 138
To the hamlet	▶ 305
To the quay in the bay	▶ 200

250

You come up through the tunnel into a cave, lit by hanging lanterns, although much of it is now covered in cobwebs. Fortunately, you do not see any spiders. A ladder built into one side of the cave leads up and up to what looks like a trap door in the ceiling, but it is a long climb, a good fifty metres. There seems no other obvious way out until you notice a faint outline of sunlight around a large man-sized rock on a cave wall.

A message on the wall reads, *'I turn once, what is out will not get in. I turn again, what is in will not get out. What am I?'* If you know the answer already, turn to that paragraph number if you want to go through the stone door. If not, and you want to try to solve the riddle ▶ **268**. Otherwise, you can take the:

Tunnel to Hades	▶ 661 in *The Houses of the Dead*
The ladder up	▶ 470

251

The clearing of the Great Green Ones has recovered well ever since you dealt with the acid dragon. Leaves have grown back; bark is scarred but healthy.

The totems are looking better too – well, still hoary,

encrusted with vines and brambles, green with moss and lichen, and ancient beyond your reckoning but unburned by acid.

Nausea sweeps over you, as they construct their thoughts using your brain to do so.

'Welcome, meat-thing, champion of the vine, saviour of trees! We are forever in your debt, and we bestow upon you the title **Friend of the Forest**.' Note it on your Adventure Sheet.

'When you are in need, call upon us and we will aid you.'

'Anything else?' you ask, your head pounding with the pain of talking to them.

'What do you mean,' says the walnut totem. And then you hear them muttering amongst themselves,

'The meat-on-sticks are greedy.'

'What?'

'You know, things, they always want things. They can't just get by on sap and sun, so they wander about getting 'stuff'.'

'Ah, yes, I understand.' and the walnut totem addresses you directly once more.

'Here, mortal, is our reward. I believe this is the sort of thing the unrooted like.'

Upon the old wooden altar appears some more **flowers of fertility**, a bag of forest nuts, and some apples.

'Hey, I'm not a squirrel!' you say, rather annoyed at such a paltry reward after everything you went through to get here.

'Eh?' says one of totems, 'I thought you *were* a squirrel.'

'No, no, this one is some kind of – what do they call it – a wolf, isn't it?'

'Fools!' says the walnut totem, 'This is one of those walks-on-two-trunks blobby flesh things, you know, the stupid ones who burn and chop and fight each other over bits of earth or coloured pebbles and metals they find buried underground.'

'One of those, really? And it saved us?'

'Yes, this is a good one.'

And so the conversation goes but listening in to them using your own brain to talk to each other is too unpleasant. You'll just have to accept what you've been given and move on. Hopefully their friendship and aid really will prove useful, when the time comes. Time to leave the forest.

▶ 148

As you are the Steward of the Summer Palace, you send for Erifili, the head chef. She arrives sometime later, stomping into the room with her heavy tread for she is built like a... well, a toilet made from brick.

'So now you're the commander of a fort, and you want to hold a banquet, eh? My, you're on the up and up, aren't you? Well, you've got the space for it, that's for sure, and the kitchens are good enough, but to do it properly I'll need to hire some staff and plenty of ingredients. I can get most of it but if you can get me a few things, we'll make something special, fresh baked bread, truffle sauce, the works,' says Erifili.

Erifili needs:

100 pyr
venison sausages
jar of hydnon truffles
pomegranate wine
pomegranate honey
farmlands grain
honey cake
fresh fish

'One of each of those should get me started. I'll provide the rest.'

If you have the money and the required ingredients and wish to proceed, cross them off and ▶ **421**

If not, or not yet, ▶ **220** and choose again.

Walking a little way upstream, you find a big branch and use it to stir up the river mud under a clump of leaves. Bubbles of trapped gas rise and break greasily on the surface.

You stroll back to find the children holding their noses in disgust. 'What's that stink?' cries one.

'Oh, there's the carcass of a dead rat just a little way upriver,' you say.

'Ew!'

They're out of the water and running home as if the Furies were after them. Job done.

Write your attributes on the Adventure Sheet:

STRENGTH 0
GRACE 0
CHARM 0
INGENUITY +1
Then ▶ **723**

❏

If you have the codeword *Pernicious* ▶ **286** immediately. If not, read on.

Put a tick in the box. If there was a tick in the box already

▶ **307** immediately. If not, read on.

The farm seems strangely quiet. Sheep bleat in their pen, but there are no children playing in the fore court and no one comes out to greet you. Odd.

You knock on the door. There is no answer, so you open the door and step in – to a terrible sight.

Tied up and gagged to two chairs are Krio and Selene! Behind each of them stands a thug, one tall and thin with a horribly burned face, the other short but well-muscled with a shock of bleached white hair and patterned whorls tattooed on his bare chest. A Celt by the look of him. Behind them stands... Deridedes!

'You think I would really let you steal my cock, free my slave and destroy my livelihood with impunity? No, you stinking dog, it's time for payback!'

'Payback!' echoes the man with the burned face.

Deridedes flicks his eyes over at burned face with irritation.

'Let them go now, and I will make your death swift,' you say through gritted teeth.

'Hah, I don't think so!' says Deridedes.

'Don't think so!' echoes burned face.

Deridedes glares angrily. 'Put down your weapons and surrender to me now, and I'll let them go. Or else I'll have their throats slit,' he says.

'Yeah, throats slit!' says burn face, much to Deridedes' irritation. What will you do?

Attack	▶ **383**
Surrender	▶ **466**

The forest is dark and dense, and the heat is stifling but you must go on. You can hear your pursuers closing in on you but the statue of Artemis is nowhere in sight. You need to buy yourself more time.

Make an INGENUITY roll at difficulty 8.

Succeed	▶ **195**
Fail	▶ **502**

'Satyrs?' says Kaustikia sneeringly. 'They don't even taste that good, and the thick hair on their legs is like string, it gets stuck in my teeth! No, I can do without them, and I can do without you wittering on anymore. Time to break your head for my bread, don't you worry, you'll soon be dead.'

If you have the **Nemean bagh nakh** ▶ **817**

If not, ▶ **783**

'Ah, if it isn't the great hero! Greetings, my Steward. Oh, and Archon of... well, and the rest of them. Perhaps I should give you a new title – mortal of many titles, hah, hah, hah!'

You smile wanly. You do have several titles but each and every one of them was earned through blood and death.

'Anyway, it's always a pleasure to see you and you will have my eternal thanks for bringing Arcadia back to life but I have no more tasks for you. All I can do is offer you the full hospitality of the Palace, for you richly deserve it.'

If you have not a single pyr to your name ▶ 760

Otherwise there is nothing left to discuss with the King other than pleasantries, so you take your leave; ▶ 282 and choose again.

258

You come to the base of the altar to Pan. There is a note in the altar niche. One side reads, '*These pipes, when played by the truly skilled, can inflame the passions of those who hear it – from wild rage to reckless abandon in the face of danger.*'

Orphea has left a message on the other side, '*Thanks again, my dearest friend, for the Pipes of Pan, I will play them to great acclaim, and hopefully, riches too! Although for now I am quite well off, thanks to your generosity. Don't worry, I've let you keep all your other rather magnificent things. After all, I don't want to leave you destitute, do I? Not if I want to rob you again next time… love and kisses – Lady Rapscallion xxx.*'

You heave a resigned sigh. She has tricked you again. Gain the codeword *Prankette*.

To leave this place ▶ 463.

259

❑

Put a tick in the box. If there was a tick in the box already ▶ 554 immediately. If not, read on.

A terrible howl fills the bracken-bound trail with menace. You recognize that sound – it is the daemon of Hades, Wolfshadow. He has found you, even here in Arcadia! Fear grips your heart for they that hear his howl are doomed. You also know that he no weapon made by mortal hand can harm him.

And there he is, further on down the trail his flayed body a mass of crimson muscle, the great sinews of his jaws glistening with ichor and his teeth dripping black saliva. He growls at you, and prepares to charge. You have no choice but to throw him off the scent somehow.

If you have any of **honey of Hades**, **weasel blood**, a **caged canary**, **fresh fish**, **a harpy's egg**, a **centaur's skull**, **venison sausages**, some **strix stew**, a **honey cake**, a **maggoty pie** or a **shrivelled heart** and wish to discard it ▶ 71

If not, there is nothing you can do but flee for your life ▶ 747

260

You re-appear in another ball of flaming smoke to find yourselves at the bottom of a trickling waterfall. Ahead, a thin stream runs through a grassy valley, hills rising up high on either side. Behind you rises a steep cliff.

'Welcome to the Valley of Bones,' says Myletes. 'I've no idea where we are, and I only have enough magic for one trip back, so this is it. Try or die.'

'Easy for you to say,' you remark sarcastically.

'Indeed, it is,' replies Myletes. 'I will wait here for you but if you're not back within a day, I will leave. If I see any witches, floating eyes, giants or anything else unpleasant, I will also leave or to put it another way, flee in terror immediately. Sorry, but there you go.'

'Fine,' you say. 'Wait for me here, I'll be back.' And you head off down the valley.

▶ 309

261

You have come to the Upper Tarn, home to the river god Alpheus. The lake is full to the brim with clean, wholesome river water that gushes down the cliffside to fill the lower Tarn, from whence it rushes down the Alpheus falls to run out to the great encircling seas of Oceanus.

Life has returned in full majesty to the lake – swans float like royal barges on its surface, flamingos gather in a great, pink flock of cawing birds to feed at the lakes edge, reeds, grasses and flowers proliferate everywhere.

A couple of fishing boats ply the lake-top in search of dinner. Above, a bright sun cradles the earth in her warm arms and gulls and gannets, with gimlet eye, look for fish darting through the waters below.

And all of this because of you. However, there is nothing more for you to do here, so you move on. Where to?

North to the Druid's Shrine   ▶ 463

North-west skirting past the Shrine to the woods ▶ 620

Take the stairs in the cliffside down to the lower tarn ▶ 545

262

You can see nothing untoward. Perhaps if you speak or shout your insults in the right way, you can stimulate Kraterus into crowing. Worth a shot anyway, as you've paid the entrance fee already. You shout a challenge, and Deridedes welcomes you up onto the stage.

'A challenger!' he says to the audience, 'and a hard-bitten looking one too, though this be a battle of wits rather than strength, so we shall see who triumphs today! I shall begin. Now, let me see,' says Deridedes, hand on his chin. 'Ah, I have it – adventurers like you are known to pander to the rich and powerful, doing jobs for them in return for money. That makes you an arse-kissing, apple polishing, toad loving, brown-nosed, fart swallowing lickspittle!'

The audience erupts with laughter, applauding enthusiastically. Immediately Kraterus screeches his peculiar cock-a-doodle-do, that sounds so much like he is saying in a strangled, drunken voice 'silly-old-goat.'

'First point to me,' says Deridedes. Time to strike back. What will you try?

'Some say a bowl of stewed prunes will loosen the bowels. I say – no need for prunes, just the sight of *you* will do the trick.' ▶ 645

'An arse pudding, that's what you are!' ▶ 754

263

If you have the title **Mindless Quarry Slave** ▶ 521 immediately.

You follow the wagons back to the quarry just south of the Sacred Way where Mela the sorceress mines her frozen limestone that keeps Ladon ice-bound in his prison of frost and rime. You can try and infiltrate her camp again, or come back later.

Use stealth	▶ 277
Use cunning	▶ 318
Leave this place	▶ 380

264

You pull the lever and are launched high up into the air, up and over a raised plateau from which the Alpheus river runs down to the eastern shore. You hurtle across the clear blue sky at a terrifying lick and then slowly start to descend, coming down over the verdant farmlands to the Sacred Way in the north east corner of Arcadia. The Sacred Way seems to rise up to meet you – will your bones be shattered on the hard paving stones of the Way? But then you see the catch-net that you're supposed to fall into safely. If you do *not* have the codeword *PatchupThree* ▶ 763 immediately. If you do have it, read on.

You plummet into the webbing of the catch-net safely. After you take a moment to catch your breath, you climb down and look around. ▶ 526

265

'I have already made you a batch of the cure,' says Chiron. 'Surely you don't need another?'

▶ 90 and choose again.

266

It is lightly wooded here, at the outskirts of the Dales of Leaf and Stream. Colourful flowers are everywhere, birds sing songs of joy in the trees, bees buzz and dragonflies glitter like jewels in the summer sun. A clear-watered brook babbles by, and you can smell thyme, mint and basil on the air. It is the very picture of an Arcadian paradise. And yet, something feels odd… you can't put your finger on it. Perhaps it is in your imagination. Will you go:

Deeper into the Dales	▶ 2
North-east to the Trail	▶ 728
North-west to the Trail	▶ 455
West to the hills	▶ 559

267

❑

Put a tick in the box. If there was a tick in the box already ▶ 344 immediately. If not, read on.

The morning sun is especially bright today for the sky is cloudless. Your shadow spreads long on the ground. Something starts to itch inside your head and a drowsy numbness begins to pervade your senses. You watch in horror as a writhing thing of black rags and tendrils as of night itself hauls itself up out of the earth to batten onto your shadow like a vampire bat. It begins to feed, and it feels like a part of your souls is draining away.

Once again, this stygian crow-thing, this ink-black shadow-hunter from the abyss has come for your shadow.

If you have a **lightning flint** ▶ 36

If not, make an INGENUITY roll at difficulty 7:

| Succeed | ▶ 185 |
| Fail | ▶ 102 |

268

The message on the wall reads, *'I turn once, what is out will not get in. I turn again, what is in will not get out. What am I?'*

Take each letter of your answer, give it its corresponding number in the alphabet (so A would be one, Z would be 26) add them all together and turn to that paragraph. If it is correct, it will say so, if not, return here and think again.

If you cannot solve the riddle, or do not wish to go through the door, you can take the:

| Tunnel to Hades | ▶ 661 in *The Houses of the Dead* |
| The ladder up | ▶ 470 |

269

You try to dodge and hack your way through the writhing mass of vines, but one of them wraps itself around your leg, keeping you in place long enough for another to curl around your arm, and then another around your torso and both legs. Soon you cannot move at all. And then the purple flowers batten onto your skin, small needles sinking into you and you realise they are not suckers at all, rather they are injecting some kind of soporific sap into your veins for you begin to sink into a deep sleep. Will these plants devour you at their leisure or are they injecting you with some kind of seed too?

► 398

270

If you have the title **Archon of Agriculture** ► 123 immediately. If not, read on.

If you have the codeword *Plough* ► 52 immediately. If not, read on.

You have travelled to the Verdant Farmlands, or more accurately, these days, the Once-Verdant Farmlands, for the fields are sown only with stones and weeds. Hay wagons and ploughs lie abandoned, slowly crumbling in the summer sun. Ramshackle farm buildings, broken barns and dilapidated stables litter the landscape like piles of crumbling driftwood on a deserted beach. The quern stones that ground the wheat and barley are still and the irrigation channels and water butts lie empty and dry. No chickens or goats cluck and bleat in their pens; where once hundreds worked the land, now only a handful remain.

Nearby, you see a centaur pulling his own plough, aided by two young centaur foals. Further afield, a family of humans are harvesting what looks like turnips.

At least some food is being grown but it is subsistence farming at best. If you have a **Contract: Farm Overseer** ► 186. (To check if you have it, note **270** in your Current Location box, ► 101 and then return to this section after). If you haven't got it, there is nothing more you can do here for and you will have to come back later. Further west lie impassable cliffs, so will you go:

North-east	► 365
North-west	► 380
South-east	► 419

271

You have returned to the site that Helen has chosen to build her new inn upon. She is waiting for you in a nearby copse of trees, hiding from the sun.

'Such a fierce sun,' she says coming over to greet you, parasol held up over her head. 'Feels like it'll burn my wispy shade-body away completely! Anyway, have you found an architect?'

If you have a **Contract: Architect** ► 343. If not, read on.

'Not yet,' you say.

'Ah well, come back when you do,' says Helen, squinting up at the sun.

You take your leave. From here you can go:

North-east to the Woodlands	► 60
East along the riverbank	► 138
South	► 822
West to the Wineries	► 417

272

You have come back to the grass and bush covered crater in the ground. The bushes sport rather unpleasant blood-red flowers, with vicious looking thorns that are purple and swollen, as if infused with malice.

The large stone door set into one side of the crater floor is still there. Upon it these words appear:

MURDER AT THE PHILOSOPHERS ACADEMY
Aspasia has been murdered. The culprit is one of either Epimenides the Cretan, Cleanthes the Stoic, Aristippus the Cyrenaic or Protagoras the Sophist. They make the following statements. You have been correctly informed that the guilty person always lies, and everyone else tells the truth.

Epimenides: 'Cleanthes is the culprit.'
Cleanthes: 'Protagoras is innocent.'
Aristippus: 'Cleanthes' statement is true.'
Protagoras: 'Epimenides' statement is false.'

Who killed Aspasia?

What will you say?

'Epimenides'	► 323
'Cleanthes'	► 182
'Aristippus'	► 405
'Protagoras'	► 527
Come back later	► 833

273

You return to the honey hives proudly holding the bearskin as proof of your great deed.

Sivi and King Nyctimus are there to greet you. Sivi claps her hands together, 'By the golden arrows of Artemis, well done!' she says. 'I can also tell you that the honey is now ready for harvesting.'

Nyctimus says, 'Single-handedly killed a bear! Impressive indeed. I think another title is in order – I dub thee the Apiarist!'

Lose the codeword *Pudding* and gain the title **The Apiarist**.

► 319

274

You lie there barely conscious for a few precious minutes. You hear wolf-like howls behind you, and then whooping and hollering! They are close...

You shake your head to clear it and get to your feet – to

see Alpha, the great wolf, standing in front of you, his yellow eyes bright with intelligence. You heave a sigh – is this how it is to end, chased down and killed like a hunted rabbit?

But then Alpha turns away, and heads off in the direction of a nearby gully. He pauses, and looks behind at you – he wants you to follow him! He leads you down through dead-tree covered gully, and then up the other side through a mass of brambles that has a hidden path leading to a ridge. You follow through and then run down the other side. You turn at the bottom, and there is Alpha at the top of the ridge. You wave your thanks and the wolf gives a soft, low bark before darting back into the undergrowth. You spared him, and now he has spared you…

Nevertheless, you are not home and dry yet. You can still hear the howling of your pursuers albeit a little further away.

► 255

275
You make an offering at the shrine. Pan is a wild and unpredictable god. Roll a die:

score 1	► 5
score 2-3	► 27
score 4-5	► 65
score 6	► 80

276
If you have the codeword *Nettle* ► 445 immediately. If not, read on.

You move deeper in the forest, where the trees are greener, wilder and somehow more 'alive'. As you do, you notice a path opening up before you, as if the trees were somehow deliberately parting to allow you through. You hear the sound of voices on the air, and the occasional girlish giggle. You see movement from tree to tree, a flash of wild hair here, a rainbow of wild flowers there. The path leads you to a big oak tree, and upon one of its branches sits Karya, the hamadryad.

'Hello, my mortal hero! Have you got my Davides?' she asks.

'I have not,' you say.

'What are you doing here, then? Unless you want a dryad or two to frolic with, is that it? Well, don't look at me, I have given my heart to another! Anyway, you're getting nothing, not until you bring my lover back from the dead. He's in Hades somewhere, he's tall, handsome and a hairdresser.'

'A hairdresser in Hades?'

'Yes, a hairdresser in Hades, now go, and don't come back until you've saved him for me!'

What will you do next?

Go to the old apiary	► 8
Leave this place	► 225

277
You wait until Captain Theseus leaves on another lake run, taking half the garrison with him. Then you carefully observe the routes the remaining guards take on their patrols.

You skulk in the bushes until you see an opportunity to dart in behind the stone cabin unseen… hopefully.

Make a GRACE roll at difficulty 8.

Succeed	► 479
Fail	► 337

278
You make good progress, darting and weaving through the woods but then trip up over a tree root, and land flat on your face. One of the stags gallops across your back, pounding your body with its hooves.

If you are already wounded, your skull is trampled too, and your brains are spilled all over the forest floor. Death is at least instant ► 111

Otherwise, tick the Wound box on your Adventure Sheet and read on.

You lie where you are and play dead. Soter and his gang snuffle around your body for a time but soon they head back into the wild woods. It is just as well they are not predators. You pick yourself up and look around. During the chase you have become hopelessly lost.

► 242

279
Your mother holds the coins tight, but she is pitifully weak in her old age. You take them from her as she once took sharp objects from your pudgy baby fingers.

'I have deeds I must do in the wider world,' you tell her. 'The gods know this is little enough coin to get me started, but it is better to set out even with old shoes than to go barefoot.'

Record 20 pyr on your Adventure Sheet, then ►753

280
You step through the small postern door beside the Great Northern Gate of Vulcan City and into Arcadia, where it is forever summer, or so they say.

From here the Sacred Way runs north up to the coast. To the west, massive mountains rise up to the heavens, snow-peaked and ice bound. To the east all you can see are trees and trees and trees, the Deep Forest of Arcadia. You are not sure, but perhaps you can see the ruins of a tower of some kind, poking up over the treetops in the forest depths. From here you can go:

North along the road	► 804
East into the Deep Forest	► 710
South to Vulcan City	► 222 in *Workshop of the Gods*

You retrace your steps through the dark forest as fast as you can. You can hear the Nemean lion crashing through the trees but it soon gives up when you near the edge of the forest and the world of man. Well, man, centaurs, satyrs, dryads, nymphs and werewolves that is, to name but a few of the Arcadian folk. Better leave the deep forest for now. You can always come back later ▶ **148**

If you have the codeword *Plight* ▶ **322** . If not, read on.

You have come to the entrance of the Summer Palace. It gleams white in the sun. Two guards stand at the door, satyr guards by the look of them – half goat, half man. They've got rudimentary armour, including helmets with holes for the horns on their heads. One of the satyrs leans against a pillar snoring, the other is lazily munching on some kind of kebab but at least he's awake. As you walk past them, he nods a greeting.

Inside, you find that since the Palace has been refurbished, new sections have opened up, and now there is a working kitchen, and even an art gallery! Nyctimus is at his desk busy running things. Will you visit:

Your suite of rooms	▶ **100**
King Nyctimus	▶ **197**
The palace kitchens	▶ **310**
The art gallery	▶ **409**
The bulletin board	▶ **101**
Examine the onager	▶ **471**
Go to the lagoon	▶ **345**
Leave this place	▶ **547**

If you have the codeword *Propeller* ▶ **367**. If not, you have no idea how to build a travel catapult. ▶ **220** and choose again.

You are readying yourself for a nice spell of relaxing fishing when once again the waters boil and up surges a raging Ladon, river weed hair spraying water across your face as he tosses his head angrily.

'Ah, you again. Fine, carry on.' With that he sinks beneath the waters and is gone. This time though it seems the god has scared some of the fish away, for you only catch two. Note two **fresh fish** on your Adventure Sheet.

When you have finished fishing, you decide to move on. Where will you go?

West on the Way	▶ **20**
South-west into the forest	▶ **189**
East on the Way	▶ **380**
South, into the lush river valley	▶ **403**

You have returned to the parched vineyard of the wineries. Everything is dried up and dead. Well, except for Maron the satyr who is lying nearby propped up against an old cart, snoring loudly. Two empty jugs of dandelion wine lie discarded beside him.

You nudge him awake with your foot. 'What, what is it? Can't you see I'm sleeping?' mumbles Maron.

'Drunk again, eh?'

'Yes! Yes, drunk again. Now leave me alone – I told you, can't do anything about nothing until the rivers are flowing again. Now, have you brought me a lovely nymph or two to comfort an old satyr? No? Well, bugger orf, then.' With that he turns over and goes back to his snoring sleep. What can you do but leave? From here, you can go:

North to the Arcady Trail	▶ **238**
West to Treycross on the Arcady Trail	▶ **728**
South on the Trail	▶ **338**
East to the bridge over the river Alpheus	▶ **14**

❏

Put a tick in the box. If there was a tick in the box already ▶ **327** immediately. If not, read on.

You return to the sheep farm of Krio and Selene with some trepidation. You're not sure whether Deridedes kept his word and left them alone, after you gave yourself up and got hanged to death.

But from a distance, all seems well, the kids are playing in the forecourt, and Krio is shearing sheep in the pen. At the sight of you the entire family stops to stare in astonishment.

'How… how can this be? We buried you in our garden with a headstone and everything, because you gave your life to save ours!' says Selene.

'The gods move in mysterious ways,' you say enigmatically.

'Well, whatever,' cries the boy Magnes, 'it's great to see you alive!' The whole family runs up to you and they all hug you.

For a moment you feel loved. It was almost worth getting hanged for…

They explain that Deridedes left them alone after he'd had his revenge. He had no interest in 'woolly-minded sheep shaggers, and their shit-stink children' and he left with his thugs to pursue a life of highway robbery, apparently. Since then the farm has been thriving, though they put flowers on your grave every day and sacrifice to Hades regularly, so that he will make sure you go to Elysium.

You don't mention any of your visits, or planned visits to Hades or who you really are, instead you just ask they remove

the headstone and ignore the grave from now on, as it is rather disturbing to stand at your own resting place, despite all that you know.

Magnes takes you out back to show you the collection of lodestones and other metals that stick together or sometimes repel each other. He thinks their special property is in some way like light or fire or gravity, a new concept he's named after himself. He calls it magnetism. He's planning to study these metals and then write up his discoveries and send them to the Philosophers' Academy. You give him as much encouragement as you can.

Later, you dine with the happy family. Grateful for your sacrifice, Krio will sell you **bales of wool** at cost price – 15 pyr each. Note that you can't carry more than three bales at a time.

When you are ready, you say your farewells and take your leave. ► 822

287

If you have the codeword *Plenty* ► 811 immediately. If not, read on.

You have come to a bridge along the Sacred Way that encircles the world, as do the waters of Oceanus. From here, it runs east and west along the coast. The bridge spans the River Ladon that comes down from a great lake to south and into the sea but the river bed is dry and parched, for the waters have long since dried up. The gods or spirits of the Arcadian rivers, Ladon and Alpheus have not been seen in an age or more. To the south-west are the wooded outskirts of

the Deep Forest and the ruins of a castle of some kind, jutting up over the treeline. From here you can:

Go to the bridge ► 741
Head south, into the dried-up river valley ► 403

288

Gain the codeword *Plundered*. You do not find a mark or a track anywhere. You have to admit, this Autolycus is good. But then you catch a scent of something. It's the note, it has a faint fragrance, not unpleasant. You hand it to Erifili. Perhaps her gourmet nose will be able to tell what it is.

'Amaranth oil,' she says instantly. 'Used in cooking, but not much, for it has a very subtle taste. Mostly it's used for oiling metals or... Wait, if I remember right, also used in Vulcan's workshops to make his Kourai Khryseai, his Golden Maidens, the automatons of Vulcan City.'

It seems if you want to get your money back or get your revenge, you will have to search for Autolycus in Vulcan City.

For now there is nothing you can do but get some rest.
► 220

289

The battle is hard, but your skill at arms keeps the wolf at bay. You manage to nick its jaw, a painful blow, it seems you are getting the better of it. Alpha snarls and then howls, not so much a bestial roar as a summons.

Seconds later, out of the trees, step several bushwhack wolves, a full pack, maybe two, of at least ten feral beasts. You cannot fight that many. You turn and run for your life.

Make a GRACE roll at difficulty 8.
Succeed ▶ 454
Fail ▶ 375

The east coast of Arcadia ▶ 200
The north coast of Arcadia ▶ 444
Head for open ocean (if you have an **astrarium**) ▶ 316

290

You have returned to the upper Tarn of Alpheus on the high river plateau. It is as dry as dust here, and heat roils up from the surface of the lake bed, wafting out and around the lake like a stifling blanket. Up above, birds ride the thermals, cawing and wheeling in the azure skies. If you have the codeword *Pumped* ▶ 201 immediately. If not, read on.

There is nothing more for you to do here, so you move on. Where to?

North to the Druid's Shrine ▶ 463
North-west skirting past the Shrine to the woods ▶ 620
Take the stairs in the cliffside down to the lower tarn ▶ 578

291

You reach down and cut his bonds, freeing him. 'Now get out of my sight, I never want to see you again, you thieving goat!' you say.

'Thank you for not killing me, for showing mercy!' says Jas, bowing and scraping as he backs away.

'Go!' you shout, raising your dagger. He turns tail and flees, his hooves throwing up divots of earth from the grassy ground – but the look that he gives you as he runs away makes you think that perhaps this is not over yet...

Lose the codeword *Prisoner* and gain the codeword *Proscribe*. You find amidst the abandoned detritus of their little camp: a **brazen trumpet**, a **box of paints**, a lock of **water nymph hair** which looks more like straggly seaweed than anything else, and 25 pyr in a pouch. There is also a raw venison steak. If you have a **book of recipes**, you can turn the venison into **venison sausages**. Note them on your Adventure Sheet as well. If you do not have the book, the steak will go off very quickly in this Arcadian summer heat, so is of no use to you. When you are done, you move on.

Go back to Treycross market ▶ 728
Leave this area ▶ 12

292

The crew are keen to put to sea. 'All I need is a course,' says the helmsman.

You must hug the coast unless you have an **astrarium**, in which case you can navigate in open seas.

North coast of Boreas ▶ 444 in *The Pillars of the Sky*
West coast of Boreas ▶ 200 in *The Pillars of the Sky*
The city of Iskandria ▶ 837 in *The Hammer of the Sun*
The Shores of Psamathe ▶ 328 in *The Hammer of the Sun*
The east coast of Notus ▶ 200 in *The Hammer of the Sun*

293

Being a bamboozling charmer and dissembling hoaxer yourself, you recognise the techniques she is using to disguise her identity.

'Who are you really?' you say accusingly, glaring at her. She balks, for you are very intimidating.

'I'm sorry, I'm sorry, it's me, Damara!'

You recognize her now – the water nymph who worked with Jas your butler to defraud and rob you.

'He made me do it, it was all him!' she squeals.

'I don't believe that for an instant, all three of you were as thick as thieves. Well, that's because you were thieves, in fact, but anyway, tell me why I shouldn't just cut you down right now?'

Damara goes an even paler green. 'Er... because, because... a kiss, I'll give you a kiss!'

'A kiss? I let you go in exchange for a kiss? Why would I do that?'

Damara tosses her seaweed hair, looking a tad miffed. 'Well, I'm hurt you don't think a kiss from me is worth much, but on the other hand, you know what they say about the kiss of the water nymph, right?' She gives you an alluring smile, revealing sharp, pointy little teeth. 'My kiss will let you breathe underwater for a while.'

That could be useful. What will you do?

Kiss her ▶ 708
Kill her ▶ 561
Let her go ▶ 399

294

The gallery is quite full today. A dryad has left muddy footprints across the floor, nearby a couple of mortals are having a heated argument about a particular piece of pottery, and a drunken satyr lies passed out in one corner. He looks a little like your butler, Jas, in fact. Could it be? But then in comes Erifili from the kitchen, wiping her hands on a cloth.

'Have you got something for me?' she asks.

If you have a **masterpiece by Apelles** and wish to sell it to her ▶ 789

If not, you explain you are just spending some time looking at the art. When you are ready ▶ 282 and choose again.

295

Desperately, you comb out your hair, rearrange your clothing so it resembles a woman's chiton, and hunch yourself up as if a Bacchante filled with the frenzied spirit of the mad god; but it is a hopeless effort and doesn't fool any of them for a moment, for they can smell your man-musk. Moments later you are engulfed by a pack of shrieking, frenzied furies, tearing, biting and ripping at you with nails, teeth and bare hands, intent on sacrificing you to the mad god. You are overwhelmed and literally torn to pieces in a matter of seconds, and your body scattered to the four winds. Well, those bits of it that weren't eaten that is.

▶ 111

296

You have been given permission to hunt in Arcadia by the goddess Artemis but the killing of the deer uses up your hunting quota. Cross the **hunting permit** off your Adventure Sheet.

▶ 148

297
❑

Put a tick in the box. If there was a tick in the box already ▶ 271 immediately. If not, read on.

You spot a figure pacing out a wide space near the bridge. She is heavily robed, wearing a wide brimmed hat to keep the sun off. Even so, she also sports a parasol – clearly she's not a fan of the eternal summer sun of Arcadia. As you draw near, you recognize Helen, the innkeeper of the Inn of the White Poplars in Hades. You'd found the Silver Seal of Hades and given it to her, so she could leave Hades and set up another inn in the lands of the living, for she is a shade, and has been long dead for many years.

She looks up at you, 'Hello there, I was hoping you'd turn up soon,' says Helen. She waves a black-robed arm expansively, 'The perfect spot for an inn!' she says, 'By a bridge for enhanced footfall, on the banks of a beautiful river and near to the vineyards from which we can source our wine!'

'Clearly you know your business,' you comment.

'Indeed,' says Helen. 'I hope you're still up for the deal. Help me build this inn, and we'll be joint owners. I know you're not the type to settle down, but if you set me up here, you can come and stay whenever you like, obviously, but also collect your share of the profits.'

'What do you need?' you ask.

Helen looks around. You can see her shadowed features squinting in concentration. 'Well, an architect to design and build it all, then a painter and decorator to tart it up, then a living innkeeper to run it, as I can't be front of house, as I'm… well, a shambling shade from Hades is not the best look for an inn, don't you think?' She looks around. 'I suppose technically I'm one of the undead now,' she says wistfully.

If you have a **Contract: Architect** ▶ 343

If not, you will have to come back later. You say your farewells to Helen and travel on. From here you can go:

North-east to the Woodlands	▶ 60
East along the riverbank	▶ 138
South	▶ 822
West to the Wineries	▶ 417

298
❑ ❑ ❑

Put a tick in a box.

If two boxes are now ticked ▶ 428 immediately. If one box or all three boxes are now ticked, read on.

Here in the temple of Demeter you can ask the Priestess Thekla to bless some Arcadian soil for you. Any earth from round and about will do, but you will have to donate 15 pyr to the temple coffers to get it. If you do, add one **blessed soil of Arcadia** to your Adventure Sheet for every 15 pyr you spend.

When you are ready, you leave the temple. You can go:

West along the coast	▶ 380
South along the coast	▶ 419
South-west into the farmlands	▶ 270

299

You see on the table a letter that Mela was writing. You take a few moments to look through her correspondence. It seems she is working with someone called the 'Master of Twilight' and that they have been tasked with keeping the river gods, Ladon and Alpheus, imprisoned so that the rivers run dry, and thus Arcadia can be kept weak and powerless. But who does the Master of Twilight work for, and why?

Anyway, Evadne's heart is starting to freeze up your backpack; you need to return it before you get frostbite. You make your way back to her stone cage.

▶ 680

300

You have left the hot, burning desert of Notus behind you. Although there is a hot summer sun here in Arcadia the air is filled with fresh sounds and smells. Birdsong, the hum of the bee, the buzz of the dragonfly, glinting in the sunlight, the heady scents of herbs and the sweet bouquet of wild flowers. But what terrible dangers lie hidden behind this pleasant mask of Arcadian paradise?

If you have the codeword **Neveragain**, lose the codeword **Projectile** and then ▶ 832

301

'By the Muses' mammaries, I can't believe you found yet another Apelles – looks so fresh too! Anyway, I'll give you a hundred and twenty-five pyr for this one.'

'Only a hundred and twenty-five?' you say.

'I'm afraid so. There's a limited market for this sort of thing, you know. Only so many collectors and that.'

You shrug resignedly. 125 pyr is 125 pyr. Add the money and cross off the **masterpiece by Apelles**.

'The market is getting a little flooded, so I'll only buy one more, even if you do manage to find another.' says Erifili, and you take your leave. ▶ 282

302

You play a rather sad but touching funereal song you heard the shades of bargemen sing on the bayous and rivers of Hades. You play it well, and it brings a tear or two to the eyes of some audience members.

'Nice,' says Velosina. 'Well, not *nice* exactly but definitely good. Very good. Game on, then!'

Velosina steps up and play an old centaur folk song, telling the story of how the centaurs were driven from their ancestral homelands by a tribe of cruel and savage... well, humans. It's clever for it pleases the audience, while also turning them against you. You will have to hope that Chiron really is as honourably impartial as they say he is. It is your turn to play again.

Make a CHARM roll at difficulty 7. If you roll snake eyes (two) ▶ 228 immediately. If not, read on.

| Succeed | ▶ 376 |
| Fail | ▶ 407 |

303

You roar in righteous anger, and charge straight at them, brandishing your weapon.

With a scream of terror, Damara shrugs off her black robes, including a wooden shoulder rack, designed to make her look like a misshapen ogre, revealing a web-fingered and footed, rather shapely water nymph underneath it all. She catches some of her seaweed-like hair in the wooden rack, but her fear of you is so great that she pulls it out in her haste to get away. Timandra also wails in fear, and trips over, falling out of her royal robes, and sending her mask tumbling, revealing the stilts she was walking on! She has hair like long grass with yellow daisies growing though it, clearly a dryad of the meadow. You recognize them in fact, having seen them in Jas's company before.

The water nymph and the meadow dryad run off as fast as they can, but Jas is still tied up, and cannot run anywhere.

'Umm... I can explain...' splutters Jas.

'Hah, don't even try, you scheming little shit-bag!' you say. You draw your dagger. Jas gulps.

'No, wait,' he cries in terror, 'let me make it up to you, I'll be the best butler ever, no more tricks or lies, I promise!'

You reach down, dagger hovering near his throat. Jas whimpers, and then a terrible smell wafts up – he's shat his pants.

You wrinkle your face in disgust but his fear softens your anger. You can't bring yourself to kill the hopeless coward but that doesn't mean you can't fire him. Or maybe keep him on but there will have to be conditions.

| Never darken my door again | ▶ 291 |
| Forgive and forget | ▶ 243 |

304

You flee into the trees. It is hard for Soter and his herd to get through the densely packed trees, even if it is their home ground, and you are able to lose them in the dark forest, for they are not hunters like the wolves. You heave a sigh of relief. You are safe.

Or are you? You look around and realise that during the chase you have become hopelessly lost.

▶ 242

305

If you have the codeword *Plenty* ▶ 48 immediately. If not, read on.

The hamlet is called, rather oddly, Bridgadoom. It seems half empty, no doubt caused by the drying of the rivers and the economic hardship that has caused. Still, there are a few places still open for custom, a tailor's shop, the local ruler's hall, and such like, and there is an unusual shrine in the village square – a shrine to Moros, he who brings doom to men. Who will you visit?

Cressida the magistrate	▶ 120
Phineas the rumour monger	▶ 153
Gelos the tailor	▶ 187
Leave the hamlet	▶ 801

306

You pull the lever and are lobbed high up into the air, hurtling across the sky like a shooting star. It is terrifying but also a big thrill. Down below you can see the wineries and vineyards of Arcadia and the course of the Alpheus river that runs to the eastern shore, and then you start plummeting downwards toward the Sacred Way in the south-eastern corner of Arcadia. The heavy grey flagstones of the Way do not seem very welcoming as you hurtle towards them... But then you see the catch-net that you're supposed to fall into rushing up to meet you at breakneck speed. If you do *not* have the codeword *PatchupFive* ▶ 233 immediately. If you do have it, read on.

You fall into the webbing of the catch-net safely. After you take a moment to catch your breath, you clamber down and take a look at your surroundings.

► 622

307

The farm is deserted and crumbling and sheep roam the hills, wild and untended. Krio and Selene are buried out the front, and fresh flowers have been laid on their graves but there is no sign of Magnes and his brothers. There is nothing more you can do at this tragic place, but mourn their lives and your own choices. Will you go:

North to a bridge	► 14
South to the Sacred Way	► 832
East to the Sacred Way	► 833
West on the Arcady Trail	► 338

308

Alpha leaps at you, but you fall onto your back deliberately, weapon ready. The wolf realises what is about to happen but it is fully committed and cannot avoid impaling itself on your blade. Its own weight forces your weapon up into its heart, killing it instantly. A lucky blow. You get up and stare down at the body. Such a powerful, magnificent beast, yet so easily slain.

You skin it, and take the beautiful white pelt as a trophy. Gain the codeword *Pelt*.

When you are done, you stand up – and see that you have been surrounded. A pack of bushwhack wolves, and their handlers are just standing there, staring at you. The handlers, at least four or five of them, are human but heavily bearded and hairy, wearing clothes made from deer hide. They carry goads with which they control the wolves, but no weapons that you can see. You notice that their eyes are tinged with yellow.

One of them gestures, and the wolves step apart, forming a pathway through the forest. He indicates that you should walk that path.

You can see ten or more wolves, but you can tell there are even more of them amidst the trees, including more men.

You have no choice but to follow the path they have laid out for you.

► 4

309

As you follow the stream down the river valley, you notice that nearly everywhere you look there are bones jutting out of the earth or lying scattered around. Many look like they've been gnawed on by the same set of teeth – or perhaps a single tooth. Others look as if they've had all the flesh boiled off them. Many of the bones are clearly human…

A feeling of mounting dread creeps up inside of you. After a while you come to mounds of discarded equipment. Weapons, helmets, rusting armour, rotting leather sandals and such like. This fills you with unease. Who has taken the time to pile all this up, and where are the original owners?

Further on, you realise who the owners were, for you find mounds of human skulls, three of them piled in a row. There must be a hundred or more. The sense of dread grows stronger within you…

Beyond the skull piles you come to a ford with some stepping stones and from behind a copse of three trees steps a crook-backed old crone, grey from the top to the bottom – grey robes, grey hair, grey skin. She is toothless, spittle dribbling from her half open mouth, and eyeless, not just blind, but without even any eye sockets. She starts up a wailing cry, like a kind of paean to despair, and you feel that terrible sense of dread rising up within you, threatening to overwhelm you.

You have found Enyo, the Creeping Dread, one of the Grey Ones… You try to marshal your powers and strike her down but then beside her appears another grey crone, similar to the first. She steps out behind her sister, one hand holding an eye, with which she observes you. Suddenly she triples in size, turning into a creature so foul and hideous that your heart explodes with terror and fear in an instant. Even though you are a great hero you cannot control yourself, and you turn and flee from Deino the terror, whimpering as you run as fast as you can.

And from behind a mound of skulls steps Persis the wall-shaker, another socket-less, dribbling crone of grey malice. Leaning on a staff with both hands, she stamps one foot down upon the ground and from it ripples a quaking force that rattles your body and shivers your bones so that your feet fly out from under you and you fall backwards. The ground rises up to meet your head and you are smashed into unconsciousness.

► 379

310

The palace kitchens are huge, for once they catered for hundreds, including the very gods themselves. Now the palace has been re-decorated, there are quite a few people working or visiting but nothing like the old days. Still, there are about ten or so kitchen staff, most of them ordinary humans. Satyrs, nymphs, faeries and dryads are considered too unreliable for this sort of work, as they'd probably end up drinking the wine stocks and eating the food.

The head chef is a large, stocky woman, muscled like a blacksmith, clearly once an Amazon. She sees you looking her up and down and says, 'Yes, yes, I was an Amazon warrior once, by Apollo's pink painted arse, but I just prefer cooking to fighting, and art too, and that's that. I'm Erifili and you're the Steward, right? Well, then, you can help yourself to anything you like,' and she gestures to a table laden with baskets of food and drink.

You can take a **Summer Palace picnic hamper** if you want. Note it on your Adventure Sheet.

You also spot a small jar, labelled 'Ambrosia'. You are reaching for that when Erifili shouts, 'No! Stop! I should have said *anything but that* as it's ambrosia, you know the food of the gods, meant only for them. If a mortal eats it, their blood turns to ichor and they die in agony.'

'But I thought Herakles the great hero was given some and it made him immortal?' you say.

'Yes, he was *given* some. That's the point, given it by a god, with the permission of Zeus, that's the only way. But it seems the gods sleep, and I really should put that somewhere safe, as it will likely kill some idiot or another!'

She turns back to her work. If you have the codeword *Retrieve* and wish to ask Erifili about ophidiaroot ▶ 498. If not, when you are done ▶ 282 and choose again.

311

The stranglevines seem unstoppable, so you throw down a **lava gem** and shatter it. There is a flash of fire, and the vines recoil in a writhing mass of purple suckered creepers. You are able to move forward, but soon the vines close in around you once again and you have to use more lava gems. Roll a die.

score 1- 4	Use two more
score 5-6	Use one more

Cross off the **lava gems** as required. The bursts of fire keep the vines off you, and you manage to get past them and out of the woods.

Will you go:

North-east to the Trail	▶ 728
North-west to the Trail	▶ 455
West to the hills	▶ 559

312

The boys carry on playing, glancing up at you from time to time and smirking… Eventually, Lefkia comes back.

'Ah, hello, you're back! Do you have the things we need to start work?' she says.

If you have:

box of paints x 2
vinegar of hades x 1
bucket of gypsum

and wish to hand them to Lefkia, cross them off your Adventure Sheet and ▶ 715

If not, you tell Lefkia you will come back when you do, and take your leave. 'Don't take too long,' she says, 'My crew will get impatient.' ▶ 547

313

❑

Put a tick in the box. If there was a tick in the box already ▶ 339 immediately. If not, read on.

After an hour or so, the trapdoor opens once again to vent more heat. Shielding your face from the hot air, you peer down. It is very dark, but at the bottom you can make out something glowing redly. You spot a ladder nearby and start climbing down.

You descend into darkness, your hair and clothes ruffled upward by the onrushing heated air. Sweat breaks out on your brow. It is so hot you can barely breathe.

After a few minutes, you reach the bottom. You are in some sort of huge underground cavern, dug out relatively recently by the look of it.

The red glow comes from a large pool of lava, bubbling slowly in the centre of the cavern. Suspended above it is a massive glass beaker or amphora, filled with what looks like a blueish green vapour. It is stoppered and sealed by a bronze cap, inscribed with strange symbols. The heat from the lava keeps whatever is in the glass beaker as steam, but you presume the heat build-up is so great, it has to be vented from time to time either to protect whoever else may be down here or to prevent the enormous glass beaker from over-heating and exploding.

You look around. Other than the lava, everything is darkness and shadow.

▶ 372

314

Deridedes nods in mild approval and the crowd laughs uproariously. You hear a few people commenting on it 'Oh, very good,' 'Start a war to shut down bad breath? Why not!' and such like.

'Good stuff for a beginner I suppose, but I doubt it will impress the judge,' says Deridedes dismissively. But then Kraterus suddenly crows 'silly-old-goat!' and the crowd claps in appreciation. Deridedes eyes widen in surprise.

'Cock likes it though,' you mutter. 'One point to me!'

Deridedes can hardly believe it, but he puts the mask up to his face, which amplifies his words a little, and counters with:

'You pie-faced loon, where'd you get that numpty chump-head from — yer mutant mum?'

The crowd laughs uproariously and Deridedes steps back, expecting Kraterus to give his approval too, but the cockerel remains silent.

Deridedes' face falls. You smile with grim satisfaction. Now it's your turn to launch an insult.

'A malodorous whiff of rot surrounds you like a cloak of dung, so it's no surprise you are shunned like the skunk.' ▶ 469

'You reek of ass!' ▶ 549

315

You have returned to the dryad infested regions of the woodlands of Ambrosia. This is where Phearei the dryad bewitched you into loving her, a spell so strong you were able to break it only by killing yourself. To confront her again may be rash –but on the other hand, you lived and served as her slave for weeks, and you know all the forest paths, the songs the dryads sing and Phearei's habits and movements. You could seek revenge but you'd better not go any further unless you are properly prepared or you will simply succumb to their beguiling song once again. Will you:

Return to Sivi's apiary ▶ 8
Leave this place entirely ▶ 225
Seek out Phearei ▶ 82

316

If you have the codeword *Ovation* ▶ 348
Otherwise ▶ 423

317

You clamber to a high point and dive in, cutting the water like a knife blade. Broken crystals of sunlight dance in the stream as you surface.

'Wow. I wish I could do that.'

'I can teach you.' You look around. 'Actually, not here. It's too shallow. You might hurt yourselves.'

'*Please…*'

With a sigh you pretend to relent. 'All right, let's move a few hundred yards that way where the water's a bit deeper.'

After you've been coaching them for a few minutes, they start to lose interest. Little kids have the attention span of gnats. You leave them cavorting in the stream and go back to your favourite spot.

Write your attributes on the Adventure Sheet:

STRENGTH 0
GRACE +1
CHARM 0
INGENUITY 0
Then ▶679

318

You consider the situation. Perhaps you can come up with a cunning plan. Make an INGENUITY roll at difficulty 8.

Succeed ▶ 374
Fail ▶ 402

319

You have completed one of the Great Labours of Arcadia. Write the number **360** (not *this* paragraph number) in the Current Location space on your Adventure Sheet in place of the number already written there, if any, and then ▶ 38

320

You manage to outrun the angry mob of villagers without out too much difficulty once you have crossed the bridge over the Alpheus but not before one of them, a particularly fast young girl, manages to spear you in the thigh with a pitchfork, before she falls back, exhausted. Tick the Wound box on your Adventure Sheet. If you are already wounded, then you fall to the ground to be overwhelmed by the mob who beat you to death ▶ 111 (note that in this case, you don't get to keep the 600 pyr, as they take that back before you expire).

If you are still alive, despite your wound you are able to run on and the farmers and peasants, unused to such running, give up, and return to their homes. Something tells you that you may not be welcome in their village anymore… Still, at least you made 600 pyr.

You look around. The course of the river runs out into a bay with a low wooden quay for the docking of boats. From here you can go:

North ▶ 774
South ▶ 833
West along the river ▶ 138
To the quay in the bay ▶ 200

321

If you have the title **Master of Mockery** ▶ 117 immediately. If not, read on.

You enter the gaudy pavilion of Deridedes, priest of Momos. Inside a large crowd is laughing hysterically at two men on the stage. One is clearly Deridedes the priest, the other a local farmer, by the look of him. At the front of the low stage is a cockerel in a cage, a big, loud one too. A sign over the cage reads:

'*Judge Kraterus the Cockerel*'

The priest says something rather insulting, and Kraterus pipes up with a loud screech that sounds very much like 'silly old goat!'

The crowd roars with laughter, applauding madly as the farmer, ruefully shaking his head, walks down off the stage.

Deridedes addresses the crowd.

'So, who wishes to enter the Tournament of Taunts? Fifteen pyr buys you a shot at the title. If you beat me, you win the Judge himself, Kraterus the Cockerel, prize money of a hundred pyr, and the coveted title of Master of Mockery! Any of you cock-slimers, dangle-berries and scrotum-rattlers want to give it a go? Rules are simple, we take it in turns to insult each other, if Kraterus calls the caller a "silly old goat", they score a point. First to three points wins.'

If you want to enter the Tournament of Taunts, cross off your 15 pyr and ▶ **91**

If not, or you'd like to come back and try again later, you can head back to the market (▶ **728**) or leave the area (▶ **12**).

322

A strange languor starts to numb your mind. You look around puzzled. What are you doing here? What were you about to…no, you should be… confusion dogs your path. In a fog-like dream you begin to wander away from the Palace, following the Arcady Trail south until you come to the Treycross market. ▶ **716**

323

☐

Put a tick in the box. If there was a tick in the box already ▶ **78** immediately. If not, read on.

'Epimenides is the murderer!' you say out loud. With a rumbling, clanking sound, as of ancient wheels turning, the door slides to the side. Inside, is a low platform carved with a frieze of Typhon, the many head Father of Monsters, battling against Zeus, the Father of the Gods.

Upon it lies a stone tablet, a fragment of spell that can be used to call upon the power of Typhon himself.

Note that you have the third fragment of Typhon on your Adventure Sheet (in your notes, not as an item, as you cannot lose it – write the spell down too, if that helps). This one reads:

'Come to me, Typhon, Earth Child, Spawn of the Abyss, Dread-filled Dragon, come forth from the Abyssal Vaults of the Vulcanverse! I command thee!

'I bind thee by the power of the Gods and Titans. In the fires of Thanatos, I make sacrifice, I bind thee by flame, venom and fang, I bind thee by Gaia, Tartarus and Zeus. Typhon, you are mine to command!'

If you now have the **Eye of Typhon** and the other two spell fragments, get the codeword *Neophyte* in *The Houses of the Dead*. You can then return to the shrine of Typhon in Hades to cast the spell.

You step back out of the alcove, and the door slides shut once more. There is nothing more for you to do here but leave. Where will you go?

North to the bridge   ▶ **801**
West to the low hills   ▶ **822**
South on the Sacred Way ▶ **600** in *The Hammer of the Sun*

324

If you have the codeword *PatchupSeven* ▶ **154** immediately. If not, read on.

You have arrived at the end of the Sacred Way that leads to the great northern gate of Vulcan City. To the west, massive mountains rise up to the heavens, snow-peaked and ice bound. To the east all you can see are trees and trees and trees, the Deep Forest of Arcadia. You are not sure, but perhaps you can see the ruins of a tower of some kind, poking up over the treetops in the forest depths.

Nearby, a structure of wooden poles and webbing is in a poor state of repair. Repairing it will cost you 20 pyr. If you wish to do so, cross off the money and get the codeword *PatchupSeven*. Either way, from here you can go:

North along the road   ▶ **804**
East into the Deep Forest   ▶ **710**
Follow the walls south-eastward to some low hills ▶ **559**
South to Vulcan City   ▶ **222** in *Workshop of the Gods*

325

The fountain is low and wide, made out of time-stained marble, as is the statue above it. The statue is of a beautiful young woman, exquisitely carved from white marble. Judging by her sleeveless dress, and the cup she holds in one hand, it is of Hebe, cup bearer to the gods, and also the goddess of youth. In her other hand, she holds out a little casket with three empty indentations, as if expecting an offering of some kind. Lava gems, perhaps?

Water bubbles up out of the fountain, and down to fill the wide marble bowl to the brim. The water has a silvery sheen to it, and smells wholesome and sweet. You take a sip – it is refreshing and wonderful to drink.

If you place three **lava gems** in her hand ▶ **346**
If not there is nothing else you can do here, so will you:

Investigate the cliffside door   ▶ **235**
Climb the stairs up the cliff   ▶ **370**
Go south along the river   ▶ **684**
Go south west to the old arch   ▶ **340**

326

You have returned to the temple of Demeter. Thekla, the priestess you paid to work here is waiting. She greets you and reminds you that once the temple has been repaired she can re-consecrate it.

'Perhaps then the people can farm the land again, with Demeter's blessing.'

If you have the title **Steward of the Summer Palace** ▶ **567**. If not, read on.

There is nothing you can do here for now. Will you go:

West along the coast	▶ **380**
South along the coast	▶ **419**
South-west into the farmlands	▶ **270**

327

You have come back to the sheep farm of Krio and Selene. All is well, the family seem happy, and Magnes is a shepherd boy by day, and a natural philosopher the rest of the time, it seems.

You dine with the happy family. After, you can buy **bales of wool** at cost price: 15 pyr each. Note that you can't carry more than three bales at a time. When you are ready, you say your farewells and take your leave.

▶ **822**

328

You bellow a challenge, deep and guttural, an ancient sound, nature's challenge, red in tooth and claw, a sound that has been heard across all the forests, plains and mountains where life thrives for millennia, where all living things strive in the battle of the survival of the fittest. Or the luckiest…

The wolf turns, terrifyingly calmly and paces towards you. Close up, you can see he is large for a wolf, but not especially so. His fangs are white and sharp, his fur also white, and remarkably clean. No, it is not his wolf body that is so terrifying, it is his eyes, yellowed like the wolf, but full of a terrible intelligence, bright with cunning, like that of a man.

Alpha looks down at the trap, and then up at you, amusement in its eyes. It knows exactly what you have tried to do. Then it snarls and jumps over the trap, and tries to rip out your throat. You will have to fight him. Make a STRENGTH roll at difficulty 9.

Succeed	▶ **308**
Fail	▶ **289**

329

The Blackgate Travel Catapult is ready to go, oiled and polished. You crank up the catapult arm and get into the leather lined bucket seat. A winch on one side lets you choose the direction and destination, and a lever on the other will propel you up into the air. Where to?

North-western Arcadia	▶ **107**
North-eastern Arcadia	▶ **264**
South-eastern Arcadia	▶ **306**
South-western Arcadia	▶ **406**

Or, if you decide against using it ▶ **220** and choose again.

330

If you have the codeword *Parapet* ▶ **220** immediately. If not, read on.

If you have the codeword *Punition* ▶ **694** immediately. If not, read on.

The old Arcady Trail leads up the hill to the ruins of an old fort. It overlooks the valley below but most of the battlemented walls have crumbled away, or are covered in

vines. It was once called the Fortress of the Black Gates or simply Fort Blackgate but now its great bronze doors, black paint flaked and patched, hang askew, its heraldic symbols long since faded into dust, its flags and banners nothing but threadbare tatters. Where once none could pass its warlike walls, now anyone can simply walk into it, except... around the archway over the shattered gates, several severed heads have been nailed. Some are now flesh-scoured skulls, but others are still fresh, one even dripping blood. On closer inspection, you see that it is the head of young woman. Also, you notice that some of the skulls are charred and blackened, as if by fire.

Clearly, a hideous monster of some kind is now living in Fort Blackgate. Will you:

Enter the Fort   ▶ 608
Go back   ▶ 85

331

You play a rather sad but touching funereal song you heard the shades of bargemen sing on the bayous and rivers of Hades. Unfortunately, half way through you forget how the refrain goes and the crowd turns from tearful appreciation to mocking laughter.

'Hah! Well, a good try, but you should practice more,' she says, smirking.

Velosina steps up once more and plays a song of summer meadows and blue skies, animals gently grazing by riverbanks and flower beds, an ancient song of Arcadian paradise, and she plays it very well indeed. The crowd love it. Soon it is your turn once more. You'd better get it right this time.

Make a CHARM roll at difficulty 7. If you roll snake eyes (two) ▶ 228 immediately. If not, read on.

Succeed   ▶ 376
Fail   ▶ 407

332

There is a door here, set into the side of a low mound of earth. A door knocker, in the shape of an owl, hangs from it. At the top of the door, words are carved in wood:

A SHRINE TO ATHENA
GODDESS OF WISDOM

You knock on the door, and it swings open to reveal a small room dug out of the cliffside with an altar to Athena inside. You can get blessings here. If you are a worshipper of Athena, blessings are free. If not, you must pay 10 pyr per blessing. You can only have a total of three blessings at a time.

When you have finished here, you return to the lower tarn.

▶ 578

333

You are standing in the sacred treasure Vault of Vulcan in Arcadia, a place on the cusp of life and death, set apart from the world, blessed by the god Vulcan himself. Shimmering pillars hold up the ceiling, itself a black shroud filled with glimmering stars. The floor is of black marble inlaid with intricate red mosaics that writhe and glow as if they were made of rivers of lava. Gingerly, you walk upon it, for it feels both unreal, as if you might fall through it at any moment and also dangerously hot, like walking on molten marble. Everywhere there are heaped piles of unimaginable treasures of all kinds. Coins, gems, silver, gold, armour, weapons, vases – inconceivable wealth. Yet it is all insubstantial and unreal. You cannot hold any of it, no matter how you try. Only that which you have left here yourself can you touch.

If you are alive, then you can take any items or money that you have left here previously out of the Vault and add them to your Adventure Sheet or store any items in the vault also – simply cross them off your Adventure Sheet and add them to the box below or vice versa. (Note that you cannot store the **sceptre of Agamemnon** or the **Arcadian vault key**, if you have them. They must remain on your Adventure Sheet).

If you are dead, you can put any possessions and money you like into the Vault to retrieve later. However, if you have the **sceptre of Agamemnon** or the **Arcadian vault key** do *not* put them into the Vault. They stay with you even after death.

Also if you are dead, lose any companion and, if you were wounded, untick that box on your Adventure Sheet.

ITEMS IN VAULT

If you are alive   ▶ 555
If you are dead   ▶ 666

334

You set the **golden dog** loose (cross off a charge) and it barks at the basilisk angrily. The huge lizard seems confused for a moment, but then it breathes another cloud all over the golden dog – which has no effect whatsoever of course, for it is already made of gold. The dog darts forward and sinks its golden teeth into the basilisk's throat. It tries to shake it off, but in the meantime you circle around and leap onto its back, driving your blade into the top of its skull over and over again, until you hit the brain and it dies.

You have slain the Midas basilisk! Gain the codeword *Precious*.

You look around the town, and search the basilisk's nest behind the statue of Gaia but there is not much to be found. The golden statues are too heavy to move and seem bound in place by whatever force turned them to gold. The town has been long abandoned and it seems the basilisk did not hoard or covet anything material. All you find of use is a pouch of 20 pyr, a **box of paints** and some **copper ore**.

Still, the basilisk is dead and you take its head as a trophy. You head back down to the Inn of Swollen Mammaries.

▶ **530**

335

Deridedes gives a nod of appreciation and the crowd laughs, but not uproariously.

'Not bad for a beginner, I suppose, but not great either,' says Deridedes dismissively but then Kraterus suddenly crows 'silly-old-goat!' and the crowd chuckles some more. Deridedes eyes widen in surprise.

'Cock likes it though,' you mutter. 'One point to me!'

Deridedes can hardly believe it, but he puts the mask up to his face, which amplifies his words a little, and counters with:

'You pie-faced loon, where'd you get that numpty chump-head from – yer mutant mum?'

The crowd laughs uproariously and Deridedes steps back, expecting Kraterus to give his approval too, but the cockerel remains silent.

Deridedes' face falls. You smile with grim satisfaction. Now it's your turn to launch an insult. What will you go with?

'A malodorous whiff of rot surrounds you like a cloak of dung, so it's no surprise you are shunned like the skunk.'
▶ **469**

'You reek of ass!' ▶ **549**

336

'Lovely!' says the voice, and a pale, green-hued arm reaches out to pluck your offering off the altar. You notice the fingers of her hand are more like gnarled twigs than human fingers.

Sounds of slurping echo out of the tree.

'Yum, yum,' says the dryad of the shrine.

You shake your head and cross your arms. 'The golden arrow of Artemis?' you ask once more.

'What? Oh yes, of course. I've never heard of a *golden* arrow of Artemis, but there are most certainly arrows of Artemis, for the goddess makes her own. It is said that Lykaon, the wolf king of the Deep Forest once stole a quiver of arrows from the goddess herself, curse him for his audacity! Perhaps you should talk to him. Assuming he doesn't eat you first, of course.'

You thank the dryad of the shrine and take your leave. Will you:

Go north on the Way	▶ **419**
Go south on the Way	▶ **801**
Go west into the Woodlands	▶ **60**

337

You creep out of the undergrowth, timing a short dash to the rear of the stone cabin when you trip over a bramble, and fall to the ground in a clattering bundle of noise.

'Ho, ho! What have we here?' says a hoplite guard, stepping over, a couple more men behind him. You leap to your feet ready to fight, but within seconds you are surrounded by five or six armoured soldiers. You are knocked to the ground, and one of them readies his spear to finish you off when a loud voice sounds out

'Stop, you oaf!' A woman in a pale white mask under a wide-brimmed black hat, and long yellow robes shoulders her guards aside. She holds a tall ebony staff topped with a snake, a dagger and a key, made from bronze.

'Don't just kill them willy-nilly, we need every slave we can get. Hold this one down while I cast the spell,' says the masked woman.

'Yes, Mela,' says one of the guards, clearly terrified of her, and he signals to the others.

You struggle but there are simply too many of them and they pin you to the ground. Mela the Sorceress stands over you, gesturing with her staff and making arcane symbols in the air with her other hand.

'I bind the soul, the work, the hands and mind: all of these I bind by Hecate the Saffron Cloaked!' she intones ritually.

You find your eyelids drooping and your mind numbing. She continues on, chanting a spell that begins to tighten around your very soul, like chains of iron. 'I bind thee by the sword of Ares, the grace of Artemis, by Apollo of the silver tongue, and the wisdom of Athena!' she continues.

If you have a **heart of ash** or a **heart of oak** ▶ **191** immediately. If not, ▶ **446**

338

If you have the codeword *Plantation* ▶ 15 immediately. If not, read on.

Here, the Arcady Trail winds round the eastern edges of the of woods known as the dales of leaf and stream. Where will you go next?

West to the Dales	▶ 266
South to the Sacred Way	▶ 832
North on the Trail	▶ 728
North-east to the Wineries	▶ 417
East on the Trail	▶ 14
South east to some hills	▶ 822

339

You have been down this path before – and last time it did not end well. Are you certain you are ready to try again? If so ▶ 394. If not, you can leave and come back later.

Go north to the Druid's Shrine ▶ 463

North-west skirting past the Shrine to the woods ▶ 620

Take the stairs in the cliffside down to the lower tarn ▶ 578

340

You have come to a crumbling monument, a triumphal arch of some sort built upon the south western clifftops of the Alpheus river plateau. The monument seems to depict centaurs and humans welcoming strangely garbed foreign priests. Much of the words that have been carved into the stone have been worn away, but you see the words 'metic' (a term for a foreigner given basic rights of citizenship in Greece), 'druid' and 'Celts'.

Looking around, you see that the Arcady trail runs up to a trap door set under the arch in the ground, and then north a short way to the Lower Tarn of Alpheus. To your west, you can look down over the cliffs to the Arcady Trail, the Summer Palace and the Wineries below. They look beautiful in the bright sunshine of eternal summer. From here you can go:

Down the hatch	▶ 771
North-east to the Lower Tarn	▶ 578
East to the river	▶ 684

341

❑

Put a tick in the box. If there was a tick in the box already ▶ 382 immediately. If not, read on.

A terrible howl comes from the trees to the west of the trail. You know that sound – it is the lupine daemon of Hades, Wolfshadow. Somehow he has tracked you down, even here in the wooded trails of Arcadia! Cold fingers of fear wrap around your heart for you know that no weapon made by mortal hands can kill that foul beast.

And then he appears, blood dripping from his flayed flesh onto the grey paving stone, desecrating the Sacred Way. Wolfshadow is a mass of raw, red muscle, sinews and jaws glistening with ichor and the slime of grave rot and undeath. He breaks into a fast trot, and then into a full-blown charge, howling all the time. You have no choice but to throw him off the scent somehow.

If you have any of **honey of Hades**, **weasel blood**, a **caged canary**, **fresh fish**, **a harpy's egg**, a **centaur's skull**, **venison sausages**, some **strix stew**, a **honey cake**, a **maggoty pie** or a **shrivelled heart** and wish to discard it ▶ 17.

If not, there is nothing you can do but flee for your life. ▶ 165.

342

Kaustikia pauses. 'Dryads. Hmm, they are sweet and delicious, that's true, but not easy to catch, hiding in their trees and that. In fact, if the trees go, I'll be able to eat lots of dryads, so bonus! For now, though, I think I'll just have a plate of seconds – you.' Kaustikia closes in to the attack.

If you have the **Nemean bagh nakh** ▶ 817

If not ▶ 783

343

'I have engaged the services of an architect, hopefully he will be along soon,' you explain to Helen and sure enough, after a short time you see a figure approaching the bridge from the west. As it draws near, you see it is a woman of middle age, her hair tied back in a greying bun, and a red cap on her head. She wears a light green *peplos*, a kind of long armless dress, from shoulder to ankles, tucked in at the middle, and edged with a geometric yellow pattern. You spot a nice pair of heavy leather boots under the peplos. Sensible walking boots, a little out of step with the patrician style of her dress. She looks pretty fit, and strides up to you confidently. Her eyes are bright with intelligence, and of a grey-green colour. You can't help noticing that her eyes match the colour of her hair and her peplos.

'Greetings, you must be the Steward of the Palace. I am Hypatia of Iskandria, the architect,' she says waving a hand and giving a perfunctory bow.

You greet her with a bow in return. 'That is one of my many titles,' you say, acknowledging her greeting.

'Many titles, eh? What, am I supposed to be impressed?' she says waspishly, but with a jaunty grin on her face.

'You're a woman,' says Helen in a surprised ghostly voice.

'Yes, yes, I am indeed a woman' says Hypatia, 'You

should be pleased – I had to outperform all the men at the architects' school in Iskandria, and that was just to get in, let alone graduate. I'm better'n most of the male architects you'll ever meet, I can promise you that.'

'OK then,' rasps Helen.

Hypatia's brow furrows as she looks Helen over. 'You seem a little… odd. Where are you from?' she asks.

'Very far away,' you say, hurrying things on, 'and we've no time for that, we've got an inn to build.'

'An inn! Wonderful, I haven't designed one of those in a long time,' says Hypatia enthusiastically, her inquiry into Helen's background forgotten for now.

Helen hands her a papyrus scroll. 'Here are my special requirements,' says Helen in her haunting, sepulchral voice of the dead.

Hypatia eyes her askance, but takes the scroll, unfolds it and reads. 'Terrace overlooking the river…'course, yeah, three floors, sure, no problem, garden for clients, plus herbs, vegetables… cellar for wine and ale storage…yes, yes, sewage pipes into the river, uh-huh, right, and… nine bedrooms, one "royal suite", kitchens, yeah, yeah, can do that…' She looks up. 'Yup, I can do all this, not a problem.'

'Great, so when will it be ready?' you ask.

'Let's meet up here later on. I should be able to get the plans drawn up and the foundations pegged out in a few days. I'll get to work straight away.'

Gain the codewords **Proprietor**. There is nothing else you can do here, so you move on. From here you can go:

North-east to the Woodlands	▶ 60
East along the riverbank	▶ 138
South	▶ 822
West to the Wineries	▶ 417

344

The sun beats down from a cloudless sky. Your shadow is strong on the grassy ground. Last time you were attacked here by the Shadowhunter. You look around, ready for another attack, but nothing happens. Perhaps you are too alert. Anyway, quickly you move on. From here you can go:

East to the eastern bridge	▶ 801
West to the western bridge	▶ 14
North to the Woodlands	▶ 60
South to some hills	▶ 822

345

If you have the codeword **Plenty** ▶ 131 immediately. If not, read on.

The lagoon was once a pleasure pond for the palace but now it is completely dried out. A lingering smell of rotting fish permeates the air. Punts and sail boats are drawn up on the banks, laid out like the bodies of the dead, ready for burial in some mass grave, their timbers peeling and cracked.

There is nothing here for you. Will you:

Enter the Palace	▶ 96
Examine the onager	▶ 471
Leave this place	▶ 547

346

The lava gems disappear in a flash of light, and the water turns from silver to gold. Cross off the **lava gems** from your Adventure Sheet.

You drink of the delicious, golden waters and feel them healing you. You can either untick your Wound box or remove one scar. If you have neither, than you have wasted your lava gems this time.

For every three lava gems you sacrifice to the goddess Hebe you can cure yourself if wounded or heal one scar. When you are done, will you:

Investigate the cliffside door	▶ 235
Climb the stairs up the cliff	▶ 370
Go south along the river	▶ 684
Go south west to the old arch	▶ 340

347

You place the meat just behind the wolf-trap you have already laid. Cross it off. Hopefully the sight of you and the meat will be enough to lure the beast onto your trap.

Then you bellow a challenge, deep and guttural, an ancient sound, nature's challenge, red in tooth and claw, a sound that has been heard across all the forests, plains and mountains where life thrives for millennia, where all living things strive in the battle of the survival of the fittest. Or the luckiest…

The wolf turns, terrifyingly calmly and paces towards you. Close up, you can see he is large for a wolf, but not especially so. His fangs are white and sharp, his fur also white, and remarkably clean. No, it is not his wolf form that is so terrifying, it is his eyes, yellowed like the wolf, but full of a terrible intelligence, bright with cunning, like that of a man.

Alpha looks down at the meat and the trap, and then up at you, amusement in its eyes. It knows exactly what you have tried to do. Then it snarls and jumps over the trap, and tries to rip out your throat. You will have to fight him. Make a STRENGTH roll at difficulty 9.

Succeed	▶ 308
Fail	▶ 289

348

You have the option to steer a course out to the island you saw from the lighthouse near Iskandria. Your navigation device allows you to triangulate its position simply by adjusting some dials.

Head for the island ▶ **481** in *The Pillars of the Sky*
Not this trip ▶ **423**

349

If you have the codeword *Plenty* ▶ **241** immediately. If not, read on.

Drosos, the handsome young farm overseer you hired is waiting for you, here in the once verdant farmlands.

'Good day to you, but until we get the Ladon and the Alpheus flowing once again as a water source for our crops, I can do nothing.'

It seems there is nothing more you can do here until you have restored the rivers of Arcadia to their former glory. You will have to come back later. Further west lie impassable cliffs, so will you go:

North-east ▶ **365**
North-west ▶ **380**
South-east ▶ **419**

350

❑

Put a tick in the box. If there was a tick in the box already ▶ **805** immediately. If not, read on.

You walk into what looks like an ordinary inn. There are tables, chairs, a fireplace, and a bar, though it is deserted. It is clean and well swept, but it doesn't look like there have been any customers in a while.

A woman stands up from behind the bar and looks at you in surprise, cleaning cloth in hand. She is middle-aged, tall, slim, long-haired, and rough round the edges a bit, from years of hard work but also fit and healthy looking.

'Oh,' she says, 'A customer! Welcome to the Inn of the Swollen Mammaries.'

'The... the what?'

'Ah, yes, of course, let me explain. the Inn of the Swollen Mammaries is named for, well, these hills, they're actually the breasts of Gaia, the earth mother, or so it is said, hence the sacred Mamilla-stones. One day, so swollen with the divine mother's milk were they, the hills sprayed Gaia's blessing all over the land. From her milk sprang a tribe of women known as the Galgyni, strong and rather martial. They went out and... ah... kidnapped some men, and so founded the town you can see up in the Udder Hills, Galanthropos. Well, that's the short version, for the tourists.'

'They're called the Udder Hills? Really?'

She shrugs. 'Well, yes.'

You stare, nonplussed, for a moment. 'All right, then. And where is everyone now?' you ask. 'The town looks deserted.'

The innkeeper nods sadly. 'It is. Since the rivers dried up, the traders and the tourists and the Gaia worshippers stopped coming. Without the river water we couldn't grow enough food anyway, so many left. And then came... the monster, and now all have fled or are dead.'

'The monster?'

'Yes, a basilisk, but not any kind of basilisk. One of the heroes told me it was a Midas basilisk. Instead of its breath shrivelling people up or turning them to stone, it turns them into gold.'

'Heroes?'

'Yes, since the town was abandoned, no one comes here save the occasional hero, intent on slaying the basilisk. It's what keeps me going, just about. I put them up for a night, so they can base here, but none has ever returned from the town, not even that trio who fought as a team, not one of them came back. I assume you're one of those? A glory hunting hero? Or maybe it's not the glory but the money – if what they say is true, there must be quite a few golden statues up there, though some say they cannot be moved and will remain forever.'

'Well, I hadn't heard of this monster, but now that you have told me, perhaps I will assay the task.'

The woman shakes her head. 'What a shame, you're such a fine-looking hero, it'll be a sad loss, but there you go. I can give you a nice room and a delicious final meal... er, supper! Delicious supper. Ahem.'

'And you are?'

'Oxygala, landlady of the Inn of the Swollen Mammaries.'

'Pleased to meet you,' you say politely, 'I'm the Hero of the Age.'

''Course you are, that's what they all say,' she says with a smile.

Anyway, you can buy and sell a few things here.

	To buy	To sell
Fresh fish	20 pyr	15 pyr
Venison sausages	15 pyr	10 pyr
Honey cake	–	50 pyr
Pomegranate wine	–	35 pyr

When you are done, you can:
Search for the basilisk ▶ **792**
Return to the Sacred Way ▶ **20**

351

You duel the champion of Death on the banks of the river Ladon, a titanic battle that swings back and forth like a wrathful tide. Luckily for you, Death Dealer has to take you alive, for if you die, you'll just be brought back to life by the gods, so that gives you an edge. Eventually, you land a blow that sends him sprawling backwards to the ground, where you are able to finish him off quickly.

As he dies, he rasps, 'Thanatos will bring me back, and I will come for you once again, mortal!'

You sigh resignedly. Will you never be rid of the Death Dealer? Anyway, you have triumphed once again – for a time. Where to now?

West into the forest	▶ **189**
North to the bridge	▶ **517**
South to Ladon's Lake	▶ **37**

352

❏

Put a tick in the box. If there was a tick in the box already ▶ **401** immediately. If not, read on.

You enter the tent of Zenia the fortune teller. Inside you find a rather flustered old lady, with a long warty nose, and wisps of silvery hair hanging down from her chin, eyes rheumy with age, sitting at a table upon which rests a few cups and a pottery jug. Behind her is a small fire with a cauldron of water bubbling away.

She welcomes you. 'I'm terribly sorry but I'm out of mushrooms, I can't make the tea! I know, I know, hopeless and all that, but I really wasn't expecting so many customers today,' she says in an old cracked voice.

You notice that her nose seems to be out of place, somehow. You can't help yourself, and you lean forward and give it a tug.

It comes off in your hand...

'Oi!' she shrieks, 'what have you done?' in a voice now rather shrill and strong.

She blinks for a moment. 'Oh, what the Hades,' she says, and starts pulling at her silvery hair, removing a wig that made her look bald, and wiping off her make up, revealing a young blonde woman who appears perfectly fit and healthy.

'By Hecate's teeth, it's all an act – it's what they expect you see, an old witchy woman, telling their fortunes, brewing up magic tea, dispensing wisdom and the like. But actually, I'm twenty-six, and married with two kids. I can't even tell fortunes, I just brew up some tea, and the mushrooms do the rest, but I've run out, so what does it matter, eh?'

'I'm sorry I ruined your disguise,' you say.

'Oh well, I'm done for the day anyway. Unless *you've* got some kykeon mushrooms that is?' she says.

If you have some **kykeon mushrooms** ▶ **810**; if not, read on.

'Ah well,' says Zenia, 'come back when you've found some, and I'll show you your future – or a possible future. Or maybe the past, it all depends really.'

For now, you can head back to the market (▶ **728**) or leave the area (▶ **12**).

353

The journey has left you groggy and confused. You cannot help yourself and fall into a deep sleep. When you recover, you realise you have been robbed. What a disaster! Cross off all your money. Perhaps you will be able to recoup your losses later.

▶ **410**

354

The apiary is alive with bees a-buzzing, under a clear blue sky and a bright, bone-warming sun. You spot Sivi tending to the bees, her braided hair like juicy pomegranate seeds, now hanging down behind her and across the ground like a bridal train.

'By the gods, Sivi, get a haircut!' you say, half in jest. She turns and smiles at you, revealing pale teeth the colour of pomegranate pith.

'And do you know of a hairdresser?' she asks.

'Actually, I have heard of one, but he's in Hades.'

'Dead? How sad!'

'No, not really... well, anyway, I could cut it for you,' and you heft your blade.

'I don't think so!' says Sivi emphatically. 'Anyway, no need,' and she gives a curious whistle. Out of the trees several squirrels scuttle down, run over to her and start nibbling the trailing braids. Soon they have shortened it considerably.

'My "hair" tastes like pomegranate seeds,' she explains.

'Right. OK then,' you say, rather astonished. Anyway, if you are here to see if there is any pomegranate honey available for you ▶ **513**. If not, will you:

Go deeper into the woods	▶ **176**
Leave this place	▶ **225**

355

You realise even you cannot beat such a creature when he has so many other stags with him. No, the wisest course is to beat a hasty retreat. Perhaps they won't come after you.

You back away slowly, but Soter barks a command and he and his gang of stags charge right at you, intent on trampling you into mincemeat.

You turn and flee as fast as you can hoping they will be hindered by the trees more than you will. You can hear their hooves thundering on the forest floor as they give chase.

Make a GRACE roll at difficulty 8.

Succeed	▶ **304**
Fail	▶ **278**

356

You manage to inflict a wound or two, but eventually your luck runs out, and a small drop of acid gets into your eye. The agony is too much, and you are unable to parry the dragon's next blow which rips off some of your armour and sends you sprawling to the ground. In an instant, she has wrapped her serpent coils around your torso, holding you in place as she vomits acid all over your head. It starts burning out your eyes, nose and mouth, as you squirm in utter agony.

Slowly, Kaustikia begins to eat you, starting with your feet and legs and then your arms. You cannot tell which is worse – the burning acid, or having your limbs torn apart, bite by bite. Death is a welcome relief when it comes.

► 111

357

If you have the codeword *Praise-Apollo* ► 413 immediately. If not, but you have a **Contract: Priest of Apollo** ► 643 immediately. (To check if you have it, note 357 in your Current Location box, ► 101 and then return to this section after). If you have neither, read on.

You have come to a kind of domed gazebo, like a small circular temple, on the top of little hill. Atop the dome rests a rusty, sun-shaped weather vane. Inside, there is an altar of some kind. Leaves and clumps of earth litter the floor. The skeletal remains of a squirrel lie up against the altar. It is an abandoned shrine to Apollo but you do not have the means to re-consecrate it at the moment. Perhaps you can return later. ► 20.

358

A few well-aimed clumps of earth put paid to their fun. They charge up the river bank towards you, mud-spattered and furious, but you have no patience for infant tantrums. You box a few ears, kick a few rears, and the pack of them run crying back to their mothers.

Write your attributes on the Adventure Sheet:

STRENGTH +1
GRACE 0
CHARM 0
INGENUITY 0
Then ► 723

359

Kakas will no doubt try to breathe fire all over you. Fortunately, you have a fireproof hide, made from the skin of a mammoth and vinegar of Hades. Quickly you stretch it over your shield; it should make for an excellent fireguard.

You enter the courtyard of Fort Blackgate and shout a challenge at Kakas. He looks up, and then does a double take,

looking from the body he is roasting on a spit and then back at you, and back at the body several times. You laugh out loud.

'Didn't I… haven't I… what the–?' he rumbles.

'I'm back. I told you, I'm no ordinary hero,' you say.

'I see. Well, then, I guess I'll have two heads on my wall, and a second dinner!'

Once again, you cannot afford to be hit, you will have to rely on your wits and agility.

Make a GRACE roll at difficulty 7.

Succeed　　　► 453
Fail　　　　　► 720

360

You come round from your encounter with a god, to find Sivi and Nyctimus looking at you with concerned expressions on their faces.

'Are you well?' says Sivi.

'Yes, yes, I'm fine,' you say shaking your head to clear it.

'Was it the gods? What did they say?' asks Nyctimus.

'Another… great labour finished…' you manage to say as you recover from your encounter with divinity.

'Excellent! Excellent,' says Nyctimus, 'that is good.'

'That must be rather harrowing, talking to the gods! I've got some nice honey for you though, that might help,' says Sivi. ► 513

361

You are following the banks of the river Alpheus. It rushes merrily by, nourishing the life around it. A mother duck leads her chicks through the reeds, bees buzz around the wildflowers, frogs croak and birds hunt for insects under the bright blue Arcadian sky. If you have the codeword *Parted* ► 21. If not, read on.

If you have the codeword *Penumbra* ► 267. If not, from here you can go:

East to the eastern bridge　　► 801
West to the western bridge　　► 28
North to the Woodlands　　　► 60
South to some hills　　　　　► 822

362

You can feel the hot, carrion-reek breath on your heels as you dash between the trees, but you are not fast enough and the demon's jaws grip your leg in an unbreakable vice, and he twists you down to the ground. Almost casually, Wolfshadow pins you with his forepaws, his legs twin piledrivers of flayed muscle, and rips out your throat. You die vomiting blood – the last thing you see is the wolf daemon lapping it up.

► 111

363

You manage to outrun the angry mob of villagers without too much difficulty once you have crossed the bridge over the Alpheus. They soon give up, and return to their homes but something tells you that you may not be welcome there again... Still, at least you made 600 pyr.

The course of the river runs out into a bay with a low wooden quay for the docking of boats. From here you can go:

North	▶ 774
South	▶ 833
West along the river	▶ 138
To the quay in the bay	▶ 200

364

You think maybe she's hiding something but you can't put your finger on it.

Anyway, you apologise saying you meant to catch a fish, not a nymph. She nods and hands you back your hook, a strange look in her eyes.

You turn away to put your hook and line back onto the fishing rod, when you hear a cry of triumph from behind you. You turn to see the nymph going through your back pack.

'This is my hair!' she shouts, holding up the water nymph hair. You recognise her now, of course. It is Damara, who'd conspired with Jas your butler to trick and rob you! In her other hand, she has some of your money.

'Hah! I can't wait to my lover, Jas, that I've finally outwitted you!' With that she dives over the side of the bridge and into the river. You step up to take a shot at her, but she turns into a fish, and swims out of sight. You shake your head ruefully. You should have killed them all when you had the chance, you think to yourself.

Cross off the **water nymph hair** and up to 100 pyr, if you have it, and give yourself the title **Tricked by a Water Nymph**. As that's ruined your fishing trip, you decide to move on. Where will you go?

West on the Way	▶ 20
South-west into the forest	▶ 189
East on the Way	▶ 380
South into the lush river valley	▶ 403

365

If you have the codeword *PatchupThree* ▶ 526 immediately. If not, read on.

You are on the Sacred Way. From here, it runs west along the northern coast, and south along the eastern shore. The terrain around about is lightly wooded with much bush and bramble. To the south-west, it gives way to the verdant farmlands, the grain basket of Arcadia. Or at least it used to be.

You also notice a small temple, surrounded by a copse of trees to the south west.

Nearby, a large net is slung between four wooden poles, clearly designed to catch something falling from the sky but it in a state of disrepair. It will cost you 20 pyr to have it fixed. If you wish to do so, cross off the money and get the codeword *PatchupThree*. Either way, from here you can go:

West along the coast	▶ 380
South along the coast	▶ 419
South-west into the farmlands	▶ 270
Investigate the temple	▶ 55

366

You can feel your shadow draining away, and it is horrible. You hack down at the thing but before your blow hits, it fades away, like ink down a plug hole. All that is left is a small patch of black dirt in the ground.... And thankfully, your shadow which appears fully intact. Gain the codeword **Penumbra**.

You wonder what sort of creature it was. Some kind of shadow-hunter? And was it chance it chose your shadow or was it sent? Perhaps you will find out later but for now you decide to move on, checking on your shadow as you do. Will you go:

West into the forest	▶ 189
North to the bridge	▶ 517
South to Ladon's Lake	▶ 37

367

You send for Mandrocles the boy engineer who is actually fifty-six years old but fell into a fountain of youth and now has the body of a nine-year-old boy. He fixed up the travel catapult at the Palace. It is not long before he arrives.

'Impressive, an entire fort as a house!' he says. 'You have come far, haven't you?' he says. You nod, and explain that you'd like him to build a travel catapult here like the one at the Palace.

Mandrocles nods, 'I can do that,' he says, 'but I'll need a few things.'

100 pyr
timber x 1
copper cog x 2
lava gem x 1

If you have one **timber**, two **copper cogs**, one **lava gem**, and 100 pyr and wish to give them to the boy engineer, then cross them off and ▶ 392

If not, you explain that you will send for him again later when you have what's needed. ▶ 220 and choose again.

368

You pull the lever and are lobbed high up into the air, speeding through the blue skies of Arcadia like an arrow shot from the bow of Apollo. It is terrifying but also thrilling. Down below you can see the dales of leaf and stream, so pretty in the bright sunlight. As you fly on, you spot a curious temple-like structure in a woodland clearing before you begin to drop out of the sky at an alarming rate, falling towards some grass-covered foothills. At this rate, you will be smeared like strawberry jam across the hilltops!   But then you see the catch-net that you're supposed to fall into rushing up to meet you at breakneck speed. If you do *not* have the codeword *PatchupSix* ▶ 647 immediately. If you do have it, read on.

You fall into the webbing of the catch-net safely. After you take a moment to catch your breath, you clamber down and take a look at your surroundings.

▶ 663

369

You slay the beast with a quick thrust to the heart so that it will not suffer, and then you skin it, and take the beautiful white pelt as a trophy. Gain the codeword *Pelt*.

When you are done, you stand up – and see that you have been surrounded. A pack of bushwhack wolves, and their handlers are just standing there, staring at you. The handlers, at least four or five of them, are human but heavily bearded and hairy, wearing clothes made from deer-hide. They carry goads with which they control the wolves but no weapons that you can see. You notice that their eyes are tinged with yellow.

One of them gestures, and the wolves step apart, forming a pathway through the forest. He indicates that you should walk that path.

You can see ten or more wolves, but you can tell there are even more of them amidst the trees, including more men.

You have no choice but to follow the path they have laid out for you.

▶ 4

370

❑

If you have the codeword *Plenty* ▶ 261 immediately. If not, read on.

Put a tick in the box. If there was a tick in the box already ▶ 290 immediately. If not, read on.

Here is where the Upper Tarn of Alpheus, the source of that ancient river, is to be found. But the lake is now little more than a dry dust bowl. Strangely, it is also stiflingly hot and dust devils dance across the baked and cracked mud of the lake bed, as hot air swirls skyward. In the high blue, birds ride the thermals, soaring majestically across the heavens.

As you draw near to the lake, you can feel gusts of hot wind blowing up and out, bathing you in heat. Where is that coming from, you ask yourself?

In the sky, dark grey clouds gather. You are reminded of what the bards and story-tellers say of the famous summer storms of Arcady.

'Arcadia's lush greenery is forever thirsty so the gods decreed many rainstorms: sudden, thunderous and bright with lightning.'

And sure enough, soon the heavens open and a storm-fall of water crashes down upon you. Lightning flashes in the sky, and thunder booms so loud it leaves your ears ringing. But it is short and sharp and soon the summer storm has moved on. It is just as well – these storms are the only source of water in Arcadia these days, ever since the river gods disappeared.

Around you the rains soaks into the earth but at the lake-bed, it starts to steam. Whatever is heating the bottom of the lake it's hot enough to evaporate water.

Nearby you notice the torrential rain has washed away a small mound of earth where someone had recently buried something. You find a curious stash inside – a jug of dandelion wine, a bag of bones, and a pouch with a gemstone worth about 50 pyr. Note the **jug of dandelion wine**, the **bag of bones** and 50 pyr on your Adventure Sheet. When you are ready, if you have the codeword *Pumped* ▶ 201 immediately. If not, read on.

There is nothing more for you to do here, so you move on. Where to?

North to the Druid's Shrine   ▶ 463

North-west skirting past the Shrine to the woods ▶ 620

Take the stairs in the cliffside down to the lower tarn ▶ 578

371

The woods grow darker still, and the trees seem to crowd in around you, as if trying to block your path in silent outrage that you should dare to come here.

You find the clearing with the two dead hunters, and now the remains of the Nemean lion itself, its flayed carcass long since devoured by wolves, ants and flies. You pause for a moment, perhaps a pang of sorrow touching your heart for the poor lion. True, it was a man-eater, and probably killed hundreds, including satyrs, centaurs, nymphs and dryads, devoured over the years but still, it was a noble beast. Or perhaps you feel it got what it deserved, and the Vulcanverse is better off without it. Perhaps you feel pride that you defeated such a beast. Or perhaps you feel all those things.

Anyway, when you are ready, you can continue on in search of the heart of the forest or head back to 'civilisation'.

To the heart of the forest   ▶ 602

Leave the green gloom   ▶ 148

Out of the dark a face looms, lit by the red lava glow. The face is painted black on one side, white on the other. You fire up a lamp, and in the flickering light you see a man in grey robes stitched with a pattern of silver moons and golden suns.

'Ah, it is you. How fortunate,' he says in a soft whispery voice. If it weren't for the cavernous echo you might not be able to hear him at all, what with the bubbling sound of the lava and the rushing of hot air.

'Tell me who you are and what you are doing here, tell me quickly or you won't be feeling very fortunate at all,' you say threateningly.

'Hah! An entirely predictable response. Still, I will indulge you. I am the Master of Twilight, a son of Nyx, and I took the river god Alpheus and boiled him up. Now I keep him in a flask,' and he nods at the great glass jar hanging over the lava pool.

'The people of Arcadia need their river gods, release him immediately!' you demand.

'Laughably predictable as ever! You think that you, a run of the mill fortune-hunting mercenary, a deluded rogue who thinks they're a hero chosen by the gods, can defeat me? Bah, I am the Master of Twilight, and I have captured a god. You though, you I will destroy.'

With that he raises his arms and shouts, 'Destroy this fool, my deadly Nightshades!'

And out of the shadows black shapes swarm, rushing towards you like flickering shadows cast from an open fire.

If you have a **lightning flint** ▶ 414

If not ▶ 460

Put a tick in the box. If there was a tick in the box already ▶ 326 immediately. If not, read on.

A woman steps through a door at the back of the temple. She is dressed in a long white chiton, with a cloak and head scarf, edged with a green and yellow pattern and is of middle-age. Rather matronly one might say.

'Greetings, young hero,' she says, 'I am grateful you took up my contract. My name is Thekla, and I am a priestess of ever-green Demeter, apple-bearer, corn-mother and mistress of this house.'

You nod politely. If you have the codewords *Oedipus* or *Olifant* ▶ 691 immediately. If not, read on.

'But as you can see, the temple is in dire need of repair. If you can see to that, then I can open it up to the people and serve the goddess. Perhaps then they can farm the land again, with Demeter's blessing.'

If you have the title **Steward of the Summer Palace** ▶ 567; if not, read on.

You tell the priestess you will look into it but for now there is nothing you can do but move on. You can go:

West along the coast	▶ 380
South along the coast	▶ 419
South-west into the farmlands	▶ 270

374

You find a wagon stacked with several bodies of quarry slaves – worked to death it seems. Cruel indeed, but you take some of their clothes and, disguising yourself as a slave, and you are able to shuffle across the quarry unnoticed. ▶ 479

375

Even you cannot outrun so many wolves. They fall upon you in a frenzy and rip you apart like a pack of hunting dogs pulling apart a fox. You die in horrific, blood-drenched agony, but at least it is relatively quick.

▶ 111

376

You start playing a *hyporchema*, or festival dance tune, and it begins well, with the audience enjoying the rhythmic joy-filled melody, and you are able to build it up to a thrilling musical climax.

The crowd applauses enthusiastically. Velosina folds her arms with a 'humph!'.

'Well, then,' says Chiron, 'it's come right down to the wire, the final face-off.'

Velosina takes her last turn and plays a beautiful love song, a melody rich in heart and soul. After she's done, she nods at you. 'Beat that, then, mortal!' she says with a grin.

If you have the codeword *Quoit* ▶ 574; if not, read on.

One last play. Make a CHARM roll at difficulty 8.

Succeed   ▶ 412
Fail   ▶ 468

377

You have returned to the Wineries, and what a change! Everywhere, many satyrs are at work, either tending to the trees, or squeezing out the juices from the pomegranates – a fussy, labour-intensive job. On the other hand, many satyrs seem to want to do it, as break time includes plenty of pomegranate wine. If you have come to see if your share of the latest bottling of the harvest is ready ▶ 58. If not, from here, you can go:

North to the Arcady Trail   ▶ 238
West to Treycross on the Arcady Trail   ▶ 728
South on the Trail   ▶ 338
East to the bridge over the river Alpheus ▶ 14

378

You've brought down a decent sized deer, and you are able to harvest venison for five packs of venison sausages before the smell of the meat draws the wolves of the forest. There are too many of them to deal with so you take what you can, and leave. Note **venison sausages x 5** on your Adventure Sheet.

If you have a **hunting permit** ▶ 296
If not ▶ 232

379

You dream that you are trapped in a grey house where the walls, the furniture, the doors and ceiling – everything – is grey. You cannot get out and are beginning to panic when you wake up with a start.

You are lying on a slab at the back end of a cave. It is a kitchen of some kind, and three old crones are arguing.

'I'm sick of soup, sick of it!' says one in an ancient voice like dust and dirt.

'Well, I'm sick of roasts – trying to chew with just the one tooth takes forever. I want soup!' says another in a voice like dried-out mud.

'Oh, be quiet,' says a third, 'I'm trying to find a new recipe for a change,' her voice like iron filings mixed up with black treacle.

You risk lifting your head and looking around. The Grey Witches are sitting around a large cauldron. One of them is holding up an eye with which she is reading from an enormous book. If they have only one eye between them, and that is occupied, presumably they cannot see you.

Gingerly, you sit up, careful not to make a sound as the Grey Sisters continue their bickering.

'This one's strong. The meat'll be tough so we want something long and slow to tenderise it.'

'Bah, just stick her on a spit and roast her.'

'How do you know it's a her?'

'I don't! Who knows? I can't tell the difference anyway, and actually who cares? They're all vermin.'

'Tasty though.'

While they bicker, you consider your options.

Try and grab the eye   ▶ 624
Try and kill them quickly   ▶ 430
Run for it   ▶ 477

380

If you have the codeword *Plenty* ▶ 396 immediately. If not, read on.

You are on the Sacred Way on the coast of Arcadia. A fresh sea breeze comes off the waters of Oceanus to the north, and the scent of wild flowers and tree blossom wafts across the air. A summer sun warms your bones. To the south, impassable cliffs rise up to a plateau. From here, you can go:

West to a bridge   ▶ 517
East on the Sacred Way   ▶ 365
South-east to the Farmlands   ▶ 270

381

You snap out of the vision of your god. Out of the waters is rising a great figure, man-like with translucent skin that is also faintly scaled in silver, eyes like orbs of black ice, hair like thin tendrils of brown seaweed, sprouting out of the top of his head like a carrot-top, his fingers webbed and taloned. It is Alpheus, the river god, restored to life!

'What... what... what?' he intones in long, slow groans.

'You were imprisoned in a gigantic glass flask that was so hot, it turned you into steam,' you explain.

'Ah, yes, I remember now, that little twilight chap, what a tedious fellow.'

'Yes, he's dead now. I slew him in battle and released you,' you say.

'Hmmm? Oh, how dull to be back here again, though I must admit, better than that stuffy glass thing, it's true,' rumbles Alpheus.

'But you're the river god, surely that's a great thing to be?' you ask, surprised.

'At first, yes, it was, but it's been a long, long time. You wouldn't understand being a mere mortal, but for me...' He heaves a great sigh. 'Just same old, same old, day in day out.'

'Well, this must have been a bit of an adventure, then?' you say.

'I suppose so, but then again, I was boiled up in a jar for most of it, so who knows?' he moans.

'I freed your brother, Ladon, too,' you say, 'And now you and he can fill all the rivers and lakes again, and the people will be able to grow crops once more, and make wine and all of that.'

'Oh, that's what all this is about is it? Well, all right, then, I suppose, yes, we can do that. Nothing else to do anyway.'

'Why do you think you were imprisoned like that?'

'I don't know but something is afoot. A conspiracy, a plot – someone wants to spread chaos around, so they can take advantage, no doubt. But as to who? That I cannot tell you.'

With that he begins to fall back into the great lake that now fills the old tarn. The lake water is now gushing downriver over the falls to the lower tarn too.

'Wait! Don't I get a reward?' you ask.

'Eh?' says Alpheus. 'Umm.. well, I guess so. Let me see what I can find buried under all this mud at the bottom of my lake.'

Roll a die to see what he gives you:

score 1	**golden lyre** (+2)	
score 2	**winged sandals** (+2)	
score 3	**abacus** (+2)	
score 4	**iron spear** (+2)	
score 5	2 **lava gems**	
score 6	250 pyr	

Add your prize to your Adventure Sheet and gain the codeword *Plenty*.

When you are done, from here you can:

Go north to the Druid's Shrine ▶ 463
North-west skirting past the Shrine to the woods ▶ 620
Take the stairs in the cliff down to the lower tarn ▶ 545

382

You hear a faint howl in the distance, a wolf of some kind, they are common enough here in Arcadia. At least you hope it's a wolf and not that undead horror from Hades... You wait in trepidation but you do not hear it again. It is safe to move on.

You are on the Sacred Way. From here, it runs north and south. To the west, impassable cliffs rise up to another ridge of cliffs, upon which rests the Alpheus river plateau. From here you can go:

North on the coastal Way ▶ 365
South on the coastal Way ▶ 774
North-west to the Verdant Farmlands ▶ 270
South-west to the Woodlands of Ambrosia ▶ 60

383

You simply charge at the nearest thug – burned face. Burned face's eyes widen in fear and he just cuts Krio's throat there and then – you chop him down, and turn to the Celt, but he too has slit Selene's throat before you can save her either. You cut him down too, and turn to Deridedes. He squawks in terror and simply runs for the door. You chase after him and cut one of his legs out of from under him.

He rolls on his back, and begs for mercy, but there is none in your heart, not after what he has done, so you drive your blade deep into his guts and twist until he is dead.

It brings some satisfaction, but it will not bring back the lives of the Krio and Selene, innocent farmers both.

You return to the farmhouse to a terrible sight. Krio and Selene tied to chairs, blood soaking the walls, the floor, and them. They stare through sightless eyes, faces fixed in horror, at the ceiling, their throats yawning open like a second grin of death.

And there is Magnes and his brothers, staring in horror at their murdered parents.

What a terrible mess. You try to move their bodies, but Magnes won't let you. He won't even look you in the eye, it is clear he blames you. He and his brothers slowly begin to clear up, preparing their parents for burial, and simply burning the bodies of Deridedes and his thugs.

You can do nothing here. Magnes, without saying a word, makes it clear you are not wanted. It is time to go. With a shake of your head, you move on. Where will you go?

North to a bridge	▶ 14
South to the Sacred Way	▶ 832
East to the Sacred Way	▶ 833
West and the Arcady Trail	▶ 338

384

Lose the codeword **Prisoner**.

You are sneaking your way to the tree line when a shout goes up, and you see that Timandra has spotted you. Out from the trees emerges Damara of the black robes, dragging Jas along behind her on a chain. She yanks him up close and puts a long dagger to his throat...

Timandra, strides over towards you, and points to the ground. 'Put the money here!' she booms in a trumpeting voice and then steps back a few paces.

What choice do you have? You put down the 200 pyr (or as near as you can get) – she gestures with her swords for you to back away, and you do. Then the curiously humped and misshapen black robed figure comes forward, picks up the money, throws Jas to the ground and then the two of them disappear into the woods.

You untie a relieved Jas, who is suitably grateful. 'Thank you, great one, supreme hero of the age! Thank you, thank you,' he says, fawning all over you.

'Yes, yes, enough already,' you say.

'But you saved me, you did, you saved me! I was worried you'd just leave me to rot.'

'Unfortunately, I couldn't bring myself to do that, though I did think about it.'

'Oh, very funny, very funny.' Jas hesitates for a moment and eyes you uncertainly. He then shakes his head, 'No, no, my most beloved captain is joking, of course.'

'Hmmphh,' you grunt.

'Well, anyway, it's still a happy day,' he says, 'happy day indeed! I'll see you back home when you're ready, my captain!' he says. Then he capers off, singing happily. It is not long before he's bought himself a jug of wine at the market, before you see him heading onto the Arcady Trail back towards the Palace. You wonder where he got the money to buy wine? Surely his kidnappers would have taken it?

Anyway. The task is done, you have your butler back. Time to move on.

▶ 12

385

You leave the Palace behind. As you walk, something doesn't sound quite right in your pyr pouch. The coins don't rattle in the way they usually do. You look inside and realise that the money you took off of the two boys is counterfeit! It's just cheap painted copper... Somehow during the game, they replaced the pot with fake coins. The little swines have ripped you off – so much for playing by the rules, no, they played you instead. Remove 75 pyr from your Adventure Sheet.

You consider returning to Lefkia to demand your money back but then again, you don't want to disturb her in her work or upset the schedule in any way. Also, it's rather embarrassing to have to admit to being outsmarted by a couple of ten-year-old kids. Best leave it, put it down to experience and a lesson learned. Though if you ever find the little bastards again...

Time to move on. ▶ 547

386

You manage to dart into the cover of the trees with the screaming Bacchantes snapping at your heels. You dart away through the trees, but they surge after you. Many trip and fall, but are there so many of them it doesn't really matter. They fan out, fast, fuelled by frenzy, unheeding of the whip of the branch, the ripping thorn, the sting of the nettle. Soon they will be on three sides of you.

They are closing in. You can:

Try and pass yourself off as a woman	▶ 295
Climb up into the treetops	▶ 231
Hide in a bush or forest gully	▶ 133

387

❑

Put a tick in the box. If there was a tick in the box already ▶ **725** immediately. If not, read on.

You land a large river fish. Something appears to be bulging inside it, and you decide to gut it there and then. In its stomach you find an old clay tablet, a prayer tablet probably thrown into the river as a supplication to the river god, Ladon. It reads:

'I, Polycrates, killed her, my wife. The farm is mine now, as is my beloved but guilt gnaws at my soul. Please, O river, take my confession, and my guilt with it! O Ladon, although I may not be forgiven, let my crime be forgotten and let it rest on the river bed for all eternity!'

Well, it seems his crime has not been forgotten after all. Note the **confession of Polycrates** on your Adventure Sheet. No doubt you will find someone to show it to later. You decide to move on. Where will you go?

West on the Way	► 20
South-west into the forest	► 189
East on the Way	► 380
South, into the lush up river valley	► 403

388

You look for tracks but your wood craft is not up to the task and you are unable to find a way. The shrine is lost to you. For now. You can always come back and try again later. Will you go:

North on the Way	► 419
South on the Way	► 801
West into the Woodlands	► 60

389

The fountain is low and wide, made out of time-stained marble, as is the statue above it. The statue is of a beautiful young woman, exquisitely carved from white marble, though it is mottled with lichen and moss now. Judging by her sleeveless dress, and the cup she holds in one hand, it is of Hebe, cup bearer to the gods, and also the goddess of youth. In her other hand, she holds out a little casket with three empty indentations, as if expecting an offering of some kind. Lava gems, perhaps?

Could this be some kind of fountain of life or youth? Not that it matters for without the flowing waters of the Alpheus it clearly ran dry a long time ago. There is nothing else you can do here, so will you:

Investigate the cliffside door	► 235
Climb the stairs up the cliff	► 370
Go south along the river	► 684
Go south west to the old arch	► 340

390

You cut your arm with your dagger. Tick the Wound box on your Adventure Sheet.

The wolf's ears prick up. He can smell your blood, sense your weakness. He turns, terrifyingly calmly and paces towards you. Close up, you can see he is large for a wolf but not especially so. His fangs are white and sharp, his fur also white, and remarkably clean. No, it is not his wolf body that is so terrifying, it is his eyes, yellow like the wolf, but full of a terrible intelligence, bright with cunning, like that of a man.

But his eyes fill with feral blood lust and the urge to finish off a weakened prey – he leaps at you. Instinctively, you step back, but with a snap, the trap shuts around his leg, and he yelps in agony.

Alpha bites down at the wood, but it is too sturdily built, so the wolf turns its attention to the cords that tie the trap to the tree. You step up, ready to deliver the killing blow.

Realisation dawns in the wolf's eyes, just like it would if he were human. He cannot bite through the cord in time. Immobilised as he is, he would not be able to avoid the thrusts of your blade. Alpha sinks to the ground, and looks up you, resignation in his eyes. He is readying himself for death. He knows he has been beaten.

| Kill the wolf | ► 369 |
| Let him go | ► 408 |

391

You've bagged a rather small deer, and you are only able to harvest venison for 3 packs of venison sausages before the smell of the meat draws the wolves of the forest. There are too many of them to deal with so you take what you can, and leave. Note **venison sausages x 3** on your Adventure Sheet.

If you have a **hunting permit** ► 296
If not ► 232

392

It takes a couple of days of hard work until Mandrocles is finished. He proudly presents you with the Fort Blackgate travel catapult, set inside the walls, on a large circular moving platform that you can crank around to target the four corners of Arcadia.

'It's all calibrated perfectly,' says the boy Man, 'I've checked.'

'I hope so!' you say. 'I don't want to end up smeared all over something like tomato purec.'

'Fear not, I am Man, the boy engineer! I know what I'm doing, trust me.'

You nod. ► 220 and put a tick in the box marked travel catapult.

393

Your uncle scoops you up and draws his sword, which he holds up to the window. You are spellbound by the play of yellow fire across the dark brown metal.

'See those chips in the blade?' says Nicomachus in a tone that is half a laugh, half a snarl. 'Each a foe who'll never trouble me again!'

He holds you up to the family as you run your fingers over the bronze sword. 'See? Our little one is a true follower of the Abundant One, the Leader of Armies, the Blood-Stained Bane of Mortals.'

On your Adventure Sheet, mark Ares as your god and then ► 769

394

You descend once again into the cavern that holds the imprisoned Alpheus, who has been reduced to vapour.

At the bottom of the ladder you look around and spot the man in grey robes, stitched with patterns of silver moons and golden suns, looking up at the great alembic containing the vaporised Alpheus.

'Hello again,' you say. The Master of Twilight turns to face you.

'What? You again?' he says in his whispering voice. 'Well, then, so it is true what they say!'

You nod with what you hope is a chilling smile.

He just laughs and says, 'So, I must destroy you again. Kill this fool, my deadly Nightshades!' he shouts, pointing at you with his staff.

This time you are ready for him. Or are you?

If you have a **lightning flint** ▶ 414

If not ▶ 460

395

You step towards the young man with his flowing locks of lustrous black hair, beautiful brown eyes and alluring good looks. He nods in greeting and smiles a slow, enigmatic smile, white teeth bright like sun on snow. He turns, and walks away through the crowd with you following on behind. Even his gait is graceful and balletic. Every now and then, he looks behind at you and smiles. You find your breath catching in your throat when he does, for he is so unavoidably captivating.

He leads you to a simple square canvas tent at the edge of the market. He lifts the tent flap, and gestures for you to enter. Your heart skips a beat when he smiles reassuringly at you, and you find it hard not to stare in wonderment at his divinely handsome good looks. You think that perhaps he is a god, but then again, perhaps not. There is something about him you can't quite put your finger on…

Anyway, will you enter the tent? Your heart aches with longing to be with him but then again, your head is the ruler of your heart. Isn't it?

Enter the tent ▶ 765
Walk away ▶ 742

396

You are on the Sacred Way on the coast of Arcadia. A fresh sea breeze comes off the waters of Oceanus to the north, and the scent of wild flowers and tree blossom wafts across the air. A summer sun warms your bones. To the south, impassable cliffs rise up to a plateau. Nestled at the foot of the cliffs is the limestone quarry, now run by Archimedes (but not that Archimedes). From here, you can go:

West to a bridge ▶ 517
East on the Sacred Way ▶ 365
South-east to the Farmlands ▶ 270
South to the quarry ▶ 641

397

'You are truly an enterprising adventurer, and I am honoured to have you as my captain!'

You nod. 'It wasn't easy to get all this stuff.'

Suddenly Drosos yelps out loud – Kraterus has pecked him through the bars of his cage!

'Silly old goat!' screeches Kraterus.

You stifle a smirk and say, 'So, how long do you think it will take?'

'Well, I've got to fertilize the fields, get the quern stones working and hope Kraterus treats the hens better than he treats me, but that's the easy bit, really. The hard part will be getting all the farmers and farmhands to come back. That will take time.'

Gain the codeword **Plough**. There is nothing more to be done here, you'll have to come back later to check on progress. For now, where will you go?

North-east ▶ 365
North-west ▶ 380
South-east ▶ 419

398

You wake to find yourself sitting at a long banqueting table, in the middle of a wooded dale. A bouquet of yellow lilies and their seed pods sit in a vase by your side, filling your nostrils with their musky scent.

It is early evening, the moon is rising, and tall lantern poles illuminate the scene. In front of you is a silver goblet, and a big silver bowl with a fork and spoon.

You look up, and your vision swims. You blink to try and clear your eyes but your mind is fogged still, full of conceits and fancies that do not seem to be yours. You look around, everywhere there are revellers drinking at their seats or cavorting wildly or making love at the edge of the clearing under the shadow of the trees. There are dryads, nymphs, satyrs and… but wait. They have the heads of animals: cows, deer, stags, dogs, wolves, even fish. There is much talk but it seems to be a language you recognize but cannot understand. You stare in fascination, looking around wide eyed and barely sensible.

A young woman with the head of a cat, giggling and purring, fills your cup with an amber liquid. '*Drink!*' says a booming voice in your head, and you lift your goblet and drink without thinking. The golden wine is so delicious, you quaff it all in one long draught. Around you, the other guests applaud wildly. Some, you cannot help but notice, appear to be clapping with hooves that clack like castanets, others with clawed paws that barely make a sound.

Another woman, this one with the head of a mouse, squeaks at you, and slops some kind of meat stew into your silver bowl.

'*Eat!*' says the booming voice in your head. You spoon the spicy stew into your mouth without demur. It is utterly delicious, sweet and tender, although you cannot tell what kind of meat it is, as you have never tasted it before.

Soon a group of dryads, covered in leaves and weeds, dance a slow, swaying *Apollonian*, an ancient ritual dance usually performed at funerals.

You drink and eat the entire evening away, the wine clouding your mind even more, so that you look around, wide eyed, smiling wanly, taking in the extraordinary scenes, like a child at a wedding. The revels go on 'til dawn, when you finally crawl under the table and fall into a long, deep, dreamless, sleep.

▶ **432**

399

You reach for the hilt of your weapon, and she quails back in fear, but then you shake your head.

'It's all right, I'm not going to kill you, nor will I demand a kiss. You can go.'

Damara heaves a sigh of relief. 'Thank you for your mercy,' she says, and turns to go. But then she hesitates.

'I couldn't... you wouldn't... I shouldn't ask after all that's happened but... would you give back my hair? It's just that... it's a living part of me, do you see?'

You shrug your shoulders. You haven't found any other use for it, so why not? You hand her the **water nymph hair**. Cross it off your Adventure Sheet.

'Thank you again!' she says, as she puts it up to her head. You watch, fascinated as it seems to burrow into the rest of her sea-weed hair, as if making itself at home.

'And I'm glad you didn't kiss me, as my kiss doesn't let you breathe underwater at all. You'd a probably drowned if you'd tried it!' With a raucous laugh, she dives over the side of the bridge, turning into a fish on the way down, and disappears into the river. Such a trickster! Anyway, there is nothing more to be done here, you're feeling fished out for the day, so where will you go?

West on the Way	▶ **20**
South-west into the forest	▶ **189**
East on the Way	▶ **380**
South into the dried-up river valley	▶ **403**

400

You have come down out of the high mountains of Boreas along the Sacred Way into Arcadia. The contrast could not be more different. Ice bound mountains have given way to seas of trees under bright blue skies and a summer sun. The sounds and smells of summertime fill the air – birdsong, the hum of the bee, the buzz of the dragonfly, glinting in the sunlight, the heady scents of herbs and the sweet bouquet of wild flowers. But what deadly dangers and hidden snares await beneath this Arcadian paradise?

▶ **158**

401

You walk into the tent of Zenia the fortune teller – or, more accurately, her tea shop. She is behind her counter, wearing her full 'old witch' disguise – long warty nose, wig of baldness, nails painted to look cracked and blackened, wisps of silvery hair hanging off her chin and so on.

'Ah it's you!' she says vigorously, not bothering with her old lady voice. 'I hope you've brought some mushrooms?'

If you have some **kykeon mushrooms** ▶ **810**; if not, read on.

'Ah well,' says Zenia, 'come back when you've found some, and I'll show you your future – or a possible future. Or maybe the past, it all depends, really.'

Head back to the market	▶ **728**
Leave the area	▶ **12**

402

As you are considering your options, one of the guards spots you hiding in the bushes!

'Ho, ho! What have we here?' says the hoplite guard, stepping over, a couple more men behind him. You try to make a dash for it, but trip over some brambles and within seconds you are surrounded by five or six armoured soldiers. You leap to your feet only to be knocked back down again. One of them readies his spear to finish you off when a loud voice sounds out

'Stop, you oaf!' A woman, dark eyed, with red hair under a wide-brimmed black hat, and long yellow robes shoulders her guards aside. She holds a long ebony staff topped with a snake, a dagger and a key, made from bronze. Over her face she wears a pale white mask.

'We need every slave we can get, hold them down while I cast the spell,' says the masked woman.

'Yes, Mela,' says one of the guards, clearly terrified of her, and he signals to the others. You struggle but there are simply too many of them and they pin you to the ground. Mela the Sorceress stands over you, gesturing with her staff and making arcane symbols in the air with her other hand.

'I bind the soul, the work, the hands and mind: all of these I bind by Hecate the Saffron Cloaked!' she intones ritually.

You find your eyelids drooping and your mind numbing. She continues on, chanting a spell that begins to tighten around your very soul, like chains of iron. 'I bind thee by the sword of Ares, the grace of Artemis, by Apollo of the silver tongue, and the wisdom of Athena!' she continues.

If you have a **heart of ash** or a **heart of oak** ▶ 191 immediately. If not, ▶ 446

403

❑

If you have the codeword *Plenty* ▶ 795 immediately. If not, read on.

Put a tick in the box. If there was a tick in the box already ▶ 775 immediately. If not, read on.

The river-bed is desiccated, baked in the Arcadian summer sun that beats down on your face. Fish bones rot in the dried-up mud. You contemplate climbing down the banks and rooting through the crumbling dirt, looking for lost treasures, but it would be messy work indeed, and likely all you'll find are fish heads and stink.

And then you feel a curious itch. You reach to scratch it, but realise that somehow the itch is inside your head. Make an INGENUITY roll at difficulty 8.

Succeed	▶ 501
Fail	▶ 719

404

Deridedes sighs in disappointment. There's a titter or two from the audience, but not much more than that.

'Poor, very poor,' says Deridedes, 'a school boy insult.' but then Kraterus suddenly crows 'silly-old-goat!' and the crowd laughs. Deridedes eyes widen in surprise.

'Cock likes it though,' you mutter. 'One point to me!'

Deridedes can hardly believe it, but he puts the mask up to his face, which amplifies his words a little, and counters with

'You pie-faced loon, where'd you get that numpty chump-head from – yer malformed mum?'

The crowd laughs uproariously and Deridedes steps back, expecting Kraterus to give his approval too, but the cockerel remains silent.

Deridedes' face falls at which you smile with grim satisfaction. Now it's your turn to launch an insult but which one?

'A malodorous whiff of rot surrounds you like a cloak of dung, and that's not the only reason nobody likes you!' ▶ 469

'You reek of ass!' ▶ 549

405

'Aristippus is the murderer!' you say out loud.

'Stupid mortal,' says a stony voice in your head, and you are suddenly transported elsewhere. Roll a die:

score 1-2	▶ 222 in *The Hammer of the Gods*
score 3-4	▶ 222 in *The Pillars of the Sky*
score 5-6	▶ 222 in *The Houses of the Dead*

If you do not have all the books, simply re-roll until you are transported to a book you do have.

If you do not have any of the other books in the Vulcanverse, you are transported to the north-west corner of Arcadia. ▶ 158

You pull the lever and are hurled up into the blue like an arrow shot from Artemis's bow. Your heart leaps into your mouth and your legs turn to jelly but soon fear turns to exhilaration as you fly across the sky. You see the Arcady Trail down below, like chalk marks on stone and then nothing but trees, until you start to plummet downwards toward the Sacred Way below. At this rate, you will be splattered over the grey stone like a rotten tomato!   But then you see the catch-net that is designed to break your fall safely rushing up to meet you at horrifying speed. If you do *not* have the codeword *PatchupSeven* ▶ 143 immediately. If you do have it, read on.

You fall into the webbing of the catch-net safely. After you take a moment to catch your breath, you clamber down and take a look at your surroundings. ▶ 154

You start playing a 'hyporchema' or a festival dance tune, and it begins well, with the audience enjoying the rhythmic joy-filled melody, but you miss a note or two on the chorus and they shake their heads, tutting in irritation.

'All right, all right, that's it, I'm afraid,' says Chiron. 'I call Velosina the winner,' says Chiron.

'But there's another round to go!' you protest.

'Nevertheless, it is clear to me, Velosina just isn't going to make the mistakes she'd have to make to lose this now, so there's no point continuing.'

You sigh resignedly, as Chiron gives her the scroll. 'Here is Sappho's poem, rather a sad, tragic piece but beautiful all the same. It's called "My lover lies with Ladon".'

Velosina accepts it with a bow, as the crowd applaud. She turns to you, 'Ah well, you gave it your best shot,' says Velosina, slapping you on the back heartily, 'and I've won a fine Sappho original, and without having to do much at all, really, so thank you.'

'I'm sorry you lost,' says Chiron, 'but is there anything else I can help you with?'

▶ 90

Suddenly filled with sympathy for the magnificent creature, you reach down and open the trap, releasing it. For a second or two the wolf doesn't move, before it realises what you have done.

Then it leaps up, and stares at you, yellow eyes blazing, before uttering a short, sharp bark, and out of the trees step more wolves, a full pack of at least ten of them. Have you been a complete, soft-hearted fool, you wonder to yourself?

▶ 418

If you have the title **Arcadian art dealer** ▶ 294 immediately. If not, read on.

If you have the codeword *Painter* ▶ 478 immediately. If not, read on.

The gallery is a long rectangular room. Along one wall is a great mural, running the entire length of the gallery, depicting scenes from the Trojan war from a fleet of ships, to the wooden horse and the sack of the city. In between Achilles battles Hector, Ajax wields his great shield, the gods intervene aiding their chosen favourites and soldiers fight and die under a cruel sun, time and time again.

On the other wall paintings are hung in the more traditional manner, while in the middle, on several stands are some beautifully painted pots and cast bronze sculptures. Most of them have been created by the great masters of ancient Greece – Agatharcus, Eupompus, Zeuxis, Parrhasius and Apelles to name but a few. Most of the paintings are for sale, at quite high prices in fact.

Just then a door bursts open at the back and in rushes a tall, stocky woman, muscled like a blacksmith, dressed in a food-stained chef's outfit.

'Hi there, I'm Erifili, the head chef and also the curator of this wonderful gallery! Yes, yes, I'm built like a marble shit-house, it's true, as I was once an Amazon warrior but food and art are my true passions not all that fighty stuff!' She shows you around the gallery and tells you some of the stories behind the art and the mural. It seems all the painters are long dead, except for one, Parrhasius, who has an art studio in Arcadia somewhere.

If you are carrying **the portrait** by Apelles ▶ 181

If not, there is nothing else you can do here, so ▶ 282 and choose again.

You wake to find yourself beside a track, the Arcady Trail, that runs through this wooded land. Nearby birds twitter loudly in the trees.

Arcadia is a woodland paradise – or at least it was once, until its rivers ran dry. But still, it is home to centaurs, dryads, nymphs, the fae, satyrs, wolves, bears and mankind too, amongst other creatures. Many adventures await you.

▶ 686

You have returned to the woodlands of Ambrosia. As you go deeper into the trees, you find nothing and no one. All is silent, as if all of the forest folk, even the woodland animals, are avoiding you and they probably are, out of fear no doubt, for you slew the oldest and most ancient of the dryads of the

Woodlands, Phearei. There is nothing more for you here.

Return to Sivi's beehives ▶ **8**
Leave this place ▶ **225**

412

You decide on difficult piece written by Limenius, composer of the Delphic Hymns. It's reasonably well known but is also known for its complexity. You begin well, and manage to pull it off without making any mistakes. Velosina and the audience are impressed.

It is time to find out who has won. You and Velosina stare up at Chiron expectantly. The old master pulls a hand down his beard several times, thinking. And then he pronounces judgement.

'I think the human has just edged it, I'm sorry Velosina,' he says. 'That last song, what skill!'

The crowd applaud, and Velosina takes her defeat with good grace.

'Fair enough,' she says, slapping you on the back heartily. 'You did well – for someone with only two legs,' and she laughs.

Chiron presents you with the musical scroll of Sappho. 'Here is Sappho's poem, rather a sad, tragic piece but beautiful all the same. It's called "My lover lies with Ladon".'

Note **Sappho's song** on your Adventure Sheet. When you are ready, Chiron congratulates you and says, 'Is there anything else I can help you with?' ▶ **90**

413

You have successfully reconsecrated this shrine, by hiring a priest to look after it. He greets with you with a cheery wave, and offers to pray to Apollo on your behalf. You can get blessings here. If you are a worshipper of Apollo and do not have the title **Unfriended by Apollo**, blessings are free. If not, you must pay 10 pyr per blessing. You can only have a total of three blessings at a time. Once you've decided on your blessings, read on.

If you have the codeword **Plight** ▶ **480** immediately. If not, read on.

When you are finished here, you can return to the Sacred Way ▶ **20**

414

Thinking fast, you pull out the lightning flint and strike it. A great flash of white light illuminates the entire cavern for a second or two.

Instantly the Nightshades are blown away, and the Master of Twilight staggers back, blinded for a moment.

'Now we'll see who's the fortunate one,' you say through gritted teeth, hefting your weapon.

'I wasn't expecting that, true, but I am no mere master of shadows, oh no!' With that he draws two swords, one dark and dripping with venom, the other bright, with flickering flames along its edge.

The Master of Twilight grins at you. 'These are my swords, Sunsmoke and Duskvenom.'

You must fight. Make a STRENGTH roll at difficulty 7.

Succeed ▶ **516**
Fail ▶ **483**

415

You are making your way through the woodlands, heading back to your mistress, your love and the light of your life, Phearei, hoping to gift her with some food of the gods. Surely this will please her, and she will spend some time with you? Deep down inside of yourself you are disgusted with your love-sick fawning but your heart is smitten. Yet in your heart of hearts you know it isn't real, but you are powerless.

You stumble across the grave of Karya, the dryad that was rejected by her mortal lover and killed herself to be with him. Upon her headstone reads the epitaph:

*'THE LOVE THAT LONGEST LASTS IS THE LOVE THAT IS UNRETURNED
– ANTEROS, GOD OF UNREQUITED LOVE'*

You muse on Davides, the hairdresser of Hades. He too was enchanted by a dryad and escaped by killing himself. And you won't be sent to Hades for all eternity, the gods will bring you back to life. That is your way out. But the thought of never seeing Phearei's face again, of losing that love, even though you know that love is false, fills you with trepidation. You will have to convince your own soul... Make a CHARM roll at difficulty 7.

Succeed ▶ **431**
Fail ▶ **74**

Terrified, you try to outrun them but it is no good, they are too quick. Several of them throw themselves at you, and although you are able to shake them off, they slow you down enough and moments later you are engulfed by a pack of shrieking, frenzied furies, tearing, biting and ripping at you with nails, teeth and bare hands, intent on sacrificing you to the mad god. You are overwhelmed and literally torn to pieces in a matter of seconds, and your body scattered to the four winds. Well, those bits of it that weren't eaten that is.

▶ 111

If you have the title **Archon of Wines** ▶ 377 immediately. If not, read on.

If you have the codeword *Press* ▶ 227 immediately. If not, read on.

You have come to a wide-open space of neatly arranged rectangular fields, but now they are untilled and neglected. This was once the great vineyard of Arcadia. Vines are arranged neatly in row after row after row – except they are all withered and dead, every single one. Grapes do not grow here anymore, drunken satyrs do not crush them with their hooves, the wine of Arcadia, called the Nectar of the Gods is made no more.

If you have a **Contract: Winemaker** ▶ 106. (To check if you have it, note **417** in your Current Location box, ▶ 101 and then return to this section after). If you haven't got it, there is nothing more you can do here for and you will have to come back later. From here, you can go:

North to the Arcady Trail	▶ 238
West to Treycross on the Arcady Trail	▶ 728
South on the Trail	▶ 338
East to the bridge over the river Alpheus	▶ 14

You look behind – perhaps you can make a run for it, but more wolves emerge from the forest shadows. Perhaps it is now your turn to ready yourself for death.

But the wolves form themselves into two lines, creating a path through the woods. Alpha walks down it, turns to look at you, and then points down the path with his head.

He wants you to follow him. You hesitate, but Alpha trots up to you, and actually nuzzles your hand in a gesture of reassurance before setting off down the path once more, heading into the deep forest. With a sigh, you decide to follow him. After all, what could possibly go wrong?

▶ 22

If you have the codeword *PatchupFour* ▶ 540 immediately. If not, read on.

You are on the Sacred Way. From here, it runs north and south. To the west, impassable cliffs rise up to another ridge of cliffs, upon which rests the Alpheus river plateau.

Nearby, a large net is slung between four wooden poles, clearly designed to catch something falling from the sky but it in a state of disrepair. It will cost you 20 pyr to have it fixed. If you wish to do so, cross off the money and get the codeword *PatchupFour*.

If you have the codeword *Neverending* and you do *not* have the **golden arrow of Artemis** ▶ 341

If not, from here you can go:

North on the coastal Way	▶ 365
South on the coastal Way	▶ 774
North-west to the Verdant Farmlands	▶ 270
South-west to the Woodlands of Ambrosia	▶ 60

You do battle with the champion of Death on the banks of the river Ladon. Long and hard you fight, but mighty though you are, you begin to tire. But Death Dealer, immortal spirit of battle that he is, does not. In the end, you are overcome, and he batters you into unconsciousness.

You wake to find yourself tied up in the back of a cart, being pulled along by Death Dealer on his mighty black charger that he calls Daisy, of all things…

He has dragged you all the way to hell! Up ahead looms the volcano of death, the abode of Thanatos himself.

'Almost there, Daisy,' mutters Death Dealer to his horse. You need to think fast to avoid oblivion at the hands of death himself.

Make an INGENUITY roll at difficulty 7.

Succeed	▶ 247
Fail	▶ 199

❑

Put a tick in the box. If there was a tick in the box already ▶ 83 immediately. If not, read on.

You invite many of your friends to the banquet, Maron, the wine-drinking ever-drunk Satyr, Sivi the beautiful honey dryad, Hypatia of Iskandria the architect, ever-smiling and cheerful Lefkia, Mandrocles the boy engineer, the putative King of Arcadia, Nyctimus, Drosos the farmer, Chiron the centaur and many more that you have met on your adventures.

It is a merry evening, with much pomegranate wine and a sumptuous dinner wonderfully cooked by Erifili and her team.

At midnight, you are about to propose a toast to King

Nyctimus when the hall doors burst open and in marches a figure, armed with swords and a spear. You note that he wears little armour, however, and that his skin seems to be tinged with a light blue colour, which is odd.

'I am Glaukos the Gorgon Guard and I have come to challenge the Commander of Fort Blackgate – in this case, you!'

'What? But why?' you ask, stepping down from the table.

'I seek glory, so that my name will be remembered forever along with the likes of Achilles, and Hektor and, of course, you, for you are the most renowned hero alive today. Well, until I've killed you that is, and then I will be the most renowned. Now come, to battle!'

'If you insist,' you say, gearing up for a fight, readying your weapon and so on.

'What are the rules?' you ask. 'First blood?'

'First blood? Of course not, to the death.'

'To the death? Are you sure?'

'Oh yes, anything else has no meaning, a mere practice bout. No, only by killing you will I gain glory.'

You look around, wondering as to the wisdom of this, but rather than attempting to stop the duel, your guests are re-arranging their seats to watch. You can hear some of them placing bets – most of them expect you to win, though, which is heartening of course, but still, it seems they're happy to be entertained by the possibility that you will be killed right in front of them. But then again, you are the hero of the age, right?

With a sigh, you ready your weapon, and take a duellist's defensive stance. You nod at your opponent – without warning, he instantly hurls his spear at you! But you are not so easily caught off guard and you dodge aside.

'Ah well, a long shot anyway,' says Glaukos, drawing two swords. That seems odd to you, fighting with a sword in each hand and no armour at all, but still. You circle each other, grimly. Behind you, your guests watch with bated breath, silent, expectant.

▶ 507

422

You are shown to your rooms, the 'Herodion Suite'. It's rather palatial, with a large lounge and dining area, a bedroom and a bathroom with a restful looking deep marble bath set into the floor. The walls are painted with murals – in the bedroom, salacious scenes of, well, 'Eros at work', put it that way. The bathroom has scenes of water nymphs and mermen bathing in Arcadian rivers, while the lounge area has one long mural around all four walls of a great feast in the forest at night, with dryads, satyrs and faerie folk carousing under starlight and the light of lamps hanging from the trees. The ceiling is a starry night sky.

There are fine furnishings and objets d'art and you even have your own attendant, a young satyr, a half human, half goat with the torso and head of a mortal man but with hairy goat legs and horns on his head. The satyrs are common creatures found across Arcadia; this one's name is Jas the Helot and he's your butler. Through him, you can order food from the kitchen, have a bath drawn, get your bed readied and so on.

On one wall in the lounge area, you see what looks like a cave entrance to the side of the forested banquet scene. On closer inspection you see that is in fact a door, painted to look like a cave entrance. It is flanked by two Kourai Khryseai or Golden Maidens, automatons created by Vulcan as his retainers who stand as painted guardians in the night. A plaque above the door reads 'The Vault of Vulcan in Arcadia'. It is locked – to get in you need the key.

▶ 100

423

The land drops away below the horizon and there is nothing but sky and sea all around. Climbing the rigging, you feel salt spray on your face and revel in the sensation of plunging into an unexplored cerulean realm with no limits.

When the sun is high you are a speck in blue immensity. Nights enfold the ship in a gulf of uttermost darkness flecked with moon-limned foam and starlight. When winds rise you ride through lightning-stoked storm and gunmetal swell. Dawns and dusks mix all the colours of creation on the palette of the heavens.

Your crew are uneasy so far out into the unknown, but they trust that in the mechanical motions of the astrarium you are able to read a true bearing back to harbour.

Where will you steer your course?

Iskandria harbour ▶ **837** in *The Hammer of the Sun*
The Shores of Psamathe ▶ **328** in *The Hammer of the Sun*
The east coast of Notus ▶ **200** in *The Hammer of the Sun*
The east coast of Arcadia ▶ **200**
The north coast of Arcadia ▶ **444**
The north coast of Boreas ▶ **444** in *The Pillars of the Sky*
The west coast of Boreas ▶ **200** in *The Pillars of the Sky*

424

You lie there barely conscious for a few precious minutes. You hear wolf-like howls behind you, and then whooping and hollering! They have found you…

You try to fight, but there too many of them and soon they tear you limb from limb, ripping out your entrails, and eating you up in a frenzy of bloodlust and greed. Death is agonising but quick.

▶ 111

❑

Put a tick in the box. If there was a tick in the box already ▶ **497** immediately. If not, read on.

You take out the **queen bee** you have stored carefully in your back pack and hand it to Sivi. Delete it from your possessions.

'By the Pipes of Pan, you found one! And look at her, how beautiful she is,' she says in her dark, syrupy voice.

Gently Sivi puts the queen bee into the one of the hives.

'I will nurture and protect her, and soon she will give birth to daughters and the cycle of bee life will begin,' says Sivi. 'Thank you – come back later and perhaps I will have a jar or two of pomegranate honey for you.'

Gat the codeword *Poll*. You say your farewells to the extraordinary Sivi, and go on your way. Will you:

Go deeper into the woods	▶ **176**
Leave this place	▶ **225**

426

You enter the courtyard of Fort Blackgate and shout a challenge at Kakas. He looks up, and then does a double take, looking from the body he is roasting on a spit and then back at you, and back at the body several times. You laugh out loud.

'Didn't I… haven't I… what the–?' he rumbles.

'I'm back. I told you, I'm no ordinary hero,' you say.

'I see. Well, then, I guess I'll have two heads on my wall, and a second dinner!'

Kakas moves in, swinging his club in great wide circles. Once again, you cannot afford to be hit, you will have to rely on your wits and agility.

Make a GRACE roll at difficulty 7.

Succeed	▶ **748**
Fail	▶ **720**

427

There are one or two titters in the crowd, but mostly you hear comments like 'what's a quacksalver?' and 'pettifogging? What does that mean?'

Deridedes says to you, 'Actually, I think that's your best yet, clever stuff, but wasted on this audience. And, I'm afraid, wasted on Kraterus the cockerel too!'

But then Kraterus crows a 'silly-old-goat.' Deridedes eyes narrow in anger. 'That little shit, I'll beat…'

'What was that, Deridedes?' you say at the top of your voice.

'Oh, nothing, nothing,' says Deridedes. 'Ladies and gentlemen, amazingly, and for the first time ever, we have a winner!' He raises your hand and says, 'I dub thee, Master of Mockery!'

You bow, as the crowd roars their approval. Deridedes

tries to hurry away but you grab his arm forcefully, take the money pouch off his belt, count out a 100 pyr, toss it back, jump off the stage, grab the cage holding Kraterus, and dash out as fast as you can before anyone can stop you. You race round the back, where you free the slave boy and give him his cut. He runs off with a shouted, 'thank you!' before he disappears into the crowd.

Note **Kraterus the cockerel**, the title **Master of Mockery,** and 50 pyr on your Adventure Sheet.

You are done here. You can return to the market place ▶ **728** or leave the area ▶ **12**.

428

Thekla, the priestess of Demeter is dressed differently today. She is wearing a brown chiton with a green mantle and is holding a mask on a stick, clearly the Mask of Demeter. 'Greetings! I'm afraid I can't bless any soil today, it's the festival of Thesmophoria, where we honour the goddess Demeter and her daughter Persephone.'

If you are female ▶ **150**; if not, read on.

Thekla continues, 'I'm afraid the festival is open only to women, you can't join in. It lasts for three days, so please come back when it's over. For now, I'm sorry, but I must be going, so many things to do, but thank you for your help, and may Demeter smile on you!' With that she leaves you with nothing more to do but travel onwards. You can go:

West along the coast	▶ **380**
South along the coast	▶ **419**
South-west into the farmlands	▶ **270**

429

You step forward drawing your weapon intent on slaying Soter and as many stags as you can but it only takes a second or two for you to realise your mistake.

Several more stags emerge – you strike at Soter, but your weapon gets entangled in his antlers and with a flick of his head he disarms you. From either side, stags charge in, knocking you to the ground, and trampling you underfoot. Soter gores you savagely as you lie stunned on the ground, and soon you are a mass of broken bones and bleeding flesh. You pass out. Soter and his gang trot away back into the mists of the forest.

After a while you come round to see a wolf tugging at one of your broken legs. You try to fight but you can barely move for most of your bones have been shattered. More wolves come out of the forest. You are forced to watch your own legs getting eaten before pain and blood loss mercifully ends your life. However, perhaps the gods will give you a second chance, despite your hubristic belief in your own skill.

▶ **111**

430

You leap to your feet, drawing your blade, and in an instant hack off the arm of the Grey witch holding the eye. They shriek in outrage, but now that they are completely sightless, it becomes an easy matter to finish them quickly, before they can act to fill you with fear or shake the ground around you. Heads roll and throats gush blood, as you slay them all. The Grey Witches, ancient beings from before the time of the Olympians, are no more.

You look around for loot, but, astonishingly, they have nothing save one enormous book of recipes, too heavy for even you to carry. No money, no hoard, no treasure. It seems they had no interest in such things, just in eating human 'vermin'.

You do however, pick up the eye. It is quite large, and fills your hand like a ball. And then it twists up to look at you, a white eye, in a pocket of grey skin, with a bright blue iris and a pupil that is like looking into the deep, dark depths of the ocean. You shudder and drop it into your pack.

You leave the cave of the grey witches and follow a path along the riverside, down the valley. After a while, you see a squat, stone tower off set from the stream, with a paved courtyard outside enclosed by a wall. A path runs downhill to entrance arch.

▶ 757

431

You cannot bear this moon-calf, love-sick fool that you have become. With a supreme effort of will, you put your so-called mistress out of your mind and cut your own throat. As your life's blood spills out onto the forest floor, you feel nothing but relief and the joy of freedom. Perhaps you will return and take your revenge…

▶ 111

432

You wake to find yourself sitting at a long banqueting table, in the middle of a wooded dale. It is early evening, the moon is rising, and tall lantern poles illuminate the scene. In front of you is a silver goblet, and a big silver bowl with a fork and spoon. Your brow furrows in puzzlement. Didn't you just…?

Everywhere there are revellers, cavorting, drinking, dancing, even behaving lewdly in public. They are dryads, nymphs, satyrs, and humans too but all have the heads of animals.

Once more, a young woman, this time with the head of a pigeon, appears at your side. She squawks at you and fills your bowl and goblet with food and drink. The booming voice sounds in your head again – 'Drink!' – and you are unable to resist its command, and drain your goblet.

'Eat!' says the booming voice and again, you slurp up the unknown meat, pale and pink and porky but you know it isn't pork.

Dryads dance the funereal Apollonian.

You drink and eat the entire night 'til dawn, when you finally crawl under the table and fall into a long, deep, dreamless, sleep once more.

▶ 496

433

You can see Alpha up ahead. Carefully, you lay down the wolf-trap and tie it securely to a nearby tree. Now you have to decide what to lure him into the trap with. You could try shouting a challenge, perhaps just you will be enough. Or you could spice it up with some meat – you'll need venison sausages or strix stew. Or you could use your own blood with a self-inflicted wound.

Shout a challenge	▶ 328
Put some meat down	▶ 347
Cut open your arm	▶ 390

434

The boys describe the rules of a simple game of knucklebones and you start playing, each rolling in turn. 'We keep gambling until one person has all the money,' they say.

The boys seem especially unlucky with dice, and it doesn't take long before you have it all. You feel a little bad at taking all the money in a gambling match from ten- or eleven-year-old boys, so you offer to give it back. They shake their heads, insisting you keep it.

'What sort of men are you teaching us to be when we grow up?' says Ataktos. 'Weak-willed shilly-shallyers!'

'Quite so, I mean if a boy's word is meaningless won't the man's be too?' says the other.

'But I can't take money off children!' you say.

'We set up the game and the rules, no point playing at all if you don't play by them,' says Pioataktos

'And that's the point of life, or so our mother says – there are rules, and if you live your life by them, then that is a life well lived!'

An interesting philosophical point. Maybe they are right, so you decide to keep the pot after all. The boys, looking a little dejected, take their leave, saying they are going home to their mother. You feel bad for them but then again, perhaps it is a lesson well learned. Add 50 pyr to your Adventure Sheet.

Shortly after, Lefkia comes back.

'Hello, hello! You're back! Where are the boys?'

'They went home,' you say. You don't mention that you took all their money in a gambling game.

'Ah, OK, I don't really need them anyway, I was just keeping them out of mother's hair. Anyway, do you have the things I need to start work?'

If you have:

box of paints x 2
vinegar of hades x 1
bucket of gypsum

and wish to hand them to Lefkia, cross them off your Adventure Sheet and ▶ **211**

If not, you tell Lefkia you will come back when you do, and take your leave. 'Don't take too long,' she says, 'I'm eager to get started!' ▶ **385**

435

The duel does not last long. The truth is that you are simply far more experienced a fighter than Nessus, who is just the leader of a gang of local thugs. You cut him down without even taking a wound. His men give a cry of despair as he falls to the ground, bleeding out on the forest floor.

He looks up at you, as he lies dying. 'Well fought,' he says. To his cut-throat crew he says, 'Let this one live, it was a fair fight.' He takes off his green tunic, and hands it to you.

'Here, this is yours by right of battle, take it, wear it, it will aid you.' And then he lies back, smiles up at the sky, gives one last laugh, and dies.

The rest of his warband begin packing their things up. Some start to leave. You watch them, uncertain as to their intentions, but they ignore you completely. The warband is finished. Gain the codeword *Payment*.

You also have the **tunic of Nessus**. Note it on your Adventure Sheet. If you want to put it on ▶ **509**. If not, or perhaps later, there is nothing more for you to do here, so you leave the forest.

▶ **189**

436

You have returned to the heart of the forest where the Great Green Ones are waiting for you. If you have the codeword *Purify* then ▶ **251** immediately. If not, read on.

If you have the codeword *Purged*, then ▶ **642** immediately. If not, read on.

If not, there is nothing else you can do here but make your way back to 'civilisation'. You can always come back once again, if you wish.

By following your own path back through the forest you are able to make it to the outskirts without too much difficulty. Thirsty, tired, and sweaty, you leave the deep forest.

▶ **148**

437

As you run past, you give the satyr a shove, throwing him to the ground right in front of the daemon-wolf. You do not pause to observe what happens next – the sound of screaming and the tearing of flesh is enough to tell you what is going down.

You make your escape through the woods. You try to tell yourself it was a worthy exchange, the life of a satyr for one who may well save the Vulcanverse, but guilt still gnaws at your soul. But then again, what is done is done.

▶ **60**

438

Mark your GRACE score as −1, then ▶ **459**

439

You dodge under the dragon's bite and slash upward with your Nemean claws. The ultra-sharpened talons slice through her armoured scales and rip open her throat.

Kaustikia reels back, as blood gushes like a hot crimson geyser from the mortal wound. She chokes out her life on floor of her cloud lair. At the last minute, she begins to laugh, cackling insanely, before she finally dies.

Why was she laughing? And then you realise why, for the cloud upon which you are standing simply dissolves away upon her death, leaving you falling through empty space. You hit the ground so hard that your body explodes like a ripe tomato, spraying your blood and guts across the forest floor. However, you have defeated the dragon.

Gain the codeword *Purify*.

Lose the codeword *Phosphoric*.

▶ 111

440

'Foolish mortal,' echoes the voice, and you are suddenly transported elsewhere ▶ **500**.

441

You manage to get to the treeline without getting seen. The improbably tall and terrible tyrant Timandra appears to be craning her neck trying to spot you amidst the crowd at the edge of the market.

Nearby, the hunched and twisted from of black-cowled Damara steps out of the trees as well. She hisses at Timandra, 'Where the Hades is that Steward?' she hisses.

'Sshh!' says Timandra, silencing her with a backward slash of her hand.

And then you see Jas… He's just behind Damara, tied up but standing right next to her.

'Watch out, you don't want to get in a fight with this one, believe me! We just take the money, I'll play rescued victim, and we can split the cash later.'

Hah! Why am I not surprised, you think to yourself. Probably his idea in fact, knowing him, the little sh–. In which case, who are Timandra and Damara really? Perhaps it's time to find out.

▶ 303

442

You rise the next morning to an entirely different day called *Nesteia*, the day of fasting. All the women sit in a circle around a large fire but without eating or drinking. The chairs upon which you sit are wreathed in a particular type of flower that gives off a scent that dulls your desire and numbs your senses. It is a day of subdued reflection upon Demeter's mourning at the loss of her daughter to the underworld in particular and the cycle of death and rebirth in general. You retire to your tent, tired and exhausted. A not so pleasant day.

▶ 522

443

Once again you have returned to the tent of your seducer, the handsome young man of the enchanting smile and the lustrous hair. You do not even know his name…

He welcomes you with a long, languorous kiss and ushers you into his lair once again. You are unable to resist his wiles.

If you have a **Blessing of True Sight** ▶ 528 immediately If not, ▶ 473

444

There is a sheltered cove here on the north coast of Arcadia.

> BOAT MOORED HERE? (Y/N)

If you have arrived by boat, note in the box that it is moored here. If your boat is here you can put to sea, otherwise you must go overland.

Set sail – delete the boat from the box above and then ▶ 292

Head inland to a range of hills ▶ 217

445

You move deeper in the forest, where the trees are greener, wilder and somehow more 'alive'. You notice a path opening up before you, as if the trees were somehow deliberately parting to allow you through. You hear the sound of voices on the air and the occasional girlish giggle. You see movement from tree to tree, a flash of wild hair here, a rainbow of wild flowers there. The path leads you to a big oak tree, draped in flower covered vines and creepers, and upon one of its branches stands Karya, the hamadryad.

'Hello, my mortal hero. Have you got my Davides?' she asks.

'I did find him, yes,' you say.

'Really? How wonderful! Where is he, he all right?'

'Kind of. He's a shade in Hades, true, but it's not like it used to be and he's opened a hairdresser shop, in fact.'

'Hah, hah, brilliant! And when will he be coming home?' says Karya, her eyes brimming with hopeful tears.

'Ah, well, that's the problem. He doesn't want to come

back,' you say.

'What do you mean?'

'I'm not sure I should…'

'Oh come on, tell me!'

'He… well, he said he never loved you, that you bewitched him into loving you, and that that is slavery not true love, and the only way to escape was to kill himself.'

Karya's face goes as white as a skull bleached by the desert sun. 'Wha… no… I…' stutters Karya.

Her tears of hope turn to tears of grief and she screws her face up into a mask of pain and heartbreak.

'Well, then, I will join him in Hades. Maybe he'll understand that my love is true after all!' With that, she wraps a vine around her neck, steps off the bough she stood upon and falls, the vine breaking her neck like a snapped twig.

In an instant she is gone. You stare astonished – she must really have loved her tree frog, Davides. How tragic.

Karya swings gently in a light forest breeze, her face a mask of sorrow, even in death. Leaves start to shrivel and drop from the oak. Its bark begins to harden and crumble. It too, is dying. Perhaps Karya and her oak tree were one and the same, the trees death compounding the tragedy. Gain the codeword *Perdition*.

You shake your head as your heart fills with sorrow. Such sadness, such despair. And then a sound behind you attracts your attention.

▶ 515

446

You are unable to resist her powerful magic, and you fall under the sway of Mela the Sorceress. Gain the title **Mindless Quarry Slave**.

Soon your thoughts turn to mud and you hear only the commands of your mistress and her minions. You find yourself hacking out chunks of limestone from the quarry, or loading frozen slabs of limestone and ice onto the wagons.

The work is hard and brutal – all the mindless slaves are worked into the ground and safety is of little concern. If a slave dies, Mela sends Theseus out to capture another.

This turns out to be a bit of luck for you – you are killed almost in passing by a falling limestone slab that crushes your skull, spilling your brains onto the dusty ground of the quarry. Painful and unpleasant to put it mildly but a dose of death will remove the spell you are under.

▶ 111

447

Unfortunately, Jas has been kidnapped and you have not yet ransomed him. Though he may be a rather irritating and somewhat disrespectful butler, without him you cannot get any of the true benefits of the Herodion Suite. Until he is rescued you can only:

Take a tour of your rooms	▶ 422
Enter the Vault of Vulcan in Arcadia	▶ 828
Leave your rooms	▶ 282

448

You run for your life through the trees. Fortunately for you, the bear is wounded and is limping, and you are able to outrun it. Fear gives your feet wings. Perhaps you can come back and hunt for the bear when you have healed up. For now, it is time to move on.

▶ 225

449

You manage to bring down a large, antlered stag! You are able to harvest venison for 7 packs of venison sausages and a set of magnificent antlers. Note the **stag antlers** and **venison sausages x 7** on your Adventure Sheet. Soon the smell of the meat brings several packs of wolves and you are forced to give up your kill to them and get out of there.

If you have a **hunting permit** ▶ 296. If not, ▶ 232

450

You do not find a mark, a scratch, a track or a trace anywhere. You have to admit, this Autolycus is good. Gritting your teeth in irritation you realise there is nothing you can do but retire and try and recoup your losses elsewhere tomorrow. Maybe you will encounter Autolycus again somewhere down the line and you can have your vengeance.

▶ 220

451

You try to strike at the thing but your brain feels fogged, and you are too slow. With a sound like a wine cork popping your shadow is sucked up into the black nothingness that is the creature. And with that it drains away into the earth like ink down a plug hole, taking your shadow with it.

It leaves you feeling bereft, like you'd lost a limb. Some part of you is forever weakened, although you cannot immediately tell what effect it may have upon you. All you are certain of is that you have no shadow, and no matter how you stand or move, even in the brightest summer sun of Arcadia, you no longer cast a shadow. Note the title **Hero without a Shadow** on your Adventure Sheet.

You wonder what sort of creature it was. Some kind of shadow-hunter? And was it chance it chose your shadow or was it sent? No doubt you will find out later but for now you must go on. Will you go:

West into the forest	► 189
North to the bridge	► 517
South to Ladon's Lake	► 37

452

Drosos, the farm overseer you hired to rebuild the farmlands is waiting for you.

'Good day to you, boss,' he says, 'Have you got the things I need to start work?'

If you have:

blessed soil of Arcadia x 3

grindstone x 2

Kraterus the cockerel

then ► 397

If not, you tell Drosos you will return when you have what he needs. For now, where will you go?

North-east	► 365
North-west	► 380
South-east	► 419

453

You duck under his sweeping club. Kakas is thrown off balance for a moment, and you are able to jab him with your weapon. He grunts in pain, but it is only a light wound, drawing little blood and he barely notices. There is so much fat and muscle it will be hard to hit anything vital.

And then Kakas raises his club, covering his face for a moment. You are about to take advantage of the fact that he can't see you when he lowers the club and breathes out a great cloud of fire at you!

► 523

454

You race for the safety of the woodcutter's cabin, a pack of wolves – no, two packs – yapping at your heels! Luckily for you, one of the wolves trips on a tree stump, and the others career into it in a mess of fur and claws. That gives you enough time to reach the hut but not before one of the wolves, faster than the rest, manages to bite your calf – tick your Wound box. You trip and fall against the cabin door, but the woodcutter opens it at the last second, letting you fall to the floor inside, before slamming it shut. He bolts the door behind you.

'Don't worry,' says Leonidas, 'the cabin is proof against any wolf attack, just so long as they don't bring their master.'

'Master? Alpha you mean? But I can see him, over there,' you say, tending to your bleeding leg.

'No, not Alpha, I mean Lykaon, the Wolf-King.'

'Ah....'

Fortunately, the King does not come, and after a time, the wolves give up and return to the trees.

'They will be alert and ready now, so best you leave while you can, but if you want to try again, please come back, I'll be here. Maybe you'll have better luck next time,' says Leonidas. Where will you run to?

West to the Sacred Way	► 324
East to the Arcady Trail	► 455
South east to a small wood	► 475

455

If you have the codeword *Neverending* and you do *not* have the **golden arrow of Artemis** ► 259 immediately. If not, read on.

You are following the Arcady Trail, a dusty well-walked path through the woods and overgrown hedgerows of Arcadia. The trail runs past the dales of leaf and stream and past a small wood that crowds the edges of the trail to the west. From here you can go:

North west into the Deep Forest	► 710
North	► 85
East	► 728
North east to the Palace	► 686
South east into the Dales	► 266
West into the small wood	► 475

456

You are not fast enough, and some acid catches the side of your face, causing you agonising pain. Tick the Wound box on your Adventure Sheet. If you are already wounded, then the pain makes you pass out and you never wake again, gobbled up by the dragon. ► 111

If you still live, Kaustikia cackles evilly. 'Soon you'll be my next meal,' she hisses, her voice sibilant and filled with malice.

She spits acid at you again, but this time you are able to dodge it. You realise you will have to kill her soon, or be struck by acid once more.

Make a STRENGTH roll at difficulty 11.

| Succeed | ► 439 |
| Fail | ► 356 |

457

You plummet earthward, shrieking the whole time. The forest canopy rushes up to meet you and you crash into it, smashing your way downwards through branch after branch, sending a flock of birds fluttering up into the sky, cawing in outrage at your unwanted visit – a feeling which is entirely mutual. And then you are knocked senseless.

You wake some time later to find you are hanging upside down, one leg wedged in a tangled mass of leaves and branches. Miraculously, although you are scratched and bruised, the branches broke your fall and you are not seriously injured. You look down to stare at your backpack which has fallen onto the forest floor. A squirrel scuttles up to it, sniffs, looks up at you, and then scuttles away.

Soon after, a young man steps up to the backpack. He is dressed in light leather armour, carrying a spear in one hand with a bow slung over one shoulder. He looks up at you – you can't help but notice how handsome he is. He smiles up at you roguishly. 'Well, what have we here?' he says in a rich, deep voice. 'Looks like my lucky day, free stuff!'

Desperately you try to reach up to your leg, but you are weighed down with armour and weapons, and you can't quite reach.

'Don't do it!' you bellow. 'Just help me down and I'll reward you.'

'Oh, I don't know. You look quite dangerous to me and the money in that backpack looks tempting…'

If you have the codeword *Query* ▶ 157

If not ▶ 626

458

You run for your life, terrified, as the wild women slowly gain on you. You dash into the tree-line of the dales and, to your surprise, the Bacchante horde veers away in a different direction, giving up on the chase. One of them pauses at the tree-line and hurls a skin of wine at you, before running off to join her sisters. You stop, panting for breath, leaning against a tree, and pick up the **golden wine of Dionysus**. Best not to drink of it, but it may prove useful. Note it on your Adventure Sheet.

And what turned them away? What lies within this Arcadian wood that they would not enter it? Some religious taboo? Or… something worse than them? What could that be?

▶ 266

459

There is no fire in the hearth, only ash. Outside is the cold blue of a winter's evening. The house feels as if something vital has gone out of it.

Years have passed. You are fully grown. Beside you, your mother is no longer the robust force of nature you remember but a thin little old lady.

'Two coins,' she says, holding them up. 'It's all we have to buy supper.'

It's only now you become aware of your brothers and sisters, all younger than you, huddled in silence at the back of the room.

'Give them to me, mother, and I'll fetch us something.'

'But then, how will he pay the ferryman?'

And it's with dread that you follow her eyes to the table, where the sheeted body of your father lies. Those two coins, placed on his eyes, would give his spirit the means to cross the river into the afterlife.

'Or should they go as an offering to the gods, who must look on us kindly if we are to survive?' wonders your mother. She sounds so lost and bewildered that you must surely stir and sob in your slumber.

Use the coins to buy food	▶ 32
Put them on the corpse's eyes	▶ 146
Take them to the shrine	▶ 214
Keep them yourself	▶ 279

460

The Nightshades rush at you. It is hard to tell the difference between them and the darkness. You hack at them with your weapon but they are like insubstantial phantoms and your blade just passes through them.

They overwhelm you in shadow… And then begin to drain your energy, leeching the life force out of you. You struggle but you are deep in darkness and soon you can feel your body withering up like a dead dog rotting under the summer sun.

Your death is agonisingly slow…

▶ 111

461

You find yourself sitting out on the porch of a rustic cabin, beside a babbling brook and near the edge of a wood. Birds sing in the trees, deer drink from the stream, a soft, cool breeze caresses your face. The day is fading into melancholic shadow.

Out of the woods, a figure steps. You cannot quite make him out; it is as if he were dressed in the twilight itself. He gestures, and out of the gloom, shadowy figures emerge.

Someone steps out of the cabin behind you, holding something in their hands, a stone of some kind. They strike it and there is a flash like lightning and the shadows are torn into shreds of shrieking night in an instant.

You wake, your eyes temporarily blinded by the flash. You blink your way back into the real world.

'Welcome back, nomad in the lands of dream,' says Zenia.

If you have some more **kykeon mushrooms** and 10 more pyr and want to try another vision ▶ 737.

If not, there is nothing more to be done here, so you can head back to the market (▶ 728) or leave the area (▶ 12).

462

You invite many of your friends once again to another banquet and they all turn up, this time with friends, expecting an exciting evening and, indeed, it is another merry evening, with much pomegranate wine and a marvellous feast wonderfully cooked by Erifili and her team but this time, when the midnight gong is struck, nothing untoward happens. The days of the Blackgate Banquet Spectacular, as it has come to be known, seem to be over.

Anyway, an entertaining evening is had by all. The next morning you wake up a little worse for wear but ready to continue your adventures.

▶ 220

463

You are at the Druid's Shrine on the upper part of the Alpheus river plateau. From here you can go:

North west into the woods	▶ 620
South to the Upper Tarn	▶ 370
Visit the Shrine	▶ 484

464

'Eh? How will the nymphs die? most of them live in rivers, they'll be fine,' says Kaustikia.

You stand nonplussed for a moment. 'Umm... I guess so,' you mutter. 'Bad example.'

'Anyway, whatever, nymphs, shmymphs, it's time I had my seconds – and that will be you.' Kaustikia closes in to the attack.

If you have the **Nemean bagh nakh** ▶ 817
If not ▶ 783

465

You wake refreshed, gazing at the frolicking 'games' Eros and others are getting up to on your bedroom mural.

You leap out of bed, full of new energy, gain a **benison x 1**. Note it on your Adventure Sheet. It gives you +1 on your next attribute roll. Once it has been used, cross it off.

Jas is ready with your breakfast, and he helps dress you in your armour and weapons. Every now and then he says things like, 'Oh my, how dapper you look' or 'I'm so lucky to have such a fine-looking governor' or 'Quite the hero, boss, quite the hero' or 'Me? I'm a simple slave, don't mind me.'

As you walk out the door, he pats you on the bottom with a 'there you go, chief!'

Reflexively, you reach for your weapon and Jas gulps fearfully, before scuttling away quickly with a muttered apology. Shaking your head, you move on.

▶ 282

466

'All very well,' you say, 'but how can I be sure you'll let them go if I give myself up to you?'

'Well, for a start I don't give a shit about them, it's you I want! Tell you what, put your weapons and armour over there, then lie face down, and I'll let them go.'

You decide to do as he says, ready to leap up and fight if necessary. But Deridedes does indeed untie them.

'Go on, get out of here,' he says.

Deridedes's thugs pin you down, and tie you up.

'What now?' you say. 'A beating? Robbery?'

'Oh no, much worse than that!'

'Much worse!' mumbles burned face. Deridedes raises his eyes.

'Must you repeat everything I say? Sometimes I wish that dragon had finished the job after breathing all over your face,' says Derides.

'Breathed acid, all over my face,' mutters burned face. Deridedes sighs.

'Anyway, this way,' he says to you, and he leads you out to the back of the farm to a tree, with a rope and a hangman's noose, hanging from it.

'What? I spared your life, and you're going to hang me for it!' you splutter in outrage, struggling to break free, but his two thugs know their stuff when it comes to tying people up.

Without much ceremony, Deridedes loops the noose around your neck, and his thugs hoist you up into the air, the noose tightening around your neck. You glare at Deridedes and manage to rasp a few last words,

'I'll be back!'

You choke to death with the small satisfaction of seeing Deridedes face blanch for a moment. The last thing you hear is him saying, 'Do you think the dead can come back?' and the reply from his Celtic henchman, 'Nah, 'course not.'

Well, we'll see about that, you think to yourself before everything goes black. Gain the codeword *Pernicious*.

▶ 111

467

You make your way round the eastern treeline without being noticed, but as you draw near to Alpha, you tread on a branch buried beneath some rotting leaf mulch and it cracks loudly.

Alpha turns, terrifyingly calmly, and paces towards you. Close up, you can see he is large for a wolf but not especially so. His fangs are white and sharp, his fur also white, and remarkably clean. No, it is not his wolf body that is so terrifying, it is his eyes, yellowed like the wolf, but full of a terrible intelligence, bright with cunning, like that of a man.

Alpha snarls and then howls, not so much a bestial roar as a summons.

Seconds later, out of the trees, step several bushwhack wolves. More of them emerge from the forest gloom, snarling. At least two packs, more than ten of them. You recall something someone said about bushwhack wolves – 'they lurk in the Deep Forest, ready to pounce on those foolish enough to wander through its shadowed woodlands.'

And this time it is you who are the foolish one… You turn and run for your life.

Make a GRACE roll at difficulty 8.

Succeed ▶ 454
Fail ▶ 375

468

You decide on a difficult piece written by Limenius, composer of the Delphic Hymns. It's reasonably well known but it is also very complex. You begin well, but then get into an awful mess. To be fair, it is a difficult piece, but even so Velosina and the audience are not impressed.

'I call Velosina the winner,' says Chiron.

You sigh resignedly, as Chiron gives her the scroll. 'Here is Sappho's poem, rather a sad, tragic piece but beautiful all the same. It's called "My lover lies with Ladon".'

Velosina accepts it with a bow, as the crowd applaud. She turns to you, 'Ah well, you gave it your best shot,' says Velosina, slapping you on the back heartily, 'I've got a fine Sappho original, but it was hard fought and close! Clearly you're a talented player.'

'I'm sorry you lost, but it was close,' says Chiron, 'Anyway, is there anything else I can help you with?'

▶ 90

469

There is some laughter from the audience, but not as much as you would have liked. 'Very erudite, I'll give you that, but too clever and too many words,' says Deridedes. However, Kraterus crows his approval with a 'silly-old-goat!' anyway.

Deridedes blinks in surprise. 'What the…' he mutters.

'Cock likes erudite. Cleverer than you, it seems,' you comment.

Deridedes' brow furrows. 'Well, let's see what he thinks of this.' He puts the Momos mask up to his face and says, 'You nut-brained ninny-noggined knob-headed nincompoop, no one knows your name!'

The crowd roars with laughter at that one, and Deridedes smiles broadly, awaiting the judgement of Kraterus.

But none comes. Deridedes gasps in shock. 'Two nil to me,' you say with a mocking smile. What will you try now?

'At last! I've been searching for a fool, and look what I found – you!' ▶ 568

'You pettifogging, mooncalf mountebank, quacksalver!' ▶ 427

470

You start climbing the ladder, making sure you don't look down. At the top, you heave at the trap door with your shoulder and thankfully it flips open easily and you climb out into bright sunlight.

▶ 340

If you have the codeword *Propeller* ▶ 66 immediately. If not, read on.

At the side of the Palace is an open space at the centre of which sits a large onager, a catapult usually used as a siege engine but this one is bolted onto an octagonal wooden plate that can be rotated with a winch device. An arrow is painted onto the forward edge of the octagon. A sign reads:

FUNFAIR FAST TRAVEL RIDE

The catapult has a rather fancy looking bucket seat that a person could easily fit into and can be turned to point in eight directions, each one labelled with a compass direction. Surely this isn't... is it?

On closer inspection, you see that the catapult is in need of repair. If you have the **Contract: Engineer** ▶ 50. (To check if you have it, note **471** in your Current Location box, then ▶ 101 and then return to this section after.) If you haven't got it, there is nothing more you can do here for now. Will you:

Enter the Palace	▶ 96
Go to the lagoon	▶ 345
Leave this place	▶ 547

❑

If you have the codeword *Payment* ▶ 61 immediately. If not, read on.

Put a tick in the box. If there was a tick in the box already ▶ 92 immediately. If not, read on.

As you draw near, you spot a centaur at the treeline, watching you. When you get close enough, you shout a greeting, but the centaur, bow-armed and helmeted, just turns and canters away into the wooded darkness.

You follow his trail, clearly a well-travelled path. for many hooves have churned up the forest floor. After a while, you come to a large wooden wall, a stockade built in the middle of this part of the deep forest.

You take a step towards the stockade when a head pops up on the wooden walkway. It's a man with a leather cap, holding a bow and wearing a bright green tunic that seems to sparkle with magical light. His eyes are also green, and he sports a tightly cropped black beard. Then you notice the tunic runs down to his back – a horse's back. He's a centaur.

'I'm not taking callers today!' says the centaur, 'You look like far too much trouble to even rob, so why don't you just trot off, eh?' And he gestures rudely at you.

'Who are you?' you ask.

'Me? I'm Nessus, true king of the centaurs, currently leader of this warband,' and he points down into the stockade. Does that mean there really is a warband there or is he bluffing?

'Do you know what they say about centaur warbands?' he asks.

You shake your head.

'Bow-armed, keen-eyed, and wind-swift, they can bring down a storm of arrows upon their foe in seconds!' he says portentously. And then he snaps his hand down in a cutting gesture.

And out from the centre of the stockade comes a cloud of arrows, up into the air, and then rushing down right at you.

You only just manage to dart behind a tree, as the arrows thud into the earth, the trunk, or get caught in the branches above you, before clattering to the ground. Definitely not bluffing then.

You can hear Nessus laughing, along with several others. Then he shouts 'Now get lost, unless you want an arrow in the arse!'

If you have the codeword *Punisher* ▶ 151

If not, you have little choice but to 'get lost' ▶ 189

The handsome man or whatever he truly is, leads you to the bed once more, and you find yourself unable to resist. This time you do not wake up at all, for he – or it – has been slowly drinking your soul, bit by bit. And without a soul, the gods cannot bring you back...

▶ 750.

You have returned to the wineries. The trees that the renegade centaurs burned have been removed and replanted, things are coming along. Maron has recovered from his beating, and comes up to you, offering you a swig from a jug of dandelion wine. You shake your head.

'Have you sorted out that centaur warband yet?' he asks.

'I'm afraid not,' you say. 'Where were they again?'

'Up north, east of the north-eastern ruins in the deep forest, and west of the bridge over the river Ladon. We can't really get on with the harvesting of the pomegranates until you make them go away. If you don't sort it soon, they'll be back, and I for one don't want another beating!'

You nod. Time to move on. From here, you can go:

North to the Arcady Trail	▶ 238
West to Treycross on the Arcady Trail	▶ 728
South on the Trail	▶ 338
East to the bridge over the river Alpheus	▶ 14

475

In a glade in the woods you come across a small cottage. The walls are festooned with ivy and thick moss makes the roof look like something that has grown out of the earth rather than been made by mortal hand.

If you have the codeword *Petasos* ▶ 514
If not but you have the codeword *Quest* ▶ 536
Otherwise ▶ 558

476

Drosos, the farm overseer, leads you to a nearby barn. 'I must say this has been a particularly rich harvest. Demeter or Gaia is smiling on us! Your cut is even bigger than usual.'

He hands you your portion of the most recent harvest – four bags of grain.

Note some **farmlands grain x 4** on your Adventure sheet. When you are ready, cross off the **flowers of fertility**, for their magic is used up, and gain the codeword *Planted.* Now decide where you will go next.

North-east ▶ 365
North-west ▶ 380
South-east ▶ 419

477

You jump down from the stone slab and dash for the cave mouth. Behind you, the Grey Sisters shriek their outrage, and Persis, the wall-shaker, stamps her foot…

The ground shakes beneath your feet and you tumble to the earth as several rocks fall from the cave ceiling knocking you out once again. You never wake up, not even to find out what new recipe they used to cook you up.

▶ 111

478

The art gallery has several people in it – a satyr, gazing at a portrait of Aphrodite hanging on the wall, a water nymph, who leaves wet footprints on the wood-panelled floor, and several humans, wandering amongst the works of art. Erifili the head chef and art curator is standing behind a desk at the far end of the room.

If you have a painting called **A Hero in Hell by Apelles** ▶ 24

If not, there is nothing you can do here so ▶ 282 and choose again.

479

You manage to get to the rear of the stone cabin without being seen. You tread carefully for it is very cold here and the frosted earth crunches underfoot. You find a large window at the rear of the cabin – carefully you look over its ledge.

Inside is a young maiden, with striking blue eyes and also, surprisingly, light blue skin. Her hair is white and spiked with thin icicle braids. Her lips are red but her breath is as cold as ice. The whole room is rimed with frost. An ice nymph…

You have heard of such creatures but they are rare indeed, and usually found only in the mountains of Boreas.

She senses your presence, and turns to face you. You can see frozen tears on her cheeks. A drop falls to the ground where it shatters.

'Who are you?' you ask.

'I am broken-hearted Evadne, a nymph, abducted from my home in the ice and snow to serve Mela, the witch of Hekate.'

Suddenly the door burst open, and you duck down behind the window ledge.

Mela herself walks in, instructing some of her slaves to place the limestone slabs in large water troughs. You risk peeping over the ledge. Mela wears a white mask under a wide-brimmed black hat, and is dressed in yellow robes. She holds an ebony staff in one hand, which is topped by symbols of Hekate made from bronze – a key, a dagger and a snake. Her other hand points at the nymph imperiously, and she commands Evadne to freeze the water around the limestone.

'Yes, mistress,' says Evadne submissively, and you watch as the nymph places her hand in the trough. She grunts with effort and soon the water and the limestone slabs are frozen solid.

Evadne slumps into one corner, exhausted. Mela contemptuously tosses a basket of food and drink onto the cabin floor before leaving. All this just to keep Ladon frozen in his lake. But why?

As for Evadne, you could get her out of there – the window is certainly big enough. In fact, you wonder why she hasn't already tried to escape so you ask her.

'I cannot, for the witch has my heart.'

'What do you mean, do you love her?' you ask.

'No, no, literally, she has my heart of ice in a casket. I cannot leave without it,' explains Evadne. 'She can melt it at any time. I must do her bidding or die.'

'Ah, I see.'

'If you can get it for me… bring me back my heart, then I can be free! She keeps it in her chamber in the temple.'

'I'll see what I can do,' you say.

She stares at you, astonished.

'Really?' she says, hope blossoming on her face like a flower. 'Are you some kind of hero, then?'

'Yes, actually, I am,' you reply without thinking.

▶ 538

480

The priest of Apollo speaks to you, 'You seem troubled, brave one. I can see a shadow on your heart. Perhaps the blessing of Apollo Phanaeus, the bringer of light, is what you need for his brilliance brings truth out of darkness.'

If you wish to get a blessing of Apollo Phanaeus, it will cost you 10 pyr. If you do, note the **Blessing of True Sight** on your Adventure Sheet. When you are done, you can return to the Sacred Way.

► 20

481

'Soon you'll be my next meal,' she hisses, her voice sibilant and filled with malice. She spits acid at you but you are able to dodge it. You realise you will have to kill her soon, or be struck by acid for your luck will eventually run out. You close in, trying to rake your claws across her face.

Make a STRENGTH roll at difficulty 11.

Succeed	► 439
Fail	► 356

482

After a short while, Lefkia arrives. 'Hello, hello,' she says enthusiastically, 'so glad to be working again!' You note that her once white work clothes are now splattered with paint and plaster. She and Hypatia confer for a moment and then Hypatia says, 'Well, then, here is a list of what we need,' and she hands you a scroll.

100 pyr to hire labourers
timber
limestone
vinegar of Hades x 1
bucket of gypsum x 1
box of paints x 1

'There's a woodcutter at the edge of the Deep Forest in the south-west. He should be able to provide some timber. There used to be a limestone quarry just north of the Alpheus river plateau, and I know of a gypsum mine in Boreas, though whether it's still working is another question,' adds Hypatia.

If you have *all* of these things and wish to hand them over, cross them off your Adventure Sheet and ► 552

If you don't have all of them, you say, 'I shall go forth on a quest to get everything you need!'

'Spoken like a true adventurer,' says Lefkia. You make your farewells. From here you can go:

North-east to the Woodlands	► 60
East along the riverbank	► 138
South	► 822
West to the Wineries	► 417

483

Although you are clearly the better fighter, the Master of Twilight manages a lucky glancing blow with his sword Sunsmoke on your sleeve, no more than a slight touch. It does no harm to you directly, but it does set your sleeve alight, distracting you long enough for him to nick you across the leg with his other sword, Duskvenom. Immediately you can feel poison coursing through your veins. Your muscles start seizing up, and you fall to the floor, unable to move. The Master of Twilight straddles your twitching body.

'So end all those who defy the Master of Twilight!' he whispers. You glare your defiance as he stabs you through the throat, and you die choking on your own blood.

► 111

484

If you have the codeword *Passage* ► 681 immediately.

Otherwise, if you have the title **Unfriended by Apollo** ► 706 immediately.

Otherwise, if this box ❏ is already ticked ► 585 immediately. If not, put a tick in it now and then read on.

You come to a stone archway, but done in the style of the Celts, carved with geometric whorls and patterns. Before it stands a man in long white, robes, hooded and with a belt of mistletoe around his waist and a wreath of oak leaves around his head. On closer inspection you see that the belt is in fact solid silver, painted and jewelled with green and red. Must be worth a small fortune! On either side of him stands a Celtic warrior, hair spiky, white and limed, chests bare and covered in blue painted symbols, wearing trousers, each with a finely crafted leather belt, again picked out in red and green. Each holds a spear in one hand, a figure eight shaped shield in the other, bronze bossed, and a beautifully worked iron longsword, hanging from the hip.

'Greetings, wanderer of the green, I am Amergin the Druid, Keeper of the Words of Knowledge, welcome to Pan's Arbour, or as we would call it, the Shrine of Cernunnos, for they are the same god.'

But you're Celts, not Greeks, right?'

'Indeed. Long ago there was a treaty between the Arcadians and the Galatian Celts. We shared some gods, such as Apollo the Bright One, and the Wild God, so we exchanged priests and the like. We were invited here to tend this Shrine to the Horned God and have done so faithfully for hundreds of years.'

'Can I enter the Arbour?'

'Of course, for a donation.'

Your eyes flicker down to his silver belt. Clearly they've prospered from this arrangement. The druid hitches his belt up, and coughs uncomfortably at your gaze.

'Anyway, a great warrior like you? Let me see – a **bearskin cloak** will do nicely!'

If you have a **bearskin cloak** and wish to give it to Amergin, cross it off and ▶ **664**

If not, or you don't want to do so now, you can come back later ▶ **463**

485

You manage to outrun the shrieking horde, skirting the walls of the city and heading south east towards some hills. You spot a nearby cluster of houses, and run toward them, but doors and windows have been slammed shut and secured fast – there is no succour there. Up ahead, you see a large wood, the dales of leaf and stream but they are close behind. Make a GRACE roll at difficulty 10.

Succeed	▶ **458**
Fail	▶ **416**

486

If you have the title **Spider's Bane** ▶ **77** immediately. If not, read on.

The cave is lit by hanging lanterns – who lit those, you wonder – and is covered in cobwebs but thankfully no spiders that you can see. A ladder on one wall rises up to a hatch in the ceiling, a good fifty metres up. Another hatch in the floor goes who knows where. Try as you might, you cannot open the hatch in the floor, but you could climb the ladder. Where will you go?

Up the ladder	▶ **470**
Back out onto the Arcady Trail	▶ **238**

487

The duel does not last long. The truth is that you are simply far more experienced a fighter than Nessus, who is just the leader of a gang of local thugs. Although he manages to spear you in the thigh, you cut him down shortly after. His men give a cry of despair as he falls to the ground, bleeding out on the forest floor. Tick the Wound box on your Adventure Sheet. If you were already wounded, gain 1 scar instead.

He looks up at you, as he lies dying. 'Well fought,' he says, and then to his cut-throat crew he says, 'Let this one live, it was a fair fight.' He takes off his green tunic, and hands it to you.

'Here, this is yours by right of battle, take it, wear it, it will aid you.' And then he lies back, smiles up at the sky, gives one last laugh, and dies.

The rest of his warband begin packing their things up. Some start to leave. You watch them, uncertain as to their intentions, but they ignore you completely. The warband is finished. Gain the codeword *Payment*.

You also have the **tunic of Nessus**. Note it on your Adventure Sheet. If you want to put it on ▶ **509**

If not, or perhaps later, there is nothing more for you to do here, so you leave the forest ▶ **189**

488

You are tracking a small herd of deer when you emerge at the edge of clearing. On the other side, mist wreathes the trees like a vast, writhing funereal shroud.

Suddenly out of the forest fog steps a stag. A massive stag, with antlers whose tips seem to glow with power and whose flanks are marked with magical sigils.

You have heard of this creature from myth. It is Soter, lord of the woodland herds, and protector of the Arcadian deer. Artemis herself created him, as a foil against Lykaon's wolves as they were taking too many deer. You can even recall what the bards and storytellers say about him: 'Do not disturb the herd, for Soter's hooves are like hammers and his antlers are as keen as the spear of Achilles.'

Soter brays his defiance and rage at you, and paws the ground with a hoof. It seems your deer hunt has drawn his attention.

On the other hand, if you could slay such a mythical beast, those antlers and that symbol-marked hide would make for a glorious trophy indeed.

On either side of Soter, several more stags step into the clearing, each one a magnificent specimen. What will you do?

Fight	▶ **429**
Just run	▶ **355**

489

If you have the codeword *Plenty* ▶ **659** immediately. If not, read on.

'Ah, it's the Steward, greetings!' says Nyctimus. 'What can I do for you?'

'A question, what is it you wanted me to do again?'

'Me! No, no, it's the gods, *they* want you to do it. And it's to rescue or find or somehow save the river gods, Ladon and Alpheus. Start by visiting Lake Ladon, maybe you can pick up some clues from there. The Lake is to the north of here. After that, try Tarn Alpheus, up near the Druid's Shrine.'

'Is it really the gods though? Or are you just saying that so you don't have to give me a reward if I pull this off.'

Nyctimus puts a hand to his mouth and coughs.

'No, no, of course not, it's really the gods, they told me in a, well, in a dream.'

'Hmm....' you mutter. Still, there is nothing more to be done here, so you take your leave.

▶ **282** and choose again.

490

Euphorbos shakes his head. 'You hang onto it for safe-keeping. We know where it is. When you've got full use of it you can bring it back. I'll still be here. Or… wait, do I mean *was* here? This backwards living is very confusing.'

Do *not* remove the **bag of Aiolos** from your list of possessions just yet. ▶ **759**

491

You run for your life but the bear is too fast for you and he swipes your legs out from under you with one paw. You fly face first into the loamy mulch of the forest floor. Stunned, you can do nothing as the bear holds you down with one paw while the other rips off the back of your skull and scoops out your brains. Death is mercifully quick.

You died while fleeing like a coward, nevertheless, perhaps the gods will still take pity on you.

▶ **111**

492

Hermes has sent you in your sleep to Arcadia once again. You wake with a start, fearful of thieves, bizarre visions or some other catastrophe but nothing untoward occurs. You find yourself in quiet, sun-dappled woodland, warm and cosy… but you know that won't last for long.

Nearby, you can see the pillared portico of the Summer Palace, rising up above the trees.

▶ **686**

493

The catch-net is a net made of twined vines, stretched across four wooden poles like an enormous spider's web. Unfortunately for you, it's not been maintained for years and one of the poles has fallen, bringing the net down with it.

You simply crash into the ground with bone breaking force.

Tick the Wound box on your Adventure Sheet. If you are already wounded than your skull is shattered and your brains are spilled all over the Sacred Way. ▶ **111**

If you still live, you stagger to your feet and look around. ▶ **517**

494

'Ah, Ladon and Alpheus, the river gods of Arcadia. For an age have they run and roared across Arcadia, bringing life to the land, until dark forces locked them up somehow. Without them, the rivers dried up, and Arcadia began to perish slowly, day by day. Without the rivers to water the fields, there wasn't enough bread and wine to go around, and the Arcadians starved or fled.

'But why? Who would want such a thing? I have heard that a powerful divine force is behind it all, and it is they who are responsible for putting the gods to sleep so that they can take control of the Vulcanverse. But first they must weaken it, or so the rumours go. But who are "they"? An Olympian god? A titan? An alliance of such gods? Or one of the primordial gods, the ancient ones who birthed the titans? Who can say? And that is all I have to tell you about the rivers of Arcadia. Anything else?'

If you have the title **Mayor of Bridgadoom** ▶ **118**
If not ▶ **153**

495

It wasn't how you planned to spend your afternoon, but you play some games with the children. They're delighted to have the attention of somebody a bit older.

Write your attributes on the Adventure Sheet:
Strength 0
Grace 0
Charm +1
Ingenuity 0
Then ▶ **679**

496

You wake to find yourself sitting at a long banqueting table, in the middle of a wooded dale. It is early evening, the moon is rising, and tall lantern poles illuminate the scene. In front of you is a silver goblet, and a big silver bowl with a fork and spoon – again! This goes on for several nights in a row, until one evening you wake to find that the moon is full and bright enough that lanterns are no longer needed to illuminate the scene.

A stone altar has been set up in the glade, and a large fire has been built up, with a rotary spit across it, waiting for whatever carcass is to be stuck upon it and roasted.

Two figures in cowled robes stand on either side of the altar, holding a staff in one hand, entwined with vines flowers, and a sickle in the other. The priests begin to intone the words of a ritual…

'O Despoina, mistress of animals, she who is the flower and the fox, the grass and the goat, the wood and the wolf, she who is the wilding, the *physis,* the earth, accept our sacrifice so that in death, there will be re-birth!'

Behind you, all the animal headed people sitting at the table reply.

'From death comes the seed, from the seed comes life, the circle turns and the world spins.'

The ritual goes on in this vein but you are distracted by the clothes you are wearing – a simple white shift with what looks like a seed painted on your chest.

You look around suspiciously. Where is the sacrifice here? Normally it would be a bull or a goat or... or is it... but your thoughts slip away from you like an eel in a river and you find yourself drinking from a goblet of wine, your mind fog-filled and forgetful, your nostrils filled with the scent of the yellow lilies of the lake.

If you have the title **Tricked by a Water Nymph** ▶ 722
If not, but you have a **heart of oak** ▶ 770
If you have neither title nor heart ▶ 610

497

You return to the Apiary of Sivi the dryad of the pomegranate trees. You find her sobbing in the corner, her long crimson braided hair looping around her ankles, looking to trip her up at any moment.

'You need a haircut,' you say, 'before you have an accident.'

'What? Who cares about such things, when disaster has befallen us!' says Sivi, pointing at one of the hives. It has been cracked open and ransacked. 'A bear came, and it ripped open that hive and ate all the lovely honey. Many bees died trying to defend their home, but their stings could not penetrate the bear's thick fur.'

'Oh dear,' you say, 'So no honey, then?'

'No!' says Sivi, 'not until you've killed the bear.'

'What, me? A bear?'

'Yes, you, who else? Me? I'm a dryad, as like to trip over my own hair as kill a bear!'

'Hmm... good point. Well, OK then, I can't promise anything, but I'll see what I can do.' Gain the codeword *Pudding*. What now?

Hunt for the bear right now	▶ 752
Go deeper into the woods	▶ 176
Leave and come back later	▶ 225

498

Lose the codeword *Retrieve*, and gain the codeword *Pennywort*.

You ask Erifili, the palace chef, what she knows about the herb ophidiaroot.

'Ah, ophidiaroot, an interesting herb indeed, very rare and hard to find! It can be used in cooking for it has a rich flavour that is both tart and savoury. However, one must be careful, for too much of it will cause vomiting and diarrhoea which is why it is used in medicine as an emetic to that effect. But even then one must be careful, for if you ingest small amounts daily, it won't be enough to cause vomiting, and over time it will build up inside of you and eventually kill you. A slow, horrible death, for it looks like nothing else than the Black Blight or the Bubo Plague.'

'Interesting indeed,' you say. 'Do you have any here?'

'Oh no, I don't need exotic herbs to make my cooking taste good, and in any case, it's far too dangerous.'

'Where can I find some?' you ask as innocently as you can. She stares coolly at you. 'Special recipe is it?'

You nod. But you don't mention that is for the wife of the Grumble King for you are beginning to suspect what she really wants it for...

Erifili shrugs. 'Anyway,' she says, 'ophidiaroot likes fresh water and shade, too much sun will kill it. So the best place to look for it is under a wide spreading tree like the willow, on a river bank. Or even better, under a bridge.'

You thank Erifili. ▶ 282 and choose again.

499

Suddenly Alpha's ears prick up and he sniffs the air. He can sense your weakness, your wound! Alpha turns, terrifyingly calmly and paces towards you. Close up, you can see his is large for a wolf but not especially so. His fangs are white and sharp, his fur also white, and remarkably clean. No, it is not his wolf body that is so terrifying, it is his eyes, yellowed like the wolf but full of a terrible intelligence, bright with cunning, like that of a man.

Alpha snarls and then howls, not so much a bestial roar as a summons.

Seconds later, out of the trees, step several bushwhack wolves. More of them emerge from the forest gloom, snarling. At least two packs, more than ten of them. You recall something someone said about bushwhack wolves – 'they lurk in the Deep Forest, ready to pounce on those foolish enough to wander through its shadowed woodlands.'

And this time it is you who are the foolish one. You turn and run for your life but your wound slows you down.

▶ 375

500

There is a flash of light which feels like a veil of shadow has been lifted from your face, and you find yourself... somewhere else. Roll two dice:

score 2-4	▶ 380
score 5-6	▶ 559
score 7-8	▶ 728
score 9-11	▶ 774
score 12	▶ 353

501

Some sixth sense makes you turn to look behind – and there you see something so unnerving it makes your hair stand up on end. Some *thing* is hunched over your shadow, seemingly sucking it up off the ground! The thing is shapeless and utterly

lightless, as if a formless blob of black ink had oozed up out of the earth or a crooked stygian crow-creature had dropped out of the sky to feed on your shadow.

You can feel your shadow draining away, and it is horrible. You draw your weapon but before you can strike, it fades away like ink down a plug hole. All that is left is a small patch of black dirt in the ground.... And thankfully, your shadow which appears fully intact. Gain the codeword *Penumbra*.

You wonder what sort of creature it was. Some kind of shadow-hunter? And was it chance it chose your shadow or was it sent? Perhaps you will find out later but for now you decide to move on, checking on your shadow as you do. Will you go:

West into the forest	▶ 189
North to the bridge	▶ 517
South to Ladon's Lake	▶ 37

502

You look around the shadowed greenery, the heat closing in around you like a hot, sticky hand, stifling your thoughts. You rack your brains for an idea, but nothing comes to mind. Your wood-craft is simply not good enough.

You can hear the whoops and snarls of your pursuers closing in on you. All you have left is to run as fast as you can and hope for the best. You offer up a prayer to the gods and throw yourself on their mercy. Roll a single die and pray.

score 1-4	▶ 627
score 5-6	▶ 557

503

The horde of howling Bacchantes gain on you fast, as they cut across the Sacred Way towards you, blocked by the walls of the city as you are. Terrified, you try to outrun them, but it is no good. Several of them throw themselves at you, and although you are able to shake them off, they slow you down enough until you are engulfed by a pack of shrieking, frenzied furies, tearing, biting and ripping at you with nails, teeth and bare hands, intent on sacrificing you to the mad god. You are overwhelmed and literally torn to pieces in a matter of seconds, and your body scattered to the four winds. Well, those bits of it that weren't eaten that is.

▶ 111

504

'Seems the villain has an ego,' says Erifili handing you a note she found in the storeroom.

'To the mighty hero -
    I did it! Right under your nose, I, the greatest thief of the age, robbed the greatest hero of the age. The bards will sing of it forever.
    Yours insincerely,
    Autolycus
    PS I left you your stuff, too difficult to fence. Prefer hard cash anyway.'

You search the storeroom for clues. Make an INGENUITY roll at difficulty 7.

Succeed	▶ 288
Fail	▶ 450

505

Kaustikia rises up on her coils and says, 'I don't know how you came back from Hades, and even though you didn't taste very nice last time, to be honest, I'll happily eat you again.'

'Wait, wait, I have some more arguments I think you should hear!'

'What, more blather?' She folds her arms and glares down at you, fluttering her wings in irritation. 'Fine, go on, see if you can talk me round, but while you're at it, perhaps you could sprinkle a little salt over your head, and drape some thyme around your neck for me, eh?'

'If the Great Green Ones die, so will all the sheep, and I think you're rather fond of sheep, aren't you?

'Yes, I'm very fond of sheep, true, but I'm happy to take my chances. Sure, I'd prefer a sheep, but still, eating you for seconds won't be such a hardship.'

'Wait!' you say, 'what about the...'

'Wine, the vines will die too.'	▶ 144
'Dryads, they'll die too.'	▶ 342
'Nymphs, they'll die too.'	▶ 464

506

You rack your brains, but try as you might you can't think of way to turn the tables, and now time has run out. You'll just have to pay up after all.

▶ 632

507

Glaukos hacks at you and you riposte fast and true, slicing him across the arm, but your blade simply bounces off his skin.

'Your skin is as hard as bronze, that's cheating!' you say accusingly.

'What do you mean cheating? Was Achilles a cheat because he was invulnerable, save for a small spot on his heel? What about Heracles? He poisoned most of his weapons, that's how he killed so many, was he a cheat? And Ajax! Did he cheat by having a god-blessed shield so large no one else could wield it? Is that cheating?'

You circle your foe, reassessing your strategy. 'What is it that makes your skin like bronze?' you ask, to buy a few seconds.

'A gorgon's blood, suitably treated, can be ingested, hardening the skin like stone for a time,' says Glaukos as he readies another flurry of attacks, heedless of his defence. Behind you, you can hear rapid chattering as people change their minds about the outcome and thus their bets accordingly. Thanks for the vote of confidence, you think to yourself.

Make a STRENGTH roll at difficulty 7. Note that the only weapons that will give you a STRENGTH bonus in this fight are the **hardwood club +1** or the **Nemean bagh nakh + 3**; blessings and benisons still work, though.

Succeed	▶ 556
Fail	▶ 619

508

You have completed one of the Great Labours of Arcadia. Write the number **573** (not *this* paragraph number) in the Current Location space on your Adventure Sheet (in place of the number already written there, if any) and then ▶ 38

509

You pull the tunic of Nessus over your head, and smooth it down over your torso. It feels prickly, but also very green and very sparkly. You frown. You can't feel anything magical, or anything at all really.

And then you realise that's because your skin has gone numb. And then you stagger, falling to one knee. Your blood feels like it is boiling! It's a trick, Nessus has tricked you, even in death. Desperately you try and pull the tunic off, but it is too late, its poison is coursing through your veins. Your blood, hot like lava, bursts out of you, ripping open your skin, erupting from your mouth, nose and anus. Even your eyes burst out of their sockets like exploding bolts. Death is at least quick.

▶ 111

510

The great beast swings a massive paw at your head but you block it with your shield... however big though it is, the shield of Ajax is very ancient, and it explodes into shards under the force of the blow. Luckily for you, one of the splinters catches the Nemean Lion in the eye, and it flinches for a second, giving you enough time to crack it across the head. That stuns the great beast just long enough for you to bring your club down over your head in a great two-handed blow that stuns it a little more. You proceed to hammer its skull over and over again, as hard and as fast as you can until, incredibly, the lion is dead, its skull bashed in.

You pause to catch your breath. You can hardly believe you pulled it off. Now the glory and the spoils are yours. Skilfully, you manage to skin the lion and remove its talons, both of which you take as trophies. The head itself is so mangled as to be of no use.

Cross off the **shield of Ajax** from your Adventure Sheet, it is destroyed but you take the lion pelt and its terrible talons. Such a deed will not go unforgotten. Give yourself the title **Lion Slayer**.

When you are ready, you can continue on in search of the heart of the forest or head back to 'civilisation'.

Into the heart of the forest ▶ 602
Leave the green gloom ▶ 148

511

❑

Put a tick in the box. If there was a tick in the box already ▶ 537 immediately. If not, read on.

'Well, well, yet another work by Apelles, by Pan's pink throbber!' says Erifili. 'I'll give you 100 pyr for it.'

Trying not to think about what Pan's pink throbber might be, you hand over the painting. Add 100 pyr to your Adventure Sheet and cross off the **masterpiece by Apelles.**

'Thank you, you're a real art dealer now,' says Erifili, 'but that's got to be it. I'm not sure I'll be able to sell this one on, so no more, even if you manage to find one, OK?'

You nod and take your leave. ▶ 282 and choose again.

512

You cannot break out of your dazed reverie until it is too late. With a sound like a wine cork popping out of the bottle your shadow is sucked up into the black nothingness that is the creature. And with that it drains away into the earth like ink down a plug hole, taking your shadow with it.

It leaves you feeling bereft, like you'd lost a limb. Some part of you is forever weakened, although you cannot immediately tell what effect it may have upon you. All you are certain of is that you have no shadow, and no matter how you stand or move, even in the brightest summer sun of Arcadia, you no longer cast a shadow. Note the title **Hero without a Shadow** on your Adventure Sheet and lose the codeword *Penumbra*.

The Shadowhunter has stolen your shadow. Was it chance that it chose your shadow or was it sent? No doubt will find out later but for now you must go on. From here you can go:

East to the eastern bridge ▶ 801
West to the western bridge ▶ 14
North to the Woodlands ▶ 60
South to some hills ▶ 822

513

If you have the codeword *Pure* ▶ 582 immediately. If not, read on.

'Here is your share of the honey harvest,' says Sivi and she hands you a couple of small terracotta pots of pomegranate honey. The pots are decorated with red beading around the top and bottom, like braids of Sivi's hair. 'There's some beeswax too, if you want it'.

Gain the codeword *Pure* and note **pomegranate honey x 2** and some **beeswax** on your Adventure Sheet. You thank the dryad, and make your farewells for now. Will you:

Go deeper into the woods ▶ 176
Leave this place ▶ 225

514

A note is pinned to the door:

'Gone travelling. I might go and stay in that hut that I'm going to build a few decades ago. You know the one. Drop in and see me. – Euphorbos.'

There is nothing else of interest here. You can rest at the cottage for a few days if you like (untick your Wound box if you were injured) and then press on.

► 617

515

'You killed her, then,' says a rich, resonant voice behind you. You turn to see another dryad, but this one has pale green luminescent skin and eyes, with gnarled wooden horns on her head. Sections of her body are also gnarled wood, and brightly coloured flowers grow from them. Her hands are also gnarly and woody, ending in sharpened talons like wooden stakes.

'I didn't kill her, no. It's a tragic irony – she beguiled someone into loving and serving her and then fell in love with them in turn, and when that love was unrequited, killed herself.'

'To love is to serve, it's true,' says the dryad. 'I have not loved in a hundred years but I have many servants for I am Phearei of the Meliae, those ash-dryads who were born from the blood of Uranus, castrated by Cronus, who in turn was cast down by Zeus, whom, as a baby, I and my sisters tended in the caves of Crete. I am the oldest of the dryads of the woodland glades, and, yes, you killed her.'

'With respect to your ancient lineage and all, she killed herself,' you protest.

'But you didn't have to tell her, you should have protected her from such truths and now she is gone. And for that, *you* will serve.'

Phearei waves her wood-gnarled arms and out of the trees step several dryad maidens, and they begin a soft, gentle song. Phearei begins to sway hypnotically before you.

If you have some **beeswax** ► 712

If not ► 544

516

It soon becomes clear that you are the better warrior. You draw first blood, and the Master of Twilight realises he is outmatched. He changes tactics, rather than trying to out fight you, he starts trying to touch your clothes with his flaming blade, or just trying to nick a hand or a foot with his venomous blade. You will have to be extra careful. Make a GRACE roll at difficulty 7.

Succeed ► 532

Fail ► 483

517

If you have the codeword **PatchupTwo** ► 287 immediately. If not, read on.

If you have the codeword **Plenty** ► 682 . If not, read on.

You have come to a bridge along the Sacred Way that encircles the world, as do the waters of Oceanus. From here, it runs east and west along the coast. The bridge spans the river Ladon that comes down from a great lake to the south and into the sea but the river bed is dry and parched, for the waters have long since dried up. The gods or spirits of the Arcadian rivers, Ladon and Alpheus, have not been seen for many a year. To the south-west are the wooded outskirts of the Deep Forest, and the ruins of a castle of some kind, jutting up over the treeline.

Nearby, a large net is slung between four wooden poles, clearly designed to catch something falling from the sky but it in a state of disrepair. It will cost you 20 pyr to have it fixed. If you wish to do so, cross off the money and get the codeword **PatchupTwo**. Either way, from here you can:

Go to the bridge ► 741

Head south, into the dried-up river valley ► 403

518

'Protagoras is the murderer!' you say out loud.

'Stupid mortal,' says a stony voice in your head, and you are suddenly transported elsewhere. Roll a die:

score 1-2 ► 222 in *The Hammer of the Gods*

score 3-4 ► 222 in *The Pillars of the Sky*

score 5-6 ► 222 in *The Houses of the Dead*

If you do not have all the books, simply re-roll until you are transported to a book you do have.

If you do not have any of the other books in the Vulcanverse, you are transported to the north-west corner of Arcadia. ► 158

519

Mark your CHARM score as −1, then ► 459

520

You step up to the statue, and kneel before it, giving thanks to Artemis for your survival. Suddenly, a large bear bursts into the clearing followed by a several wolf-men, snarling and roaring, their yellow-eyed faces half beast, half man, slaving with blood-lust, their bodies fur-covered and elongated, hands large and claw-like with talons like iron nails.

You wonder whether they will stick to their side of the bargain. Or even if they are able to, in their bestial state. You step back uncertain.

But the bear begins to change in front of your eyes, her snout shortening, her body shrinking and her arms and legs returning to human form. The wolves are following suit and soon Kallisto is standing before you, with her fur cap and bearskin robes. Actually her real skin, it turns out.

The wolves behind her are now naked men and women all staring at you in surprised appreciation. Kallisto actually claps.

'Well done, you are worthy prey indeed.'

'Not prey anymore, I hope?' you ask.

She smiles, and laughs, revealing heavy white teeth. 'Not prey anymore, no! Come, follow us, we will return to my father at the temple.'

'Won't I be defiling the temple again, if I do that?'

'No, not now, you have been ritually cleansed by surviving the hunt and praying to the goddess.'

You nod, and follow a bear-woman and a troupe of naked, incredibly hairy men and women down a trail through a gloomy forest. On either side of you, wolves pad along like an escort of hunter killers. Or perhaps jailers.

▶ 640

521

You were once enslaved here, working the quarry for hour after back breaking hour. Although your mind was dominated by another, and your memory of that time is patchy, you do recall the lay out of the quarry, and its paths any byways. That makes things much easier.

▶ 479

522

The third day is called *kalligeneia* or 'good birth.' It begins, thankfully, with a very hearty breakfast, but also oddly with all the women sitting around the fire once more but this time exchanging ritual insults and crudities, the more obscene the better, and usually about their husbands or other men. This also involves a lot of laughter, as the more inventive and ridiculous the obscenity, the better. You hold your own, coming up with some particularly coarse and smutty comments too rude to mention here.

The rest of the day is spent in praying at the altars to Demeter and Persephone for fertility, not just for the crops but also for the women at the festival, so that their own children might be strong and healthy.

The evening is spent around the campfire, the women having worked upon the morning's obscenities and trying to take them to the next level. Wine is also drunk, and soon there is much hilarity, though some take the insults to heart, and there is also a drunken fight or two, soon broken up by Thekla, the priestess.

You retire to your tent late that night, thinking that, all in all, you have enjoyed yourself.

▶ 721

523

You deflect most of the flames with your fire-proof shield but a few tongues of flame catch your clothes. You slap at your sleeve, and manage to put it out without difficulty.

'You're a clever little thing, I'll give you that, but you can't dance around like a little chorus girl forever,' rumbles the giant.

He is right. You will have to dodge and jab, dodge and jab for quite a time to weaken this foe enough to kill him but all it takes is one blow of that club or one fiery blast that gets past your shield, and you are likely done for. But how can he be breathing fire like that? Make an INGENUITY roll at difficulty 7.

| Succeed | ▶ 560 |
| Fail | ▶ 534 |

524

You are able to avoid the bear's clubbing swipes and savage attempts to bite your head off. You manage to land a couple of well-placed blows that cause some serious bleeding, and eventually the bear slows down enough for you to drive your weapon through its skull and into its brain.

Incredibly, you have killed a bear in a toe-to-toe stand up fight! You skin the bear, and take it as a trophy. Note the **bearskin** on your Adventure Sheet.

If you have a **hunting permit** ▶ 184

If not ▶ 219

525

To take on the dragon Kaustikia once more, you'll need the services of Pegasus again.

As you approach the trees upon which he has his nest, the legendary horse sees you and flies down to greet you. He whinnies happily – clearly Pegasus is fond of **honey cakes**. Cross all three of them off your Adventure Sheet.

You mount up and fly up and away, over the deep forest, like row upon row of green-garbed soldiers marching far down below, and up to the cloud home of Kaustikia the acid dragon, whose breath is poisoning the Great Green Ones.

Pegasus drops you off and leaves once again. Kaustikia was dozing, wrapped up in a ball, but this time she wakes instantly.

'What, you again? How can that be? I ate up every last bit of you last time.'

If you have the **Nemean bagh nakh** and wish to fight Kaustikia ▶ 817

If not, you'll have to match wits with her instead ▶ 505

526

You are on the Sacred Way. From here, it runs west along the northern coast, and south along the eastern shore. The

terrain around about is lightly wooded with much bush and bramble. To the south-west, it gives way to the verdant farmlands, the grain basket of Arcadia. Or at least it used to be.

You also notice a small temple, surrounded by a copse of trees to the south west.

From here you can go:

West along the coast	▶	**380**
South along the coast	▶	**419**
South-west into the farmlands	▶	**270**
Investigate the temple	▶	**55**

527

You run pell-mell for the treeline to the south east. The mob of howling Bacchantes pursue you in a frenzy of rage – they are heading in a straight line, following the edge of the forest, but you are having to cut across their path. It will be a close-run thing, and the sight of the snarling blood-frenzied women is quite terrifying. Make a GRACE roll at difficulty 7.

Succeed	▶	**386**
Fail	▶	**416**

528

That small part of you that is still you remembers the words of the priest of Apollo, how the god of light can reveal truth in darkness. With a great effort of will you call upon his aid, and suddenly, in a great flash of bright white light all is revealed...

The tent is shabby and tattered, the intoxicating scent is really a foul-smelling concoction of herbal black magic, the fineries are cheap and chipped, the bed a straw pallet. And the handsome young man....

....is really a woman. Or her top half is, for one leg is made of bronze, and the other is that of a donkey or horse. Her torso is misshapen and twisted, her eyes black coals in a pasty white face covered in warty protrusions. Her hair is but a few wisps of ropey black strands that hang down off her liver-wort stained, balding pate like dead snakes.

You realise she is a creature called an empousa, a shape shifter that feeds on those young men and women foolish enough to fall for her cunning wiles.

And now that you can see the truth, her enchantment is broken. With a cry of rage, you draw your weapon, and the empousa, realising the game is up, shrieks, 'Bah, Zoupa will still drink your soul, but I'll just have to do it the old way!'

As she speaks, her mouth reveals dirty yellow fangs, and her breath reeks of grave rot. So much for teeth of sunlit snow, and honey breath... You shudder at the thought of kissing her. At least you finally know its name.

Time to take your revenge, if you can. She circles you, clawed hands at the ready. You must fight Zoupa the empousa. Make a STRENGTH roll at difficulty 7.

Succeed	► 581
Fail	► 551

529

You meet with Drosos the farm overseer. 'I'm sorry, my Archon,' says Drosos, 'but the wheat and barley are not yet ready to harvest. Give us some more time.'

You'll have to come back again later. For now, where will you go?

North-east	► 365
North-west	► 380
South-east	► 419

530

You return to the Inn of the Swollen Mammaries and Oxygala is there behind the counter to greet you.

'So, you haven't been up to the town yet?' she says.

'I have indeed, and I have slain the basilisk,' you say proudly.

'Hah, I don't believe you!' she says.

'I thought you'd say that, so...' You haul out the head of the basilisk and hold it up before her.

'By Gaia's teats, so you have!' exclaims Oxygala excitedly. 'Now we can... well, maybe now the people will come back to live in the town, and the tourists, and all the rest. My inn will prosper once again, I cannot thank you enough.'

'Here,' you say. 'Put the head on the wall above the bar as a trophy.'

She accepts it gratefully. 'You can stay here whenever you like,' says Oxygala, 'in the Earth-mother suite, the best place in town!'

If you want to stay here the night ► 633

If not (you can always come back later) you take your leave and head back to the Sacred Way and into Arcadia, in search of more adventures ► 20

531

You fall into a dream, and find yourself landing in a forest clearing, where a wolf has been caught in a vicious looking trap. It is no ordinary wolf though, for its fur is like molten silver or mercury and its eyes are like stars. A dream wolf.

Your dream self frees the wolf but in doing so you drop

the trap, and it snaps shut on your own leg, wounding you badly. The wolf melts away in a river of silver. You are able to remove the trap, but one leg is badly damaged.

Behind you, hunters come, and it is you who are their prey. You limp on, and it looks like you are doomed until a howl in the distance leads you to a trail of silver, which you follow safely to freedom.

You sit up suddenly, grimacing at the savage pain in your leg, but you soon realise it is nothing.

'Hope that journey into dream was fun,' says Zenia. You have returned to reality. If you have some more **kykeon mushrooms** and 10 more pyr and want to try another vision ► 737

If not, there is nothing more to be done here, so you can head back to the market (► 728) or leave the area (► 12).

532

You adroitly avoid his little tricks and stratagems and begin forcing your opponent back. He grows more and more desperate until you have him backed up against the lava pool.

He screams in anger and hacks at you recklessly in one last desperate attempt to beat you. You dodge under his strike, and thrust your blade into his chest. He falls back with a strangled cry into the lava.

His body goes up in flames in and instant, and then his swords explode, throwing lava up and around. You throw yourself backwards out of the way, but then the great flask above the pool begins to shake and shudder as it is bespattered with globules of molten lava.

And then the enormous glass flask explodes, and out roars a great cloud of super-heated steam, rushing upwards, blasting open the trapdoor in the roof, and bursting out into the sky above.

You stare up at the opening in the roof in astonishment. Once you've gathered your wits about you, you race up the ladder as fast as you can. Has Alpheus survived?

► 594

533

The Warrior of Ares thrusts his spear through your shoulder with such force that you fall back to the ground. Tick the Wound box on your Adventure Sheet. If you are already wounded, then this finishes you. At least you died in battle against the servant of a war god. ► 111

If you still live, the Warrior steps over you, spear held to your throat.

'You fought well, and your blood soaks this holy ground. You are worthy of the god.'

With that the Warrior of Hades fades away on a scented forest wind. Gain the codeword *Praise-Ares* and ► 178

534

You are unable to work out how Kakas is breathing fire. It seems hard to believe, looking at him, but maybe he really is the spawn of Typhon or Echidna, the father and mother of monsters and he is a creature out of myth.

You try again to see what's going on behind his club, but fail to notice the large flint in his other hand which he hurls at you, cracking your head open like an egg. You fall to the ground, pole axed. You never wake up, which is just as well probably, for your fate is grisly indeed

▶ 111

535

If you have the codeword *Pursued* ▶ 730 immediately. If not, read on.

The woodcutter, Leonidas, who is neither a Spartan, nor a King or a hero, greets you.

'Hello again, have you come to deal with that most deadly of wolves, Alpha? If so, I have another wolf-trap if you need it.'

If you want to take on Alpha	▶ 577
If not, there is nothing else to do here, so where to next?	
West to the Sacred Way	▶ 324
East to the Arcady Trail	▶ 455
South east to a small wood	▶ 475

536

❏

If the box is empty, put a tick in it and ▶ 648. If it was ticked already ▶ 687.

537

'By Pan's swollen balls, you've found another one, where the Hades are you getting these? Anyway, it's no good, the market is flooded, I won't be able to sell it, so I'm not buying. By all means, hang it on the wall if you like but that's it, I'm afraid,' says Erifili.

There is nothing else you can do here, so ▶ 282 and choose again.

538

The temple of Hekate is quite small, but has an ante-chamber attached to the back of it. You surmise that must be Mela's room. You make your way to the back of the chamber and find a small wooden door. You listen for a while, but all is silent within. You reach for the door handle.

If you have a **clockwork owl** ▶ 615 immediately. If not, read on.

You hesitate for a moment. Something doesn't seem right around the door handle. Make an INGENUITY roll at difficulty 8.

| Succeed | ▶ 571 |
| Fail | ▶ 553 |

539

❏

Put a tick in the box. If there was a tick in the box already ▶ 768 immediately. If not, read on.

You climb down under the bridge, to find a dark and shady world of mushrooms and river reeds. You rummage around until you find what you think must be the ophidiaroot – a long, sinuous stalk, ending with several white flowers shaped like the head of a hooded cobra.

You gather up the plants and harvest their roots. Note a batch of **ophidiaroot x 1** on your Adventure Sheet. When you are done, you return to the bridge where the course of the river runs out into a bay with a low wooden quay for the docking of boats. From here you can go:

North	▶ 774
South	▶ 833
West along the river	▶ 138
To the hamlet	▶ 305
To the quay in the bay	▶ 200

540

You are on the Sacred Way. From here, it runs north and south. To the west, impassable cliffs rise up to another ridge of cliffs, upon which rests the Alpheus river plateau.

If you have the codeword *Neverending* and you do *not* have the **golden arrow of Artemis** ▶ 341

Otherwise, from here you can go:

North on the coastal Way	▶ 365
South on the coastal Way	▶ 774
North-west to the Verdant Farmlands	▶ 270
South-west to the Woodlands of Ambrosia	▶ 60

541

'Disaster!' wails Drosos, your farm overseer. 'Though I suppose it's my fault for hiring a bunch of satyrs as farm workers. Cheaper, true, but, well, they got drunk, and disappeared into the woods with a bunch of naughty nymphs. We lost a couple of days I'm afraid.'

You'll have to come back again later. For now, where will you go?

North-east	▶ 365
North-west	▶ 380
South-east	▶ 419

542

You have returned to the old bandit camp of Nessus, the renegade centaur. The wooden walls are falling apart and rotting, and it has been thoroughly looted.

Nearby, you find the grave of Nessus… To your consternation you see that it has been dug up. Perhaps a woodland animal dug out his body to feed on but there is no trace of it, no blood or bones or ripped flesh.

There is nothing more you can do here. Musing as to what happened here, you move on.

▶ 189

543

If you have any or all of the codewords *Planted*, *Pure* or *Pinot*, lose them.

You lose track of the trail, and then lose track of where you are. You wander through the dark, stifling forest, unsure where you are going and soon you are lost completely.

Everywhere the trees seem to lean down in silent condemnation of your presence for violating their tranquillity. Ahead, you can hear birdsong, the bark of a fox, perhaps, or a chirruping squirrel but when you draw near, everything falls as silent as the grave. You wander for days. Luckily you come across a forest brook with freshwater, but soon you're beginning to starve. The occasional forest berry isn't going to sustain you for long.

Fortunately, one morning, you see light ahead, and hurry to the edge of the forest. You run out into bright sunlight near the banks of a river. Looking at your map, it has to be the river Ladon.

▶ 403

544

The song of the dryads starts to creep over you, numbing your senses. Phearei's dance of love and desire is as old as life itself and is captivating, you cannot look away. Even though you know exactly what is going on, you find yourself unable to resist. A peaceful calm soothes your soul, and a burning, all-consuming love fills your heart. This beautiful spirit, this princess of life itself, of the ancient forests and flowers, Phearei the immortal dryad, is all you can think of, and how you can serve her. Soon you are utterly bewitched…

▶ 584

545

The lower tarn of Alpheus is now full to the brim with life-giving water. More of it gushes down from the upper plateau, tumbling down into lower tarn almost joyously. The lake side is covered with reeds, and other flowers. Toads croak in the swampy earth, birds stoop out of the sky to snatch them up, and insects buzz everywhere. Life in all its blood and beauty has returned. And it's all down to you.

You can see the door set into the cliffside, and the stairs leading to the upper tarn. Nearby is a statue and a fountain.

Feeling rather smug, you decide what to do next.

Go to the door	▶ 235
Investigate the fountain	▶ 325
Climb the stairs	▶ 370
Go south along the river	▶ 39
Go south west to the old arch	▶ 340

546

The lion smashes at you with a massive paw which you are able to block with the great shield of Ajax but then it charges straight at you, hammering your shield with the entire weight of its massive body. You are forced back onto a tree root, and you fall to the ground. The lion springs upon you, pinning you to the ground with its forepaws while its massive jaws close around your head and bites it off. Death is instant.

You fought bravely if somewhat futilely. Perhaps the gods will deem you worthy enough to restore you to life.

▶ 111

547

The Arcady Trail leads away from the Palace. To the north is the great lake that is the source of the river Ladon. Look at your map. From here you can go:

South-west on the Trail	▶ 455
South on the Trail	▶ 728
North to the Lake	▶ 37

548
❑

Put a tick in the box. If there was a tick in the box already ▶ 590 immediately. If not, read on.

You walk further into the dales, following the thin path between the line of trees and the wide forest pool. Strange noises like the unstopping of corks from bottles fill the air as the golden lilies of the lake puff out small clouds of spores. Almost instantly, a strong soporific musk spreads across the glade and you start to feel a little dizzy. Things begin to swim in your vision. Your mind fogs up with curious thoughts, whimsical, capricious, almost random, almost as if you were thinking someone else's thoughts, those of a child perhaps, or a drunken satyr.

You realise you need to get away from here, but then a noise above your head causes you to look up – a face rushes down at you out of nowhere, and your heart nearly bursts in sudden fright but then it sweeps away, your eyes following its movement. You can barely make out her form for it is so quick, but it appears to be a young woman, running on air, her movements so fast they look to you like the movements of a jerking puppet. Mocking laughter trails after her – one of the aurae, perhaps; the nymphs of the breeze?

You turn to look over the little lake. And there, rising up out of the waters is a water nymph, dressed in soft green weeds – except that she has the head of a horse.

Behind her, out of the tree line step two young men – but one has the head of a boar, and the other a stag, complete with a full set of antlers.

With a thrill of horror, you realise that these are not masks, they cannot be for their eyes are darting about and their lips move as they talk to you but it is a language so ancient you cannot understand it. Or is it the golden lilies and their somniferous spores, twisting your senses?

The smell is everywhere, suffusing your senses; it is the scent of madness, of nightmares. You try to get away from this place but you cannot help yourself, and you sink to one knee. It is as if your body were falling asleep from the bottom up.

A fish leaps out of the water, except that it is not a fish but a long-tailed monkey with the head of a fish. It lands beside you and hugs your leg, wrapping its tail lovingly around your arm, looking up at you, as if in affection, but its fish eyes are blank and pitiless like the black, abyssal depths of Tartarus itself.

A harpy in a nearby tree – except that it has the head of a mantis – reaches into her nest and hurls an egg at you. It clatters off your chest to the ground. She hurls another. And another.

And then the first egg cracks open, and slowly, ever so slowly, a long, jointed, glistening chitinous leg emerges, followed by a second, jointed insectoid limb.

You stare, paralysed with a creeping horror, as the two legs begin to drag out a long, glutinous body behind it. A cockroach, as large as your foot, cracks out of the egg, six spiny legs beetling, two antennae questing. And its eyes… there are two of them and they look uncannily human, staring at you, knowing, understanding, recognizing. Other eggs crack open and several swollen cockroaches scuttle towards you, their limbs rustling like dry old bones rattling in a jar.

The monkey holds on tight, the stag, the boar and the horse walk slowly towards you, babbling in an unknown tongue, while a foot-long cockroach begins to caress your leg with its antennae… Uncontrollable horror rises up with in you and you begin to scream wildly until, thankfully, you pass out.

▶ 398

549

The audience bursts out into long and uproarious laughter. Deridedes acknowledges your insult with a rueful smile. 'Simple, but effective, especially for an unsophisticated audience like this but the judge is of a higher calibre, a most refined rooster and he won't fall for such crudity,' he says to you in an aside.

But the cock crows a 'silly-old-goat' and the crowd claps and whistles enthusiastically.

Deridedes looks askance at the floor. 'How can it..?' he mutters, leaving the sentence unfinished.

'That's two points to me, none for you,' you point out with a smirk.

'Hah! Well, we'll see about that,' says Deridedes. He puts the Momos mask up to his face and says, 'You nut-brained ninny-noggined knob-headed nincompoop, no one knows your name!'

The crowd roars with laughter at that one, and Deridedes smiles broadly, awaiting the judgement of Kraterus.

But none comes. Deridedes gasps in shock.

'My turn for the final round,' you say.

What will you try now?

'At last! I've been searching for a fool, and look what I found – you!' ▶ 568

'You pettifogging, mooncalf mountebank, quacksalver!' ▶ 427

550

The Iskandrian ship drops you off at a bay on the north coast of Arcadia. 'A pleasant land,' says the captain, surveying the greenery of the hills that rise up just a little way inland. 'When I retire and want to get the sand of Notus out of my throat, this is where I'll come.'

▶ 444

551

Although you have thrown off her enchantment, it is not entirely gone. Every now and then Zoupa turns back into the shape of the beautiful young man, and you find yourself unable to press your attack. She takes advantage of your hesitation to strike you down and batten her yellow fangs on your neck. You pass out, but this time you do not wake up at all, for she has been slowly drinking your soul, bit by bit, and now she drains the last of it. And without a soul, the gods cannot bring you back…

▶ 750

552

'Wow, you got it all, how brill is that!' says Lefkia, clapping her hands together excitedly.

Hypatia raises an eyebrow. 'What, some limestone and a bit of timber, how hard can that be?' she says disparagingly.

'Actually…' you begin, but then you think better of it. Hunted by werewolves led by a bear, a sorceress, a frozen lake… who would believe you anyway?

'Anyway,' says Helen, from the shadows of her lean to, the important thing is that we can start work.'

'Indeed, won't be long before you own an inn!' says Hypatia.

Soon several labourers turn up, and work begins. Gain the title **The Hotelier**.

'Come back later,' says Lefkia, 'we'll let you know when it's finished.'

You take your leave ▶ 653

553

You examine the door handle and find a small poison needle trap – which you accidentally set off! It pricks your finger, and you can feel poison coursing up your arm. You sink to one knee, gasping in pain. Is this the end?

Luckily for you, you are able to survive the toxin, but tick the Wound box on your Adventure Sheet. If you are already wounded gain 1 scar instead, as the poison leaves your hand blackened and burned by venom.

After a while you are sufficiently recovered to open the door and step into the chamber. Inside there is a bed, a table and a cabinet, full of the apparatus of sorcery – vials, alembics, a jar full of eyeballs, another full of severed fingers. There are herbs, poisons, potions and scrolls, lots of scrolls. In one corner there is a chest. It is frosted with ice. You open the lid. Inside is a casket, bitterly cold to the touch. You open that. Inside that is a beating heart of ice.

▶ 299

554

You hear a faint howl in the distance, a wolf of some kind, they are common enough here in Arcadia. At least you hope it's a wolf and not that undead horror from Hades… You wait in trepidation but you do not hear it again. It is safe to move on.

You are following the Arcady Trail, a dusty well-walked path through the woods and overgrown hedgerows of Arcadia. From here you can:

Follow the Trail west into the Deep Forest ▶ 710
Follow the Trail North ▶ 85
Follow the Trail East ▶ 728
Go north-east to the Palace ▶ 686
Go south-east into the Dales of Leaf and Stream ▶ 266

555

You step back into your suite at the Summer Palace. ▶ 100

556

He tries to overwhelm you quickly, attacking wildly, but with careful parrying and riposting you are able to wear your opponent down for he is not built for a long fight. Finally, you wear him out and beat him into submission. He falls to his knees, exhausted, bruised and beaten. Behind you, your guests cheer heartily – well, most of them.

'You are the better hero, I see that now. Please, just kill me, I cannot go on with the bitter taste of defeat forever in my heart.'

| Kill him | ▶ 662 |
| Let him live | ▶ 734 |

557

You run on, panting in the terrible heat, rivers of sweat running down your body. Your limbs begin to ache with fatigue and it is getting harder and harder to draw breath. Behind you, howls and exultant whoops fill the air – and then sheer off in another direction! Maybe a deer or two has led them astray or some other stroke of luck.

It is not long before you come to the edge of a clearing in the forest, in the middle of which you spot the statue of Artemis hunting with her bow, accompanied by two wolves, all beautifully carved in brightly coloured painted marble. At its base lie offerings to the goddess. You made it.

▶ 520

558

There is no one here. The cottage looks as if it hasn't been inhabited in years. The compost heap is a pile of green slime, the rain butt has rotted away, and the chimney is blocked with soot.

The only thing of interest is a faded note scrawled on a wall calendar next to a circled day. You peer close and gradually piece together the words:

'Move to Boreas? Pine barrens look nice.'

Then you notice the date on the calendar. It's next year's.

▶ 617

559

You have come to a range of low, grass covered hills. To the west are the great walls of Vulcan City, and to the north, the deep forest. Eastwards lies the dales of leaf and stream.

You look around the hills. Some are crowned with a few trees here and there. One hill has three tall trees on top of which rests what looks like a large nest made of reeds and branches, and draped, incongruously, with wool. Something moves – a head, peeping over the edge at you. A horse's head by the look of it! If you have the codeword *Phosphoric* ▶ 606 immediately. If not, read on.

There appears to be no way for you get up there or lure whatever is in that nest down, so you move on. From here you can go:

North-west to the Deep Forest	▶ 710
North to the Arcady Trail	▶ 455
South to the Sacred Way	▶ 119
East into the Dales	▶ 266

560

The next time he raises his club up to his face, you take a

chance and roll aside early. You are able to see what he's up to – the bottles tied into his great beard are actually full of turpentine or some other flammable liquid. He raises his club to conceal that he's sucking it up into his mouth, striking his bronze capped club with some kind of flint or other device to create a spark, and igniting his breath! He isn't some mythical flame-spewing giant, more like a common-or-garden circus fire breather. Clever, but still, you know his trick now.

You dodge a swing of his club, and then pretend to stumble, luring Kakas into going for a blast of flame. As he raises his club, you dart to the side, and hurl a rock at his beard, just as he strikes a spark. You're accurate enough to shatter a bottle, soaking his beard – it goes up in a great roar of flames!

'Aiieee!' howls Kakas, as his beard burns, followed by all of his hair. Bottles begin to explode, turning his entire head into a ball of flame.

You stand and watch as he staggers around flailing wildly, moaning in agony like some kind of demented living candle.

Eventually he hits the floor with a ground-shaking thud, all the flesh of his head burned away, leaving only a massive blackened and charred skull.

You have defeated the giant Kakas. Gain the codeword *Punition* and ▶ 592

561

You raise your weapon – she steps back with a cry of 'No!' but you are too fast, too brutal, and too experienced in the despatching of souls to hesitate and you cut her down with one swift blow. She dies at your feet, her red blood spreading around her like a crimson sheet laid out on a grey-stone bed. The pale green glow of her skin and eyes fades into black and her sea-weed hair begins to shrivel up. You notice that even the locks of her hair you were carrying start to shrivel up too. Cross off the **water nymph hair** from your Adventure Sheet.

Damara the water nymph is no more. You decide against doing any more fishing today, so it is time to move on. Where will you go?

West on the Way	▶ 20
South-west into the forest	▶ 189
East on the Way	▶ 380
South, into the dried-up river valley	▶ 403

562

That makes sense. You spent a few hours fishing and bring home a good catch for supper. You can still smell that fish frying in the pan with garlic and herbs, still taste the succulent flesh on your mother's wheat cakes with a squeeze of lemon. Of course, in a dream every meal is perfect. Now ▶ 459

563

Suddenly three figures step out from behind the ruined fountain.

'Right, then, you dung-faced maggot, this is a robbery! Give us everything or die!' says their leader, who is flanked by two thugs one tall and thin with a horribly burned face, the other short but well-muscled with a shock of bleached white hair and patterned whorls tattooed on his bare chest. A Celt.

You know all three of them. The two brigands are led by Deridedes, the priest of Momos you beat in a contest of insults, the man who kidnapped and enslaved the boy Magnes who you freed and returned to his family, and also the man who hanged you from a tree, even after you had spared his life previously.

At the sight of you, his jaw drops. 'How…how can you be still alive? I hanged you from a tree, we cut your body down, that family of sheep-shagging lackwits buried you, we saw it!'

You smile. 'I told you I'd be back.' You see that the Celt has gone quite pale. The other, the lumbering burn-faced oaf just stares at you, his brow wrinkled in puzzlement.

'But… but how?' mutters Deridedes

'I am Chosen of the Gods.'

At that the Celt just turns tail and runs.

Burned face turns to watch him, surprised, and you step up and simply run him through with a deft thrust to the heart. He drops down dead.

Deridedes eyes widen in terror. He steps back holding his hand up pleadingly.

'Wait, wait, surely we can come to some kind of agreement here, I've got money!'

'We tried that, when I spared you the last time. I'll not make that mistake again,' you say. You step forward. Time to get your revenge.

Kill him	▶ 601
Torture him to death slowly	▶ 629

564

You spot a local ragamuffin of a boy, casing the crowd, no doubt looking for a pocket to pick. Quickly you offer him 10 pyr, a princely sum to an impoverished scallywag like this boy, if he can find the strange looking misshapen woman in the black robes, and he sets off with excited glee.

You notice a figure standing a little way off on the edge of the teeming market, staring at you. She wears a theatrical mask like that of a tyrant, all white with red lips and eyes, and royal robes, again from what looks like a set of theatrical props that cover her completely. She seems unnaturally tall, at least two and half metres, and holds a sword in each hand. Presumably she is the Timandra the terrible tyrant. She

gestures at you but you pretend not to notice, trying to buy some time. A few minutes later the boy returns,

'I found her, followed her to a small clearing in the woods west of here!' he says breathlessly.

'Show me the way!' you say and you melt into the crowd so that Timandra the terrible tyrant can't see you. The boy leads you on a circuitous route around the back of the tall tyrant and towards the woods. He points in the direction of the clearing, just beyond the treeline, and holds out his hand with a cheeky grin on his face. You give him the 10 pyr and he runs off, grinning even more. It is only then that you notice he's already pick pocketed you for 5 pyr! Cross off 15 pyr. With a curse, you creep towards the woods, keeping low and out of sight.

Make a GRACE roll at difficulty 7.

Succeed	▶ 441
Fail	▶ 384

565

Immediately you fall under the dryad's spell. You are even more susceptible to it the second time round. Phearci wakes and begins to dance for you once more, laughing and chuckling the whole time, and soon you are once more beguiled, and your heart is hers. She welcomes you back to slavery with relish.

And this time there will no escape. You try self-slaughter once again, but you cannot overcome the fear of losing her this time. Phearei's magic is just too strong. Even though you know you are bewitched, and this love is a false love, you cannot bear to be without her. You go back to your mistress, doomed to serve her for all time. Your adventure ends here.

▶ 750

566

You step through the arch and into a thick copse of trees. Once you pass through them, Pan's Arbour or as the Celts call it, the Shrine of the Horned God, is a sunken glade, with an altar of oak at the centre. Offerings to the god have been left beside it – wine, ale, fruit, meats, seeds and so on. Lots of wine in fact. At the base of the altar, carved into the wood, is the face of Pan, bearded, horned and wild eyed.

If you have **Pan's amulet ▶ 781**. If not, you can make an offering and pray at the altar.

Pray	▶ 696
Leave	▶ 463

567

❑

Put a tick in the box. If there was a tick in the box already ▶ **167** immediately. If not, read on.

'I know someone who can help,' you say. You send for Lefkia, the woman who refurbished the palace, and it is not long before she arrives.

'Hello, hello!' she says breezily, ever-cheerful, greeting you and the priestess with a smile, her bright brown eyes sparkling with humour. Last time you saw her she was covered in dust and paint, but now she's looking a little neater.

She takes a look around the temple, muttering to herself and making marks on a papyrus scroll she holds in one hand.

'I can fix it up, no problem! I've still got some paint left over from the palace job, but the plaster work – well, I'll need some more **vinegar of Hades** and another **bucket of gypsum** for this.' If you have these items already and want to hand them to Lefkia, ▶ **628**.

If not, you will have to come back later when you do. For now, you can go:

West along the coast   ▶ **380**
South along the coast   ▶ **419**
South-west into the farmlands   ▶ **270**

568

Most of the audience guffaws loudly at that one, followed by a smattering of appreciative applause.

Deridedes says to you, 'An old one, but still solid, I'll give you that. But our judge has heard that before, and will remain silent!'

Just then Kraterus crows a 'silly-old-goat.' Deridedes eyes narrow in anger. 'That little shit, I'll beat…'

'What was that? Deridedes?' you say at the top of your voice.

'Oh, nothing, nothing,' says Deridedes. 'Ladies and gentlemen, amazingly, and for the first time ever, we have a winner!' He raises your hand and says, 'I dub thee Master of Mockery!'

You bow, as the crowd roars their approval. Deridedes tries to hurry away but you grab his arm forcefully, take the money pouch off his belt, count out a 100 pyr, toss it back, jump off the stage, grab the cage holding Kraterus, and dash out as fast as you can before anyone can stop you. You race round the back, where you free the slave boy and give him his cut. He runs off with a shouted, 'thank you!' before he disappears into the crowd.

Note **Kraterus the cockerel**, the title **Master of Mockery** and 50 pyr on your Adventure Sheet.

There is nothing more to be done here, so you can head back to the market (▶ **728**) or leave the area (▶ **12**).

569

As the new Mayor, you are given Cressida's old desk. You also get the key to the enormous iron strongbox that is the village 'treasury'.

Since her hefty fine, there are now 600 pyr in the strongbox.

Embezzle the money   ▶ **212**
Invest it in the village   ▶ **147**

570

❑

Put a tick in the box. If there was a tick in the box already ▶ **246** immediately. If not, read on.

You pull the lever and are thrown up into the blue like an arrow shot from Artemis' bow. Below, you can see the Arcady Trail like chalk marks on stone and then nothing but a sea of trees until you start to plummet downwards towards the Sacred Way at the western edge of Arcadia. Suddenly there is a loud squawk right in your ear, and a flurry of feathers in your eyes and mouth. You have hit a large bird! To your horror, you realise you've been thrown off course, and now you're plummeting down into the sea of trees below. You can't help yourself and you utter a loud 'Aieeeee!'

▶ **457**

571

You examine the door handle and find a small poison needle trap which you are able to disarm.

You open the door and step into the chamber. Inside there is a bed, a table and a cabinet, full of the apparatus of sorcery – vials, alembics, a jar full of eyeballs, another full of severed fingers. There are herbs, poisons, potions and scrolls, lots of scrolls. In one corner there is a chest. It is frosted with ice. You open the lid. Inside is a casket, bitterly cold to the touch. You open that. Inside that is a beating heart of ice.

▶ **299**

572

You track the deer and are able to bring one down. The rest scatter into the trees in terror. Roll a die:

score 1   ▶ **488**
score 2-3   ▶ **391**
score 4-5   ▶ **378**
score 6   ▶ **449**

573

You come round from your encounter with a god, to find Drosos and Nyctimus looking at you with concerned expressions on their faces.

'Are you all right?' says Drosos.

'Yes, yes, I'm fine, it was just…' you mutter, shaking your head to clear it.

'Was it the gods? What did they say?' asks Nyctimus.

'The labours, I… another one finished…' you stutter.

'Excellent! Excellent,' says Nyctimus, 'that is good.'

'Back to the mundane, I suppose, but your cut of the first harvest is ready for you to collect,' says Drosos.

► 793

574

You decide on a risky choice – a brand new sea shanty from the fishing ports of western Boreas. Centaurs aren't known for their seafaring, but on the other hand, it is a cracking tune and quite new. You give it a foot-tapping (or should that be hoof-tapping), finger-drumming, leg-hopping rendition and your ploy pays off, the crowd loves it.

You and Velosina stare up at Chiron expectantly. The old master pulls a hand down his beard several times, thinking. And then he pronounces judgement.

'I think the human has just edged it, I'm sorry Velosina,' he says. 'That last song, what a piece!'

The crowd applaud, and Velosina takes her defeat with good grace.

'Fair enough,' she says, slapping you on the back heartily. 'You did well – for someone with only two legs!' and she laughs.

Chiron presents you with the musical scroll of Sappho. 'Here is Sappho's poem, rather a sad, tragic piece but beautiful all the same. It's called "My lover lies with Ladon".'

Note **Sappho's song** on your Adventure Sheet. When you are ready, Chiron congratulates you and says, 'Is there anything else I can help you with?'

► 90

575

'A wise answer,' says the voice. Gain the codeword *Praise-Athena*. The door swings open to reveal a small room under the earthen mound with an altar to Athena inside. you can get blessings here. If you are a worshipper of Athena, blessings are free. If not, you must pay 10 pyr per blessing. You can only have a total of three blessings at a time.

When you have finished here ► 578

576

If you have the **kingslayer dagger** with you that the shade of Klytemnestra gave you ► 650 immediately. If not read on.

You run down the path and through the arched entrance way and charge at the giant with a war like cry. He steps back in surprise. He has four arms but is heedless of your attack, and you run him through with your first strike, right through the heart.

He falls to the ground dead. And then simply gets up again.

'You think it would be so easy? I am king of the gigantes and here, on my land, I cannot be killed,' says Alcyoneus in a booming voice. He reaches for you with all four of his massive hands…

You dodge aside and strike once more and the battle rages for a time. You kill him again, and try to drag his body off his land before he recovers, but he is simply too heavy, and you only manage to move him a foot or two.

In the end, you are forced to try and wrestle him out of his courtyard but he has four arms and you are not Heracles, and soon he has you pinned.

'Goodbye, foolish mortal,' says Alcyoneus as he slowly breaks you in two, cracking your spine like a twig. At least you died a heroic death, fighting the king of the giants.

► 111

577

You consider your options. The wind is blowing from west to east, so if you follow the wind maybe you can circle around behind Alpha without him catching your scent. Then you can lay the wolf-trap and lure him onto it.

You will have to make sure you make as little noise as possible, as well, of course.

Make a GRACE roll at difficulty 7.

Succeed	► 639
Fail	► 467

578

If you have the codeword *Plenty* ► 545 immediately. If not, read on.

The source of the Alpheus river is the Upper Tarn from where it runs down a waterfall into the Lower Tarn where you are now. But it is dried up and parched, like a desert gully, a lake of old bones and dust.

On one side of the tarn, set into the cliffside is a strange door. On the other side, stairs have been hacked out of the cliffs, climbing up the cliffs to the high plateau.

There is also an ancient fountain nearby with a statue upon it.

Investigate the door	► 235
Investigate the fountain	► 389
Climb the stairs	► 370
Go south along the river	► 684
Go south west to the old arch	► 340

579

You have returned to the clearing in the heart of the forest where the Great Greens Ones dwell. The three totems are hoary, and ancient beyond reckoning, stained with moss and lichen, wreathed in creepers and flowers but also green, very green. One has a strange mouth-like aperture on its trunk, the second has flower-like 'eyes' and the third is fecund with strange looking walnuts. The totems' faces are as wide as a man's arms stretched out to either side.

All is quiet. The wooden altar, cup, tablet and knife are still here. You take another look at the clay tablet. It is hard to read such an ancient text but you recognize certain words – the Great Green Ones, Fount of the Forest, Heart of the Vine, Mother of Trees, the First Leaf and so on. You can make a libation as a sacrifice on the altar.

Will you try a libation or leave?

Wine, or water	▶ 778
Your own blood	▶ 827
Dione's blood, if you have it	▶ 756
Daemon's blood, if you have it	▶ 806
Leave it for now	▶ 669

580

You simply turn tail and make a dash for the woods. Perhaps you can lose him in the trees.

'Hah, I knew it, a coward after all!' bellows Death Dealer and he sets off in pursuit. Hopefully his shield and armour will slow him down.

Make a GRACE roll at difficulty 8.

Succeed	▶ 116
Fail	▶ 159

581

Lose the codeword *Plight* and gain the codeword *Penalty*.

Your anger and disgust at how you have been tricked fuels your blows and soon she falls to the ground under your martial onslaught and you slay the foul creature without hesitation. Zoupa the empousa will no longer feed on the hearts of the men and women of Arcadia.

You search her tent and find a little chest in one corner. Opening it you find a small fortune. 250 pyr, and, propped up against the wall and covered in a tattered old wrap, a huge round object of some kind. You remove the covering to find an ancient shield with a placard hanging off it, like a museum piece.

'Ajax came up bearing his shield in front of him like a wall – a shield. of bronze with seven folds of ox-hide'

– Homer, the Iliad

The legendary shield of Ajax! Could it really be? It certainly looks old enough to have been in the Trojan Wars. And how did that foul, black-hearted empousa come by it? Deceit, subterfuge and murder, no doubt...

Anyway, you take the shield. Note the **shield of Ajax** on your Adventure Sheet. It is too much of an antique to be used regularly in battle, for it looks like it might fall apart at any moment, but still, no doubt you will find a use for it.

You also find a letter to Zoupa the empousa. It is from a woman called Mela, a sorceress of Hecate. It describes what you look like and instructs her to drink your soul...

When you are ready, you can return to the market (▶ 728) or leave the area (▶ 12).

582

Sivi is nowhere to be seen. Suddenly, what you thought was a pomegranate tree comes to life and you realise it was Sivi all along. 'Welcome, mortal of many titles, to my honey farm. Unfortunately, while the bees have been busy, there is no honey to harvest yet. You'll have to come back again later.'

You take your leave. Will you:

Go deeper into the woods	▶ 176
Leave this place	▶ 225

583

You are too slow, and are engulfed in flames! You howl in agony as your hair burns up in a flash, your eyes sting, your skin charred – and then you are struck by a massive blow from the giant's bronze-capped club.

'Hur, hur, hur, crispy human for dinner!' is the last thing you hear before you are hammered into unconsciousness. You never wake up. Well, not here at any rate.

▶ 111

584

So begins a life of servitude and slavery. At first you are made to attend to the funeral of Karya, where satyrs, dryads and others of the fae mourn her loss. You are blamed for her death but because you are a doting love fool, you accept the blame and are whipped for it which you also accept just to be near Phearei. You hang on her every word, and do whatever she tells you, for you love her utterly. You find yourself with other charmed mortals, men and women both. You must pleasure the dryad in her arbour at night, sometimes with other love-slaves, and entertain her according to her whims which may be a song, a poem or a 'frolic' with the other slaves while Phearei and her friends laughingly look on. Sometimes she lends you out to her friends – that makes you sad, for you are away from Phearei's light but you obey anyway, for your entire life is now dedicated to one goal – serving your mistress.

You must also serve her food and drink, help dress her in the mornings, and tend to her toilet at night. Sometimes you are sent on errands to other parts of Arcadia. There are ample opportunities to escape, but you always come back to her because you cannot bear to be away from her for too long, as your love is so deep and all-consuming, even though she often does not treat you well, compared to the other love-fools.

▶ 607

585

You arrive at the Druid's Shrine. Amergin and his two Celtic warrior guards greet you at the archway entrance. 'Ah, 'tis the wanderer in the green. Do you have the donation for the god?' asks Amergin.

If you have a **bearskin cloak** and wish to give it to Amergin, cross it off and ▶ **664**

If not, or you don't want to do so now, you can come back later ▶ **463**

586

You wake refreshed, gazing at the…er… 'goings on' in the mural on your wall.

You leap out of bed, full of new energy, gain a **benison x 1**. Note it on your Adventure Sheet. It gives you +1 on your next attribute roll. Once it has been used, cross it off.

Also, if you were wounded, you are healed. Untick your Wound box.

Your butler, Jas the Helot, helps you don your armour and equipment along with comments like, 'Oh my, what a physique,' or 'I must say, you are quite the mighty warrior!' or 'Artemis herself would die for those calves, my captain,' and so on.

You wonder whether killing your butler is a crime or not. Unfortunately, you think it probably is, so you glare at him for a moment. 'Me? I'm a simple slave, don't mind me,' he says obsequiously.

Anyway. Time to move on. ▶ **282**

587

Ladon's Lake is no longer frozen, its waters warm and inviting but the water level is much lower than it would normally be. There is not enough lake water to flow down to Oceanus, and the rest of the river is still dry. As you walk the banks of the lake, Ladon himself rises up out of the water to greet you, his green beard and hair straggly with weeds. He looks tired, and weak, but at least he is no longer trapped in a block of ice.

'Thank you again for freeing me, mortal hero, but without the strength of Alpheus, my counterpart, the river spirits cannot flow, for we are bound together by the power of water,' says Ladon. You nod your understanding.

'Free Alpheus…' he says with a tired sigh, before sinking back beneath the waves.

There is nothing else for you here.

▶ **81**

588

You have already been to the heart of the forest, and won its favour. You return to the clearing, but the Great Green Ones sleep on, oblivious, waiting for the day when you might call upon them. There is nothing more for you to do here, so you head back to the edge of the forest, and to 'civilisation'.

▶ **148**

589

You battle heroically for a time, ducking and diving, but eventually the bear catches you around the head with a massive paw. You are thrown to the ground, head buzzing.

If you are already wounded, then the bear has ripped your head right off, and death is instant ▶ **111**

Otherwise, tick the Wound box on your Adventure Sheet. You realise you cannot win this fight, and that the bear is going to kill you. You have no choice but to flee for your life. Make a GRACE roll at difficulty 7.

Succeed	▶ **448**
Fail	▶ **491**

590

You remember the last time you were here – you were ensorcelled, fattened up, sacrificed on an altar with a sickle, stuck on a spit, roasted and eaten. Are you sure you want to risk that again? If not, and you wish to try and leave ▶ **67**

If you really want to go through it all again, then ▶ **776**

591

Ladon's Lake is looking beautiful, its surface calm and peaceful in the summer sun. From the lake, the river Ladon runs to the northern shores. Somehow it looks like it is flowing happily.

You pause for a moment to bask in the glory of your own magnificence for achieving such a thing as restoring the rivers of Arcadia.

Swans glide majestically across the lake, a fishing boat, its red sail billowing in the soft breeze, courses through the waves, chasing the jumping fish and gulls caw greedily in the high blue.

Wooden lakeside cabins have sprung up on the shore, for Arcadian folk like to take their ease by a lake. Nearby, you see a nymph, laughing wildly, pursued by a priapic satyr, until she dives into the water, turns into a fish, and swims away, leaving the satyr panting sadly on the beach. He turns to look at you, hopefully.

You rest your hand on your weapon. Quickly he looks away, before galloping off into the woods.

If you have the title **Kissed by a Water Nymph** and wish to explore the lake bed ▶ **794**

If not, there is nothing more to do here ▶ **81**

592

You respectfully take down the body of the young woman Kakas had been roasting, reunite it with its head and bury it properly.

As for Kakas, you build up the fire, drag his enormous corpse and dump into onto the fire instead. It will take a few hours to render down but eventually there will be nothing left but ash. You remove all the other heads, and bury them too, before mounting Kakas's massive skull over the gates as a monument to your glorious victory.

And then you turn your attention to the bronze chest nearby. Inside you find Kakas's treasure – the **Cuirass of the Lost Hero**, 150 pyr, a **roll of canvas**, two **lava gems**, a **jug of dandelion wine** and, lodged in the corner, forgotten, some **copper ore**. Quite the haul. Add them to your Adventure Sheet.

Now that you have the **Cuirass of the Lost Hero** if you also have the **Helm of the Lost Hero**, the **Greaves of the Lost Hero**, and the **Vambraces of the Lost Hero** then you have the Panoply of the Lost Hero. Delete all the Lost Hero items from your Adventure Sheet, add the **Panoply of the Lost Hero** instead. If you have any of the items in storage/vaults make a note that once you have them all in your carried inventory, they will become the Panoply.

You are finished with Fort Blackgate for now, so you take your leave. There is only one way out, south along the Arcady Trail.

▶ 85

593
❏

Put a tick in the box. If there was a tick in the box already ▶ **655** immediately. If not, read on.

The painter and decorator whose contract you have bought is waiting for you at the gates of the Palace. It is a young woman in a white chiton and a clean white apron. Her auburn hair is tied up in a bun, under a little white hat, and her eyes are a bright brown colour that twinkle with humour. Behind her are two young boys of around ten years of age. Twins, in fact, by the look of them.

'I am Lefkia. Thank you for hiring me.'

'Your apron looks a little clean for a painter and decorator,' you say.

'Ah, well, there hasn't been any work for a long, long time, sadly. We are so grateful you have come and I look forward to getting covered in paint and dust,' she says. 'Me and my crew can fix up the palace, I just need a few things first.'

'That's your crew, is it?' you ask, pointing at the twins.

She looks behind her and the two boys grin up at her mischievously.

'Yes,' she says, turning back to you, 'my little brothers, Ataktos and Pioataktos. Don't worry, they'll do as I tell them.'

The boys exchange a look, and then giggle.

'Here,' she says, and she gives you a handwritten note. 'This is what we need to complete the job.'

box of paints x 2
vinegar of hades x 1
bucket of gypsum

If you have all these items and wish to hand them to Lefkia, cross them off your Adventure Sheet and ► **715**

If not, you tell Lefkia you will come back when you have them, and take your leave. 'Don't take too long,' she says, 'My crew will get impatient.' ► **547**

594

You haul yourself out onto the lake-bed floor. Up above, the super-heated steam that was Alpheus has roared up into the sky where it has coalesced into an enormous storm cloud. And then it rains. A great deluge of rain, all coming down in a matter of seconds. You find yourself drenched in water, as the lake begins to fill up. You dodge aside as more superheated steam erupts out of the trapdoor, as water gushes into the cavern and hits the lava. Moments later, the steam ceases, the lava no doubt solidified by now.

You run for the lakeshore, as the water level rises rapidly.

You have completed one of the Great Labours of Arcadia. Write the number **381** (not *this* paragraph number) in the Current Location space on your Adventure Sheet (in place of the number already written there, if any) and then ► **38**

595

You'll have to think fast if you're going to come up with a stratagem on the fly. Make an INGENUITY roll at difficulty 8.

Succeed   ► **564**
Fail   ► **506**

596

'It's a nice piece,' says Velosina, 'but you've shown it to me already.' You continue on to find Chiron. He greets you warmly and offers to help you in any way he can.

► **90**

597

He puts down the axe he's been using to chop wood. 'Well, that's honest at least. But if you shirk your tasks you'll never learn to apply yourself.'

'Boring.' You stroll past him into the house to see if supper's ready.

Mark your STRENGTH score as −1, then ►**459**

598

Fortunately, you know from the book how to cure the meat to make sausages – raw venison won't last in this summer heat for long.

You search for deer spoor and it is not long before you pick up some tracks. You set off down the trail, careful to make sure you're down wind, though as you progress it gets darker and more dense, the trees crowding together so much that there is little wind at all.

Make an INGENUITY roll at difficulty 7. If you have the title **Favoured by Orion**, add one to the result.

Succeed   ► **572**
Fail   ► **543**

599

'You really think I'd take a bribe? No, I think not, now, on your knees, you murderers!'

They blink at you in shock. Polycrates looks over his shoulder, as if thinking about making a run for it, but you strike a martial pose and glare savagely at him. You are a hardened adventurer after all, and can look quite terrifying if you choose to. His shoulders slump in defeat, and they both sink to their knees. The game is up.

Soon you have their hands tied behind their backs and you lead them to the raised platform in the village square where you begin to bellow loudly, calling as many of the villagers as you can to hear what you have to say.

With most of the village gathered before you, you read out Polycrates's confession, as he and Cressida stand behind you, looking crestfallen and guilty.

'That was my sister he murdered!' cries a woman from the crowd.

'Aye, and my cousin,' says a man.

'And Cressida was our magistrate, all that time, a real viper in our midst!'

You manage to stop them from lynching them on the spot, and by force of your will, persuade them to follow the law properly.

A trial is held, which they ask you to oversee. Cressida and Polycrates have little choice but to confess to their crimes. Polycrates is sentenced to death by hemlock, and Cressida is lucky enough to get away only with permanent exile from Arcadia after paying a substantial fine of 500 pyr to be paid into the village coffers.

After the sentence is carried out, the villagers come to you and, impressed by your insistence on following the rule of law, appoint you as the new *basileus* or mayor of Bridgadoom. You find yourself unable to refuse. You settle into Cressida's old office in the magistrate's hall. ► **569**

600

You have left the hot, burning desert of Notus behind you. Although there is a hot summer sun here in Arcadia the air is filled with fresh sounds and smells. Birdsong, the hum of the bee, the buzz of the dragonfly, glinting in the sunlight, the heady scents of herbs and the sweet bouquet of wild flowers. But what terrible dangers lie hidden behind this pleasant mask of Arcadian paradise?

If you have the codeword **Neveragain**, lose the codeword **Projectile** and then ▶ 833

601

Without further ado you administer swift and violent justice while also getting your revenge. One stroke of your blade and his body falls one way and his head bounces away another. Thus ends the miserable life of the villainous Deridedes, con-man, kidnapper, murderer, bandit and robber.

Once you have cleaned the blood off your hands and clothes ▶ 644

602

If you have the title **Friend of the Forest** ▶ 588 immediately. If not, read on.

You drive yourself on, into the dark and gloomy depths of the forest. The forest canopy is now almost entirely interlinked, branches entwined like a roof of ropes. What light there is comes from luminescent mosses and mushrooms rather than the sun. The air is hot, heavy and oppressive, like a pillow held down over your face. You gasp for breath, drenched in sweat. Everything is quiet, so quiet. Your nostrils are filled with strange scents and smells of flowers, herbs and fungi. Something in the air – spores, or pollen perhaps – is beginning to muddle your head with dreams and visions. You start believing that you can hear the trees thinking. And their thoughts are cruel indeed: 'Fall, meat-creature, fall, and let my roots drink your blood.'

'Die, wormling, so that my seeds can feed on your flesh and grow.'

'A manling? After all these years? Sleep, manling, sleep at my feet – for ever.'

'Dream, rootless beast, dream eternal dreams cradled in our arms.'

You stagger on, thinking that perhaps this is the end, and that you shouldn't have come here. Any moment now you will sink into unconsciousness and never wake up. The forest will eat you. But then you see light between the dense trunks up ahead, and suddenly you burst forth into a wide clearing, eyes watering in the bright sunshine. You take in great gulps of fresh clean air. Well… almost clean. ▶ 714

603

King Nyctimus greets you and thanks you for your work so far. You ask him what you know about the centaur war-band that has raided the vineyard and who are trying to extort money from you.

'Yes, I've been told about them. You see, centaurs are ruled over by Chiron, the *primus inter equos* or "first among centaurs", but Nessus, the captain of one of the centaur war-bands, rebelled against him, along with his soldiers – nothing more than a bunch of bandits and renegades, frankly. Nessus gravely wounded Chiron, who now lies on his death bed. That will be a terrible loss indeed, for Chiron is a great healer, and a mentor to mortals in the arts of civilisation, and a friend to mankind. But Nessus is wild, rebellious. He thinks Arcadia is for the beasts and the beast men, and that humans should be scoured out of the land, for to him we are as stones in a ploughed field. But most of the centaurs, appalled at what he has done to their beloved leader, have rejected Nessus and his men and thrown them out. So they have taken up residence in some kind of fortified camp in the forests to the north. From there, they raid, and plunder and pillage across Arcadia. If you can deal with them, we would all be very grateful.'

'An entire warband?'

'I know, I know it won't be easy. If I were you, I'd go and talk to Chiron first, he might be able to help you. He can be found in the centaur homelands, north of the druids on the plateau of the river Alpheus. Assuming he is still alive, that is.'

You thank the king, say your farewells and continue on.

▶ 282 and choose again.

604

'Oh my, the Golden Fleece itself!' says Gelos. 'Well now, for the paltry sum of a hundred pyr I could rework this into a magnificent golden mantle.'

If you pay the money, cross off 100 pyr and the Golden Fleece and replace it with the **Golden Himation (+1 Glory)**. It is so magnificent it adds 1 to your Glory while you have it.

When you are done ▶ 187 and choose again.

605

The catch-net is a web stretched across four wooden poles that is meant to catch anyone tossed at it from the palace onager. Except that this web of vines has been eaten away by the local insect life and rips apart as soon as you land in it. You burst through it and smash straight into the ground.

Tick the Wound box on your Adventure Sheet. If you are already wounded than your body bursts like a rotten fruit falling from a tree. ▶ 111

If you still live, you stagger to your feet and look around ▶ 419

606

The horse pops its head up again, white as snow, followed by a flutter of great white wings. Is it Pegasus himself, the great winged horse of legend? You look to the skies to the north west, above the deep forest. A huge cloud, brown and brooding, shaped like a squat, domed tower on a hill drips acid down onto the Great Green Ones below, slowly killing them.

And if they die, so does the forest. You look back at Pegasus. If only you could persuade him to fly you up there.

If you have at least three **honey cakes** ▶ **635**

If not, or if you would rather come back later, then from here you can go:

North-west to the Deep Forest	▶ **710**
North to the Arcady Trail	▶ **455**
South to the Sacred Way	▶ **119**
East into the Dales	▶ **266**

607

One day, while on an errand to fetch an aphrodisiac for your mistress you come upon a forest glade that was once the scene of a riotous picnic, suddenly and quickly abandoned. A few bronze plates and cups are scattered about, an amphora of wine long since dried up, a few tattered blankets now riddled with weeds and dirt but also an old basket, inside of which you find three small jars labelled 'ambrosia, food of the gods'. Some say ambrosia confers immortality upon mortals that eat it, others that it only brings death.

If you take them, note **food of the gods x 3** on your Adventure Sheet.

If you want to eat some of the **food of the gods** ▶ **26**

If not ▶ **415**

608

❑

Put a tick in the box. If there was a tick in the box already ▶ **630** immediately. If not, read on.

You step into the ruins of the old fort. A ramshackle crumbling keep – a crenellated stone tower atop another squat stone tower – sits in the middle of an open space where, presumably, the garrison once drilled and exercised. Now it is covered in dust and the debris of broken weapons and armour and large stains of what looks like dried blood. At the far end, a huge figure is tending a fire, a veritable giant. His hair is a shock of wild black braids, patterned with gems. He sports a huge black beard, with what look like bottles braided into it but he is so big they look like vials. An endless supply of wine or ale perhaps? A flick of the head and there's a bottle in his mouth?

He wears a simple kilt of bronze strips over leather, and little else. Beady eyes sit in folds of fat, over a lumpy, misshapen jaw, snaggle-toothed and tusked. His body is bloated with fat and muscle, and his skin covered in tattoos,

over his face, body, arms and legs. Nearby, causally propped up against a large bronze chest is a massive wooden club, capped with bronze and studded with iron bolts.

To you your horror you realise he is roasting the body of a decapitated young woman over the fire.

▶ **779**

609

Sivi, the strikingly beautiful dryad of the pomegranate tree is waiting for you. By now, the pomegranate trees she planted have already filled the edge of the clearing and rich red pomegranates are hanging down from them.

'Welcome back, it is good to see the face of the mortal without whom I would not be breathing this delightful flower-scented air, nor would I feel the soft caress of the grass beneath my feet, nor my lips taste the sweet juice of the pomegranate.'

Her golden skin seems to shine in the sun, and her crimson hair has grown even further, reaching down to the back of her ankles now.

As you take a moment to wonder at her extraordinary appearance, she asks, 'Have you got my queen bee?'

If you have a **queen bee** and wish to hand it to Sivi ▶ **425**

If not, she reminds you that you should look for one in the mountains of Boreas before bidding you farewell. Will you:

Go deeper into the woods	▶ **176**
Leave this place	▶ **225**

610

A figure appears at your elbow, places her hand under your arm and raises you up from your seat. You obey mindlessly, even though a rising sense of dread is building inside of you.

The figure, a priestess also in a cowled robe, leads you to the back of the altar.

You try to reassert your own will, but you cannot break the spell that binds your mind. In fact, you begin to giggle happily, as if all of this was a wonderful evening out or a play of some kind but you know in your heart of hearts that something much more sinister is going on and that you are to be its victim.

The two cowled figures – a priest and a priestess – begin to chant as your escort points to the altar and asks you to lie face down. With a happy, half-witted chuckle, you do so, your mind not your own, with your head jutting over the side of the altar. You look down at a wide copper bowl resting on the ground. Obviously for the catching of the sacrificial blood, but whose blood will it be?

The priest and priestess chant on, and then each places a sickle on your either side of your neck and then they yank your throat open. Your life spills into the copper bowl. In your dying moments your reason returns – your body will provide some fine gourmet dining for the fae, as well as fattening up their next victim.

▶ 111

611

'A wolf? Why not put some hunters together, go out there and kill it?' you ask.

'Because that is not an ordinary wolf. King Lykaon rules these shrouded woodlands, under him are the sons of the wolf, his dread pack leaders each a mighty wolf-lord in their own right. The mightiest of them all is Alpha, supreme hunter, devourer of dryads, slayer of satyrs, bane of men and centaurs,' says the woodcutter ruefully.

'And that is Alpha,' he adds pointing at the wolf in the trees.

'Ah, I see,' you say. 'And you are?'

'I am Leonidas,' says the woodcutter.

'What, like the Spartan king?'

'Yes, yes, like the Spartan king, but also no, for I am neither a king, nor a Spartan nor a hero, I'm just a simple woodcutter who shits his pants every time he hears that wolf howl!'

'And your family?'

'My wife and two children – I had to send them away or Alpha would have killed and eaten them. He just waits there, looking for an opening, so he can rip me apart.'

'Why you?'

'Ah… well, I may have killed a wolf-cub or two. Thought I was making the place safer for my kids, turns out the opposite is true. If I'd known he was the father… Anyway, you look like *you* could be a Spartan monarch, a true hero, will you help me?'

'Hmm… by killing Alpha?'

'Yes, or driving him away somehow.'

'What's in it for me?' you ask.

'I… I have nothing, I'm sorry. Maybe the fame will be enough? Or the pelt of such a beast, that must be worth something? I have this too that I made, maybe it will help.'

He shows you a wooden trap with sharpened stakes as its teeth.

'If you can trick Alpha into stepping on this, it'll impale a leg, immobilise him long enough for you to kill him.'

If you decide to take the wolf-trap and deal with Alpha ▶ 577. If not, you tell the woodcutter it is too dangerous and take your leave.

'Come back if you change your mind!' says Leonidas. Where to next?

West to the Sacred Way	▶ 324
East to the Arcady Trail	▶ 455
South east to a small wood	▶ 475

612

You walk into the dilapidated Summer Palace, its tattered banners giving it a rather pathetic look, like a once great queen struck down by old age and disease. King Nyctimus, also rather dilapidated-looking and gone to seed or certainly to fat, nods a greeting and waves a hand at the bulletin board. 'There is work that needs doing,' he mutters.

Examine the bulletin board	▶ 101
Come back later	▶ 547

613

Gain the codeword **Penumbra**.

You can feel your shadow draining away, and it is horrible. Thinking fast, you pull out the lightning flint and strike it. A great flash of white light flares up and simply blows the shadow crow into wisps that then drain away into the ground like ink down a plug hole. All that is left is a small patch of black dirt in the ground. And thankfully, your shadow which appears fully intact.

You wonder what sort of creature it was. Some kind of shadow-hunter? And was it chance it chose your shadow or was it sent? Perhaps you will find out later but for now you decide to move on, checking on your shadow as you do. Will you go:

West into the forest	▶ 189
North to the bridge	▶ 517
South to Ladon's Lake	▶ 37

614

'Disaster!' wails Drosos, your farm overseer. 'A sudden summer storm! Normally not a problem, but at this early stage a disaster! As it says in the Book of Vulcan, "Arcadia's lush greenery is forever thirsty so the gods decreed many rainstorms: sudden, thunderous and bright with lightning." Unfortunately, this one washed away our newly sown seeds, and we'll have to start all over again. So sorry for the delay.'

You'll have to come back again later. For now, where will you go?

North-east	▶ 365
North-west	▶ 380
South-east	▶ 419

615

The clockwork owl of Athena jumps up and twitters mechanically, warning you that the door is trapped. Carefully you examine it and find a small poison needle which you are able to disarm.

You open the door and step into the chamber. Inside there is a bed, a table and a cabinet, full of the apparatus of sorcery – vials, alembics, a jar full of eyeballs, another full of severed fingers. There are herbs, poisons, potions and scrolls, lots of scrolls. In one corner there is a chest. It is frosted with ice. You open the lid. Inside is a casket, bitterly cold to the touch. You open that. Inside that is a beating heart of ice.

▶ 299

616

You have come to the outskirts of the deep forests of Arcadia. This part is particularly ancient and hoary, the kind of primordial woods that the spirits of old inhabited before Man was even shaped from clay by Prometheus. They have resented mankind and his axe ever since.

Before you stands a vast army of trees, still, silent, brooding. From it wafts scents of spices, herbs and creatures of the forest. You glimpse some deer, flitting from trunk to trunk. Birds fly up over the trees.

If you have a **book of recipes** and wish to hunt deer for their venison ▶ 598

If not, you can:

Explore the heart of the forest   ▶ 649

Leave on the Sacred Way   ▶ 158

617

You are in the heart of the little wood. The leaping sun is quelled by leaves. Anemones line the narrow paths trampled by deer. Somewhere a lark sings. From here you can go:

North to the Deep Forest   ▶ 710

East to the Arcady Trail   ▶ 455

South to hills near Vulcan City   ▶ 559

618

'Nice try,' he says, turning back to the logs he's chopping. 'But I think you went swimming instead.'

How? Your hair is wet! Of course.

Mark your INGENUITY score as −1, then ▶459

619

You try to follow a strategy of parry and riposte, hoping to wear your opponent down but his attacks are fast and frequent, for he cares not about any form of defence. Eventually, one of his strikes gets through, cutting open a terrible wound on your arm, and you are no longer able to use it. It is followed by a series of thrusts and hacks you cannot parry, and you fall to the ground, bleeding out.

Behind you, your guests scream in horror – except for one or two, who seem to be quite pleased. Clearly they bet against you. You wonder who they might be as you choke out your life on the banqueting hall floor.

Glaukos raises his arms in triumph, 'Glaukos is the victor, Glaukos the hero! All the glory that was yours is now mine!'

he boasts. But then he kneels down beside you.

'It was a magnificent fight, you are the greatest warrior I have ever faced, I will bury you with full honours and make sure your soul goes to Elysium, along with the other heroes of the age, and one day, I will join you there.'

'Really, there's no need for all that fuss, I won't be going to Elysium, believe me,' you mutter. And finally you die.

▶111

620

❑

If you have the codeword *Prosthetic* ▶ 207 immediately. If not, read on.

Put a tick in the box. If there was a tick in the box already ▶ 9 immediately. If not, read on.

You have come to a paved road leading up to a wood in the northernmost part of the Alpheus river plateau. The road is lined with several statues of centaurs, some with lyres, some with flutes, others with bows or spears and such like. Each has a name on the plinth and a short description of their achievements and how they came to be immortalised in marble. At the end there is a half-finished statue of Chiron the Healer, first amongst centaurs. A human is working on it.

'Aren't these statues of famous centaurs, you know, dead ones from the past?' you ask.

'Yes, indeed,' says the sculptor.

'But Chiron isn't dead.'

The sculptor shrugs. 'They say he is dying, and that's why I'm here. It seems there is nothing that can be done – the physician cannot heal himself.'

Chiron is dying? That's bad news indeed for he is the greatest healer of the age. You move on into the woods where you come to a wide clearing. There are several buildings arranged around the edge, half house, half stable. Several centaurs are working here, chopping wood or cooking over a large fire in the centre of the clearing, and so on.

One of them canters up to you, tall, even for a centaur, handsome and imposing, sword on one hip, and a bone flute slung over one shoulder.

'Welcome to the Sacred Stables,' she says. 'I am Velosina.'

'They say Chiron is dying,' you ask.

She nods sadly.

'Take me to him, perhaps I can help,' you say. Velosina looks you up and down. 'You look more like a killer than a healer,' she says. 'What can you do?'

'I don't know, but what harm can it do?'

She grunts, and leads you to one of the stable houses.

▶40

621

If you have *The Houses of the Dead* then ▶ 831 in this book, *The WildWoods*. If you do not have a copy of *The Houses of the Dead*, read on.

You wake with a splitting headache. You cannot remember how you got here or what happened along the way. Worryingly, your hands are stained red with blood.

You look around. The Bacchantes lie quiescent, sleeping it off around a large fire, in a glade amidst some light woodland.

You stagger to your feet. By the fire, you see a skin of the **golden wine of Dionysus**. Best not to drink any of it, ever again in fact, but it may turn out to be useful, note it on your Adventure Sheet.

You also realise that you are completely naked, except for some **stag antlers** you have tied to your head, and some **kykeon mushrooms** threaded onto a string necklace around your neck. (Note them down if you want to keep them). Quickly you dress yourself. Perhaps it is just as well you can't remember what happened.

You are able to work out that you are near a small patch of woodland by the Arcady Trail in the south-central part of Arcadia. It is time to move on, and put this behind you.

▶ 338

622

You are on the Sacred Way. From here, it runs north to a bridge over the Alpheus river, and south into the desert of Notus. To the west, you can see a low range of grassy hills. Above the sky is blue, to your east Oceanus laps up against the shoreline, insects buzz in the air, and wild flowers dapple the roadside with many colours, for here in Arcadia it is eternal summer. There is what looks like a large crater in the ground, just north of the Sacred Way nearby. From here you can go:

To the crater	▶ 127
North to the bridge	▶ 801
West to the low hills	▶ 822
South on the Sacred Way	▶ 600 in *The Hammer of the Sun*

623

You wake up with a start. The last thing you remember is getting into bed with that handsome young man who has clearly enchanted you in some way. You will have to find a way to break whatever insidious spell he has cast upon you. Who knows what liberties he has taken? You check your belongings. Once again, your possessions are untouched, your money is safe. Your body feels tired and sore, however, but you can find no obvious wounds or marks. If only you could recall the details but it is all a blur.

You look around. You are near some low hills, with the great walls of Vulcan City to your west. This is the south-western corner of Arcadia and you have no idea how you got here, or how much time has passed. Days, possibly.

▶ 119

624

As silently as you can, you get to your feet, and edge towards the Grey One holding the eye. None of them suspects anything.

Quickly you snatch it out of her hand and instantly the three sisters shriek in outrage, and reach for you. But they are sightless and grab only empty air. You dash for the cave entrance – behind you Persis the wall-shaker stamps the ground but the rippling quake is not near enough to cause you any serious problems. Deino tries to fill your heart with dread, but you are already out of the cave mouth and away.

You run down the valley until their screams of despair fade away. The eye twitches in your hand. It is quite large, and fills your hand like a ball. It twists up to look at you, a white eye, in a pocket of grey skin, with a bright blue iris and a pupil that is like looking into the deep, dark depths of the ocean. You shudder and drop it into your pack.

After a while, you see a squat, stone tower off set from the stream, with a paved courtyard outside enclosed by a wall. A path runs downhill to entrance arch.

▶ 757

625

You examine the trees on either side of the paved way – there must have been a track or path to it once, surely? Make an INGENUITY roll at difficulty 6. If you have the title **Favoured by Orion**, add one to the result.

Succeed	▶ 755
Fail	▶ 388

626

The good-looking but roguish young man reaches for your backpack, smirking up at you. You shout at him, struggling to free yourself, threatening him with all sorts of dire endings, punishment beatings and horrible deaths but he ignores you, laughing. He just hitches your pack up onto his back and walks away.

After some time, you are finally able to get free and lower yourself to the ground. You look around, hoping to pick up the young thief's trail. And then you hear a scream of horror. You hurry over to the source of the sound and see the ruins of some kind of ancient temple, vine-bound, leaf-choked and crumbling.

As you draw closer, you see the partial remains of a frieze depicting a bright, shining sun, and the words 'Temple of Hyperion.'

You have heard of the legendary lost temple of Hyperion. This must be what the young man was looking for. Was that cry of terror him? Perhaps you will find him – or what remains of him – inside.

► 809

627

You run on, panting in the terrible heat, rivers of sweat running down your body. Your limbs begin to ache with fatigue and it is getting harder and harder to draw breath. Behind you, howls and exultant whoops fill the air. Soon they are snarling and yapping at your heels. A taloned hand knocks your legs out from under you and you tumble to the ground. The wolf people fall upon you, ripping, tearing, biting and slashing. Mercifully, death is quick, as your body is ripped apart in seconds, like pork at a hog roast.

Perhaps you gods will take pity on you and give you another chance.

► 111

628

Cross of the **vinegar of Hades** and the **bucket of gypsum** from your Adventure Sheet.

'Great, I'll start work immediately,' says Lefkia. She starts by sketching all the murals. 'I'm going to have to replaster all the walls,' she explains, 'which means I'll have to redo all the murals as well. I'll try my best to capture the style of the original artist!'

'And I shall bless your work!' says Thekla.

'That should speed things up, though if you mix up a bucket of plaster, that'd be even better,' says Lefkia with a cheeky grin.

The priestess nods, hikes up her robes and gets to work. You could help too, but on the other hand, you have employed them both and you have other things to do, such as battling monsters, performing heroic deeds, and saving the world. You will have to come back later to check on progress.

Gain the codeword *Priestly*. You can go:

West along the coast	► 380
South along the coast	► 419
South-west into the farmlands	► 270

629

You overpower Deridedes easily and tie him to the statue of Hermes.

And then you torture him. Slowly, the death of a thousand cuts. He suffers terribly, constantly begging for mercy and then for a quick death but you give him neither and eventually he dies a long and agonising death.

While it may satisfy your vengeful blood lust – and some

would say he deserved it – it is not justice. Nor is it noble or befitting the actions of a hero. People will hear of this, and while they will fear you more, they will also think less of you. Lose 1 Glory.

Once you have cleaned the blood off your hands and clothes ► 644

630

As you approach Fort Blackgate once more, you notice a new addition to the grisly trophies nailed to the battlements above the broken gates – your own head! You stare at it in horrified fascination for a while, before carefully entering the fort as quietly as you can. There in the far corner, tending his fire, is Kakas the giant, once again roasting a human body over the flames. And to your further horror you realise it is your own body he is roasting!

Hopefully this time you can avoid such a fate. You know some of Kakas's tricks – if you have a **mammoth hide** and some **vinegar of Hades**, you can make a **fireproof hide** by soaking the mammoth skin in the vinegar. (Delete them and replace them in your possessions with **fireproof hide**.)

If you do that or you already have a **fireproof hide** ► 359
If not ► 426

631

You head back to the Palace to see how the work has progressed once more. It's looking good – as you walk in you can see the floors are clean and well swept, the murals as good as new, crumbling walls re-plastered and old rotting wood replaced with new. You find Lefkia putting the finishing touches on a mural in one of the bedroom suites.

'Hello again. Look, I've finished, isn't it great?' and she points up at the mural. It is a graphic scene of an orgy in the forest with dryads and satyrs romping rather rudely together. Lefkia realises what she's pointing at and starts blushing profusely.

'Oh, I didn't... I mean... well, you know, this was Aphrodite's suite, um, oh dear!'

Quickly you change the subject.

'Great work, Lefkia, you have worked so hard and done a great job.'

'Oh, yes, thank you, thank you!'

'Mind you, for the money it cost me I would expect nothing less.'

Lefkia coughs, 'Well, pay more, get more. A simple aphorism but generally true.'

You nod. She has done a great job. You thank her once more, say your goodbyes and go to visit King Nyctimus.

► 697

632

Lose the codeword **Prisoner**.

You notice a figure standing a little way off on the edge of the teeming market, stating at you. She wears a theatrical mask, like that of a tyrant, all white with red lips and eyes, and royal robes, again from what looks like a set of theatrical props that cover her completely. She seems unnaturally tall, at least seven or eight feet, and holds a sword in each hand. Presumably she is the Timandra the terrible tyrant.

She gestures for you to follow and she turns and strides away towards the tree line of the Dales to the west.

She leads you to an out of the way spot and points to the ground. 'Put the money here!' she booms in a trumpeting voice and then steps back a few paces. You put down the 200 pyr. She gestures with her swords for you to back away, and you do. Then the curiously humped and misshapen black-robed figure comes out, leading a bound and gagged Jas. She picks up the money, throws Jas to the ground and then the two figures disappear into the woods.

You untie a relieved Jas, who is suitably grateful. 'Thank you, great one, supreme hero of the age! Thank you, thank you,' he says, fawning all over you.

'Yes, yes, enough already,' you say.

'But you saved me, you did, you saved me. I was worried you'd just leave me to rot.'

'Unfortunately, I couldn't bring myself to do that, though I did think about it.'

'Oh, very funny, very funny.' Jas hesitates for a moment and eyes you uncertainly. He then shakes his head, 'No, no, my most beloved captain is joking, of course.'

'Hmmphh,' you grunt.

'Well, anyway, it's still a happy day,' he says, 'happy day indeed! I'll see you back home when you're ready, my captain.' Then he capers off, singing happily. It is not long before he's bought himself a jug of wine at the market, before heading onto the Arcady Trail back towards the Palace. You wonder where he got the money to buy wine? Surely his kidnappers would have taken it?

Anyway. The task is done, you have your butler back. Time to move on.

▶ 12

633

The Earth Mother suite is luxurious indeed, with a sunken bath, a wide, comfortable bed and a balcony with a view of the rolling (and especially round) Udder Hills. Roll a die, and on a score of 5 or 6 you wake especially refreshed; gain a **benison x 1** (note it on your Adventure Sheet) which gives you +1 on your next attribute roll. Once the benison has been used, cross it off.

When you are ready, you say goodbye to Oxygala and head back to the Sacred Way and into Arcadia, in search of more adventures.

▶ 20

634

You find both Maron and King Nyctimus waiting for you at the vineyard. Maron is looking especially drunk, his beard stained red with wine, his glasses askew on his nose, his goat legs looking rather wobbly. He holds up a bottle and swigs from it.

'It's pomegranate wine and it's absolutely, divinely delicious,' he says. 'No more dandelion wine, not for me, never again. To our health!' and he takes another swig.

Nyctimus takes a sip from a glass of wine he is holding on one hand. He hands you a glass with the other.

'Here, try it,' he says.

You take a sip, and it is indeed delicious, sweet and also full of fruity flavours, as you'd expect from a wine grown from Persephone's garden, the goddess of the underworld, true, but also the goddess of spring growth and the daughter of Demeter. The Wineries of the Nectar of the Gods are back up and running.

'Thank you, adventurer, for making this possible,' says Nyctimus. 'You slew Nessus in single combat like the great hero of the age you are, and his band have dispersed. Now we can celebrate in true style, this wine is even better than the stuff we grew before. Arcadia is blessed.' He puts a hand on your shoulder and says, 'I dub thee Archon of Wines!'

Lose the codeword **Punisher** and gain the title **Archon of Wines**.

'And now you can take your share of the first vintage,' says Maron.

If you also have the title **Archon of Agriculture** ▶ 689
If not, ▶ 58

635

❑

Put a tick in the box. If there was a tick in the box already ▶ 525 immediately. If not, read on.

You lay down one honey cake on the ground. You notice the horse perks its head up, clearly interested. You put another down, and it stands up in its nest, a magnificent white stallion, with great white wings. It must be Pegasus himself!

You lay down the third cake, and the horse whinnies.

'Come, Pegasus, come!' you say.

The horse spreads its wing and leaps into the air, swooping around the trees and down to land nearby.

It whinnies once more, scenting the honey cakes. You point to the strange, tower-shaped cloud in the sky, and then at the cakes. Pegasus, being a horse of unusual intelligence, understands your meaning and kneels down to let you mount him. You put the cakes back in your pack, and straddle the magnificent beast. You have to be careful, for there is no saddle, so you cling to his beautiful white mane, as it leaps into the air, its wings lifting you skyward with each massive wing-beat, cracking through the air like a whip.

Soon the wind is blowing through your hair, and the ground below falls away. Pegasus takes you on a heart-stopping ride, across the deep forest, and up, and up to the cloud tower in the sky. As you draw near, you see it looks like a low, squat domed tower of stone, resting upon a wide cloud bed, solid as the earth, but of a brown and yellow colour. There is an acrid smell that almost chokes you, as you draw near.

Pegasus flies to the cloud, and, hovering, gently paws at it. It is indeed solid. You dismount onto the 'cloud'.

Pegasus neighs demandingly and you take out the **honey cakes**. Cross all three of them off your Adventure Sheet. The horse snaps them up in an instant, and then jumps off the cloud and falls away.

You blink in uncertain surprise. You were hoping he'd wait for you. How are you going to get down now? With a gulp, you turn to examine the low, domed tower in the clouds. And realise it isn't a tower at all.

▶ 673

636

You are setting up a trap in the hope of immobilising the bear when you hear a sudden roar. The bear has spotted you and is charging across the glade! There is no time to finish your trap, you will have to fight the bear. You do manage to get a shot off with your bow that wounds it before it is upon you, but still, you will have to fight it in hand-to-hand combat, hardly the best option when hunting bear. This will be a tough battle.

Make a STRENGTH roll at difficulty 9.

Succeed   ▶ 524
Fail   ▶ 589

637

Gain the codeword *Purloin*.

'All right, then, yes, I can keep quiet and sell you this document,' you say. 'How much are you offering?'

'Fifty pyr,' says Polycrates.

You just laugh.

'One hundred,' says Cressida. You shake your head.

'Two hundred and fifty or I take you in right now,' you demand.

'Two hundred and fifty!' gasps Polycrates.

Cressida however says 'Done!' immediately. She sends Polycrates out back, and he returns with a pouch containing 250 pyr, muttering about all his life savings.

'At least you'll still have a life. If I turn you in for murdering your wife, it's execution time, so stop complaining and hand over the money,' you say brutally.

Note the money on your Adventure Sheet. You hand over the scroll, and satisfied with the deal, take your leave.

'Never come back!' says Cressida.

Well, we'll see about that, you think to yourself as you head out.

▶ 801

638
❑

Put a tick in the box. If there was a tick in the box already ▶ 651 immediately. If not, read on.

There is no answer. You hear a retching sound from the bathroom and you find Jas throwing up in your bath.

'What the Hades…' you say.

'Eurrgh, sorry, boss, sorry, too much dandelion wine,' gurgles Jas.

'You're drunk!'

'Well… bleurgh… you could say I was just worshipping Dionysus, you know, piously respecting the god, and that… reurgghghh!'

The stink of dandelion scented vomit is quite sickening, so you leave the room before you join him.

'Don't worry, boss, I'll clean it up, I promise, just… just not now… hrueurgh!'

You shake your head. Perhaps you should talk to Nyctimus and get a new butler. Anyway, there's no way you'll be getting a quiet night's sleep or a bath today, so will you:

Enter the Vault of Vulcan in Arcadia   ▶ 828
Leave your rooms   ▶ 282

639

You manage to creep up to within fifty feet of Alpha without making a sound, your step as light as arrow-loving Artemis herself.

If you are wounded   ▶ 499
If not   ▶ 433

640

You arrive at the temple of Artemis in the deep forest. Lykaon, Wolf-King, sits on his throne. Kallisto goes to sit beside him. He welcomes you with an expansive gesture and says, 'Impressive, very impressive. I can hardly believe it!'

'Thank you,' you say.

'You are clever and also fit and fast, a good combination if you hope to survive the Sacred Hunt. So… your reward. I had to check in the holy texts, been so long since anyone actually made it through!'

Lykaon waves a hand, and a priestess of Artemis, dressed in a wolf-skin (or perhaps her actual skin) steps forward and lays a finely crafted quiver at your feet. Inside you find three arrows of Artemis.

'These aren't just named for the goddess, these are the arrows she used when she hunted in this forest, all those years ago,' says Lykaon. 'With a gold one of these you could even kill the demon Wolfshadow.'

Note **arrow of Artemis x 3** on your Adventure Sheet.

The priestess also lays a **recurve bow** and a wooden casket inside of which is 200 pyr and 3 **lava gems** at your feet.

'Not a bow of the goddess but a fine weapon, nonetheless,' says Laykaon. Note it all on your Adventure Sheet.

'And will you leave Leonidas the woodcutter in peace?' you ask.

Lykaon nods. 'As long as he kills no more cubs, we will live in peace with him.'

Lykaon stands and walks up to you, putting his hands on your shoulders and intones loudly so that all can hear:

'I, Lykaon, king of the wolves, hereby bestow upon you the title Wolf-runner!' Note the title **Wolf-runner** on your Adventure Sheet and get the codeword *Projectile* too.

That night, there is a feast in your honour, with much drinking and partying. The next day you are escorted back to civilisation with your loot, a new title and a terrible hangover.

▶ **656**

641

The limestone quarry is now a busy working concern. Whilst there are still some slaves working here – Mela's hired thugs – the vast majority are free men and women, looking healthy and well fed. Even the slaves look well enough, which is more than can be said of the treatment they meted out when they were in charge.

Archimedes greets you with a friendly smile. You can buy a consignment of building limestone here.

'Normally I charge a hundred and seventy-five pyr but as it's you I'll only charge a hundred pyr which just about covers my costs,' says Archimedes the overseer.

If you want to buy a consignment, cross off 100 pyr and add the **limestone** to your Adventure Sheet.

When you are done, you leave ▶ **396**

642

You enter the clearing of the Great Green Ones. But something is wrong – the ground is covered in patches of brown, shrivelled up grass. The leaves on the nearby trees have fallen away, and their bark is sickly and pitted with sores.

The three great wooden totems are no longer wreathed in moss or vines, but covered in patches of what looks like burns or a parasitic fungus.

The Great Green Ones stir at your arrival, and you feel your brain once again being used to think a message to you.

'Help us, meat-thing,' groans the walnut totem. 'Our roots are free, they nourish us, we thank you for it, but it is the sky, it is killing us!'

You look up. There is a strange cloud in the sky, shaped

like a squat domed tower on top of a hill and a dull brown in colour. From it falls droplets of yellow-brown rain, in little gusts and flurries. A drop lands on your hand – and burns! Acid. Acid rain.

'Please, it burns us, withers us. Soon we, the Heart of the Vine, will be burned away, and when we die the whole of the deep forest will die also, and all that lives within it. And after that, all the trees in Arcadia. You must save us, meat-walker, us and all the land!'

How are you supposed to get up there, you wonder? But you'll have to try, the fate of the wild woods depends on it.

Gain the codeword *Phosphoric*. When you are ready, you make your way out of the forest.

▶ 148

643

You have paid for the services of a priest of Apollo. He has cleaned up this small domed temple, sweeping up the leaves and dirt, removing the squirrel skeleton and hanging some round sun-shaped lanterns, giving the place a bright clean look, worthy of the god. He greets you with a cheery wave, and offers to pray for you each time you visit. Get the codeword *Praise-Apollo*.

You can get blessings here. If you are a worshipper of Apollo and do not have the title **Unfriended by Apollo**, blessings are free. Otherwise you must pay 10 pyr per blessing. You can only have a total of three blessings at a time.

When you are finished ▶ 20

644

Behind the ruined fountain you find Deridedes' stash of stolen goods. You take 150 pyr, a **box of paints**, a **hornbook (+1)** and a **lava gem**. Note them on your Adventure Sheet if you want to keep them.

Where to now? If you have the codeword *Parapet* and want to go north ▶ 220

If not, will you go:

South on the trail	▶ 455
South-west to a small wood	▶ 475
South and then east to the Deep Forest	▶ 710
North on the trail	▶ 330

645

That elicits a good groundswell of laughter from the crowd but it is not enough. The judge, Kraterus, remains silent.

'I appreciate the artistry in that one it's not bad but what hope have you got against me, the prince of piss-takes, eh?'

And so it goes. Deridedes comes up with a few choice insults, and every time Kraterus crows, but yours are just ignored entirely, even though one of them gets the most laughs of all.

It's clear the game is fixed in some way, but you're not sure how. There is nothing you can do for now. When you are ready, you can return to the market (▶ 728) or leave the area (▶ 12).

646

❏

Put a tick in the box. If there was a tick in the box already ▶ 683 immediately. If not, read on.

Gelos can make a **wolf headdress** from Alpha's pelt for 25 pyr. If so, add the **wolf headdress** to your Adventure Sheet. When you are ready ▶ 187 and choose again.

647

The catch-net is a web stretched across four wooden poles that is designed to catch anyone cast into it from the palace onager. Unfortunately it hasn't been maintained in a long while and has collapsed in a heap on the ground. There is nothing for you to fall into and you plough straight into the ground.

Tick the Wound box on your Adventure Sheet. If you are already wounded than your body is smeared across the ground like raspberry jam on toast. At least death is quick. ▶ 111

If you still live, you stagger to your feet and look around ▶ 832

648

Euphorbos comes to the door to greet you. He is still old, but seems hale and hearty despite that.

'The years are flowing off me,' he says, noticing your look. 'The only trick is remembering to talk backwards when I meet somebody heading the other way in time.'

'Have you remembered why you were chopping all those blocks out of the glacier?'

'I have, as a matter of fact. Did you ever hear the story of how Hermes's hat blew off in the wind? That was me – or will be me, from my perspective. The hat landed in the river – that is, the glacier – and I was looking for it to give it to you. Which I did. Or I will do, when I can remember where I come across the bag.'

If you have the **bag of Aiolos** and are willing to give it to him ▶ 724

Otherwise ▶ 759

649

You set forth into the depths of the forest. Everywhere, the trees stand as if in serried ranks like an army, hoary, ancient, gnarled and twisted, branches intertwined overhead like dancers at a wedding.

As you progress it gets darker with barely any sunlight filtering down to the forest floor. The air is humid, and stiflingly warm. You can hear birds high up above, but you cannot see them, and the occasional skitter of woodland animals fleeing the tread of your feet but mostly it is strangely, oppressively quiet. After a while, you come to an area of the forest that is carpeted with mushrooms. Will you:

Harvest some mushrooms	► 16
Press on into the gloom	► 49
Leave the forest while you still can	► 148

650

You run down the path and through the arched entrance way and charge at the giant with a war-like cry, **kingslayer dagger** in hand. He steps back in surprise. He has four arms, but seems heedless of your attack, and you stab him in the arm. But as he is a king, and you have the dagger, he falls to the ground dead. And then simply gets up again.

'You think it would be so easy? I am king of the gigantes and here on my land I cannot be killed,' says Alcyoneus in a booming voice. He reaches for you with all four of his massive hands.

You dodge aside, and jab him once more and he dies instantly, but then recovers. This goes on for a while, with you dragging him a few feet towards the courtyard, for he is very heavy, and then stabbing him again as soon as he comes back to life, until you drag him out of the archway and off his land, where at last he remains dead.

You can't help but feel a little sorry for him, for it must have been a hard way to go, dying and being brought back to life and then dying again before you could say or do anything. If you have any scars then you know what it is like.

But still, it is done. You search his body and find the Book of Seven Sages in one of his voluminous pockets but nothing else. You search his tower but again, not much to speak of. 100 pyr or so, some **venison sausages**, **fresh fish** and a **honey cake.** Alcyoneus' lunch by the look it.

But he was the king of the gigantes. Surely he has some treasure stashed somewhere? You search again but to no avail. So much for the promise of riches untold.

There is nothing left to do but head back to Myletes at the waterfall.

► 163

651

You call for Jas but there is no answer. Then from the bedroom you hear the sound of loud snoring. You poke your head round the door. There he is, passed out on your bed, snoring, a trickle of vomit running down the side of his face and staining your pillows. Two empty jugs of wine and two goblets lie on the floor. And lying next to him… a dryad, dressed only in diaphanous underwear, passed out too, her head resting on Jas's chest.

You shake your head. The randy old goat! To be fair, he *is* half goat but still, these are your rooms not his. Perhaps you should talk to Nyctimus and get a new butler. Anyway, there's no way you'll be getting a quiet night's sleep or a bath today, so will you:

| Enter the Vault of Vulcan in Arcadia | ► 828 |
| Leave your rooms | ► 282 |

652

You wake with a splitting headache. You can taste blood in your mouth, and your hands are stained red with it. You cannot remember how you got here or what happened along the way.

You look around. The Bacchantes lie quiescent, sleeping it off, around a large fire in a glade amidst some light woodland. And then with a thrill of horror you see the body of a young man nearby. Or at least his head… he has been torn limb from limb, and much of his flesh has been eaten raw by the look of it.

Desperately you wash out your mouth with water, hoping against hope that it is not the young man's blood that you can taste. You wash your hands too, trying to tell yourself it's probably the blood of some woodland animal.

By the fire, you see a skin of the **golden wine of Dionysus**. Best not to drink any of it, ever again in fact, but it may turn out to be useful, note it on your Adventure Sheet.

You are able to work out that you are, incredibly, on the other side of Arcadia, near a bridge over the river Alpheus. You hurry away, trying to put this whole thing behind you.

► 801

653

After some time you get a message from Hypatia that the inn is finished, so you head back to the bridge.

The inn is indeed finished, a rather fine-looking building of limestone and timber, three stories high, flat roofed, and with a painted frieze by Lefkia around the top, showing centaurs, dryads, and satyrs gambolling at a merry Arcadian picnic. The exterior walls are painted in pastel pinks and greens.

Lefkia, Hypatia and Helen are waiting at the entrance to greet you. You can't help but notice that Hypatia and Lefkia are standing a little apart from Helen. Clearly she makes them uncomfortable. Well, she is technically undead.

You notice a sign post on the outside with the picture of an armed and armoured warrior, smiling broadly, hair blowing carefree in the wind – wait a minute, it's you! And the name of the inn, picked out under the picture, is the Happy Hero.

It is rather flattering but still, you're not really known for your happy smiles, more for blood and battle, really. Anyway, they show you around. The inside is rather fine, with more of Lefkia's murals on the walls. Helen has a kind of office at the top, and you have free use of the Archon Suite, a well-appointed set of rooms. You thank Hypatia and Lefkia and they say their farewells, Helen promising them they can stay whenever they like but the two of them don't look that keen. After all, it's an inn that was haunted before it was even built.

Helen tells you that before they can get the place properly up and running, she'll have to hire a front of house manager, and some staff, but that you can leave all that to her.

You nod, and take your leave too. You can return later to rest and also see how the business is going, and whether there are any profits to be had.

From here you can go:

North-east to the Woodlands	▶ 60
East along the riverbank	▶ 138
South	▶ 822
West to the Wineries	▶ 417

654

'Ah, Kaustikia the dragon! I heard she was one of many daughters of Typhon, the father of monster, and that she has built some kind of nest in the clouds around here somewhere, and is terrorising the locals. And that her spit is like, of all things, acid. Not only that, a sheep farmer from down south claims that she likes to eat mutton marinated in wine. Which is fortunate, I suppose, for what if she preferred humans, eh?

'Anyway, I hope that helps, for that is all I have to say about that dragon. Is there anything else?' says Phineas.

If you have the title **Mayor of Bridgadoom** ▶ 118
If not ▶ 153

655

❑

Put a tick in the box. If there was a tick in the box already ▶ 807 immediately. If not, read on.

You return to the palace. Lefkia, your painter and decorator, is nowhere to be seen but her 'crew', her little twin brothers, are sitting on a blanket playing a game of some kind by rolling knucklebones. It seems they're gambling with real money!

Wait for Lefkia	▶ 312
Join the game	▶ 34
Leave this place	▶ 547

656

Having said your farewells to Lykaon and his daughter Kallisto, you find yourself once more at the outskirts of the Deep Forest. Where to now?

Leonidas' cabin	▶ 693
Sacred Way to the west	▶ 324
Arcady Trail to the east	▶ 455

657

Your battle with Phearei is a long one – you start hacking off bits of wood, at which she grimaces in pain and anger.

'Once you are mine, I will never, ever let you go,' she vows. 'You will be my slave for all time.'

Her words are a distraction, and with the beeswax in your ears you fail to hear the dryads behind you – suddenly a vine is looped around your leg, hobbling you. Phearei steps in and stuns you with a blow to the head, and soon you have been bound tightly with vines and creepers.

'Now we will see who is the mistress and who the slave,' mutters Phearei, pulling the wax from your ears. She resumes her dance and the dryads sing once more.

▶ 544

658

Kakas will no doubt try to breathe fire all over you. Fortunately, you have a fireproof hide, made from the skin of a mammoth and vinegar of Hades. Quickly you stretch it over your shield, it should make for an excellent fireguard.

Meanwhile, Kakas moves in, swinging his club in great wide circles. One blow will be enough to floor you. You cannot match him in strength, you will need to be fast, agile and cunning to beat him.

Make a GRACE roll at difficulty 7.

Succeed	▶ 453
Fail	▶ 720

659

If you have the codeword *Pheon* ▶ 257 If not, read on.

If you have the codeword *Punisher* ▶ 603. If not, read on.

If you have either or both of the titles **Archon of Agriculture** or **Archon of Wines** ▶ 707. If not, read on.

'My steward, and my hero,' says King Nyctimus, welcoming you with open arms. 'The rivers are running once more, Ladon is playing his tricks on unsuspecting river-folk, and Alpheus is his usual, grumpy self. All is well in Arcadia!' You take a bow.

'But now that the waters of life flow across the land, there are other things to be done. To get Arcadia back to its glory days, we'll need the farmlands up and running and, of course, we'll need plenty of wine to celebrate it all with. Perhaps you can turn your considerable talents to that,' says the King.

'What do I need to do?' you ask.

'Well, you could check out the Wineries and the Verdant Farmlands, also look at the bulletin board, you'll need specialists to help you out. In the meantime, feel free to enjoy your suite of rooms, and help yourself to anything in the kitchens and such like.'

You take your leave of the King. ▶ 282 and choose again.

660

You enter the main road that runs through the town. There are houses, shops, a temple or two, and what looks like the house of the town's Archon but all are falling into disrepair. Dust devils are all that walk the streets these days. That and several more statues of golden warriors, including three clustered together, one about to hurl a javelin, another shooting an arrow, the third, hands help up in a hieratic gesture, as if casting a spell or a curse.

You come to the town square, with a statue of Gaia, the earth mother at its centre.

And then something shuffles out from behind the statue of Gaia. It is an enormous lizard, over six feet long, bright yellow in colour with a long black and red crest that runs from its head to its tail. Its eyes are yellow too, its mouth wide and fanged, its feet taloned. It hisses at you and then breathes out a cloud of black vapour, sparkling with tiny golden particles. You think it will be easy enough to avoid, but then the cloud suddenly doubles in size like an enormous opening flower, and rushes down to engulf you, now more Venus fly trap than black-petalled flower! Make a GRACE roll at difficulty 9.

| Succeed | ▶ 7 |
| Fail | ▶ 42 |

661

'Excellent, another will come,' says the bulky, misshapen cowled figure and she disappears into the crowd. You put a hand to your chin. Now is the time to decide. Will you just hand over the money, get Jas back and be done with it? Or try some stratagem to outwit the kidnappers, even though that might be risking his life?

| Hand over the ransom | ▶ 632 |
| Never! Make *them* pay | ▶ 595 |

662

You don't want him coming back to challenge you again, perhaps with even more enhanced abilities, so you give him his wish, and finish him off quickly. The room falls silent as he dies on the floor of your banqueting hall...

But then the room erupts into a flurry of shouts and cries of triumph or woe as bets are won or lost followed by in depth discussions of this move or that parry, and so on.

You clear away the body of Glaukos the Gorgon Guard and retire to bed. It has been an eventful day.

The next morning you rise refreshed and ready for another day of adventuring.

▶ 220

663

You have arrived at the foothills of a range of low Arcadian hills. To the south and east you can see the Sacred Way, and to the west some more hills leading to the massive cyclopean walls of Vulcan City. To your north are the dales of leaf and stream. The ground is lush with grass, the sky a bright blue, and sunshine bathes the land in warmth. From here you can go:

Visit the Shrine to Ares	▶ 64
North-east into the hills	▶ 822
North-west to the dales of leaf and stream	▶ 266
West towards Vulcan City	▶ 119
East to the coast	▶ 833
South to the Sacred Way	▶ 300 in *The Hammer of the Sun*

664

'The horned god accepts your donation, wanderer in wilderness! You may enter the shrine of Pan.'

Amergin the druid steps to the side, and gestures through the archway.

Gain the codeword *Passage* and ▶566

665
❑

Put a tick in the box. If there was a tick in the box already ▶ 835 immediately. If not, read on.

A young woman steps out of the treeline – an unusual looking young woman. Her skin has a golden sheen to it, her hair is crimson and braided in cornrows that hang all the way down her back to her legs, braided to look like seeds threaded together. Her lips are crimson too, and her eyes a bright yellow colour with dark red pupils. She is almost naked, save for the bushy leaves that cover her upper body and hips, like a green-leafed bikini.

'Hello,' she says, 'You must be the Archon of Wines and the Steward of the Palace, yes?'

'Yes, those are some of my titles,' you say.

'Then it is you I must thank for my very existence!' she exclaims, clapping her hands together excitely.

'Really, how so?' you ask.

'It was you that brought the seeds of Persephone from

Hades, and gave them to that lecherous old drunk, Maron to plant.'

'I did.'

'Well, being seeds of the goddess, the trees flourished, and out of them, I too grew, for I am Sivi, dryad of the pomegranate trees,' she says with a bow.

'How wonderful,' you say. 'Assuming… umm…from what I've read the relationship between creator and created can be, well, difficult. Murderous even.'

'Hah, fear not on that account! No, I am here to ask for your help. I've already planted some seeds here, and with me to nurture them, more trees will grow quickly. But it is the hives I am interested in. If we can rebuild the bee colony, with me to tend them lovingly, we'll be able to create divinely delicious pomegranate honey. All I need is a queen bee. The best ones are the mountain honey bees, so I was hoping you would go to the mountains of Boreas in search of one.'

If you already have a **queen bee** ▶ **425**

If not, you tell Sivi you will see what you can do, and take your leave. Will you:

Go deeper into the woods	▶ **176**
Leave this place	▶ **225**

666

None can walk the land of the dead as a shade without feeling its mark – add one to your total scars. Also lose all cash and items except for the **Arcadian vault key** and the **sceptre of Agamemnon**, if you have them. 'Where do you wish to return to, mortal?' whispers a voice in your head.

The underworld of Hades	▶ **500** in *The Houses of the Dead*
The deserts of Notus	▶ **500** in *The Hammer of the Sun*
The fields of Arcadia	▶ **500** in *The Wild Woods*
The peaks of Boreas	▶ **500** in *The Pillars of the Sky*

667

You take the book from his hands and flip through it, feeling like a watcher of the night skies when a new planet soars into view.

As your uncle meets your look of wild surmise his thoughtful, often-serious face crinkles into a broad smile. 'Yes, you see it. She is the true goddess of beauty, the beauty of understanding that is seen with the mind rather than the eye.'

Note on your Adventure Sheet that your god is Athena, then ▶ **769**

668

You flee for your life, a horde of rabid, frenzied Bacchantes, intent on ripping you limb from limb, close behind your heels. Whatever intoxicated state they are in, it gives them speed, for they are slowly closing with you.

You run for the great northern gate of Vulcan City, but as you draw near, you see that it slams shut with a great clang. You run up to the gate, banging on it.

'Open up, in the name of mercy, open up!' you shout.

A guard leans down from the battlements 'What, with a horde of Bacchantes behind you? Are you as mad as they are? No way! Sorry, lad, but you're on your own, can't risk that lot getting in here.'

They are closing in – impassable walls to the south, impassable mountains to the west, what can you do but dash eastward, following the walls. But your attempt to get into the city has lost you precious seconds. They are almost upon you. Make a GRACE roll at difficulty 9.

Succeed	▶ **485**
Fail	▶ **503**

669

You decide against any dealings with the Great Green Ones at this point. Who knows where that may lead?

You have found the heart of the forest but there is nothing else you can do here but make your way back to 'civilisation'. You can always come back again, if you wish. Time to retrace your steps. By following your own path back through the forest you are able to make it to the outskirts without too much difficulty. Thirsty, tired, and sweaty, you leave the deep forest. ▶ **148**

670

You see Leonidas and a couple of hired hands working at the wheel and pulley machine, sawing recently felled wood. Two children are playing together, and from the inside of the cabin you can hear a woman singing.

It seems altogether a much happier place now that you have managed to come to an agreement with Lykaon, the King of the Wolves.

Leonidas greets you warmly, and offers you some soup and a mug of tea. His wife comes out and brings it to you, she too is very grateful for all that you have done.

You can buy wooden logs and planks from Leonidas here. Every batch of **timber** will cost you 50 pyr. You don't actually carry the timber around with you as it is quite a lot of wood, rather you carry a promissory note. Whoever you give the note to can use it to get Leonidas to deliver them the actual wood. However, for ease of use, just record the **timber x 1** for each 50 pyr that you spend (eg 100 pyr gets you **timber x 2**) on your Adventure Sheet.

Where to next?

West to the Sacred Way	▶ **324**
East to the Arcady Trail	▶ **455**
South east to a small wood	▶ **475**

671

Gelos can make a bearskin cloak from your **bearskin** for 25 pyr. If so, cross off the **bearskin** and the money and add the **bearskin cloak** to your Adventure Sheet instead. When you are ready ▶ 187 and choose again.

672

You find some bear dung between two trees. It doesn't smell as bad as you'd expect which probably means a recent meal of a lot of sweet honey. And then you spot it, up ahead! The bear is standing up against a tree in a small glade, raking its claws across the bark. Fortunately, it's not that big a bear, and even better, you are down wind of it, and it has not smelt you yet.

Make an INGENUITY roll at difficulty 8.

Succeed	▶ 244
Fail	▶ 636

673

What you thought were great stone blocks of the tower are in fact brown scales, the scales of a great dragon, curled up into a ball, and sleeping. It is winged and at least fifteen feet long, its body like that of a serpent. It has two forearms ending in clawed and taloned hands. Its breath wafts out in long, slow gusts like an enormous bellows in the sky. And its breath is laden with droplets of acid that float down to the forest below.

An acid dragon, sleeping in the sky, and raining its breath onto the forest below, poisoning the trees. What will you do?

Attack immediately while it sleeps	▶ 743
Wake it up	▶ 704

674

❏❏

If both boxes are ticked ▶ 740 immediately. If not, read on.

Nothing like a little fishing to relax the soul and all. Roll a die:

score 1-2	Nothing, put a tick in a box
score 3-5	one **fresh fish**
score 6	one **fresh fish** with a **moon pearl** inside

You can fish here as many times as you like until you decide to leave, or until both boxes are ticked. Note any catches on your Adventure Sheet. When you are done here, you can:

Enter the Palace	▶ 96
Examine the onager	▶ 471
Leave this place	▶ 547

675

You decide it is probably better to join them than refuse, so you snatch the wineskin and gulp down the golden wine of Dionysus. It tastes absolutely divine, and can barely stop yourself from drinking it all, until one of the Bacchantes, somewhat less intoxicated than the others, snatches it back.

'Hey, careful there, sister,' she says. 'Too much will kill you.'

The wine warms your belly. You can feel the warmth spreading out across your body, along with a sense of ecstatic release from all your cares and worries until you are suffused with a hot, burning madness that fills your soul with wild, howl-at-the-moon freedom.

Soon you descend – or is it ascend? – into a state of transcendent frenzy, at one with the mad, drunken god, and with nature at its wildest, red in tooth and claw. The last thing you remember is running to join the rest of the Bacchantes, shrieking in joyful abandon.

Roll a die.

score 1-2	▶ 690
score 3-4	▶ 652
score 5-6	▶ 621

676

If you have the codeword *Penalty* ▶ 698 immediately. If not, read on.

If you have the codeword *Plight* ▶ 716 immediately. If not, read on.

Treycross market is bustling with satyrs, humans and centaurs and even the occasional dryad and nymph. Everywhere there are street food stalls, tents, pavilions, hucksters, fortune tellers and mountebanks. Three things attract your attention. One: a canvas, gaudily painted pavilion with a sign that reads 'Deridedes, Priest of Momos, challenges all comers to a contest of insults and crude banter!' Momos the mocker is the god of ridicule and scorn and it is said he can incite rage in any heart with a single word. Some say it was he who helped to start the Trojan Wars, in the hope of culling the numbers of mankind.

Two: you see an astonishingly handsome young man, his lustrous black hair flowing across his shoulders like the glitter-black waters of the Styx, his features almost perfect in their symmetry, his eyes brown and shining like fresh chestnuts, his lips red like cherries, glowing with vitality. He is tall and slim and walks with the grace of Hermes himself. He beckons for you to follow him…

Three: a tent with a sign outside that reads 'Zenia the Fortune Teller'. Visions of things to come and a nice cup of tea'.

Visit Zenia	▶ 352
Visit Deridedes	▶ 321
Follow the beautiful man	▶ 395
Return to the market	▶ 728
Leave the area	▶ 12

677

□□□

Put a tick in a box.

If all three boxes are now ticked ▶ **541** immediately.

If two boxes are now ticked ▶ **614** immediately.

If not, read on.

'Disaster!' wails Drosos, your farm overseer. 'Kraterus, that spawn of Typhon, that devil-cock, that little monster, has escaped his coop, slashed to the bone the legs of my best plough-hand and run off with three of our prize hens! It's delayed everything, I'm afraid. Try again later.'

You'll have to come back and check on his progress again later. For now, where will you go?

North-east ▶ **365**

North-west ▶ **380**

South-east ▶ **419**

678

You follow Cressida as she hurries down the street. She heads out of the village a little way, to a farmhouse, looking behind her guiltily from time to time. You have to dodge behind a tree, and then a farm cart.

You follow close behind as she steps through the doors and into an open courtyard.

'Polycrates! Polycrates, you fool, where are you?' she shouts.

'Yes, my darling,' says a burly, half bald and bearded middle-aged farmer, turning to greet her.

'I can't believe you wrote this and threw it into the river, how could you be that stupid?' she says, throwing his confession at his feet.

'What do you mean?'

'Some idiot fished it out of the river. Thank the gods they handed it to me, or we'd be up for murder – or at least you would be.'

You step into the courtyard, and draw your weapon. 'I may be an idiot,' you say, 'but I am also armed and extremely dangerous.'

Cressida blanches, and Polycrates, like all bullies, steps back in fear.

You walk forward and snatch up the incriminating document. 'It's one thing to murder your wife, another to take on someone like me, isn't it, you cowardly maggot!'

'I didn't mean to do it, I... it was just... I... I loved another...' he mumbles.

'Bah, of course he meant to do it because he is hopelessly in love with me, and I went along with it because I wanted the farm. Satisfied? Now, let's cut to the chase, shall we? How much do you want to stay quiet, eh? As I assume that's what this is about.'

Blackmail them ▶ **637**

Turn them in ▶ **599**

679

You're heading home. The shadows are long and cool after the heat of the day. As you come through the gate, your father sees you across the yard. 'Did you do your chores?'

What is your reply?

'Yes' ▶ **618**

'No' ▶ **597**

680

You find Evadne asleep in her cabin. You hiss at her from the window and she wakes with a start. You hand her the casket.

'No, can it be?' she says, in surprise. And she starts smiling broadly. Quickly she opens the casket, and with a shout of joy, takes out her heart. It dissolves back into her like snow on warm earth.

'Evadne is no longer broken-hearted,' she says looking at you gratefully.

'Come,' you say, 'let's get out of here.' Without Evadne to freeze things, Ladon Lake will thaw under the summer sun of Arcadia pretty quickly and Mela will have no other means of re-freezing it.

'No, wait,' says Evadne, her face darkening. 'I have something I must do first.'

'What do you mean? Let's go, there's no time to waste!'

Evadne shakes her head, resolute. You heave an exasperated sigh and start to explain that Mela has a small army, but then the door bursts open and in walks Mela herself, and her minion Captain Theseus.

'Time for you to do your job, Evadne, you worm!' says Mela. Theseus laughs sneeringly.

'I think not,' says Evadne, through her cold, gritted teeth of ice.

'What! Have you forgotten I have your heart? One word and your life is over,' says Mela.

Evadne steps up and lays a hand on her shoulder. Mela slams her staff down, and calls out a spell. She stands there expectant, but nothing happens.

'My heart is not yours anymore,' says Evadne, as icy frost starts to run up from her hand and over Mela's neck. Theseus moves to help, but Evadne just rests her other hand on his arm, and soon he too is rimed in frost.

Mela's mask falls away with a frozen crack – revealing a pale white face almost identical to the mask but this time contorted into a mask of horror. And then her face frosts over, the eyes freezing up and cracking open, falling to the ground like shattered marbles. There is barely time for them to call out their agony, for they are frozen to death in seconds.

Soon all that is left are two frozen ice sculptures.

'Revenge is indeed a dish best served cold,' says Evadne with a chilling laugh.

She turns away, and climbs out of the window to stand beside you. Waves of cold waft over you, but as long as you don't get to close, you will be all right. In fact, it's quite refreshing in the hot, humid heat of Arcadia.

'Thank you for saving me,' she says, 'but now I must get home as fast as I can, for this summer sun does not love me. Come find me in the frozen wastes of Boreas. Farewell, hero!'

▶ 736

681

Amergin the Druid is waiting to greet you at the archway to the Shrine.

'Welcome, wayfarer in the wild, to the Shrine of the Horned God. You are welcome here,' and he gestures to the entrance, and steps aside.

The two warriors remain silent and still. You can't help but notice they have enormous bushy moustaches. Anyway, you enter the Shrine.

▶ 566

682

You have come to a bridge along the Sacred Way that encircles the world, as do the waters of Oceanus. From here, it runs east and west along the coast. The bridge spans the River Ladon that comes down from a great lake to south. Its waters are blue and bright, gurgling and rushing by joyously. Wild flowers, herbs and fresh green grass grows on its banks, an otter frolics in the water, the croaking of frogs and the buzzing of insects fill the air, the sky is blue and the sun warms you pleasantly and all because you brought the river gods of Arcadia back to life.

To the south-west are the wooded outskirts of the Deep Forest, and the ruins of a castle of some kind, jutting up over the treeline. Nearby, a large net is slung between four wooden poles, clearly designed to catch something falling from the sky but it in a state of disrepair. It will cost you 20 pyr to have it fixed. If you wish to do so, cross off the money and get the codeword *PatchupTwo*. Either way, from here you can:

Go to the bridge	▶ 126
Head south, up the river valley	▶ 591

683

'I can't make anything without a pelt, and I've already made you a wolf headdress, there's nothing more I can do for you regarding wolves.' When you are ready ▶ 187 and choose again.

684

If you have the codeword *Plenty* ▶ 39 immediately. If not, read on.

The once gushing river Alpheus is as dry as bone here, its riverbed littered with skeletons of fish, old leather shoes and the general detritus of decay. You can see where the water once ran down the cliff side in a great waterfall and then down to the eastern coast and the great encircling sea of Oceanus. Nearby, several bronze-banded barrels rest on a wooden quay. Surely people didn't... Anyway, whatever, the waterfall rapids are long dried out. From here, you can go:

North to the lower Tarn of Alpheus	▶ 578
West to an ancient monument arch	▶ 340

685

You remember what happened the last time you came to the dales – you were ensorcelled, fattened up and almost sacrificed, roasted and eaten. You were saved at the last minute but you cannot expect that to happen again. Time to get out of here. Will you go:

North-east to the Trail	▶ 728
North-west to the Trail	▶ 455
West to the hills	▶ 559

686

You have come to the near centre of Arcadia, following the Arcady Trail, a dusty pathway through the wild and rampant greenery that leads to the Palace, set in a deep valley, flanked by impassable towering cliffs to east and west. To the north is the great lake that is the source of the river Ladon. From here you can go:

South-west on the Trail	▶ 455
South on the Trail	▶ 728
North to the Lake	▶ 37
To the Summer Palace	▶ 10

687

Euphorbos is carrying a huge armful of ferns and grass clippings to put on his compost heap. 'This beats chopping blocks of ice out of a glacier,' he says, ushering you into the cottage for a cup of tea.

'I'm surprised you're still here.'

'I keep wondering where I'm going to come across that magic bag of winds,' he says. 'Or rather what I should say is, I wonder where I'm going to have come across it.'

If you have the **bag of Aiolos** and are willing to give it to him ▶ 724

Otherwise ▶ 759

688

It would be hard enough to outrun an insect swarm in open ground, let alone in a dense forest with trees and undergrowth hindering your passage. It is not long before they are upon you, stinging and biting. You trip over a root, and are soon covered in head to foot with wasps, bees, midges, mosquitoes and then, ants. It only takes moments for all your flesh to be stripped from your bones. After such a painful death, perhaps the gods will take pity on you.

▶ **111**

689

You have completed one of the Great Labours of Arcadia. Write the number **726** (not *this* paragraph number) in the Current Location space on your Adventure Sheet (in place of the number already written there, if any) and then ▶ **38**

690

You wake with a splitting headache. You can taste blood in your mouth and your hands are stained red with it. You cannot remember how you got here or what happened along the way.

You look around. The Bacchantes lie quiescent, sleeping it off around a large fire, in a glade amidst some light woodland. A deer lies nearby – or at least its head. The rest of it has been torn to shreds, and eaten raw, by the look of it.

You stagger to your feet. By the fire, you see a skin of the **golden wine of Dionysus**. Best not to drink any of it, ever again in fact, but it may turn out to be useful, note it on your Adventure Sheet.

You are able to work out that you are in the far north eastern quarter of Arcadia, near the farmlands. It is time to move on, and put this behind you.

▶ **365**

691

'I have seen her, the goddess. I have knelt at her feet!' you say, recalling your time in the mountain kingdom of Saesara in Notus.

'What? How… no, wait, I can see in your eyes that it is true!' says Thekla, amazed. 'What was it like?'

'Terrible and exhilarating all at once, like lightning,' you say.

'Well, then, I imagine you will not need much persuading to help in the reconsecrating of the temple. As you can see it is in dire need of repair. If you can help with that, then I can open it up to the people and serve the goddess. Perhaps then they can farm the land again, with Demeter's blessing.'

'Of course, for the honour of the goddess I will do anything I can.'

If you have the title **Steward of the Summer Palace**

▶ **567**. If not, read on.

You tell the priestess you can't help right now, but you will return when you can. For now there is nothing you can do but move on. You can go:

West along the coast	▶ **380**
South along the coast	▶ **419**
South-west into the farmlands	▶ **270**

692

'There is indeed a winged horse in these parts, or at least several folk who claim to have seen it, which I have not. Some say it is the legendary Pegasus himself, returned to Arcadia after the hero Bellerophon fell from his back to his death in hubristic pursuit of Olympus itself. Others that it is just another child of the Gorgons and not the real Pegasus – who can say for sure? What is certain, though, is that this winged horse is very fond of honey cakes and no less than three will do. Is there anything else?' says Phineas.

If you have the title **Mayor of Bridgadoom** ▶ **118**
If not ▶ **153**

693

If you have the title **Wolf-runner** ▶ **670**. If not, read on.

Put a tick in this box ❑. If there was a tick in the box already ▶ **535** immediately. If not, read on.

The dwelling is a long low cabin of forest wood. A wide clearing surrounds the cabin with several felled trees at its edge, where the dense forest begins once more.

At the front of the cabin is a wheel and pulley system, set up to power a wood saw, making the job of cutting timber much easier. But no one is working the machine at the moment.

You walk up to the cabin and knock on the door. A nearby curtain twitches as the inhabitant checks you out, and then the door opens a crack.

A middle-aged man looks out, fit and well-muscled for his age, with a tanned and weathered face, and grey hair and eyes that seem haunted by something, making him look like a grizzled veteran of some horrific war or other.

'Yes?' says the man, looking over your shoulder uncertainly, as if expecting an ambush or other unwanted surprise.

'Judging by the clearing and the saw machine, I'm guessing you're a woodcutter, right?' you say.

'Yes, but it's not safe out there, hasn't been for a while now,' says the man.

'Why's that, then?' you ask.

The woodcutter looks you up and down, and then seemingly satisfied by what he sees, opens the door further and leads you into his house, a pleasant, welcoming home that smells of freshly baked bread. Although he is alone, you can see he must have – or had – a wife and children. He leads you to a window on the other side of the cabin, and points at a spot in the tree line at the edge of the clearing. You can see the face of a large wolf, gazing hungrily at the cabin.

▶ 611

694

Fort Blackgate stands lonely and deserted, its walls cracked and crumbling, its gates lying like unburied corpses in an abandoned graveyard. Over the battlements is mounted the charred and fleshless skull of Kakas the giant who used to terrorise the land, until you slew him and mounted his head as a trophy.

A faint smell of burned flesh pervades the air. If you have the codeword *Pheon* ▶ 11 immediately.

If not, there is nothing more you can do here and the only route out is south ▶ 85

695

You dash into the outskirts of the woodland dells, Wolfshadow hot on your heels. In your haste, you collide with a tree and dislodge a small sprite, who falls to ground with a terrified squeal! The daemon wolf turns his attention to the unfortunate creature, biting off an iridescent wing before snapping up the rest of her. Nearby, you can hear the shrieking of other faeries and sprites, lamenting the loss of one of their own.

You run on as fast as you can before the fae realise you have brought this doom upon them, and curse you for it! Soon you have left Wolfshadow behind but best not to go back that way. From here you can go:

Into the Dales of Leaf and Stream	▶ 266
North-east on the Trail	▶ 728
South-west into the hills	▶ 559
South to the Sacred Way	▶ 119
East into woodland	▶ 338

696

What will you sacrifice to Pan?

If you have either some **pomegranate honey**, a **honey cake**, a **bunch of grapes**, **farmlands grain** or **pomegranate wine** and wish to put one of these on the altar, cross it off and ▶ 275

If not, or if you don't want to right now you can leave and come back later ▶ 463

697

You find Nyctimus sitting behind his wide desk in the main hall which now looks rather magnificent like a proper Palace with brightly coloured murals, refurbished banners, and a polished marble floor.

Nyctimus leaps to his feet at the sight of you, runs round the desk and grabs you by the hand.

'Thank you, thank you,' he says, 'this is wonderful, look at it! I have to admit when I saw you'd hired a mere girl, I thought… well, anyway, she has done a magnificent job.'

You agree. 'Wasn't cheap, though,' you mutter.

'Hah, maybe so, but worth every pyr,' says Nyctimus.

'For you, maybe,' you retort.

'Now, now,' says Nyctimus, admonishing you with a wagging finger, 'I think you'll find it was worth it!' He puts a hand on your shoulder and intones sonorously, 'I, King Nyctimus of Arcadia, hereby appoint you Steward of the Summer Palace!'

Note the title **Steward of the Summer Palace** on your Adventure Sheet.

'And of course, the title of Steward comes with a rather fine suite of rooms in the Palace,' and he hands you a key. 'Now, go and settle in. Come and see me at some point, and we'll see how things are.'

▶ 422

698

Treycross market is bustling with satyrs, humans, and centaurs and even the occasional dryad and nymph. Everywhere there are street food stalls, tents, pavilions, hucksters, fortune tellers and mountebanks. The gaudily painted pavilion of Deridedes, Priest of Momos, is still here, hard to miss with its bright colours.

The tent of Zoupa the empousa is long gone but Zenia the fortune teller is still selling her tea from her tent.

Visit Zenia	▶ 352
Visit the pavilion of Deridedes	▶ 321
Return to the market	▶ 728
Leave the area	▶ 12

699

If you have the codeword *Negate* ▶ 576 immediately. If not read on.

You run down the path and through the arched entrance way and charge at the giant with a war like cry. He steps back in surprise. He is tall with four arms but seems heedless of your attack, and you run him through with your first strike, right through the heart.

He falls to the ground dead. And then simply gets up again.

'You think it would be so easy? I am king of the gigantes and here, on my land, I cannot be killed,' says Alcyoneus in a booming voice. He reaches for you with all four of his massive hands…

You dodge aside and strike once more and the battle rages for a time. You kill him again, and try to drag his body off his land before he recovers, but he is simply too heavy, and you only manage to move him a foot or two.

In the end, you are forced to try and wrestle him out of his courtyard but he has four arms and you are not Heracles, and soon he has you pinned.

'Goodbye, foolish mortal,' says Alcyoneus as he slowly breaks you in two, cracking your spine like a twig. At least you died a heroic death, fighting the king of the giants.

▶ 111

700

You return to the Happy Hero Inn, looking up at your own grinning face on the sign that hangs over the front door.

Inside, the innkeeper, a tall, thin, bald as a coot, cadaverous man called Sosages greets you.

If you are wounded you can rest in the Archon Suite and untick your Wound box.

You can also buy and sell a few things here:

	To buy	To sell
Fresh fish	20 pyr	15 pyr
Venison sausages	15 pyr	10 pyr
Honey cake	–	50 pyr
Pomegranate wine	–	35 pyr

When you are ready you can visit Helen in her office ▶ 738 or leave and head:

North-east to the Woodlands	▶ 60
East along the riverbank	▶ 138
South	▶ 822
West to the Wineries	▶ 417

701

This is place you are supposed to meet the kidnappers who have demanded a ransom for the return of your butler. You are making your way through the crowded marketplace, taking in the sights, sounds and smells when someone tugs at your arm. You turn to see a figure heavily robed and cowled, the face obscured in shadow. The robes are strangely shaped, as if the body beneath them was not human.

'I am Damara the destroyer,' says the figure, her voice strangely muffled and resonant. 'If you want to see Jas the Helot again, show me the money!'

If you have 200 pyr and wish to reveal it ▶ 661 immediately.

If not, or you do not have the money ▶ 773

702

Something seems off about Cressida's demeanour, as if there was something she isn't telling you.

| Follow her surreptitiously | ▶ 678 |
| Wait for her to come back | ▶ 745 |

703

Your deity brings you into their presence. It is like hearing the sound of a celestial choir, filling your heart with awe. You fall to your knees, as the god's words boom in your ears: 'That was the third and last of the labours of this realm.'

Note the codeword **Pheon** and give yourself + 1 Glory. If you also have the codewords **Ode**, **Nomad** and **Quince**, immediately ▶ 93. Otherwise read on.

'When you have completed all twelve labours you will have proved yourself the greatest of my champions,' says your god. 'But to do that you must travel to the other realms of the Vulcanverse.'

Now turn to the section number written in the Current Location space on your Adventure Sheet.

704

Gingerly, you prod the sleeping dragon with a stick. It stirs and flicks open one eye. And then the other, staring at you with yellow snake eyes.

'What... a mortal? How did you get here, and what are you doing? I mean, I was sleeping.' The dragon raises its head and looks around. 'And you're on your own? Are you mad?'

'Actually, I thought I'd try and discuss things with you, out of courtesy,' you say.

The dragon rises up to rest on its coiled serpent body, wings furled and arms folded, long, snouted head looking down at you, in an almost comical version of a philosopher talking in an agora or forum.

'Really? Such bravery! Or is it stupidity? Well, normally I would simply tear you limb from limb and eat you but I, Kaustikia the dragon, welcome a little politeness for a change, and I am curious as to how stupid you are. Speak, then. Perhaps I might not eat you after all.'

'Well, thank you for your time,' you say.

Kaustikia nods, 'Thought to be honest, I am a daughter of Typhon and Echidna, and I'll probably eat you anyway – but go on, have your say.'

'All right, then,' you say, trying to sound confident and assured. 'It's where you're sleeping, your... well, your acid breath, it's dripping down onto the forest below, directly onto the Great Green Ones.'

'So?' says Kaustikia.

'It's killing them.'

'And your point is?'

'Well, they're the Great Green Ones, the Heart of the Vine, the Mother of Trees, and if they die, so will the forests and then eventually all that is green in Arcadia.'

'Oh, that's what they said is it, those pompous old bores! And you believed them?'

'I do. After all, they were here even before Gaia herself. They are the first roots and all that.'

'Even if it's true, what do I care?'

What will you say – that without the Great Green Ones, all the trees will die, and the land will be bare, or that all the grass will dry up, and animals like sheep and goats will die or that if all the greenery dies, so will the humans for they won't be able to grow crops or raise cattle?

All the trees will die	► **51**
All sheep and goats will die	► **13**
Mankind will die out	► **94**

705

You open the hatch and climb down a long ladder, at least fifty metres or so into a cave lit by hanging lanterns. It is covered in cobwebs but thankfully no spiders that you can see. You notice a faint outline of sunlight around a large man-sized rock on a cave wall.

A message on the wall reads, *'I turn once, what is out will not get in. I turn again, what is in will not get out. What am I?'* If you know the answer already, turn to that paragraph number if you want to go through the stone door. If not, and you want to try to solve the riddle ► **268**. If not, read on.

You know the hatch in the floor leads to a tunnel that leads all the way to the temple of Arachne in Hades, where you found the tapestry. Where will you go?

Back up the ladder	► **470**
Through the tunnel to Hades	► **661** in *The Houses of the Dead*

706

❑

Put a tick in the box. If there was a tick in the box already ► **732** immediately. If not, read on.

You come to a stone archway but built in the style of the Celts, carved with geometric whorls and patterns. Before it stands a man in long white, robes, hooded, and with a belt of mistletoe and a wreath of oak leaves around his head. On closer inspection you see that the belt is in fact solid silver, painted and jewelled with green and red. Must be worth a small fortune! On either side of him stands a Celtic warrior, hair spiky, white and limed, chests bare and covered in blue painted symbols, wearing trousers, each with a finely crafted leather belt, again picked out in red and green. Each holds a spear in one hand, a figure eight shaped shield in the other, bronze bossed, and a beautifully worked iron longsword, hanging from the hip.

'Greetings, wanderer of the green, I am Amergin the Druid, Keeper of the Words of Knowledge. Welcome to Pan's Arbour, or as we would call it, the Shrine of Cernunnos, for they are the same god.'

But you're Celts, not Greeks, right?'

'Indeed. Long ago there was a treaty between the Arcadians and the Galatian Celts. We shared some gods, such as Apollo the Bright One, and the Wild God, so we exchanged priests and the like. We were invited here to tend this Shrine to the Horned God and have done so faithfully for hundreds of years.'

'Can I enter the Arbour?'

'Of course, for a donation.'

Your eyes flicker down to his silver belt. Clearly they've prospered from this arrangement. The druid hitches his belt up, and coughs uncomfortably at your gaze.

'Unfortunately, it seems you are in disfavour with Apollo, cursed by the Bright One. We would be fools to risk his wrath by allowing you in freely, or indeed cheaply. So, a great warrior like you? Let me see – a **bearskin cloak** and 100 pyr will be enough to assuage the gods and give you passage to the shrine.'

If you have a **bearskin cloak** and 100 pyr and wish to give it to Amergin, cross them off and ► **664**

If not, or you don't want to, or you want to come back later ► **463**

707

'Ah, my Steward, and Archon! You are doing such great work, I cannot thank you enough,' says Nyctimus. You and the King exchange pleasantries, but for now there is nothing more to be said so you take your leave.

Perhaps you can come back later, when things have changed. ► **282** and choose again.

708

'I'll be able to breathe underwater?' you say.

Damara grins. 'Oh yes, for a while. And I'm sure my kiss will be lovely too,' she says.

You wonder about that, given her teeth, but the kiss of a magical water nymph may prove useful. You nod your agreement. She steps up to you, and gives you a long, lingering kiss and then steps back, awaiting your response.

'Nice, except for that slight fishy flavour,' you say.

Damara raises her eyes. 'Whatever. You hero types are so hard to please! Anyway, our bargain is done, thank you for your mercy,' she says, and turns to go. But then she hesitates.

'I couldn't... you wouldn't... I shouldn't ask after all that business with Jas but... would you give back my hair? It's just that... it's a living part of me, do you see?'

You shrug your shoulders. You haven't found any other use for it, so why not? You hand her the **water nymph hair**. Cross it off your Adventure Sheet.

'Thank you again,' she says, as she puts it up to her head. You watch, fascinated as it seems to burrow into the rest of her sea-weed hair, as if making itself at home once again.

'Hopefully we won't meet again,' she says, and with a raucous laugh, dives over the side of the bridge, turning into a fish on the way down, and disappearing into the waters.

Note the title **Kissed by a Water Nymph** on your Adventure Sheet. There is nothing more to be done here, you're feeling fished out for the day, so where will you go?

West on the Way	▶ 20
South-west into the forest	▶ 189
East on the Way	▶ 380
South, into the dried-up river valley	▶ 403

709

You turn down her offer as nicely as you can. You expect the worse but the wild Bacchante just turns away with a shrug.

'Don't know what you're missing, girl,' she mutters. Another, perhaps less intoxicated than the others, says, 'It makes us strong. Women together like this, nothing can stand in our way. But as you wish, sister.'

'I am already strong,' you say. They stare at you for a moment, and then grin wildly. One of them hands you a skin of the **golden wine of Dionysus**. If that's the stuff that drives them wild, it's best not to drink any of it, but it may come in useful later. Note in on your Adventure Sheet.

The two Bacchantes race away to join the others, leaping and whirling, howling at the sky. Soon the maniacal mob are gone, and you are alone again.

▶ 826

710

The Deep Forest is a vast sea of trees that takes up most of the western half of Arcadia. You have come to the outskirts of the forest in the south, via the Sacred Way or the Arcady Trail. Ahead of you, tree after tree marches into the deep, dark centre where it is said dire wolves and other fell creatures dwell. A track skirts the southern edge of the Forest, heading east and west.

You notice a curl of smoke from a chimney stack, just beyond the treeline. There appears to be a dwelling there of some kind. Where will you go?

The dwelling	▶ 693
The Sacred Way to the west	▶ 324
The Arcady Trail to the east	▶ 455
South east to a small wood	▶ 475

711

❏

Put a tick in the box. If there was a tick in the box already ▶ 596 immediately. If not, read on.

You show Velosina your own flute. She looks at it closely. 'An excellent piece,' she says. 'The bones of the dead make fine flutes, where did you get this one?'

'In Hades,' you say.

She looks at you, eyes wide. 'Amazing...' she mutters.

'And where did you get yours?' you ask.

'I carved it myself,' she says, 'from...' She looks down at you guiltily. 'Umm... a human I... er... killed in battle.'

'I see,' you say. 'I shall ask no more.'

She brightens. 'How about a flute duel? Chiron will be the judge!'

'Chiron? Hardly a neutral judge,' you say.

'Oh, trust me, if anything he will lean to you just to be

sure he is impartial. He is the most honourable being I have ever known, more so than the gods who are fickle.'

If you want to 'fight' a duel of flutes with Velosina ► **751**

If not, you continue on to find Chiron. He greets you warmly and offers to help you in any way he can ► **90**.

712

Make an INGENUITY roll at difficulty 7.

Succeed	► **766**
Fail	► **544**

713

'Ah, the legendary Nemean lion, who dwells in the desert – or at least he did, until relentless hunters from Iskandria, glory seekers, drove him out of the deserts of Notus. No matter how many heroes he slew, still they came. Now he hunts in the depths of the deep forest, as far from man as he can be. Some say his claws can cut through everything, save perhaps the shield of Ajax himself but where that shield lies today, no one knows for generations have passed since Achilles and Hector fought on the plain before Troy.'

And that is all that Phineas has to say on the Nemean lion. 'Anything else?' he asks.

If you have the title **Mayor of Bridgadoom** ► **118**

If not ► **153**

714

❑

If you have the codeword *Plantation* ► **436** immediately. If not, read on.

Put a tick in the box. If there was a tick in the box already ► **579** immediately. If not, read on.

You shake your head to clear your senses. You are in a wide forest clearing, in the heart of the deep forest. Arranged around the edge of the clearing are three large wooden heads. Or perhaps 'head-like' would be a better description They are hoary and ancient beyond reckoning, stained with moss and lichen, wreathed in creepers and flowers; the wood is old, but hardy and very green. Their faces are misshapen, only vaguely man like. One has a wide mouth like that of a baleen whale, carved or perhaps even grown, another has a pair of deep-set eyes, with what looks like bright blue cornflowers growing inside them. The third has a crown of leaves and branches growing out of its top from which hang many shrivelled chestnuts or perhaps walnuts.

These statues or totems or wooden standing stones, whatever you want to call them, are several feet taller than a man, and as wide as a man's arms stretched out to either side.

The clearing is filled with a profound silence. It is as if the earth itself was asleep.

At the middle point of the triangle created by the three totems is a low stump of a once great tree, wide enough for a man to lie on it.

It is covered in ancient stains, like sap, or tar but its dull russet colours seem more like blood to you. Old, old blood. The stump is moss covered. You notice a battered wooden cup, weed-bound and lichen-stained, lying beside it along with an ancient rusty blade of some kind. Beside them is an old clay tablet. You clear the filth and grime of the tablet to see that there are words carved into it in a very ancient

version of Greek. It is hard to work out what is written but you recognise a few words here and there – the Great Green Ones, Fount of the Forest, Heart of the Vine, Mother of Trees, the First Leaf and so on.

Is this old stump a sacrificial altar perhaps where libations were poured? You could try a libation on the altar. If so, what will you use?

Wine, or water	► **778**
Your own blood	► **827**
Dione's blood, if you have it	► **756**
Daemon's blood, if you have it	► **806**
None of the above	► **669**

715

'Brilliant!' says Lefkia, and she hands you a papyrus scroll detailing the money you have paid, the items you gave her etc. Add **Lefkia's receipt** to your Adventure Sheet.

'How long will it take?' you ask.

'Hard to be certain but check in from time to time and I'll keep you posted.'

You watch for a while as Lefkia starts work, laying out her paints, organising her brushes, mixing up some gypsum plaster and so on. It's a big job so there's no point hanging around, best leave her to it. ► **547**

716

❑

If the box was already ticked or if you have a **Blessing of True Sight** then ► **443** immediately. If not, tick the box and read on.

A miasma of confusion rises up inside you and fogs your brain completely. You find yourself walking as if in a dream to the tent of the beautiful young man who stole a kiss from you and then… you cannot recall. He is there again, his long black hair shining like moonlight on the still waters of the black bayou, his face as beautiful as a god. He smiles as you draw near, and once again, your heart melts at the sight of it. A small part of you, detached, separate almost, watches in horror as you smile back, walk up to the beautiful young man and give him a long, lingering kiss. You are no longer in control of yourself…

You struggle to re-assert your will but it is no use, you cannot fight the yearning in your heart. He ushers you into his tent – although 'lair' maybe a better word. He leads you to the corner bed, covered in red and purple drapes…

► **623**

717

Hyperion was the primordial sun god, he who came before. Some say Helios is his son, others that Hyperion *is* the sun.

Either way, much of the temple has fallen into ruin now, for most of those ancient gods are long forgotten, their worshippers and their rituals long gone. Together you and Theron step through the broken portal.

Inside, you find a gloomy, high-ceilinged hall, its roof open to the skies in places, its pillars cracked and fallen and vine-entwined. There is a great statue of Hyperion in the middle of the room, stained with lichen and mould, one arm long since fallen to the ground. You can't help noticing that the eyes are of bright yellow amber, still glowing in a shaft of light that spears down from the shattered roof.

'That's what we're here for,' says Theron. 'Those eyes. Worth a fortune!'

And then you see the creature. A great serpent, twined around the statue, seemingly sleeping, but your presence has woken it. The serpent's tongue flicks out, tasting the air. Its eyes snap open, its head sways around until it fixes on you both. It uncoils itself from the statue and, with a hiss, slithers towards you… It is at least twenty feet long, its head as big as your torso, its scales red, blue and green and sparkling like burnished silver.

Theron pulls out his bow. Together you are able to kill it quite quickly – Theron puts an arrow through its body just below the neck, pinning it to the statue long enough for you to hack off its head. He grins at you. 'We make a good team!' he says before capering up the statue like a monkey and taking both eyes. He drops down at you, stuffing one eye into his pocket. The other he holds in his hand. He looks at the exit, then at you, then at the exit again. You narrow your eyes and shake your head slowly.

He grins. 'Hah! Only joking,' he says, and hands you the amber eye. Note the **Eye of Hyperion** on your Adventure Sheet.

'Well, that was fun, and, to be honest, I'm not sure I could have taken that beast on my own, so thank you but now I must go. A hero's welcome awaits me in Boreas. Farewell, hero!' With that Theron jogs away, whistling a cheerful tune.

You follow him soon after. It becomes clear that the temple was built at the bottom of a gully through which runs a lively brook. It is actually quite near the western edge of the Deep Forest, although hidden from view. You are able to step out into open ground, near your original target for the Fast Travel Catapult.

► **804**

718

Drosos and King Nyctimus are waiting for you, big grins on their faces. 'It's finished, all finished!' says Drosos and he waves a hand to indicate the scenes behind him. The barns and hay wagons have been repaired, workers till the fields, the quern stones are ready to grind up the first grain crop, chickens cluck happily in their coups, smoke billows up from the chimneys of the farmers cottages and all is well in the bucolic paradise that is Arcadia.

'Thank you, adventurer, for making this possible,' says Nyctimus. 'Now we can feed our people, and they will grow, until Arcadia is once again the happy paradise it once was.' He puts a hand on your shoulder and says, 'I dub thee Archon of Agriculture!'

Lose the codeword *Plough* and gain the title **Archon of Agriculture.**

'And now you can take your cut of the first harvest,' says Drosos.

If you also have the title **Archon of Wines ▶ 508**
If not ▶ **793**

719

Some sixth sense makes you turn to look behind – and there you see something so unnerving it makes your hair stand up on end. Some *thing* is hunched over your shadow, seemingly sucking it up off the ground! The thing is shapeless and utterly lightless, as if a formless blob of black ink had oozed up out of the earth or a crooked stygian crow-thing had dropped out of the sky to feed on your shadow.

But the tickling sensation inside your head confuses you, and you stare in a horrified fugue of indecision. But if you do not act, it will suck away your shadow… you reach for your weapon; already half of your shadow is gone.

If you have a **lightning flint ▶ 613**
If not, make a GRACE roll at difficulty 8:
Succeed ▶ **366**
Fail ▶ **451**

720

You stumble on a broken spear and Kakas's club slams into you, shattering your bones and sending you flying across the courtyard. The last thing you hear is 'hur, hur, hur,' before you hit the ground, and pass out. You never wake up. Well, not here at any rate.

▶ **111**

721

The next day the women rise and say their farewells, returning to their homes and farms across Arcadia. Thekla, the priestess of Demeter, takes you back to the temple, where she hands you a blessed garland of **flowers of fertility**. Note them on your Adventure Sheet.

Now that you are back in the temple of Demeter you can ask Thekla to bless some Arcadian soil for you. Any earth from round and about will do, but you will have to donate 15

pyr to the temple coffers to get it. If you do, add one **blessed soil of Arcadia** to your Adventure Sheet for every 15 pyr you spend.

When you are ready, you leave the temple. You can go:
West along the coast ▶ **380**
South along the coast ▶ **419**
South-west into the farmlands ▶ **270**

722

A figure appears at your elbow, places her hand under your arm and raises you up from your seat. You obey mindlessly, even though a rising sense of dread is building inside of you.

The figure, a priestess also in a cowled robe, leads you to the back of the altar.

You try to reassert your own will, but you cannot break the spell that binds your mind. In fact, you begin to giggle happily, as if all of this was a wonderful evening out or a play of some kind but you know in your heart of hearts that something much more sinister is going on and that you are to be its victim.

And then, while the other two priests begin to finalise their ritual, calling on Despoina to give them bountiful crops and some kind of eternal spring, your escort leads you away unseen into the trees and away from the glade.

'Hurry,' she hisses, 'we must get away from here!'

You laugh, enjoying the game, but she whispers harshly, 'Shut up, you deluded fool or they will hear you, and you'll be roasting on that spit in moments!'

After a short while, your mind begins to clear at last. You stagger for a moment, sickened by days of drinking, and sleeping while drugged out of your mind but you are able to ask in a dry, cracked, voice, 'Who are you?'

The figure pulls back her cowl to reveal the face of Damara the water nymph, who has tried to trick and rob you several times and indeed, nearly tricked you into drowning by pretending her kiss would let you breathe underwater. Testily, you point this out and ask what she is doing.

'I didn't mean for you to drown, I just wanted… well, to get away safely, and, to be honest, steal a kiss.' With that she actually blushes. Or is that a trick too?

'But… but why take the risk to save me of all people?' you ask, as you both hurry through the moonlit woods.

'I know we've not been the best of friends as it were, but although I have wronged you, you have always been merciful, so I couldn't just let you die.'

'Well, thank you,' you say. 'So, they were going to sacrifice me, then?

'Oh yes, cut your throat, pour your blood over the altar as a libation and then skewer you on that spit and roast you in a honey and rosemary glaze.'

'What was… what did they serve me to eat?'

'Their last victim… I think her name was Mintha, so they marinaded her in a minted tzatziki sauce.'

You stop for a moment to throw up in disgust. Now you can add cannibalism to your achievements, even if it was forced upon you.

You notice that you have just thrown up next to a heaped pack of rations and equipment.

'It's the high priest of Despoina's supply stash!' mutters Damara excitedly. 'I'm sure they won't notice a little bit of this and a little piece of that going missing.' She helps herself to some cash, a jug of wine and one or two other gewgaws and accoutrements.

You notice a rather fine-looking horn, engraved with various animal headed figures, armed for war. It is the **Horn of the Fae**. Note it on your Adventure Sheet. Nearby, you hear the sound of approaching footsteps.

'Come, we must away,' says Damara fearfully, in a hoarse whisper. Quickly, she leads you safely out of the Dales of Leaf and Stream and the Snares of the Fae to some low hills, just to the south-west.

'Thank you for saving me,' you say.

'I hope that means all that was between us can be forgotten?'

You nod your agreement. 'If you need me, I will come,' you say, acknowledging that her wrongs against you are more than righted for she saved you from being sacrificed, cooked and then eaten.

She smiles at you, revealing her little shark teeth, white and needle sharp. Then she leans forward and kisses you once more. You can't help but notice that her breath smells faintly of fish.

'Until we meet again,' and with that she skips away back into the woods.

Cross off the title **Tricked by a Water Nymph** and replace it with the title **Saved by a Water Nymph**.

▶ 559

723

Now you have this part of the river all to yourself. The water rolls past, the sunlight hangs in droplets amid the leaves. It is a perfect day. The perfect day of your early life.

But there is one cloud in the otherwise clear sky. Why? Why didn't you want the children to stay? You can be honest with yourself, especially in a dream.

'I didn't want them to see I can't swim.' ▶438

'They're just annoying. That's reason enough.' ▶519

'I came to catch some fish and they were scaring them away.' ▶ 562

724

If you have the codeword *Neophyte* or *Nephew* ▶ 797

If you have neither of those codewords ▶ 490

725

Something has taken the bait. Something big. You pull but this thing is far too strong and it rips the rod right out of your hands and away into the river. You can hardly believe it. Cross off the **rod of Phainos** from your Adventure Sheet; it is lost forever.

So much for a nice day out fishing. What can you do but move on? Where will you go?

West on the Way	▶ 20
South-west into the forest	▶ 189
East on the Way	▶ 380
South, into the dried-up river valley	▶ 403

726

You come round from your encounter with a god, to find Maron and Nyctimus looking at you with concerned expressions on their faces.

'Are you all right?' says Maron.

'Yes, yes, I'm fine, it was just…' you mutter, shaking your head to clear it.

'Was it the gods? What did they say?' asks Nyctimus.

'The labours, I… another one finished…' you stutter.

'Excellent! Excellent,' says Nyctimus, 'that is good.'

'Back to the mundane, I suppose, but your share of the first vintage is ready for you to collect,' says Maron.

▶ 58

727

'A limestone quarry? Yes, there used to be one in the north, just south of the Sacred Way and north of the Druid's Shrine, but I've heard no one goes there now, for armed men have seized it and they turn ordinary folk away. Dark rumours of black magic and frostbitten slaves, of all things, fly around in the taverns and inns, but they are too outlandish even for me! Anyway, my advice is to stay away, although I can tell from the look of you that you will do no such thing.

'And that is all I have to say about mines and quarries. Anything else?'

If you have the title **Mayor of Bridgadoom** ▶ 118

If not ▶ 153

728

There is a three-way crossroads on the Arcady Trial here. A great market has been set up around and about the crossroads, called the Treycross Market.

A Hekation, a statue of the goddess Hecate as a trinity of

women, stands at the exact centre of the trail. It represents Hecate in her aspects as Hecate *Trimorphe* and Hecate *Trioditis* or the three-formed goddess of crossroads.

There are many stalls, tents, wagon-shops, fortune tellers, pie sellers, fire-eaters, jugglers, mountebanks, singers, fiddlers, farmers selling their produce, smiths, charlatans, surgeons, barbers, kebab-sellers, inns, brothels and all the rest. You can buy and sell a lot of things at the Treycross Market at the following prices:

	To buy		To sell
Fresh fish	20 pyr		15 pyr
Lava gem	100 pyr		80 pyr
Phoenix tears	–		50 pyr
Laurel wreath	–		50 pyr
Recurve bow	–		50 pyr
Hardwood club	–		50 pyr
Hornbook	–		50 pyr
Golden lyre	–		80 pyr
Winged sandals	–		80 pyr
Abacus	–		80 pyr
Iron spear	–		80 pyr
Weasel blood	–		50 pyr
Honey of Hades	–		250 pyr
Statuette of Ares	75 pyr		50 pyr
Strix stew	25 pyr		20 pyr
Vinegar of Hades	20 pyr		15 pyr
Venison sausages	15 pyr		10 pyr
Honey cake	–		50 pyr
Pomegranate wine	–		35 pyr
Box of paints	50 pyr	25 pyr	
Copper cog	–		15 pyr
Copper ore	10 pyr		5 pyr
Stag antlers	–		25 pyr
Moon pearls	–		30 pyr

When you've completed your business at the market, read on.

If you have the codeword *Prisoner* ▶ 701

Otherwise, will you:

Explore the tents, pavilions, inns and entertainments of the Treycross market ▶ 676

Leave the market ▶ 12

729
❑

Put a tick in the box. If there was a tick in the box already ▶ 265 immediately. If not, read on.

'Excellent, well done. I'll get to work.' Chiron goes out back into his workshop and after an hour or so comes out with a vial of sparkling blue liquid.

'Here you are, a cure for the black blight,' he says, handing it to you. Gain the codeword *Panacea*. You thank him. 'Anything else?' he asks.

▶ **90** and choose again.

730

The last time you were here you were able to deal with the threat of Alpha. Leonidas is still alive, trying to keep his woodcutting business going, but he is still persecuted by the followers of Lykaon and his werewolves. He can't leave the house long enough to chop enough wood to sell any timber.

And Lykaon put you through the Sacred Hunt, and you were torn apart by those very same werewolves...

If you wish to try your hand at the Sacred Hunt again ▶ **749**. If not, you can always come back again later.

Go west to the Sacred Way ▶ **324**
Go east to the Arcady Trail ▶ **455**

731
❑

Put a tick in the box. If there was a tick in the box already ▶ **735** immediately. If not, read on.

You call for Jas the Helot, your half-goat, half-man satyr butler. Roll two dice:

score 2-4 ▶ **638**
score 5-8 ▶ **744**
score 9-12 ▶ **802**

732

You arrive at the Druid's Shrine. Amergin and his two Celtic warrior guards greet you at the archway entrance. 'Ah, 'tis the wanderer in the wilderness. Do you have the donation for the god?' asks Amergin.

If you have a **bearskin cloak** and 100 pyr and wish to give it to Amergin, cross them off and ▶ **664**

If not, or you don't want to do so now, you can come back later ▶ **463**

733

You battle the bear heroically for a short while, but in the end it is just too strong and fast, its fur like armoured bronze. The bear pins you to the ground and bites off your face. You scream in agony, unable to see as your eyeballs have been eaten. The bear toys with you for a few minutes more, raking its claws done your back, and biting off one of your hands. Mercifully, you bleed out on the forest floor. At least it was a warrior's death so perhaps the gods will take pity on you.

▶ **111**

734

'I cannot bring myself to kill you like this,' you say. 'I give you your life.'

Glaukos looks up at you, his face a mask of conflicting emotions.

'But... but... I... deserve to die...to die in battle.' He grimaces angrily. 'Well, then, perhaps I will return with vengeance in my heart...and...'

But then his face falls and he shakes his head. 'No, no, you beat me fairly, so although Glaukos may not be the glorious hero of heroes, I will not let it be said he was not a man of honour. No, I pledge myself to you, if you should need me, just call for me, and I will be there to fight by your side.'

You nod. 'I accept your oath of loyalty. When the time comes I will send for you,' you say in answer. Gain the codeword *Pledged*.

With that, Glaukos gets up and leaves the banqueting hall. The room erupts into a flurry of shouts and cries of triumph or woe as bets are won or lost followed by in depth discussions of this move or that parry, and so on.

You clear away the detritus of battle and retire to bed, leaving your guests to their revels. It has been an eventful day and you are tired.

The next morning you rise refreshed and ready for another day of adventuring. ▶ 220

735

If you have the codeword *Prisoner* ▶ 447 immediately. If not, read on.

You call for Jas the Helot, your half-goat, half-man satyr butler. Roll two dice.

score 2-4	▶ 638
score 5-8	▶ 744
score 9-10	▶ 802
score 11-12	▶ 43

736

Gain the codeword *Pumped*. Evadne is gone, but you carefully make your way to the front of the stone cabin for there is still the matter of Mela's soldiers.

However, with her death the spell that bound the quarrymen is broken and they are free and there were more than thirty of them. They have rounded up her hoplites and stripped them of their weapons and armour. A couple of them have been killed and the rest it seems are being made to work mining limestone, themselves now the enslaved.

A man approaches you, tired, middle-aged, half starved, but with a determined look in his eye.

'I am Archimedes...' he starts to say.

'What, *the* Archimedes?' you interject, astonished.

'No, of course not! Really, how can you be that stu—' He stops himself from saying more and changes tack. 'Umm... anyway, thank you for rescuing us all, and releasing poor Evadne. I used to be the overseer here, before Mela ensorcelled us all. I'm going to try and re-start the business. Those who wish to leave may do so, the others I will employ on a fair wage, with fair food and lodging, plus a bonus from Mela's pay chest.'

'A good plan,' you say.

Archimedes nods. 'If you ever need to buy some building materials like limestone and rock, come back once we're up and running, and we'll be open for business' he says. 'I'll give you a discount.'

A discount? Is that all, you think to yourself, but anyway, perhaps that will turn out to be worth something in the end. Should you ever need limestone, that is.

Your work here is done. It is time to see what has happened to Ladon Lake.

▶ 772

737

You hand over the **kykeon mushrooms** (cross them off your Adventure Sheet along with the money) and Zenia goes to the cauldron at the back of the tent, and starts making tea. She pulls a wooden screen across to shield her from your view.

'Have to preserve my trade secrets, or everyone'll be making the tea, right?' says Zenia. 'And that'd be my livelihood up in smoke. Who'd feed my kids then?'

A short while later she emerges with a hot, steaming cup of tea that smells, frankly, like dog dung.

'How does it work?' you ask.

Here is a deck of cards. Leaf through them, and pick an image or phrase, think about it a bit and when you're ready, drink the tea, lie on that couch, and then... well, you'll have visions. Some nice, some... nightmarish.'

You look through the deck of pictures showing various characters, places and things. You make a choice and then gulp down the tea, grimacing at the foul taste, and lie on couch. Already you can feel things going fuzzy inside your head. What card did you choose?

Arrows of Artemis	▶ 54
Chiron, first amongst centaurs	▶ 128
The river god Ladon	▶ 192
The river god Alpheus	▶ 248
The Master of Twilight	▶ 461
Alpha the wolf	▶ 531

738

You find Helen in her office at the top of the inn, somewhat out of the way. She delegates most of the work to Sosages because she is technically a ghost from Hades which seems to make the living uncomfortable, to say the least.

Anyway, she is happy to see you. Roll one die. If you score a 5 or a 6, ▶ 787; if not, read on.

Helen explains that things have been going well, the inn will soon be making money, and that you should keep visiting to see how things are shaping up. There is nothing more to do here, so you take your leave. From here you can go:

North-east to the Woodlands	▶ 60
East along the riverbank	▶ 138
South	▶ 822
West to the Wineries	▶ 417

739

There must be thirty or more of them, and they give a whooping cry at the sight of you, surging towards you, faces feral masks of bloodlust and ecstatic rage.

The Bacchantes will typically tear to shreds in a wild frenzy of blood-letting any lone wayfarer who they regard as male. They may even eat you raw. Time to leg it, as fast as you can.

Will you run:

South to the gates of Vulcan City	▶ 668
Try to lose them in the forest	▶ 527

740

The lagoon has been completely fished out of edible catch. There is nothing for you to do here. Will you:

Enter the Palace	▶ 96
Examine the onager	▶ 471
Leave this place	▶ 547

741

❏

Put a tick in the box. If there was a tick in the box already ▶ 35 immediately. If not, read on.

The bridge is built of old stone, time-worn and mottled with lichen. As you draw near, an unpleasant smell assails your nostrils. Soon you see why – a body hangs from the bridge, slowly swinging in the breeze, the rope around its neck creaking back and forth. Beneath the bridge, lying on the dried up river bed amidst the long-rotted skeletons of many fish, is a package and a scroll. You open the scroll.

'Read, traveller, the tragic tale of Phainos, the best fisherman in all Arcadia. Daily I fished off this beautiful bridge, with the blessing of Ladon, and great was the catch! But then the river died and so have all the fish. What is there left for one such as me but to follow them? O Thanatos, give me your sweet kiss and release me, for my life has no meaning anymore.'

It seems Phainos the fisherman hanged himself from the bridge he loved, to be with his fish. A sad tale indeed. You spot a fishing rod and tackle amongst his things. Note the **rod of Phainos** on your Adventure Sheet. You take the bloated, rotting corpse down and give him a decent burial. When you are done, there is little else to do but move on. Where will you go?

West on the Way	▶ 20
South-west into the forest	▶ 189
East on the Way	▶ 380
South, into the dried-up river valley	▶ 403

742

Caution gets the better of you, and you turn away. His handsome face falls, the sight of which almost breaks your heart and for an instant you want to cover those perfectly formed features in apologetic kisses but after a moment reason prevails, and you regain control of yourself. What's happening here, you think to yourself?

'Come back later, please,' he says in rich mellifluous voice. 'I'll be waiting for you.'

Even his voice is like honey. Quickly you leave while you can.

Visit Zenia	▶ 352
Visit Deridedes	▶ 321
Return to the market	▶ 728
Leave the area	▶ 12

743

You sidle up to the sleeping dragon. Raising your weapon, you ready a great blow to drive down through its massive skull and into its brain, hopefully killing it in an instant. But you have misjudged just how tough its scales are, and your blade skitters off to the side.

The dragon wakes with an angry roar. 'Who dares try to murder Kaustikia as she sleeps!'

The dragon's eyes, yellow and snake-like, fix you with a terrible glare.

'A mortal? How did you get here? No matter, you will make an excellent snack for breakfast!'

If you have the **Nemean bagh nakh** ▶ 817
If not ▶ 783

744

You call Jas. Somewhat surprisingly he appears promptly.

'What can I do for you, my most glorious captain?' A tad over the top, you think, but at least he was on time. He continues, 'Some food from the kitchen, a bath and then bed, perhaps, for the greatest hero of the age?'

As ever, you are unsure as to the sincerity of his words but you say, 'Thank you, Jas, that'll do nicely,' anyway.

Jas brings you a plate of delicious food from the palace kitchens, bowing in a ridiculous over-the-top-manner the whole time. You shake your head. It's hard enough being the 'greatest hero of the age' without having a mickey-taking butler, but on the other hand, at least you have a butler.

After dinner you take a long hot bath after which Jas massages your aching muscles, and tends to any cuts and bruises – making it just about worthwhile to put up with him. Then you go to bed for some much-deserved rest. Roll a die:

score 1-4	▶ 465
score 5-6	▶ 586

745

After about twenty minutes or so Cressida returns. 'Well, that was interesting – there was indeed a Polycrates in the village, and his wife did die under suspicious circumstances, but Polycrates himself drowned in a boating accident a few years later. Divine justice, I suppose,' she says. 'Anyway, thank you for this, but I guess the matter is closed. Still, I'll put it in the town records.' Cross off the **confession of Polycrates** from your Adventure Sheet.

There is nothing else to be done, so you take your leave.
▶ 48

746

You have come to an ancient abandoned shrine once dedicated to Ares, god of war, the man-slaughterer, insatiable in battle.

However, you are not welcome here. You cannot re-consecrate this Shrine while you have the title **Accursed of Ares**. There is nothing else you can do but leave.
▶ 832

747

Wolfshadow is approaching fast. Your only way out is to try and lose him in the nearby dales.

Make an INGENUITY roll at difficulty 7.

Succeed	▶ 695
Fail	▶ 362

748

You duck under his sweeping club. Kakas is forced off balance for a moment and you are able to jab him with your weapon. He grunts in pain, but it is only a light wound, drawing little blood and he barely notices. There is so much fat and muscle it will be hard to hit anything vital.

And then Kakas raises his club, covering his face for a moment. You are about to take advantage of the fact that he can't see you, when he lowers the club and breathes out a great cloud of fire at you! Make a GRACE roll at difficulty 7 as you try to avoid getting engulfed in flames.

Succeed	▶ 818
Fail	▶ 583

749

❑

Put a tick in the box. If there was a tick in the box already ▶ 808 immediately. If not, read on.

You enter the forest once more and announce your presence loudly. It's is not long before several trackers arrive. They are astonished at the sight of you. They begin to mutter and jabber excitedly amongst themselves before more of them turn up, forming a large crowd around you, leading you back to the temple at the centre of the forest. You arrive in the clearing to be greeted by Lykaon, seated on this throne and his daughter, Kallisto, beside him.

'The last time I saw you,' says Kallisto, 'you were being torn apart in front of my eyes, and then I ate your heart! How can you be here?'

'Did you escape from Hades? Incredible!' says King Lykaon.

'No, no, I… it's a long story, but, well, sometimes I get to come back,' you say vaguely.

'Amazing. Still, by coming here you've defiled the temple – again! We're going to have to have another Sacred Hunt once more,' says Lykaon, giving you a puzzled look.

However, his subjects take a different view – they start cheering loudly, looking forward to another hunt with comments like: 'Nice, this one had a tasty liver!' or 'Brains were delish,' and 'Can't wait to eat that arse again!' and so on…

'All right, quiet now,' says Lykaon. He turns to you. 'Why?'

'I believe surviving the Sacred Hunt is necessary to complete certain tasks I have to finish.'

'Very well, then,' says Lykaon. 'Let the hunt begin!'

Once again, Kallisto begins her transformation into a bear, as do the sons and daughters of Lykaon. You waste no time and flee into the forest, hunted once more, the prey of werewolves.
▶ 110

750

Your character is no more. Thanatos, whose touch is death, has claimed you. You will have to start all over again. Delete all codewords, titles, items, wounds, scars, ticks, blessings, companions and so on from your Adventure Sheet and from all of the Vulcanverse books you own. You will also have to delete all items in storage in vaults, houses, villas and palaces. When you are done ▶ 1 in any book to start again.

751

A wooden dais is set up near the centre of the clearing. Chiron stands upon he dais, and you and Velosina stand below on the ground. Many centaurs gather round, including a few humans who also live and work in the Sacred Stables.

'Each will play three tunes on the flute, and after, I will decide the winner,' announces Chiron.

'There should be a prize!' someone yells from the crowd.

Chiron tugs on his beard, running his hand down its impressive length.

'Yes, you're right. Hmm, let me see...' he says. 'Ah, I know, whoever wins gets a lyric poem written and set to music by the great Sappho herself. How about that?'

'Perfect,' says Velosina, glaring at you comically.

You make a face back at her. She laughs, and then she composes herself, and raises her flute to her lips.

She plays a happy dancing jig of a song, and soon the crowd are hopping and prancing along to it. When she's done, the audience clap enthusiastically. Now it is your turn. Note that you must play with your bone flute, and cannot use any other instrument.

'Not bad, I'll give you that, but how about this?' You raise the bone flute of Koré to your lips – it was a gift from Persephone herself – well, you hope it was. Surely that will count for something?

If you have the codewords *Oedipus* or *Olifant* or the title **Favoured of Demeter** you can add 1 to your CHARM rolls in this contest, for you have pleased Persephone.

If you have the title **The Gardener,** you have offended Persephone and must subtract 1.

If you qualify for both then they cancel each other out.

Make a CHARM roll at difficulty 6. If you roll snake eyes (two) ▶ 228 immediately. If not, read on.

Succeed   ▶ 302
Fail   ▶ 331

752

You're going on a bear hunt. What could possibly go wrong? You start by looking for bear spoor in the vicinity of the apiary.

Make an INGENUITY roll at difficulty 7. If you have the title **Favoured by Orion**, add one to the result.

Succeed   ▶ 672
Fail   ▶ 798

753

The dream breaks and flies apart like smoke in a strong wind. All that you have seen is in your past, or perhaps exists only in the imagination that fuels your memories of the past.

You have now filled in your Adventure Sheet with the details of your god, your attribute scores, and perhaps one or two other things besides. It is time to enter the wild woods.

You are woken by the sound of birds singing in the trees...
▶ 410

754

The crowd erupts into uproarious laughter. Soon the term 'arse pudding' will be heard all across the Treycross market but for now, Derididedes says, 'Well done. Crude, simplistic, base and so on, but a good choice for a crowd like this one. However, Kraterus is a judge of discerning taste and requires more artistry in his insults.'

And Kraterus does indeed remain silent. So it goes. Derididedes comes up with a few choice insults, and every time Kraterus crows, but yours are just ignored entirely, even though your arse pudding quip got the most laughs of all.

It's clear the game is fixed in some way, but you're not sure how. There is nothing you can do for now, perhaps you can return later. You can head back to the marketplace (▶ 728) or leave the area (▶ 12).

755

You find the traces of an old path through the wood, now heavily overgrown. After a little hacking back of vines and brambles you find a small clearing with a single great oak in the middle. At its base is a low altar. You have found it! Gain the codeword *Praise-Artemis* and ▶ 194

756

You intone a few words in as sacred a voice as you can muster.

'I offer this libation in honour of the Great Green Ones, and to venerate the Heart of the Forest!'

You kneel down, bow your head and pour the libation onto the tree-stump altar. Dione's blood sinks into the wooden altar like water in sand. Cross **Dione's blood** off your Adventure Sheet.

The three totems appear to twitch a little, or is that a trick of the light? But then you see the moss and the lichen fall away, and they begin to become even greener. The totem with the deep-set eyes appears to shift slightly to face you. Its cornflower eyes twist and writhe out of its sockets to fix upon you like sunflowers in the sun.

The crown of leaves of the second totem begins to fill out with sap, and the chestnuts and walnuts expand and begin to pulse slowly.

The third opens its great baleen-like mouth and begins to suck in the air, creating an eerie whistling sound that makes your spine tingle. The whole thing is unnerving and strange.

Words form in your head as if someone or something was using your own brain to think and express its thoughts.

'Blood of the usurpers!'

'A daughter of she who stole everything from us!'

'Accursed Gaia, that was born from our seed!'

'It is good, this blood, like the taste of revenge.'

'How long has it been?'

'Many, many seasons…'

Your head begins to ache terribly. Your own thoughts are getting crowded out, it is hard to hold onto yourself, they are taking over your brain. You gasp in pain.

'The walking-meat thing suffers…'

'Only one should speak…'

The pain starts to fade as two of the creatures leave your mind.

'We are the Great Green Ones,' says the pulsing walnut totem.

'Those who sacrifice to the spirits of nature can call upon our aid in battle and though we are grateful for your gift, and will gift you in return, first we need one more thing from you, meat-thing.'

You nod through gritted teeth, unable to speak, but at least you don't feel like you are drowning in the mind of a forest.

'Our roots are deep. Down, down into the earth they burrow, for we are the earth and the earth is us. But something is gnawing at them, draining our sap that is to us like blood is to walking meat. Find and protect our roots and we will reward you! Take this, as a sign of our trust.'

At your feet flowers suddenly grow up out of the ground. Note the **flowers of fertility** on your Adventure Sheet.

You say – or rather think – your agreement. Gain the codeword *Plantation.*

'Walk back to us when you have cleaned our roots, meat-thing.'

The voice in your head is suddenly gone, and your thoughts are your own once more. The Great Green Ones sink back into silent sleep, dreaming their dreams of sap, root, bark and branch. You wonder what it feels like to have your roots gnawed at. Is it perhaps like having an itch that you cannot scratch away?

Anyway, there is nothing more you can do here so you decide to make your way back to 'civilisation'. By following your own path back through the forest you are able to make it to its outskirts without too much difficulty. Thirsty, tired, and sweaty, you leave the deep forest – for now.

▶ 148

757

The door of the tower opens and out steps a large man, some seven feet in height, dressed in leathers, but seemingly without any weapons. He looks powerful though, heavy set,

his head bald and beardless but gnarly and misshapen like a baked potato. A thin gold circlet rests atop the gnarly potato head. It must be Alcyoneus, King of the Giants.

And then from behind his back, two more arms appear! A four-armed giant. Tricky. What will you try?

Attack him where he is ▶ 699

Roll the eye down the slope towards him ▶ 800

Try to lure him out of the courtyard with insults ▶ 820

758

You call for your butler but there is nothing but silence. You check the bedroom – empty. Gingerly, you approach the bathroom and open the door. Your worst fears are confirmed. There lies Jas, completely naked, asleep in the bath. With him is a water nymph, one of the river spirits of the dales of leaf and stream, cradling him in her arms, both of them dead drunk and snoring. On the floor is a banquet of half-eaten sea food and several bottles of now empty dandelion wine. In fact, it looks like the bath is filled with dandelion wine! That must have cost a bit. You wonder where he gets the money from…

You shake your head and close the door, not wishing to look at a naked Jas for a moment longer. You sigh. The trials of having a satyr as a butler, you suppose. Maybe you could shove his head under, and say he drowned in the bath? Perhaps that's a bit harsh. And then there's the nymph too, you can't really just murder her as well. Ah well, what can you do?

You do however, find a **jug of dandelion wine** by the door, unopened. A little bit of compensation but still. Note it on your Adventure Sheet.

Anyway, there's no way you'll be getting a quiet night's sleep or a bath today, so will you:

Enter the Vault of Vulcan in Arcadia ▶ 828

Leave your rooms ▶ 282

759

Euphorbos invites you to stay for a few days. 'You can get a lie in,' he says. 'I already got up early tomorrow and made breakfast.'

If you are injured, you can untick the Wound box on your Adventure Sheet. When you are ready to resume your travels.

▶ 617

760

'I have done much for Arcadia, you said so yourself,' you tell the King.

He narrows his eyes suspiciously. 'Ye-as…?' he says.

'Well, I have fallen on very hard times indeed, all my money is lost!'

'What? A disaster! Well, I'm sure someone as resourceful and heroic as you will be able to recoup your losses in no time,' says Nyctimus breezily.

'Exactly so,' you say expectantly.

'I'm not sure I get your meaning,' says the king. 'Anyway, must get on with things, nice to see you and all that, until next time, and so forth.'

'Surely you can spare some money from the treasury? After all, I'm the reason there's any money in there at all,' you point out. Forcefully.

The king sighs. 'Well, I suppose that's true, yes. A hundred pyr should get you back on your feet, right?'

'A hundred and fifty pyr will do nicely, and it's the least you can do,' you say putting on your best violent warrior face.

As it is indeed a very violent warrior face, Nyctimus says, 'Yes, yes, of course, right away!'

One of his satyr clerks rushes away into the treasury and comes back with a bag of coins. Note 150 pyr on your Adventure Sheet. There is nothing left to discuss so you take your leave.

▶ **282** and choose again.

761

The Inn of the Swollen Mammaries is teeming with folk, drinking and eating, gossiping, singing. It is loud and buzzing. Over the bar, mounted on a bronze shield, is the head of the Midas basilisk, stuffed and varnished. Below it a sign reads 'Slain by the Hero of the Age'. You can't help but feel a surge of pride welling up inside you. You step up to the bar, where there are several bar staff. But then Oxygala herself, the landlady, rushes over to greet you.

'Welcome, welcome,' she says, 'look what you did!' and she gestures at the crowd. 'And the town is thriving too, the golden statues of the defeated heroes have been left in place, each hero named and respected. And they make a great tourist attraction, I have to say!' You grin, and drink a tankard or two of honey mead, on the house of course.

If you want to stay here the night in the Earth Mother suite (for free) ▶ **633**

If not, after a while you take your leave and head back to the Sacred Way and into Arcadia, in search of more adventures ▶ **20**

762

'I have heard it said that the witch-magic of Hekate is drawn from the same source as the charms and spells used by nymphs and dryads – in other words from Pan himself, as well as the goddess. A dryad's heart is supposed to ward off all such spells, if you can win one.

'And that is all I have to say about that. Anything else?'

If you have the title **Mayor of Bridgadoom** ▶ 118
If not ▶ **153**

763

The catch-net is basically a net made of twined vines, stretched across four wooden poles like an enormous spider's web. Unfortunately for you, it's not been maintained for years and there is a big hole in the middle of it. You fly straight through it and crash into the ground with bone-breaking force.

Tick the Wound box on your Adventure Sheet. If you are already wounded than your skull is shattered and your brains are spilled all over the Sacred Way ▶ **111**

If you still live, you stagger to your feet and look around ▶ **365**

764
❏

Don't tick the box until told to. If you have the title **Slayer of Truffle Hunters** ▶ **129** immediately.

If not but you have the codeword *Purged* and the box is ticked ▶ **149** immediately.

Otherwise, if you have the codeword *Panacea* and the box is ticked ▶ **234** immediately.

If none of the above apply, put a tick in the box above. If there was a tick in the box already ▶ **180**. If not, read on.

The cabin is a low building of wood and as you draw near a strong, rich smell of the forest fills your nostrils. It is a the smell of hydnon, the subterranean truffle of ancient Greece. It is a truffle hunter's hut. As you step round to the front entrance, you see a stone arch set into a low mound of earth nearby. The stone is carved with symbols and ancient letters in a lost language. None can read them today but you know some scholars that call it 'Atlantean'. Several symbols are repeated – three branches on a tree, surrounded by a circle. It looks very ancient.

From inside the wooden cabin you hear a child coughing. You open the door, and the truffle smell is overwhelming. Jars are full of them, some hang from the walls, others are drying out on special racks, or are stored in olive oil, suffusing it with flavour.

In a back room you find a child, sick in bed, her face pale, her brow wet with sweat and her eyes bright with fever. Her face and arms are covered in little black spots.

'Daddy? Is that you?' she says.

'No, no, I'm just a curious passer-by.'

At the sound of your voice the girl draws herself up in fear. 'Please don't hurt us,' she whispers.

'Don't worry, you're safe,' you say reassuringly before asking, 'Where is your mother?'

'Mummy is dead,' she says, 'the blight took her, just like it will take me if Daddy doesn't get back soon.'

'The blight?'

'Daddy calls it the black blight.'

'What is your name, little girl?' you ask.

'I am Io,' she says, barely able to stay awake.

'And where is your daddy?'

'Down the hole. In the land of roots...' she mutters before falling into sleep. You mop her brow and make sure she is comfortable before leaving the cabin. Perhaps you should look for the father in the 'land of roots' so you step up to the arched entryway and walk into the dark.

▶ 823

765

You enter his tent. Inside it is richly furnished, though small. Amphorae, goblets, a jug of wine, and other fineries, all beautifully fashioned, have been carefully placed for maximal aesthetic effect.

A statuette of three-formed Hecate, goddess of magic, stands in the middle of the space. Each of her three selves holds up an oil lamp that fills the room with a gentle, flickering light.

A triangular bed, covered in red and purple drapes fills one corner completely. An incense burner on a low marble table nearby wafts a heady, intoxicating scent through the tent. Your head is spinning.

The young man of extraordinary beauty steps in behind you. He gently places a hand on your shoulder and turns you to face him.

You find yourself gazing into his eyes, his lips inches from yours. Even his breath smells like honey. You can't help yourself, and your heart starts hammering in your chest.

He smiles his heavenly smile and then leans forward and kisses you. For a moment, you are utterly outraged, your hand reaching for your dagger, but then the scent in the air, his god-like beauty, his kiss like sweet wine, your head swimming in a confused daze – you find yourself melting into his arms.

▶ 803

766

You remember the beeswax that the altogether much nicer dryad, Sivi, gave you at the apiary – quickly you fill your ears with the wax, blocking out the song of the dryads. Phearei's hypnotic dance is captivating but without the enchanting, magical singing, you are able to throw off her bewitching wiles and take back control of your own soul.

Phearei snarls – or at least it looks like she is snarling, for you cannot hear a thing – and runs straight at you, raising her taloned hands as if to impale you upon them. You must fight!

Make a STRENGTH roll at difficulty 8.

Succeed	▶ 819
Fail	▶ 657

767

❏

Put a tick in the box. If there was a tick in the box already ▶ 813 immediately. If not, read on.

You hear the sound of iron-shod hooves thundering across the sward behind you. Turning, you see a massively muscled horse, as black as night, cantering towards you. It is terrifying enough but nothing compared to the rider. He is dressed all in black, wielding a single-bladed scythe-like axe in one hand, and a shield emblazoned with a stylized black vulture in the other. Red eyes glare at you from under a horned helm of unusual design.

Down out of the sky, black-feathered vultures swoop, circling the rider.

You heave a resigned sigh. It is the Death Dealer and he has found you again.

'I am Death Dealer, the champion of Thanatos, he whose touch is death...' says the black rider, but you interrupt him.

'Yes, yes, I've cheated death, and he doesn't like it, so he's sent you, his champ, to hunt me down, haul me off in chains to be properly killed, et cetera.'

Death Dealer's red eyes wink on and off for a moment, as if he were blinking in surprise.

'Well, yes, that's about the size of it,' he says.

'OK, then, bring it on,' you say. 'I beat you once, I can do it again.'

The Death Dealer dismounts, hefting his axe...

'We'll see about that...' he says ominously.

Fight Death's champion	▶ 125
Run for the woods!	▶ 580

768

❑

Roll a die. If you score a 1 or a 2, put a tick in the box. If there was a tick in the box already ▶ 249 immediately. If not, read on.

You are able to harvest some more ophidiaroot. Add another portion to your Adventure Sheet (ie **ophidiaroot** x 1 or x 2 if you already have some and so on). When you are done, you return to the bridge where the course of the river runs out into a bay with a low wooden quay for the docking of boats. From here you can go:

North	▶ 774
South	▶ 833
West along the river	▶ 138
To the hamlet	▶ 305
To the quay in the bay	▶ 200

769

Time is fleeting and fluid in dreams. The scene changes. You are older, not yet an adult but grown big enough to disdain the company of little children. So perhaps it irks you when, arriving at a stream shaded by willows, near a pool that is a favourite spot of yours, you find a gaggle of younger children giggling and splashing about noisily in the water.

What do you do?

Chase them off	▶ 358
Trick them into leaving	▶ 253
Show them a better spot	▶ 317
Join them	▶ 495

770

A figure appears at your elbow, places her hand under your arm and raises you up from your seat. You obey mindlessly, even though a rising sense of dread is building up inside of you.

The figure, a priestess also in a cowled robe, leads you to the back of the altar.

You try to re-assert your own will, but you cannot break the spell that binds your mind. In fact, you begin to giggle happily, as if all of this was a wonderful evening out or a play of some kind but you know in your heart of hearts that something much more sinister is going on and that you are to be its victim.

And then, while the other two priests begin to finalise their ritual, calling on Despoina to give them bountiful crops and some kind of eternal spring, your escort leads you away unseen into the trees and away from the glade.

'Hurry, you must get away from here!' she hisses in a hoarse, sepulchral whisper, as if from the other side of the veil that separates life from death.

You laugh, enjoying the game, but she whispers more harshly, her voice hollow like an empty grave, 'Silence, now, my friend, your mind is not your own, and if you make any more noise, they will hear you, and you'll be roasting on that spit in moments!'

After a short while, your mind begins to clear at last. You stagger for a moment, sickened by days of drinking, and sleeping while drugged out of your mind but you are able to ask in a dry, cracked, voice,

'Who are you?'

The figure pulls back her cowl to reveal a shadowy darkness, and you shudder, a thrill of horror running up your spine. She turns her face into the moonlight and then you recognize the ghostly shade of Karya, the dryad. She killed herself to be with her lover in Hades, but he rejected her and now she suffers eternal grief and heartbreak in the Mourning Fields of Hades. You tried to help her forget by offering her some water from the river Lethe, but she refused and gave you her broken heart instead.

'You came here for me, all the way from the Mourning Fields?' you ask, incredulous.

'I know what goes on in these Dales. I heard they had taken you and after all you have done for me, I could not let you die so horribly, especially as it was easy for one such as me to come here from the underworld, for the moon is full, and the rituals and the rites have been spoken at the altar of Despoina, an ancient aspect of the one who others call Persephone,' says Karya, her voice echoing in your head like words spoken in a great tomb.

'Well, thank you,' you say. 'So they were going to sacrifice me, then?'

'Oh yes, cut your throat, pour your blood over the altar as a libation and then skewer you on that spit and roast you in a honey and rosemary glaze.'

'What was… what did they serve me to eat?'

'Their last victim… I think her name was Mintha, so they marinaded her in a minted tzatziki sauce.'

You stop for a moment to throw up in disgust. Now you can add cannibalism to your achievements, even if it was forced upon you.

You notice that you have just thrown up next to a heaped pack of rations and equipment.

'It's the high priest of Despoina and her acolytes stock pile,' mutters Karya in her spectral voice. 'I'm sure they won't notice a little bit of this and that going missing,' she adds, inviting you to help yourself with a wave of a spectral hand, grave dust glittering in the moonlight like finely ground glass.

You notice a master crafted horn, engraved with finely various animal headed figures, armed for war. It is the **Horn**

of the Fae. Note it on your Adventure Sheet and gain the codeword **_Penance_**. Nearby, you hear the sound of approaching footsteps.

'Come, we must away,' says Karya in a hoarse whisper. She leads you safely out of the Dales of Leaf and Stream and the Snares of the Fae to some low hills, just to the south west.

'Thank you for saving me,' you say.

'I am glad to have paid my debt to you. Now I must return to the Mourning Fields, to my grief, my suffering, my heartbreak for that is my fate.'

'Perhaps we will meet again,' and with that she fades away like ashes in the wind.

► **559**

771

If you have the title **Spider's Bane** ► **705** immediately. If not, read on.

You open the hatch and climb down a long ladder, at least a hundred and fifty feet or so into a cave lit by hanging lanterns – who lit those, you wonder – that is covered in cobwebs but thankfully no spiders that you can see. Another hatch in the floor goes who knows where. Try as you might, you cannot open the hatch in the floor, but you could climb the ladder. There seems no other obvious way out until you notice a faint outline of sunlight around a large man-sized rock on a cave wall. A message on the wall reads, _'I turn once, what is out will not get in. I turn again, what is in will not get out. What am I?'_

If you know the answer already, turn to that paragraph number if you want to go through the stone door.

If not, and you want to try to solve the riddle ► **268**

Otherwise, you can go back up the ladder ► **470**

772

You make your way back to the Lake, following the Sacred Way to the bridge over the dried up river. A thin trickle of water is running down the old river bed. Not nearly enough to restore the river to its former glory, but it's a start. You follow the river, to the lake itself.

The limestone has indeed thawed out under the hot Arcadian sun and sunk to the bottom of the lake but the lake only seems half full. As you draw near, the waters begin to roil and churn and out of the lake surges a tall figure of a man, his face framed in a mass of tangled weeds that are his hair and copious beard, hanging down over his chest. His skin is tinged with green, as are his eyes, which have no whites, like emeralds set in a face of pale green ivory.

'Greetings, mortal,' booms the man, 'I am Ladon, the river god. You freed me from the ice, for which I am grateful but my strength has not returned fully for I am bound to my river brother, Alpheus. Together our power is great but until

he is freed too, neither river will run as it should. Free him, and Arcadia's fertile fields will yield their treasures once more. It won't just be water that flows, but wine and bread and honey.'

You nod your understanding.

'In the meantime, take this as a reward for your efforts,' says Ladon. 'All sorts of stuff gets thrown into the lake, let me see, what have we got here…'

Roll a die to see what you get:

score 1	**hardwood club** + 1
score 2	**laurel wreath** + 1
score 3	**hornbook** + 1
score 4	**recurve bow** + 1
score 5	2 **lava gems**
score 6	250 pyr

Note whatever you get on your Adventure Sheet. When you are done here ► **81**.

773

You are unable to prove you have the ransom money. The figure hisses, 'Bah, come back when you have it – don't take too long, or we might just send you one of his ears!'

With that the figure disappears into the crowd. You cannot do anything about Jas at the moment, so you decide to move on. Perhaps you will return with the money later.

► **12**

774

The Sacred Way runs through the Woodlands of Ambrosia here. On either side, dense forest makes for an excellent ambush. You proceed warily.

You also spot some tracks leading off into the woods to the east. Will you:

Go north on the Way	► **419**
Go south on the Way	► **801**
Go west into the Woodlands	► **60**
Follow the tracks	► **79**

775

This part of the river valley has dried up long ago, since Ladon, the river god, disappeared. It's where you encountered the horrible shadow-hunter too, so you decide to move on quickly. Will you go:

West into the forest	► **189**
North to the bridge	► **517**
South to Ladon's Lake	► **37**

776

You walk further into the dales, following the thin path between the line of trees and the wide forest pool. Strange noises, almost like the unstopping of several corks from bottles, fill the air as the golden lilies of the lake puff out small clouds of spores. Almost instantly, a strong soporific musk spreads across the glade, and you start to feel a little dizzy. Things begin to swim in your vision. Your mind fogs up with curious thoughts – whimsical, capricious, almost random, almost as if you were thinking someone else's thoughts, a child perhaps, or a drunken satyr.

You realise you need to get away from here, but then a noise above your head causes you to look up – a face rushes down at you out of nowhere, and your heart nearly bursts in sudden fright, but then it sweeps away, your eyes following its movement. You can barely make out her form for it is so quick, but it appears to be a young woman, running on air, her movements so fast they look to you like the movements of a jerking puppet. Mocking laughter trails after her – an aura perhaps, one of the nymphs of the breeze?

You turn to look over the little lake. And there, rising up out of the waters is a water nymph, dressed in soft green weeds – except that she has the head of a horse.

Behind her, out of the tree line step two young men – but one has the head of a boar, and the other a stag, complete with a full set of antlers.

With a thrill of horror, you realise that these are not masks, they cannot be for their eyes are darting about and their lips move as they talk to you but it is a language so ancient you cannot understand it. Or is it the golden lilies and their somniferous spores, twisting your senses?

The smell is everywhere, suffusing your senses; it is the scent of madness, of nightmares. You try to get away from this place, but you cannot help yourself, and you sink to one knee. It is as if your body were falling asleep from the bottom up.

A fish leaps out of the water, except that it is not a fish but a long-tailed monkey with the head of a fish. It lands beside you and hugs your leg, wrapping its tail lovingly around your arm, looking up at you, as if in affection, but its fish eyes are blank and pitiless like the black, abyssal depths of Tartarus itself.

A harpy in a nearby tree – except that it has the head of a mantis – reaches into her nest and hurls an egg at you. It clatters off your chest to the ground. She hurls another. And another.

And then the first egg cracks open, and slowly, ever so slowly, a long, jointed, glistening chitinous leg emerges, followed by a second, jointed insectoid limb.

You stare, paralysed with a creeping horror, as the two legs begin to drag out a long, glutinous body behind it. A cockroach, as large as your foot, cracks out of the egg, six spiny legs beetling, two antennae questing. And its eyes…

there are two of them and they look uncannily human, staring at you, knowing, understanding, recognizing. Other eggs crack open and several swollen cockroaches scuttle towards you, their limbs rustling like dry old bones rattling in a jar.

The monkey holds on tight, the stag, the boar and the horse walk slowly towards you, babbling in an unknown tongue, while a foot long cockroach begins to caress your leg with its antennae… Uncontrollable horror rises up with in you and you begin to scream wildly until, thankfully, you pass out.

▶ 398

777

You are struck as if by one of Zeus's bolts and you fall to the ground, stunned. Your deity appears to you in a vision, and says, 'I am pleased to call you my champion, mortal, you have accomplished much in the face of great hardship. That is two of the three Great Labours of Arcadia completed. One more remains. And now, your reward…'

When you recover, you find four objects of sacred power have been laid out before you. 'Choose one!' says the divinity.

abacus
golden lyre
iron spear
recurve bow

After recording the item you picked, turn to the section number written in the Current Location space on your Adventure Sheet.

778

You intone a few words in as sacred a voice as you can muster.

'I offer this libation in honour of the Great Green Ones, and to venerate the Heart of the Forest!'

You kneel down, bow your head and pour the libation onto the tree-stump altar.

Nothing happens… all is as silent as it was before. You could try again or leave and come back later. What will you try now?

Your own blood	▶ 827
Dione's blood, if you have it	▶ 756
Daemon's blood, if you have it	▶ 806
Take your leave	▶ 669

779

The giant looks up.

'Aha, another so-called hero looking for glory. I shall enjoy nailing your pretty head to my battlements,' rumbles the giant in a voice like an avalanche of rocks.

He picks up the massive club as if it were a quill pen and lumbers towards you.

'I am Kakas the giant,' he rumbles, 'what is your name?'

You tell him your name and that you are no ordinary hero.

'That's what they all say, either way, I shall tattoo your name on my skin – mind you, I'm running out of room, hur, hur! Maybe I'll have to feast a bit, stretch me skin out a bit more.'

And then he snorts fire out of his nose. 'I like to toast me dinner a bit first, hur, hur.'

If you have a **fireproof hide** ▶ 658. If not, read on.

Kakas moves in, swinging his club in great wide circles. One blow will be enough to floor you. You cannot match him in strength so you will need to be fast, agile and cunning to beat him.

Make a GRACE roll at difficulty 7.

Succeed   ▶ 748
Fail   ▶ 720

780

Your battle with Phearei is a long one – you start hacking off bits of wood, at which she grimaces in pain and anger.

'Once you are mine, I will never, ever let you go,' she vows, 'You will be my slave for all time!'

Her words are a distraction, and with the beeswax in your ears you fail to hear another dryad sneaking up behind you – she tries to loop a vine around your leg, but you are fast enough to dodge aside. You grab the dryad, and throw her against Phearei and they both stumble to the ground, at which point you deftly drive your weapon deep into a soft spot between Phearei's shoulder blades, killing her. The other dryad flees in horror, shrieking in fear and despair.

Phearei, the most ancient and in truth also the most wicked dryad of the woodlands, is dead. Her body begins to wither and shrivel before your eyes, leaving only her wooden heart. Note the **heart of ash** on your Adventure Sheet and get the title **Dryad's Doom**. There is nothing more to do here, so you make your way out of the forest. No one dares disturb your passage… Where will you go?

Back to the Sivi's beehives   ▶ 8
Leave this place   ▶ 225

781

You notice that the amulet with the face of Pan would fit neatly into the carved face of Pan on the side of the altar. You are examining the amulet-shaped depression when a figure steps out of the trees behind you.

'Hello again, my heroic saviour,' says a young woman and she plays a short little trill on a flute.

You turn and see that it is Orphea, the woman you saved from the frozen waters of Lake Cocytus in Hades. Later, when you were asleep, she stole all your money. Riotous red curls spill out from under her bright blue cap, lined with gold thread. She wears a fine leather jerkin, picked out in blue, over red and gold Scythian pantaloons, all looking of very high quality and brand new.

She puts out her arms and twirls, grinning wildly. 'What do you think? All new outfit, courtesy of Gelos the master tailor. No more stink of Cocytus, and all thanks to… well, you!' With that she pretends to shoot an imaginary arrow at you and laughs.

You put a hand to the hilt of your weapon, glaring at her angrily.

'Lady Rapscallion,' you mutter through gritted teeth, 'queen of thieves…'

'Now, now, let bygones be bygones,' she says.

'Easy for you to say,' you growl.

'Ah, but that's my family's amulet you have there, an old heirloom. You fished it out of the lake, didn't you?'

'Maybe it is, maybe it isn't but I found it fair and square – you know, like I didn't steal it from you while you slept.'

'Hah, hah, a fair point, but, you see, that amulet opens a secret chamber in that altar, inside which is a great treasure.'

'What treasure?'

'The very pipes of Pan himself, whoever plays upon those can enchant any who hear. Not to mention the money…'

'And what's to stop me from killing you, looting your corpse to get my own money back and then taking the pipes for myself?'

'Because it is cursed, and whoever opens it without knowing the magic words will be blinded, deafened and struck dumb!'

'Don't tell me – only you know the magic words, right?'

'Correct!'

You stare at her for a moment, thinking. She flicks her eyebrows up and grins.

'So… a deal,' she says. 'I'll say the words, you open it up, I'll take the money, you have the pipes.'

You narrow your eyes suspiciously, 'You'll give up the pipes of Pan?'

'Yes, yes, I have my flute, and anyway, it's money I really want.'

'How do I know you haven't just made it all up? Perhaps there is no curse. I mean, after last time, how can I trust you?'

'And how can I trust you?' she replies.

'Except that when I give my word, I honour it,' you say.

'Well, you would say that, wouldn't you? Although I think you may be telling the truth. But actually, think about it – it's me taking the risk here isn't it? You're the great warrior, you can kill me at any time, right?'

You shake your head. The nerve of the woman. 'I hope there are no more like you,' you say, as you consider her offer.

'Actually, I have a sister,' she says with a grin. 'Just as bad as I am. Her name is Lauria.'

You look around, expecting another, but Orphea says, 'Oh don't worry, I haven't seen her in years, she's in... well, another place.' She frowns. 'I'm not really sure where to be honest.'

Two of them, what a thought. But she has a point, you probably could kill her at any time.

What will you do? Let her say the words and then you place the amulet in the shallow depression on the side of the altar? Or ignore her completely, assume she is lying, and put the amulet in place without her?

Agree to the deal	▶ **190**
Go it alone	▶ **104**

782

Gain the codeword ***Propeller***. Man, the boy engineer, enthusiastically takes the cogs and the gem and begins work immediately.

'It'll be done in a jiffy, as quick as Hermes taking a leak!' says the boy.

After a little banging, sawing and hammering, he has it all fixed up. He steps back.

'All yours, boss,' he says pointing at the bucket seat. 'I hope you've checked all the catch-nets, made sure they're up to scratch. If not, I strongly advise you to do so before using it! Anyway, job done, let me know if you need anything else,' and with that Mandrocles takes his leave. If you want to use the catapult now ▶ **66**.

If not, you can come back later when you're ready. Will you:

Enter the Palace	▶ **96**
Go to the lagoon	▶ **345**
Leave this place	▶ **547**

783

With mounting horror you realise that you have no weapon that can penetrate the dragon's scales. Your only hope is to strike an eye, but the dragon is snake-fast and also keeps spitting acid at you, so you are unable to get near enough. Even her underbelly is scaled and armoured.

Eventually, you fail to dodge a gobbet of acid, and it burns your face, blinding you.

'Breakfast, yum!' says Kaustikia, as she knocks you down with her tail and then pins you to the cloudy ground with one taloned claw. She bites off your arm, and slowly chews it, savouring every morsel, as you writhe beneath her, acid burning out your eyes, and your arm pumping blood. Slowly she rips off your other arm, and starts eating that.

'Quite tasty as far as humans go but still, I'd rather eat a sheep,' she mutters, as she starts gnawing on your leg.

Mercifully you bleed to death before you can suffer any more.

▶ **111**

784

'As you're providing the mushrooms, it'll only cost twenty-five pyr,' Zenia says.

'And how much would you get if I were to go out there and tell them all you're really a young mother just making tea, rather than some kind of wizened old prophetess?' you reply.

'Ah... well, in that case, ten pyr. I need to cover the costs of the other ingredients after all.'

If you want to pay the 10 pyr ▶ **737**

If not, you can head back to the market (▶ **728**) or leave the area (▶ **12**).

785

❑

Put a tick in the box. If there was a tick in the box already ▶ **170** immediately. If not, read on.

You have returned to the parched vineyards of Arcadia. Everything is withered and dry but perhaps not for long. Maron, the winemaking satyr, approaches you somewhat unsteadily and greets you with a hiccup or two.

'Shorry, sorry,' he mumbles. 'I was trying to say hello but, you know, too much to drink and all that. Anyway, well done for getting the river water sorted.' He points at a nearby irrigation channel that is being dug by several satyr workers.

'We can source the water we need but now we need seeds. It's been so long since any work was done here, all the roots and the vines are gone, I've got nothing to plant at all, not a single seed. So, if you can find something like grape vine seeds – doesn't even have to be that, actually, we could make elderflower or whatever wine. Just not dandelion, that stuff's rank!' says Maron, taking a swig from a jug of that very kind of wine and grimacing. 'Still, any port in a storm,' he mutters.

If you have the codeword ***Nifty*** or some **pomegranate seeds** ▶ **208**

If not, you promise Maron you will come back later when you've got something suitable. From here, you can go:

North to the Arcady Trail	▶ **238**
West to Treycross on the Arcady Trail	▶ **728**
South on the Trail	▶ **338**
East to the bridge over the river Alpheus	▶ **14**

786

'Why is there a druid's shrine in the middle of Arcadia? Druids are Celts, not Greeks. What are they doing here? A common question.

'Well, a tribe of Celts settled up north in Galatia, and we Greeks and the white-haired Gauls, those painted men, began to trade. Turns out the Gauls worshipped Apollo too, but they call him Belenus which in their language means the bright one, just as we call our own Apollo. Treaties were signed, and some druids were made *metics*, or honorary citizens of Arcadia, and given charge of a shrine to Pan who is like their own horned god, Cern... Cernun... ah, some barbarian tongue twisting name for Pan. Anyway, so it is there are druids in Arcady.

'And that is all that Phineas has to say about Celts and druids. Anything else?'

If you have the title **Mayor of Bridgadoom** ► 118
If not ► 153

787

Helen explains that things have been going well, and she has just done the books. Your share of the profits is 100 pyr. Add the money to your Adventure Sheet. There is nothing more to do here, so you take your leave. From here you can go:

North-east to the Woodlands	► 60
East along the riverbank	► 138
South	► 822
West to the Wineries	► 417

788

The swarm of intoxicated Bacchantes surges north, but several race toward you, 'Join us!' they shriek, capering and cavorting, tearing at their hair, eyes rolling wildly, drinking from wineskins or chewing on psychotropic plants. One of them offers you some golden wine of Dionysus.

Drink	► 675
Politely refuse	► 709

789
☐☐☐

Put a tick in a box.

If all three boxes are now ticked ► 511 immediately.
If two boxes are now ticked ► 301 immediately.
If not, read on.

'By Polymnia's teats, a masterpiece by the great Apelles himself!' says Erifili. 'I'll give you 150 pyr for it.'

'You paid me 175 the last time,' you say.

'Yes, well, Apelles is dead, it's true, so his paintings go for a premium but still, the greater the supply, the lower the price, that's just the way things work.'

You grunt in irritation but still, 150 pyr is not bad, so you take the money. Add 150 pyr and cross off the **masterpiece by Apelles** from your Adventure sheet.

'Come back with another, if you can get one,' says Erifili, and you take your leave.

► 282

790

You return to the magistrate's hall but this time it is empty. A letter has been left on the table addressed to you. It reads:

'We knew you would be back for more money, just like the low-down, blackmailing, extorting, villainous, despicable fraudster

you truly are. So we have moved on to pastures new, and you will never take money from us again. One day we will find you and be avenged.

- Polycrates and Cressida.'

Ah well, it was nice while it lasted, you think to yourself. There is nothing else to be done here, so ▶ **48** and choose again.

791

Gain the codeword *Provenance*.

'All right, then, tell me what you know, and you can go,' you say, blade levelled at his throat.

Deridedes blurts it all out in a rush of terrified confessions. He doesn't know the boy's name, but he snatched him a couple of years ago from a small farmstead in some hills to the south east to be his slave assistant without having to pay for one.

You shake your head in disgust. It would be nice to kill this wretch, but a deal's a deal.

'If I ever see you again, I will kill you,' you say through gritted teeth. Deridedes nods vigorously, and then takes to his heels. He is gone.

There is nothing more you can do here so you head back to the market (▶ **728**) or leave the area (▶ **12**).

792

You follow the path up to the small town of Galanthropos in the Udder Hills. The road snakes up past a few hills of unusual perfect roundness, each topped with a small, rune-scribed standing stone, the Mamilla-stones as Oxygala called them, dedicated to the earth mother, Gaia, from which her milk burst forth to fertilise the land, out of which sprang the Galgyni tribe, the founders of the town or so the legend goes.

As you draw near to the town, you see some statues scattered about, in dynamic poses of extraordinary similitude and made of solid gold. So, it is true, then; there really is a Midas basilisk that turns people into gold.

You see that one carries a bow, another a great shield and spear, and another is an Amazon warrior woman, with a sword in each hand. Heroes and warriors all, and each has fallen to the power of the basilisk. You had better be careful.

Press on ▶ **660**

Give up and head back to the Sacred Way ▶ **20**

793

If you have the codeword *Planted* ▶ **529** immediately. If not, read on.

If you have some **flowers of fertility** ▶ **476** immediately. If not, read on.

Drosos, the farm overseer, leads you to a nearby barn where he hands you your portion of the most recent harvest – two bags of grain.

Note some **farmlands grain x 2** on your Adventure sheet. When you are ready, gain the codeword *Planted* and decide where you will go next.

North-east	▶ **365**
North-west	▶ **380**
South-east	▶ **419**

794

Damara the water nymph gave you a kiss which will let you breathe underwater for a while. Perhaps you can search the lake bed for treasures, maybe find a ship-wreck full of gold.

You take a deep breath and dive deep. You ready yourself and take a breath…

…and instantly begin to choke and drown! Damara lied to you, the little…

Tick the Wound box on your Adventure Sheet. If you are already wounded then you are too weak to swim up to the air, and you drown like a rat in the lake, not even Ladon himself can get to you in time. ▶ **111**. If you are still alive, read on.

Desperately you swim for the surface, choking. Ladon, the river god, sees you are in trouble, and he comes to your aid, heaving you up out of the waters and onto the bank of the lake in seconds. You retch and cough up water from your lungs, a horrible experience but you will live.

'Were you trying to kill yourself?' asks the river god curiously.

'No! It was a water nymph…'

Ladon bursts out laughing, 'Ah, the old kiss of the nymph will let you breathe underwater trick, eh? Can't believe you fell for that one! What did she get out of you for that?' he asks.

'Her life,' you mutter.

'Hmm… sounds like there's a tale there, and I'd like to hear it one day but I've got rivers to manage, and nymphs of my own to tend to!'

With that Ladon dives back onto the water and is gone.

Cursing Damara roundly, and vowing an as yet unspecified vengeance, you pick yourself up and move on. Delete the title **Kissed by a Water Nymph** and replace it with the title **Tricked by a Water Nymph**. When you are done ▶ **81**.

795

Where this river valley was once dried up and desiccated now roars a great river. The banks are lush with flowers and plants, fish are jumping with joy, a pack of deer are drinking deep on the other side. It is a beautiful, idyllic scene. If you have the codeword *Nemesis* ▶ **767**.

If not, you pause to enjoy the scenery and then move on. Where to?

West into the forest	▶ 189
North to the bridge	▶ 517
South to Ladon's Lake	▶ 37

796

You must fight the Warrior of Ares. Make a STRENGTH roll at difficulty 6.

| Succeed | ▶ 230 |
| Fail | ▶ 533 |

797

Lose the **bag of Aiolos** and get the codeword *Petasos*.

Euphorbos plonks the bag down on his lap and strokes it like a long-lost pet. Normally it is forever writhing and wriggling, but under his touch it loses its restlessness and lies quiet for once.

'Ha ha, when I age all the way back to mythic times I'll blow Hermes's hat clean off with this.'

'Hang on, though. Isn't this whole world a construct by Vulcan? So anything you did – or will do – back in the time of the gods doesn't apply, surely?'

He winks. 'It's a *perfect* construct. Like that switch that turns the sun on and off to replicate Hermes's original curse. Vulcan thinks of literally everything.'

▶ 759

798

You find some bear dung between two trees. It doesn't smell as bad as you'd expect which probably means a recent diet of honey.

Suddenly there is a terrific roar behind you. The bear has found you! You spin around but it has caught you by surprise and clubs you around the head with a massive paw. You are thrown to the ground, head buzzing. Tick the Wound box on your Adventure Sheet. If you are already wounded, then the bear has ripped your head right off, and death is instant ▶ 111

If you still live, you will have to fight the bear in hand-to-hand combat, hardly the best option when hunting bear! This will be a tough battle. Make a STRENGTH roll at difficulty 10.

| Succeed | ▶ 814 |
| Fail | ▶ 733 |

799

You flee into the woods, but you know the odds are against you, as it would be hard enough to outrun an insect swarm in open ground, let alone in a dense forest with trees and undergrowth hindering your passage. However, your forest lore is good, and you are able to find a certain tree, hurriedly slash at its bark, and smear its sap all over you. It acts as an insect repellent, and that gives you enough time to lose the swarm in the gloom of the forest.

Unfortunately, the sap smells so bad, it puts off people too. Note that you have **stink x 1** on your Adventure Sheet. Your next CHARM roll is at −1. After that is resolved, the smell wears off, and you can cross the 'item' off. However, that is the least of your problems, for in your headlong flight, you have lost your way and you have no idea where you are. ▶ 242

800

You roll the eye down the path, aiming for the arched entrance, and then step aside, hiding behind a tree. The eye rolls away, turning and looking back at you with every cycle, as if it were winking at you. And then it rolls through the archway to come to a stop at Alcyoneus' feet.

'What this?' he says in a booming voice, 'The eye of the grey ones, that's odd.' He picks up the eye and looks up the hill, and you duck back behind your tree.

Moments later you can hear the tread of heavy feet as he walks back up the path. He walks past you, eye in one of his four hands, pausing to look up once more.

'I hope they're all right,' he mutters.

He has his back to you. You take your chance, creep up behind him, and drive your blade right through his back and into his heart.

He dies instantly.

You have slain the king of the gigantes! Albeit not very honourably but still, no need to mention the words 'back' or 'stab' when you tell the tale.

Anyway, it is done. You take back the eye, search his body and find the Book of Seven Sages in one of his voluminous pockets but nothing else. You search his tower but again, not much to speak of. 100 pyr or so, some **venison sausages**, **fresh fish** and a **honey cake**. Alcyoneus' lunch by the look it.

But he was the king of the gigantes, so surely he has some treasure stashed somewhere? You search again but to no avail. So much for the promise of riches untold.

There is nothing left to do but head back to Myletes at the waterfall. ▶ 163

801

You have come to an old bridge across the river Alpheus. Nearby there is a small hamlet, a cluster of houses and workshops around the approaches to the bridge. The course of the river runs out into a bay with a low wooden quay for the docking of boats.

If you have the codeword **Pennywort** and want to search for ophidiaroot ▶ 539

If not, from here you can go:

North	▶ 774
South	▶ 833
West along the river	▶ 138
To the hamlet	▶ 305
To the quay in the bay	▶ 200

802

❑

Put a tick in the box. If there was a tick in the box already ▶ 758 immediately. If not, read on.

You call for your butler and hear a strangled cry from the bedroom. Quickly you open the door – to see Jas pulling up his trousers, and two – yes two – dryads, quickly covering themselves with their robes! Plates of half-eaten food and jugs of wine litter the floor. The bedsheets are stained with what you hope is food and drink.

'What the Hades were you…?' you retort angrily.

'Me? I'm a simple slave, don't mind me!' splutters Jas.

'In my bed as well!' you say, outraged.

'Sorry, governor, sorry but you know… satyr and that, what can I say?'

You shake your head and close the door, trying to shut out the sight. All right, he is half goat, nevertheless, these are your rooms not his! You know murder is wrong, but still… Or perhaps you should talk to Nyctimus and get a new butler. Anyway, there's no way you'll be getting a quiet night's sleep or a bath today, so will you:

Enter the Vault of Vulcan in Arcadia	▶ 828
Leave your rooms	▶ 282

803

Gain the codeword **Plight**. You wake up to find yourself on a part of the Sacred Way somewhere. What just happened? The last thing you remember is kissing a handsome young man. What is going on? You're supposed to be a hardened adventurer, not some lovesick mooncalf, seduced by an easy smile, brown eyes and a pretty face, no matter how beautiful.

Quickly you check your stuff. Nothing is missing. Your clothes seem in place, your money is all there. You look around to find your bearings. There is a forest to the south, hills to the north with Oceanus beyond that. It seems you have ended up in the north west of Arcadia.

▶ 20

804

❑

Put a tick in the box. If there was a tick in the box already ▶ 826 immediately. If not, read on.

You are on the Sacred Way that runs from Vulcan City to

the northern shore of Arcadia. To the east is a sea of trees: the Deep Forest. Sounds of shrieking, wailing and howling fill the air, and out the treeline bursts a crowd of women screaming in a wild, feral rage. They wear a strange assortment of animal skins – fox, deer, bear, and bull. Some have horned bull hats, others wolf masks, others wreaths of vine leaves. Some carry sticks wrapped in leaves and pine cones. Some have live snakes writhing around their arms.

All seem to be in a state of ecstatic rapture, savage and ferocious. You realise they are Bacchantes, the Raving Ones, worshippers of the god Dionysus. One of their rituals involves whipping themselves up in a state of intoxicated madness, so that they might channel the spirit of Dionysus, the mad god. In their madness, they have been known to rip up trees, tear animals apart, and also, it is said, men. They have seen you…

If you are female ▶ **788**

If not ▶ **739**

805

You have returned to the Inn of the Swollen Mammaries, in the foothills below the abandoned town of Galanthropos where the Midas basilisk has made its lair. Oxygala the innkeeper welcomes you once more.

'Will you try to kill the basilisk this time? I hope not, for you are a rather fine-looking adventurer and it would be a shame to lose you, not to mention your custom.'

You smile wanly at her lack of confidence in you but there you go. You can buy and sell a few things here.

	To buy	To sell
Fresh fish	20 pyr	15 pyr
Venison sausages	15 pyr	10 pyr
Honey cake	–	50 pyr
Pomegranate wine	–	35 pyr

When you are done, you can:

Search for the basilisk ▶ **792**

Return to the Sacred Way ▶ **20**

806

You intone a few words in as sacred a voice as you can muster.

'I offer this libation in honour of the Great Green Ones, and to venerate the Heart of the Forest!'

You kneel down, bow your head and pour the libation onto the tree-stump altar. Trapjaw's blood sinks into the wooden altar like water in sand. Cross the **Daemon's blood** off your Adventure Sheet.

A strange sound belches up out of the earth, like a cough or a retch. The trees around the edge seem to shudder for a moment and the totems change colour as if stirring in their

sleep. Words or thoughts begin to form in your head…

'Blood of Hades!'

'The taste of death….'

'Blasphemy!'

More words appear in your head.

'We are defiled!'

'Spawn of Tartarus!'

'Abominable, grave-cold, blight!'

And then out of the trees rises up a great cloud of buzzing, biting insects. They form into a swarm overhead, and then swoop down towards you. With a cry of despair, you take to your heels and run for your life.

Make an INGENUITY roll at difficulty 9.

Succeed ▶ **799**

Fail ▶ **688**

807

Lefkia, your painter and decorator is waiting for you when you return.

'Ah, hello, you're back! Do you have the things we need to start work?' she says, getting straight down to business.

You look around. 'Where are the boys?' you ask suspiciously.

'I don't know,' says Lefkia. 'They just ran off, and I haven't seen them since. Mother says they are very naughty boys and have been spending quite a bit of money on cakes and sweets and stuff. Hades knows where they got the money from! Don't worry about the work though, I don't really need them to be honest, it was just to get them out of mother's hair. Anyway, have you brought the things I need?'

If you have:

box of paints x 2

vinegar of hades x 1

bucket of gypsum

and wish to hand them to Lefkia, cross them off your Adventure Sheet and ▶ **715**

If not, you tell Lefkia you will come back later and take your leave. 'Don't take too long,' she says, 'I'm eager to get going.' ▶ **547**

808

King Lykaon and his daughter Kallisto are waiting for you at the temple of Artemis.

'Here you are defiling the temple yet *again!*' says Lykaon, visibly irritated this time. Even the others are somewhat deflated at the sight of you.

'Not another hunt,' mutters one of them. 'Not sure I can stand to munch on that liver again,' mutters another, 'I need a change of diet!'

You shrug. 'I have to do what I have to do,' you say.

'Couldn't we just pretend they made it?' someone says.

'No, unfortunately, we can't. That would anger the goddess. I mean, rules are rules, we are the sacred keepers et cetera,' says Lykaon. He heaves a great sigh and continues, 'Let's get on with it, then. Let the hunt begin!'

Once more, you flee into the forest. Maybe this time you won't get torn to pieces and eaten by werewolves. ▶ **110**

809

Hyperion was the primordial sun god, he who came before. Some say Helios is his son, others that Hyperion *is* the sun. Either way, much of the temple has fallen into ruin now, for most of those ancient gods are long forgotten, their worshippers and their rituals long gone.

Inside, you find a high ceilinged, gloomy hall, its roof open to the skies in places, its pillars cracked and fallen, and vine entwined. There is a great statue of Hyperion in the middle of the room, stained with lichen and mould, one arm long since fallen to the ground. One eye is of bright yellow amber, still glowing in the shaft of light that spears down from the broken roof, the other an empty socket its gem long since looted or shattered.

And then you see the creature. A great serpent, twined around the statue, seemingly sleeping, perhaps after its last dinner for you see a large bulge in its stomach. Man-shaped in fact. Nearby you see your backpack.

It seems the young thief met a sticky end, deservedly so, perhaps. You retrieve your stuff but in doing so you make a noise, and the serpent's tongue flicks out, tasting the air. Its eyes snap open, its head sways around until it fixes on you. It uncoils itself from the statue and, with a hiss, slithers towards you… It is at least twenty feet long, its head as big as your torso, its scales red, blue and green and sparkling like burnished silver.

If you have the **bone flute of Koré** and try using it to soothe the serpent ▶ **53**

If not, you have no choice but to fight the gigantic snake, not an easy battle. Make a STRENGTH roll at difficulty 9:

Succeed	▶ **25**
Fail	▶ **99**

810

Zenia will buy your mushrooms or make kykeon tea for you to drink, and enter a visionary trance. She will buy each batch of **kykeon mushrooms** for 20 pyr each. Cross them off your sheet if you sell them.

If you want Zenia to make you some tea so that you can have a vision of what may be, or what is, or what was ▶ **784**

If not, you can head back to the market (▶ **728**) or leave the area (▶ **12**).

811

You have come to a bridge along the Sacred Way that encircles the world, as do the waters of Oceanus. From here, it runs east and west along the coast. The bridge spans the River Ladon that comes down from a great lake to south. Its waters are blue and bright, gurgling and rushing by joyously. Wild flowers, herbs and fresh green grass grow on its banks, an otter frolics in the water, the croaking of frogs and the buzzing of insects fill the air, the sky is blue and the sun warms you pleasantly and all because you brought the river gods of Arcadia back to life.

To the south-west are the wooded outskirts of the Deep Forest, and the ruins of a castle of some kind, jutting up over the treeline. From here you can:

Go to the bridge	▶ **126**
Head south, up the river valley	▶ **591**

812
❑

Put a tick in the box. If there was a tick in the box already ▶ **790** immediately. If not, read on.

You walk in to see Cressida behind her desk. 'I knew it,' she says bitterly. 'Polycrates was right, he said you'd just come back for more and that we'd never be rid of you!'

You shrug, hand on your weapon. 'He isn't as stupid as he looks,' you say, holding out your hand. 'Another hundred or I have you both arrested for murder.'

Cressida sighs in resigned frustration and hands you a pouch of 100 pyr. Add them to your sheet.

'Now get out, I've got work to do,' she says.

You leave with a smirk. Blackmail really is the gift that keeps on giving!

▶ **48** and choose again.

813

This is where Death Dealer, the champion of Thanatos, came for you, but there is no sign of him now. You are travelling on the banks of the river Ladon. The river rushes by, birds twitter in the forest nearby, the sun is warm. A lovely day in Arcadia. Where will you go?

West into the forest	▶ **189**
South to Ladon's Lake	▶ **37**
North to the bridge	▶ **517**

814

Despite the severity of your wound, you are able to avoid the bear's clubbing paw swipes and savage attempts to bite your head off. You manage to land a couple of well-placed blows that cause some serious bleeding and eventually the bear slows down enough for you to drive your weapon through its skull and into its brain.

Incredibly, you have killed a bear in a toe-to-toe, stand-up fight! You skin the bear, and take it as a trophy. Note the **bearskin** on your Adventure Sheet.

If you have a **hunting permit** ▶ 184

If not ▶ 219

815

'The black blight! A hideous disease, newly come to Arcadia. Some say it came out of the deep, dark places under the earth or from Hades itself or the land of roots. Either way, it will take beggar or king, quarryman or queen. Some say Chiron, first amongst centaurs, has found a cure, but he has not been seen in a long while.

'And that is all that I have to say about that horrible blight. Anything else?'

If you have the title **Mayor of Bridgadoom** ▶ 118

If not ▶ 153

816

You find that Mandrocles the boy engineer is working on the catapult.

'Hi, Man,' you say.

'Greetings, boss,' says the boy engineer. 'I've tweaked it a bit, but I can't do anything more without those parts I asked for. Have you brought them with you?'

If you have 2 **copper cogs** and one **lava gem** and are willing to give them to Mandrocles, the fifty-six-year-old boy engineer ▶ 782

If not, you will have to come back later. Will you:

Enter the Palace	▶ 96
Go to the lagoon	▶ 345
Leave this place	▶ 547

817

The claws of the Nemean lion are the only thing that could cut through the dragon's scales.

You land a blow that draws blood, and Kaustikia hisses in shocked surprise, her overweening arrogance fading away in an instant.

She pauses, reassessing the situation. 'I shall have to take a little more care with you,' she growls, and then spits a gobbet of acid right at your face.

Make a GRACE roll at difficulty 8.

Succeed	▶ 481
Fail	▶ 456

818

You throw yourself to the side in a forward roll, and up to your feet, just managing to avoid the flames. You slap at your sleeve, which caught fire for a moment, just as Kakas turns to face you.

'You're fast, I'll give you that, but you can't dance around like a little chorus girl forever,' rumbles the giant.

He is right. You will have to dodge and jab, dodge and jab for quite a time to weaken this foe enough to kill him but all it takes is one blow of that club or one fiery blast in the face and you are likely done for. But how can he be breathing fire like that? Make an INGENUITY roll at difficulty 7.

Succeed	▶ 560
Fail	▶ 534

819

The battle rages on. If seems she is not trying to kill you, rather take you alive, and this gives you the advantage. You begin to press your attack.

Make a GRACE roll at difficulty 7.

Succeed	▶ 780
Fail	▶ 657

820

You stand just outside of the courtyard, and challenge him to a duel. He looks up at you in surprise and then just smiles, and shakes his head.

'Come in, little one, and then we can fight,' he says.

You call him a four-armed freak, a six limbed ant, and a gigantic embarrassment to man, beast and giant.

Alcyoneus smiles again, folds one set of arms, and puts the other two behind his head, listening politely.

You try a few more of your choicest insults, but he actually laughs and says, 'You don't think I've heard this before? Many a hero has come here and tried to lure me out with insults. At first, with some success, I admit, but now, well, now I just enjoy them. You're inventive, I'll give you that, but you're going to have to fight me here.'

You shake your head in annoyance. It seems you have no choice but to attack.

▶ 699

821

☐☐☐

Put a tick in a box. If two boxes are now ticked ▶ 59 immediately. If all three boxes are now ticked, ▶ 492 immediately. If only one box is ticked, read on.

Hermes has sent you across the world in your sleep. You wake with a start. You find yourself trapped in a kind of box, one side of which is made of glass, the other sides of a strange material you have never seen before. Staring down at you are two enormous figures – one a grey bearded oldish man with a wild look in his eyes, clearly tinged with madness, the other a red-haired woman, pale skinned and lean. They wear curious clothes of browns, blacks and greys that barely cover their bodies, with trousers in the Scythian style and white shoes tied up with string. The man holds an odd black device of some kind in one hand.

'What… what is it?' says the woman.

'I dunno – I think we've been hacked,' says the man.

And then suddenly you wake up – again. Thankfully it was just a fevered dream, no doubt of the gods. But which ones?

Anyway, you look around. You have arrived in Arcadia, the land of eternal summer. A warm haze washes through the air, birds and insects chirrup and whirr in the trees. But this is the Vulcanverse… what horrors lie hidden in this verdant paradise?

Nearby, you can see the pillared portico of a great palace, jutting up over the treeline. ▶ 686

822

You are trekking across the Arnion Hills, a range of low hills in the south of Arcadia. Rich grasses blanket these hills, and you can see flocks of many sheep dotted about, grazing. Nearby is a farmstead, with sheep in pens. Smoke curls up lazily from a chimney and children play in the fore court.

If the boy Magnes is your companion ▶ 226 immediately. If not, read on.

Will you go:

To the farm	▶ 3
North to a bridge	▶ 14
South to the Sacred Way	▶ 832
East to the Sacred Way	▶ 833
West and the Arcady Trail	▶ 338

823

You step into the cavernous entrance – and find it is reasonably well lit. Oil lamps have been placed at regular intervals along a sloping natural tunnel that leads down into the depths. Beside each lamp is a small jug of oil, some spare wicks and flint and tinder. Someone has gone to a lot of trouble of making sure that they will never be without light.

You move on, as the slope steepens, down, ever down. The smell of hydnon truffles wafts up from the depths, until you come to a cave. The walls are lined with the roots of trees from the forest above, and around them grows the hydnon truffle. But Io's father is nowhere to be seen.

On the other side of the cave, you see another opening, heading deeper into the earth. It seems quite recent, and not that safe either, as if shaken open in a quake of some kind. Rocks trickle down the uneven walls. Recently added wooden supports hold the roof up, and torches are set in brackets along the way.

You head down to emerge into a small space but with a roof so high you cannot make it out in the flickering light.

Along one wall enormously massive roots come down from the shadow-shrouded roof to burrow deep into the ground. They are like huge wooden cables, each root as wide as ten men roped together.

A man is working at one of the roots, cutting into it and gathering the sap in a bottle. He wears dirt-stained brown robes, and is of middling years with a pale white face and salt and pepper beard and hair.

This must be the roots of the Great Green Ones, the roots they want you to preserve.

You step into the chamber. The man starts in surprise.

'What the…' he says. 'How did you..?'

'You have to stop,' you say.

'What? But I can't, my child, only the sap of this tree, or whatever it is, keeps the black blight at bay.'

'Nevertheless, you must stop, for you are killing the Great Green Ones.'

'What? Who?'

'The Great Green Ones, the Heart of the Vine, the Mother of Trees. From whom Gaia herself sprang. If you kill them, all life in Arcadia will die.'

The man stares at you.

'But my baby. The blight took my wife, I can't let it take my little Io too, and only this stuff works. No, I'm sorry, I've no idea what you're talking about, I've never heard of any Great Green Ones, and in any case, surely the small amounts I'm harvesting couldn't cause so much harm. No, I'm sorry, but I'm just going to take what I need, and that's that.'

What will you do? You could just kill him and be done with it. Or see if you can find a cure for the black blight elsewhere though you're not sure how much time you have. You can see that the sap continues to 'bleed' for quite a while once it's been cut for there are lumps of dried sap around and about.

Kill him	▶ 97
Quest for a cure	▶ 63

824

You enter the old pavilion of Momos. It is empty, the stage long gone, a cold, hollow wind blowing in from the entrance and out through a large tear in the fabric at the rear of the tent, making a low, wailing sound, as of a chorus of the shades of Hades. There is nothing left for you to do here. You can head back to the market (▶ 728) or leave the area (▶ 12).

825

Sivi, the dryad of the pomegranate, wants you to hunt down and kill the bear that is ransacking her beehives of all their honey.

Until you do, there will be no honey for you either. What will you do?

Hunt for the bear right now ► 752
Go deeper into the woods ► 176
Leave and come back later ► 225

826

You are on the Sacred Way that runs across and through the Vulcanverse. This part is on the western edge of Arcadia. To the west, massive mountains rise up to the skies, white-hatted and ice bound. To the east is a sea of trees, the Deep Forest of Arcadia.

Nearby, a structure of wooden poles and webbing has been built, clearly to catch something. It is in good repair.

Will you go:

North on the Sacred Way ► 158
South on the Sacred Way ► 324
North-east into the Deep Forest ► 616
South-east into the Deep Forest ► 710

827

You cut your arm and fill the old wooden cup with your blood. When you are ready, you intone a few words in as sacred a voice as you can muster.

'I offer this libation in honour of the Great Green Ones, and to venerate the Heart of the Forest!'

You kneel down, bow your head and pour the libation onto the tree-stump altar. Your blood sinks into the wooden altar like water in sand.

A sudden wind seems to rise up out of nowhere, soughing through the trees, creating a strange wailing sound. You can't be sure but out of the corner of your eyes, you can have sworn you saw some of the trees in the forest swaying.

The totems seem to change colour too their green becoming brighter and more vibrant. Words or thoughts begin to form in your head.

'Blood of a meat-thing!'
'A particularly foul meat-thing…'
'Sacrilege!'

You look around, unsure as to what is happening. More words appear in your head.

'Poison!'
'Desecration!'
'Loathsome, squalid, filthy!'

And then out of the trees rises up a great cloud of buzzing, biting insects. They form into a swarm overhead, and then swoop down towards you. With a cry of despair, you take to your heels and run for your life.

Make an INGENUITY roll at difficulty 9.

Succeed ► 799
Fail ► 688

828

If you have the **Arcadian vault key** you can unlock the door and enter the vault of Vulcan in Arcadia ► 333

If you do not have the **Arcadian vault key** ► 100 and choose again.

829

You are taking a risk, returning to the village you stole so much money from but it seems the streets are deserted and no one has spotted you. Perhaps they have forgotten all about it? But no – suddenly howls of rage fill the air, and out from a side street surges a mob of angry villagers, men, women and children, armed with pitchforks, and clubs but some have spears and swords, perhaps just for you! There must be fifty of them.

With a resigned sigh, you take to your heels and run for your life. Cries of 'Thief! Villain! Liar! Mountebank! Charlatan! Impostor!' and such like are hurled after you. Still angry it seems. You flee for your life. Make a GRACE roll at difficulty 7.

Succeed	▶ 363
Fail	▶ 320

830

You wake with a splitting headache and a mouth like sandpaper. What have you been eating, sand? You look around, groggy and disorientated. The last thing you remember is foraging for mushrooms in the deep forest.

You are under a large bougainvillea and to your horror you realise you are completely naked. Not only that, you are lying next to a snoring goat-legged satyr who is also completely naked!

You try not to think about what might have happened under this colourful bush last night, and gather your things, getting dressed as fast as you can. The satyr starts chuckling in his sleep.

You hurry away, but then you realise you have lost *all* your money. Cross it off. On other hand, you have gained a rather slimy **lava gem** you have to wipe clean, a **moon pearl** uncomfortably lodged somewhere it shouldn't be, and a **hardwood club** (STRENGTH +1).

Gathering your wits, you work out you are on the Arcady Trail not far from the Summer Palace. ▶ 455

831

You wake to find yourself alone in complete darkness, a skin of the **golden wine of Dionysus** in your hand. Note it on your Adventure Sheet.

You have no idea where you are or how you got here, nor why you are alone but your hands are stained with blood, as are your lips. You stagger to your feet and look around.

You can see nothing but you can hear a faint wailing in the distance, as of mourners at a funeral. You head towards it – and come to one of the Gates to Hades. Somehow you have entered the underworld.

▶ **686** in *The Houses of the Dead*.

832

If you have the codeword *PatchupSix* ▶ 663 immediately. If not, read on.

You have arrived at the foothills of a range of low Arcadian hills. To the south and east you can see the Sacred Way, and to the west some more hills leading to the massive cyclopean walls of Vulcan City. To your north are the dales of leaf and stream. The ground is lush with grass, the sky a bright blue and sunshine bathes the land in warmth. There is an abandoned shrine here, and from the look of it, a shrine to Ares, the man-slayer.

Also nearby is a structure of wooden poles and webbing that has collapsed onto the ground. Repairing it will cost you 20 pyr. If you wish to do so, cross off the money and get the codeword *PatchupSix*. Either way, from here you can go:

Visit the Shrine to Ares	▶ **64**
North-east into the hills	▶ **822**
North-west to the dales of leaf and stream	▶ **266**
East to the coast	▶ **833**
West towards Vulcan City	▶ **119**
South to the Sacred Way	▶ **300** in *The Hammer of the Sun*

833

If you have the codeword *PatchupFive* ▶ 622 immediately. If not, read on.

You are on the Sacred Way. From here, it runs north to a bridge over the Alpheus river, and south into the desert of Notus. To the west, you can see a low range of grassy hills. Above, the sky is blue, to your east Oceanus laps up against the shoreline, insects buzz in the air, and wild flowers dapple the roadside with many colours, for here in Arcadia it is eternal summer.

You spot a crater in the ground just north of the Sacred Way and nearby, a large net, slung between four wooden poles, clearly designed to catch something falling from the sky but it in a state of disrepair. It will cost you 20 pyr to have it fixed. If you wish to do so, cross off the money and get the codeword *PatchupFive*. Either way, from here you can go:

To the crater   ▶ **127**
North to the bridge   ▶ **801**
West to the low hills   ▶ **822**
South on the Sacred Way ▶ **600** in *The Hammer of the Sun*

834

You are in complete and utter darkness. You cannot see your own hand in front of your face. But you can hear. And in the distance you hear the slow steady step of someone – or something – drawing near. Closer they come, ever closer, until you can hear the sound of breathing.

And then someone whispers in your ear. 'No mortal should be able to cheat their fate, for I am Thanatos, and my touch is death.' He kisses you lightly on the lips, and you die.

Oblivion   ▶ **750**

835

If you have the codeword *Poll* ▶ **497**
    If not ▶ **609**

'I dwell no more in Arcady:——
But when the sky is blue with May,
And flowers spring up along the way,
And birds are blithe, and winds are free,
I know what message is for me,——
For I have been in Arcady.'

Adventure Sheet

NAME

COMPANION (maximum of 1)

ATTRIBUTES   SCORE

CHARM

GRACE

INGENUITY

STRENGTH

WOUND

−1 from all attribute rolls
when ticked

TITLES

MONEY

GOD

GLORY   SCARS

POSSESSIONS (maximum of 20)

BLESSINGS (maximum of 3)

CURRENT LOCATION

Codewords

- ❏ Painter
- ❏ Panacea
- ❏ Parapet
- ❏ Parentage
- ❏ Parted
- ❏ Passage
- ❏ Passion
- ❏ PatchupOne
- ❏ PatchupTwo
- ❏ PatchupThree
- ❏ PatchupFour
- ❏ PatchupFive

- ❏ PatchupSix
- ❏ PatchupSeven
- ❏ Payment
- ❏ Pelt
- ❏ Penalty
- ❏ Penance
- ❏ Pennywort
- ❏ Penumbra
- ❏ Perdition
- ❏ Pernicious
- ❏ Petasos
- ❏ Pheon

- ❏ Phosphoric
- ❏ Pinot
- ❏ Plantation
- ❏ Planted
- ❏ Pledged
- ❏ Plenty
- ❏ Plight
- ❏ Plough
- ❏ Plundered
- ❏ Poll
- ❏ Praise-Apollo
- ❏ Praise-Ares

- ❏ Praise-Artemis
- ❏ Praise-Athena
- ❏ Prankette
- ❏ Precious
- ❏ Press
- ❏ Priestly
- ❏ Prisoner
- ❏ Projectile
- ❏ Propeller
- ❏ Proprietor
- ❏ Proscribe
- ❏ Prosthetic

- ❏ Provenance
- ❏ Pudding
- ❏ Pumped
- ❏ Punisher
- ❏ Punition
- ❏ Pure
- ❏ Purged
- ❏ Purify
- ❏ Purloin
- ❏ Pursued

Notes

Made in the USA
Las Vegas, NV
26 May 2024

90370123R00105